Clear to Lift

Also by Anne A. Wilson

Hover

Clear to Lift

Anne A. Wilson

A Tom Doherty Associates Book
New York

CLEAR TO LIFT

A Forge Book
Published by Tom Doherty Associates, LLC
175 Fifth Avenue
New York, NY 10010

www.tor-forge.com

Forge® is a registered trademark of Tom Doherty Associates, LLC.

The Library of Congress Cataloging-in-Publication Data is available upon request.

ISBN 978-0-7653-7851-4 (hardcover)
ISBN 978-0-7653-8621-2 (e-book)

Our books may be purchased in bulk for promotional, educational, or business use. Please contact your local bookseller or the Macmillan Corporate and Premium Sales Department at 1-800-221-7945, extension 5442, or by e-mail at MacmillanSpecialMarkets@macmillan.com.

First Edition: July 2016

Printed in the United States of America

0 9 8 7 6 5 4 3 2 1

For Mom and Dad

Acknowledgments

To my editor, Kristin Sevick. You spoiled me with an all-day, live editing session for this book, a rare gift, which of course made the novel infinitely better. I can't thank you enough for taking the time with me.

To my agent, Barbara Poelle. So much awesomeness here, I'm not even sure where to begin. Thank you for your patience with me in all things.

Thank you, Seth Lerner, for creating such a gorgeous cover. Thank you also to my publicist, Emily Mullen, Bess Cozby, and the entire Tor/Forge team! And to my copy editor, Terry McGarry, thank you for your wonderfully thorough work.

To my extended military family. Once again, I turned to you for your expertise, and you responded without hesitation. To Major Jon Sablan, USMC (Ret.), fellow skid pilot and also my next-door neighbor in Bancroft Hall at the Naval Academy. Thank you for your help with all things Huey and Marine Corps. To Chief Petty Officer Jack Ruskin, USN (Ret.), a gifted SAR corpsman with a wicked wit whom I had the honor to fly with in Fallon, Nevada. You were beyond helpful when discussing "sexy" SAR scenarios! To Captain Sara Joyner, USN, thank you for sharing your F/A-18 expertise and knowledge of the Fallon Range Training Complex.

To the members of the Longhorn squadron—both past and present—stationed at Naval Air Station Fallon, who continue to uphold a long and storied tradition of excellence in high-altitude, technical mountain rescue.

To the selfless men and women who volunteer in SAR units across the country—in particular, the folks from Mono County, California—thank you.

I have to thank the crew who flew with me during the actual flood rescue that inspired the last scene in this book. Don Benson, Marty Naylor, Vince Wade, and Tom Spradlin, you guys rocked the "Devil's Own Fury"! And a special shout-out to Dean Rosnau, Mono County SAR team member, one of those we rescued that day, but only because this selfless individual risked it all to save the lives of others.

To Bela and Mimi Vadasz, mountain guides and founders of Alpine Skills International based in Truckee, California. You taught me and my husband, Bill, so much. You have no idea how much you influenced the words in this book. Bela, you left this world far too early.

To Sharmin Dominke, my authority on search-and-rescue dogs. Thank you for your help. For questions about Labrador retrievers, I turned to my brother, James Hotis, and his wife, Lisa Carlgren, and their sweetheart of a dog, Cash.

To Alison Smith, my roommate at the Naval Academy. The main protagonist was named for you.

To the band who has inspired my writing from the beginning—the always awesome, ridiculously talented Muse. I always turn to you.

To my parents, Ruth and Tony Hotis, for their love and support that is always and unconditionally there. Thanks also, Dad, for the Spanish language help! Love you immenso!

To my sons, Adam and Isaac. I love you beyond measure.

And to Bill. Always.

Clear to Lift

1

Agitated snow tumbles and whirls across the cockpit windshield. I strain to see through it, to make out three figures clinging to a vertical wall of ice. Two are unmoving, dangling like rag dolls from the ends of a climbing rope. One, wearing a bright yellow jacket and neon-orange gloves, scampers up from below, gripping two ice axes, feet and hands a flurry of movement, scrambling up, up, up, over two hundred feet above the ground, and without a . . . *rope?*

"He doesn't have a rope!" I say, squinting to be sure.

Although, wait. Maybe . . . it's an optical illusion. We *are* flying at ten thousand feet, skirting the edge of a rock buttress three thousand feet high.

Yeah, right, Alison. You know why you can't tell . . .

"You sure about that?" says Commander Benjamin "Boomer" Marks, the aircraft commander for the flight. A former offensive tackle for the University of Wyoming, he still packs every pound of his football-glory-days girth.

"No, sir, I'm *not* sure. Why? Because I can't see a flippin' thing! Which is what happens when you fly in a freakin' snowstorm! Which, by the way, goes against every—"

"You mean, this insignificant nothing of a snow squall? The one we've been flying in for all of fifteen *seconds*? The one that'll pass just as fast?"

"But what about—?"

"The deicing system is on, Malone. And look," he says, motioning with his head to the outside. "It's past history, anyway."

The snowflake assault abruptly fades to nothingness.

"See? Already through it." He flashes an I-told-you-so grin as we transition into improbably clear air, albeit in the midst of disturbingly unsettled weather—the clouds hanging heavy, threatening.

We're doing a low-speed flyby, like we always do when called to a rescue, but at least now we have an unrestricted view of the fast-moving, agile climber, who apparently does *not* require a rope when scuttling up a frozen rock face hundreds of feet above the ground. I lean in my seat as far as the straps will allow, peering into a narrow couloir— a steep tunnel of snow and ice—that splits the east face of the formidable Mount Morrison.

"That is some serious risky shit," says our ace crew chief, Beanie, otherwise known as Petty Officer First Class Billy Hilfenbein. "Soloing the Death Couloir? Jesus, Will."

"Will? Who's Will?" I ask.

"That loony!" Beanie pokes his head between the cockpit seats and points to the climber in yellow. "Lieutenant Malone, meet Will Cavanaugh, one of the best all-around mountaineers in the world."

"Like literally the world, ma'am," our star paramedic, Hap—officially Petty Officer First Class Hap Gentry—says. "The guy should like wear a cape or something."

"Is he new, Hap? I've never heard of him."

"He left for the Himalaya right after you checked in, ma'am. About four months ago, I think."

"Best climber on the Mono County SAR Team," Beanie says.

I watch, transfixed, as Will ascends Spiderman-like, quick and sure, negotiating the last few feet to the first victim.

"Rescue Seven, Mono County Sheriff, over."

"Mono County Sheriff, Rescue Seven has you loud and clear," Boomer says. "Whaddya got for us, Jack?"

"Just an update," says Jack Smith, head of the Mono County Search and Rescue Team. He briefed the rescue scenario with us via radio during our transit—two climbers stranded, hit by rockfall—and reports now from the base of the mountain, where he waits with the rest of the ground crew, watching with binoculars, over six thousand feet below us. "As you can see, Will's almost to the first victim. He passed the belayer on the way up, who's conscious, possible broken arm. But the belayer thinks the lead guy is worse off. He's been in and out of consciousness."

"Roger that," Boomer says. "We'll plan for the lead guy, first. We're rigged for rappel."

And then to me. "Ready for the controls, Alison?"

I bring my gloved hands to my mouth and give a quick blow of hot air—god bless, it's cold—before placing them on the flight controls. "I've got the controls."

"Rescue Seven, Whiskey One," a voice crackles on the radio. It must be Will. "I'm at the first victim now. He's thirty-five years old, awake, alert, oriented. He was hit by rockfall and caught by his rope when he fell. He's hanging right side up. Man reports loss of feeling from the waist down. Suspect spinal injury. After we get him off, I'll downclimb to the second victim, over."

"Whiskey One, Rescue Seven copies," I say. "Inbound."

I roll the aircraft to the left, rotor blades thwacking the air—thwack, thwack, thwack—continuing to arc around, until I arrive in a hover about forty feet away from the rocks, fifty feet above Will. I orient the helicopter parallel to the rock wall, sensing the winds more intimately now that I'm at the controls. Crap. I hate the winds in close quarters. Add to this, mushy flight controls, the result of not enough air particles at this altitude for our rotor blades to grip, and it means the aircraft is slow to react to my inputs. Crap and *crap*.

At least you're not flying in the snow. Could be worse.

Wait. Don't say that.

"Okay, ma'am," Beanie says. "Ready to slide right?"

"Ready."

"Clear to slide right thirty, right twenty, right ten . . . right ten . . . Ma'am? I need you to slide right ten."

"Beanie, isn't this close enough?"

I'd swear the rotor tips are less than ten feet from the wall now. No way we can slide farther.

"No, ma'am, we're gonna need to get closer."

My mind whirs. Rotor clearance limits. Ten feet of horizontal clearance required for the main rotor. Same for the tail rotor.

"Sir, I don't know if we can do this. I don't think we're in rotor clearance limits."

"There *are* no limits," Boomer says.

"What? It's ten feet! It's—"

"In training, yes. If it's the real deal, the only limits are your own."

"Please tell me that's not a Bruce Lee quote."

"I'm paraphrasing."

I peer out my side window at an unmoving face of black granite that is *right there.*

"I hate to break it to you, Malone, but you're rock-steady in this hover, *and* you have the ability to do this. Not to mention, the guy with a spinal injury down there would appreciate the help."

"Ma'am, why don't we try it right here to start?" Beanie suggests. "Once Hap's on the rope, he can try to swing over to the victim."

"Let's try that," I say, copping out completely. Coward.

"Roger that. Stand by," Beanie says.

I can't see Boomer, because I'm looking out my right window, but his disappointed stare bores into the back of my skull. Will and the victim below remain out of sight, as well. Instead, I focus on a deformation in the rock face and hold there. If I keep the helicopter in this relative position to the rock, we should remain clear. Should . . .

Bracingly cold air sweeps into the cockpit when Beanie opens the cabin door, doing a thorough job of penetrating the thin material of my flight suit. Even though I'm wearing long underwear, it doesn't make a bit of difference. The early-season winter storm that dropped ten inches of new snow on the Sierra Nevada yesterday also brought single-digit temperatures with it.

"Okay, ma'am, Hap's at the door. Clear to exit?"

"Clear!"

"Hap's exiting the aircraft," Beanie calls. "He's on the skids. Steady right there. I'm goin' up hot mic."

He'll have to. He'll need to be hands-free on the mic to do all the rope handling and hoisting.

The wind buffeting. There it is again. It was somewhat negligible when we were flying at speed away from the rocks, but when you're attempting to hold a hover in a confined area, tiny wind gusts seem to morph into something convincingly more violent.

"Looking good on the gauges," Boomer says. "Nice and steady on the controls."

Hap stands on the skids—our landing gear that looks like skis—facing the helicopter's open door. He wears his climbing harness, to which a rappel device is attached, and a rope runs through this, secured on one end to the anchoring system in the helicopter, while the rest of the rope hangs far below.

"Hap's ready on the rappel, ma'am."

"Clear to jump," I say.

"Copy. Man's off the skids!"

Hap leaps backward and slides several feet down the rope to arrive below the skids. From there, he lowers himself the roughly fifty feet to Will and the first victim.

"Hap's adjacent the victim," Beanie says. "Starting his swing."

"Copy," I say, imagining Hap kicking his legs out, like you would on a playground swing, to get the rope moving back and forth, so he can move into a position where he can reach the rocks.

"Swingin' good now!" Beanie says, although the call really isn't necessary, as we can all feel the helicopter rocking.

Come on, Hap. You can do this. Please do this.

As Beanie makes his calls, informing the crew of Hap's progress, I blink my right eye, trying to clear the drop of sweat—*sweat?*—that just dripped there. It irritates, stings a bit, but I can't move my hands from the controls to wipe it.

"Ma'am, I'm gettin' a negative hand signal from Hap!"

"What?" *Oh, no.* "Can't he—?"

"No, ma'am. He can't reach the victim! We're gonna have to slide closer, if we're gonna make this happen!"

Closer . . .

"Sir?" I ask, reaching for a lifeline.

"You got this, Alison. You haven't budged since we started. I know you can do it."

I grind my teeth, and a steady trickle of sweat—oh yeah, it's running now—slides down the back of my neck.

"Ma'am?" Beanie asks.

Deep breath in. *Oh . . . all right. Shit.* "Call me right."

"Okay, ma'am, you're clear to slide right eight," Beanie says, using the number of feet to the stopping point he's chosen. "Clear to slide right five, right four, three, two, one, steady. Steady right there, ma'am. We've got two feet of clearance at the blade tips."

"Copy," I say, my jaw throbbing because it's clenched so tight.

Two feet from blade tip to solid rock. Sweat-inducing for sure, and by far the most difficult rescue scenario I've faced in my short tenure with this squadron.

"And only one foot of clearance at the tail," Beanie continues. "Do *not* move the tail rotor right."

Gulp. "Copy."

The icy chill I felt earlier disappears as I become the literal embodiment of the phrase "You're in the hot seat." Perspiration blooms. I try not to think about the men in this aircraft who are entrusting their lives to me. Trusting I won't waver. Trusting I won't move the cyclic those tiny few millimeters to the right that would send us smashing into the side of this mountain. Trusting I'll be able to manipulate the rudder pedals in time, if hit by a downdraft, before the tail spins. My grip tightens on the controls, my body rigid from the toes up.

"Hap's at the victim," Beanie says, continuing the play-by-play. "Hover's lookin' good. No rise, no drift. Nice and steady, ma'am."

"Still good on the gauges," Boomer says. "You're a rock on the controls."

"Tying off the belay!" Beanie says, huffing. On hot mic, you hear everything. Grunting, breathing, and the occasional stress-induced epithet. "Belay line is tied. Lowering the litter. Nice and steady on the hover, ma'am. Lookin' good."

As Beanie lowers the litter on the hoist cable, Hap is able to tug on the trail line below, keeping it taut so the litter doesn't swing. The litter is oriented vertically to match the position of the victim. This way, Hap and Will can slide the litter behind the victim and keep him in an upright position while strapping him in.

I blink continually to keep the rock deformation in focus. The longer I stare at it, the more the eyes play tricks. From where I sit, I have no reference to a straight horizon. So easy to drift without a horizon. . . .

Damn it. My hands, slick with sweat, are slipping inside my gloves.

The wind gust hits, and I'm already pressing right pedal when Beanie's oh-so-calm voice comes through my helmet. "Pivot the nose easy right, ma'am. That's it. Still a foot of clearance at the tail. Nice and steady. Hap's loading the man in the litter. Stand by."

I start to wonder if I might draw blood, gnawing as I am on the inside of my cheek. My head pounds, straining from the concentration. *Keep it steady, Ali. You've got this.*

"Nice and steady, ma'am," Beanie calls. "Man's in the litter. Bringing tension in the hoist. We have a thumbs-up. Victim's on the way up . . . he's halfway up . . . he's at the skids. Stand by. Bringing the litter in. . . ."

Hap remains on the rock below, still secured to the helicopter by his rappel rope and the belay line, as Beanie hauls the litter into the helicopter. After the victim is secure inside, Beanie will send the hoist down to get Hap, which means I only need to hold the helicopter in this tenuous position just a few more minutes.

"Shit!" Beanie shouts. "The guy's not breathing! No pulse! We gotta go ASAP!"

Shit! Hap is still fifty feet below us.

"Hap, the victim just crashed!" Boomer says. "Strap in, Doc, you're goin' for an e-ticket ride!"

"Ma'am, you're clear to slide left! Starting CPR!"

"Copy, sliding left!"

I sweep the cyclic to the left as Hap hangs on tight, attached to the ropes below us. He'll "fly" like this all the way to the hospital, because we have no easy way to bring him up.

". . . and twelve and thirteen and fourteen and fifteen . . . ," Beanie huffs as he counts out chest compressions. ". . . twenty-one, twenty-two, twenty-three, twenty-four . . ."

"Jack, we're gone," Boomer reports. "The guy went into cardiac arrest. Be back for the second guy shortly."

"Mono County copies."

"Mammoth Hospital, Rescue Seven," I say.

"Rescue Seven, Mammoth, go ahead."

"Mammoth, we've got a thirty-five-year-old man who was ice climbing and hit by rockfall," I say. "He was caught by his rope when he fell. Awake and alert when we got to him, complained of no feeling in his legs. While hoisting him up, he went into cardiac arrest. We've initiated CPR. Inbound. ETA four minutes."

". . . fifty-four, fifty-five, fifty-six, fifty-seven . . ."

And then to Will, "Whiskey One, Rescue Seven, over."

"Go ahead, Rescue Seven."

"Be advised, victim stopped breathing, and we've initiated CPR. En route to Mammoth Hospital."

"Rescue Seven, Whiskey One copies. Climbing down to second victim now."

I stretch my fingers, while still holding the controls, in an effort to relieve the tension. My toes remain numb, even though the rest of my body is soaked in sweat.

But who am I to complain? I peer around my cockpit seat to view Beanie in the cabin. He's hunched over the victim, arms locked and straight, the model of concentration, banging out chest compressions. Sweat drips from his face, even though the main cabin door remains wide open, the grunts and huffs ringing loud and clear.

". . . ninety-three, ninety-four, ninety-five, ninety-six . . ."

2

"All right, Alison, what's my heading?" Boomer asks as our bright orange helicopter lifts from Mammoth Hospital to fly to Naval Air Station Fallon, Nevada, home to our squadron—the navy's premier search and rescue squadron, the Longhorns.

We're flying home after safely delivering the second climber to the hospital. When we arrived with him, Beanie received a hero's welcome. It turns out that, owing to the CPR he performed in flight, he saved the first climber's life. Technically, it's all in a day's work for us, but still. *Major* kudos for Beanie.

We shut down just long enough to get our litter back, and now we're airborne, and Boomer is asking directions, even though he already knows the answer. A legend in the U.S. Navy's search and rescue community, Boomer knows the extended area around Fallon like the back of his hand. It's a mystery to all as to how he's been able to finagle three tours of duty here. But it's even more of a mystery—to me, anyway—why you would want to.

I've cursed my detailer daily for sending me to this godforsaken outpost of a navy base, located in the Middle of Nowhere Dust and Salt Flats, Nevada, to serve as a station search and rescue pilot—career suicide in the navy helicopter community. But while I lament, the local sheriffs rejoice. They rely on our team and its technical expertise to execute the most difficult mountain rescues.

I exhale loudly, keying the mic to ensure Boomer hears my exasperation, as I pull the map from its case. "Sir, we could just plug the coordinates into the GPS. It would make it a lot easier."

"Wha—?" Boomer turns his head to look at me directly, the decal on the front of his helmet now clearly visible—a cowboy on a bucking horse, worn with Wyoming alumni pride. "Hear you nothing that I say, young one? How long have you been here now? Three months? Four?"

I roll my eyes, a gesture becoming far too commonplace when I'm around Boomer.

"For the hundredth time, all you need is a map and your eyeballs. Good god, what are they teaching you new pilots anyway?"

"I'm not young; I'm twenty-*eight*. And I'm not a new pilot. I've been an aircraft commander, a maintenance check pilot. I've got more than fifteen hundred hours—"

"Twenty-anything is a *baby* in my book. And as far as piloting, you're a new *breed*."

"It's worse cuz she's from sixties, sir," Beanie says.

Beanie refers to the H-60 Seahawk helicopter—the navy's finest. It does everything—antisubmarine warfare, cargo lift, special ops—all modern, all new. Beanie would know, since he's flown in them, too.

"No doubt," Boomer says. "Hell, the pilots don't even have to fly anymore. Fuckin' glass cockpits, autopilot, auto-everything." He lets out a practiced huff. "How you came out of an H-Sixty squadron with *your* stick and rudder skills is still a mystery to me."

I guess the mysteries run all the way around.

Reluctantly, I run my finger across the map, now spread on my lap. Fallon lies to the north and east of Mammoth Lakes, a drive that would take close to three hours. But in a helicopter moving at over twice the speed of a car, and tracking as the crow flies, it will take us about sixty minutes.

"Sir, your heading is zero one zero. And sir, they still teach us how to fly," I add, in defense of my fellow H-60 pilots.

"Bullshit. It's an aviation catastrophe. They're training their future drone pilots is what they're doing."

I shake my head, knowing I will never win this argument, one that only adds salt to the wound of this assignment. I *should* be back in the H-60 community, as an instructor pilot now, at the very least, well on my way to ticking off all the checks in the boxes required for future command of a squadron.

This was not the plan. Due to rotten luck and unfortunate timing, when I completed my tour at my last squadron, this billet opened in Fallon. And if you've been siphoned off here, forget it. Dreams of command? Gone. But I still cling to hope. My detailer in Washington, D.C., is actively looking for a way to transfer me early. If I can, I won't fall too far behind my H-60 counterparts, and maybe, just maybe, I'll still have a chance at command someday.

"But, damn, what you did today . . . ," Boomer says.

"Was so far outside the rules of safe and responsible flying—"

"Whatever. You were saving lives."

"But—"

"But nothing."

I throw up my hands, turning my focus to the map instead—best to just block Boomer out—as we move up the eastern flank of the Sierra, following Highway 395 north. The clouds have lifted considerably since this morning, allowing a clear view as I raise my head to check our position against local landmarks. My gaze settles on the glacially pristine waters of a high mountain lake, one I've never seen before. Eyes widening, I absorb one of the most spectacular sights I think I've ever seen.

Jagged mountain peaks, draped in white, rise from the lake on all sides, forming a rugged amphitheater. The lower slopes are thick with pine, and the lake, clear as a window, projects the reflection of the surrounding mountains—an upside-down view of a winter wonderland, just like you read about in the storybooks.

I turn to Boomer, not realizing until then that my mouth is open.

"Have we found something that impresses you, Lieutenant?"

"What is this?" I ask, ignoring the barb.

"Check your map, my dear."

Gah! Incorrigible!

Looking down, I find it. June Lake.

I pivot in my seat, watching the lake, until it recedes from view, all silver and sparkles. A jewel, secretly nested in a ring of staggeringly high peaks.

A short five minutes later, we reach the eastern entrance to Yosemite National Park, and Boomer turns slightly right, beginning a transit that will leave this dazzling high alpine world behind. Instead, we'll move into the flats and browns of the desert, an arid landscape tucked in the rain shadow of the mighty Sierra Nevada.

"God bless, it's cold!" Hap says.

But flying into the desert doesn't necessarily mean it will get any warmer.

"Beanie, any word yet on when we'll get the part to fix this heater?" I ask, wiggling my toes to regain some feeling.

"Maintenance thinks it'll be another week, ma'am."

I sigh. It's always something with this aircraft, the H-1 Huey. But with an airframe that's seen over forty-five years of service, I suppose it's inevitable. Oh, I miss the H-60. . . .

I bring my gloved hands to my face, blowing into them like I did this morning, in a feeble attempt to warm them. To my left, Boomer doesn't wear gloves, which makes me crazy. A blatant violation of the rules, and yet, he always flies like this. As a result, most of our flights include a discussion on the subject.

"Sir, your gloves? Again?"

"What about 'em?" he says, feigning ignorance.

"They provide warmth, too, you know. Not just fire protection."

"Ha! So tell me this. Were your hands slipping today?"

Damn.

"Trust me. Way better control without 'em."

"But if there's a cockpit fire—"

"Cockpit fire? *Cockpit fire?* How many documented spontaneous cockpit fires have you read about? Far more likely you'll smash the bird into an immovable slab of granite because your hands slip from the controls."

"But, sir—"

"Don't 'but, sir' me. You're flying search and rescue now. It's not a matter of *if* you'll break the rules, it's *when.*"

"Not me. Not when I'm an aircraft commander. That's not how it's done."

Not in the H-60 community, anyway.

I lean my helmeted head against my seat, staring to the heavens. *God grant me the serenity . . .* Isn't that how that one goes?

"It's gotta be below zero," Hap says. "Jee-*zus!*"

"It's minus ten," I say, glancing at the Celsius reading on the outside-air temperature gauge.

"In October," Hap says. "That's ridiculous."

"Brother, you're in the mountains now!" Beanie says.

I peek around my chair, because observing these two brings a smile to my face every time . . . which I need now. An unlikely pair—Hap from notoriously rough South Central in Los Angeles, Beanie plucked straight from a Nebraska cornfield, all red hair and freckles—these two work together seamlessly, a model for crew coordination, and the best high-altitude, technical rescue team we have.

"This is just wrong," Hap says. "Why the hell did I ever accept orders up here?"

"You know you love it!" Beanie says, laughing.

Why Hap had the luxury to *accept* orders here, that is, he had a *choice,* is beyond me. I was given no such choice. Grrr . . .

"Why don't you fly for a while, Malone. You seem a little keyed up over there." Boomer sniggers, having entirely too much fun at my expense. "And let's start a climb right here to pop over these hills."

With a glare in his direction first, I take the controls. Better than arguing about the rules. Strike that. Utter lack of rules.

"Sir, could you turn that up, please?" Beanie asks.

"My pleasure," Boomer says, a foxy grin sliding across his face.

Playing music in the aircraft. *Another* procedures violation. I swear, it's a conspiracy. A let's-gang-up-on-Alison conspiracy. But I *can't* not say something.

"Really, sir? What if we miss a radio call?"

"Have we *ever* missed a radio call?"

Not when I've been in the aircraft, anyway. But it could *happen.*

"But an emergency, sir? What happens in the event of an emergency? What happens to crew coordination if you've got—"

The aircraft jerks left as the number-one engine winds down. *Shit!* I drop the collective, increase the rotor rpm switch, and nose over to maintain airspeed.

It all happens in about three seconds.

"Sir, I—"

"Bringing the throttle back up," Boomer says.

"What!" I snap my head to look at him, incredulous, pissed, relieved, all of the above. "*You* did that?"

"Indeed."

"But you can't—! You can't just go rolling the throttles off. We didn't even brief a simulated emergency—"

"I'd say you handled an emergency quite well, while listening to the radio. Wouldn't the gentlemen in back agree?"

"I'd say she nailed it, sir," Beanie says. "Perfect execution."

"Damn, she's fast," Hap says. "I mean, respectfully speaking, ma'am."

"I *cannot* believe you did that," I say between gritted teeth . . . which only makes Boomer laugh louder, like a bellow from a walrus.

I stew, and I stew. I fly, and I stew. "It's not even real music," I grumble.

"Tell me you did not just diss country music," Boomer says, issuing a drawn-out look of disapproval. "I can see we're gonna have to make it a point to educate you on these flights."

"Not necessary."

I so don't belong here. This is just another reminder that I need to keep after my detailer to get me transferred to a 60 squadron, where pilots and aircrew actually follow the freakin' rules.

"You know, I didn't realize you'd be such a challenge, Lieutenant Malone," Boomer says. "But we'll whip you into shape eventually."

3

Tossing and turning, I finally give up, and throw off the covers in exasperation. Apple cider. That's it. I'll have some hot apple cider, and then, sweet dreams for me.

I swing my legs off the too-soft bed and shuffle to the kitchen. It's a short walk in this tiny one-bedroom apartment. All of eight hundred square feet, it's located on the second floor of the Bachelor Officer Quarters on base.

I set the water to boil, pull an apple cider packet from the faux-wood cabinet, plop the tea bag–like pouch in my mug, and drop to a seat at the kitchen table to wait.

It's just the post-rescue high, I tell myself. Recounting the mission in all of its detail, trying to process it all. The crewmen say they experience the same thing after a mission—they're *wired* for the twenty-four hours following. With me, it's just this "stuff" that builds up inside, needing a pressure release valve. Feelings that I need to push out. I just need to . . . talk.

I tried to call my just-promoted fiancé earlier today, when we were still at Mammoth Hospital, but was sent to voice mail.

Beep. "You've reached the direct line of Richard Gordon. Please leave a message." Beep.

He trades in the stock market for one of the largest financial investment firms in the world, Litton Investments. I'd forgotten when I called that the exchange was still open.

Rather than leave a voice mail, I fired off a quick text.

Tried to call. Just finished a tricky rescue. Would love to tell you about it. Need to talk about so much, in general. Can't wait to see you. Only three more weeks. Miss you!

As I try to process the adrenaline-fueled hours between 0800 and 1200 today, I realize that my world and Rich's couldn't be farther apart right now. But it'll get better. After we get married, in May, he'll remain in San Diego while I finish my tour here—*if* I have to finish my tour here—and then we'll be together again. Even though it's almost three years living apart, I have to remember, it's a small period of time in the big picture.

That's what my detailer, Commander Bigelow, told me, anyway. I cringe when I remember the conversation following the receipt of orders that unexpectedly brought me here. Out of the way, out of sight, out of the mainstream, Naval Air Station Fallon cuts counter to every reason I joined the navy in the first place. The *stable* navy. One that paid for my schooling and guaranteed a job after graduation. One that provided rank and structure, rules and regulations, just do your job, and we'll take care of you.

My mom was thrilled. My stepfather, too. They raised me to be a responsible, practical adult, unlike the louse—my biological father—who abandoned my mom and me when I was only four years old.

It's so horribly cliché. Father abandons daughter. Daughter seeks stability and security for the rest of her days. Whatever. I saw what my "dad" did to my mom, and I don't want to be left hanging like that.

I struck gold—literally—when I met Rich. Intelligent, successful, well-off. Smart choice, my mom told me.

I drag my iPad from the corner of the table and switch it on. A picture of Rich and me emerges on the wallpaper, him in his suit, me in a new dress, at his firm's anniversary party, just a month before I came to Fallon. My engagement ring takes center stage in the photo, having been placed there just moments before on the balcony of Tom Ham's Lighthouse restaurant. The lights of downtown San Diego twinkle in the background.

My gaze drifts to my left hand, the ring finger now bare. I don't wear the ring—a two-carat sparkler—when I fly, because it doesn't fit under my flight glove. I hesitate to think what it cost him. I realize, only now, that I failed to put it on when I got home, exhausted as I was.

My message folder indicates two unread messages. Opening the first, I see that Rich has finally gotten back to me.

Congrats on the rescue! Reserved the Lighthouse for the wedding reception. It's gonna be sweet as hell. Enjoy the pics!

I click on the photo attachments, smiling as I remember these same spectacular views of San Diego Bay, Coronado Island, and the downtown skyline on that mild May evening. I quickly tap out a response.

Perfect. I agree, this is the best choice. I'll try to call tomorrow. Would really love to talk.

The teakettle whistles. I fill my mug, return to the table, lean my head on my hand, and begin to lift and dunk the apple cider in its "tea bag."

Lift and dunk. Lift and dunk.

The steam drifts, and I breathe in the comforting scents of cloves and cinnamon, just as I did as a kid during the snowy Thanksgivings spent at my aunt Celia's vacation lodge on the banks of the Walker River. We'd stay in one of her eleven rental cabins and gather on the raised back porch of the main lodge to drink hot cider and listen to Grandpa Alther's navy sea stories—riveting tales of cyclones in the Bay of Bengal and port visits to faraway places like Singapore, Thailand, and Bali.

The lodge, located in the foothills of the Sierra, is only a two-hour drive from Fallon. I thought I would have made the drive there at least once since I arrived this summer, but without Celia—she turned over the day-to-day operations to a caretaker—I couldn't find a reason to go.

I don't know . . . maybe I should go back anyway. Happy memories there . . .

Tapping on the iPad screen, I see that the second unread message is from none other than Celia.

Call me when you get a chance. Dr. Grant didn't tell me anything outright—she can't, of course—but I get the feeling something's happening in your mom's therapy sessions. I'm not sure if I should be worried or excited.

Oh, boy . . .

I lift the apple cider pouch and set it to the side, bring the mug to my lips, and blow to cool the liquid.

Something odd happened to my mom after her second husband died. There's grieving, and then . . . well, there's whatever this is. I don't know what to call it. Even the resident expert, Celia—a psychiatrist—can't figure it out. Mom has put on a good face for her real-estate business, but Celia and I know otherwise.

We finally staged an "intervention." We said, therapy or else. Of course, she didn't go for it at first. Angry, hurt, it's none of your business, all of that. But now she's been seeing Dr. Grant—a referral from Celia—regularly for about seven months, and I *think* it's been going okay. She hasn't really opened up to me about her sessions, but I suppose it's easy to see what you want to see. A spark. Some hope. Just . . . some life.

I take several sips, the cider sliding warm down my throat, before touching the iPad screen to tap out a response. But I stop when the wallpaper emerges again.

Rich and me. An engaged couple.

Seven months . . .

Seven months of therapy for my mom. Seven months until I become Mrs. Richard Gordon. Alison Gordon. Lieutenant Gordon. It all rolls off the tongue nicely enough.

And then, forgoing the response to Celia—I'll just call her tomorrow—I do something I swore I never would. On the back of a grocery list, I write it out. Alison Gordon. Magdalena Alison Gordon, using my full given name. Alison Gordon in cursive. Alison Gordon in print. All caps. No caps. Big letters, small. Initials. AG. MAG. The whole wacky bride-to-be exercise for the soon-to-be Alison Gordon.

Alison Gordon . . . who will live in downtown San Diego in a high-rise loft condominium, a retirement portfolio in place, insured against every conceivable circumstance, including random acts of nature, who will enjoy a successful naval career, perhaps start a family, and live happily ever after.

I reach across the table to drop the pen back in its cup holder, knocking my mug with my elbow.

"Ow! Shit!" I push back and jump out of my chair at the same time, as hot tea splatters across my lap. *Damn it.*

Standing in my wet pajamas, I survey the floor, the table, the chair, cider sprayed over all of them, including my signature page, now soaked.

"Nice," I mutter.

I grab the sponge and wipe it all up, sweeping the remains of my ruined grocery list into my hand and tossing it into the garbage.

4

This is ridiculous. I climb into the airport manager's dented black pickup truck, about to hitch a ride from the Bishop airport to Erick Schat's Bakkerÿ. Yes, spelled with two "k"s. The Dutch bakery has won rave reviews from our crew, but really? We're supposed to be searching for *people,* not baked goods.

And, we're sitting in the *bed* of a truck. Open air. No seat belts. No way this is legal.

Boomer shakes his head as I voice my complaints. "You know, I seriously wonder about you, Malone." The truck lurches as the driver pulls out of the tiny operations building. "Let me guess. Came home from prom on time? Never ditched school? Always drive the speed limit?"

"As a matter of fact, yes."

"Boring!" he says, drawing out the first syllable. "With a capital 'B'!"

The truck rumbles over a rutted dirt road, and Boomer, Beanie, Hap, and I bump around in the back like giant Halloween pumpkins, clad in garishly bright flight suits colored rescue orange to match our helicopter. The orange suits do make our guys easier to spot once we've dropped them on-scene, and they wear their colors with rescue pride. I have no idea why Boomer, a pilot, who never sets foot outside the cockpit, would wear orange. But then again, I think he was born to wear an orange flight suit, one his extra-large self fills out a little too well. And leave it to Boomer to deem that the first order of business, when I checked into the squadron, was to exchange my drab—his words—olive-green flight suit for a more *respectable* orange.

After about fifty yards of jumping, bumping, jarring, and jerking, the tires finally find the smooth asphalt of the main road, and with a quiet *swish*, we're off. I exhale.

I also breathe more easily due to the change in weather. The cold front that had me shivering yesterday has moved on, replaced with a practically balmy day, temperatures now well over fifty degrees.

"And then college," Boomer continues. "Let me guess. . . ." He stops, waiting for me to confirm.

"I went to the Naval Acad—"

"Of course you did."

The crewmen smile, content to watch Boomer play his little game.

"And then flight school and then H-Sixties. Ughh. Did you actually pick that airframe? Tell me you didn't pick that."

"It's not like I had a lot of choice in the matter. That's pretty much all there is now. But I would have picked them anyway."

I shift my position over the wheel well as the driver turns down Bishop's Main Street, bringing my hands to the sides of my face to push my hair out of my eyes. It *used* to be in a neat bun.

I fidget, frustrated, as I try to put my hair back in place, while the crewmen point and smile. "Dude, there's that fly-fishin' shop I told you about!" "And we *have* to hit Wilson's Eastside Sports!" "Nah, man, the movie theater!" I see that the movie theater comprises just one screen. No surprise in this out-of-the-way town of Bishop, population just over three thousand.

"I hesitate to ask," Boomer says. "Favorite ice cream?"

With one look, he knows.

"Vanilla? Are you serious?"

I nod.

"Beanie, favorite ice cream," Boomer says.

"Rocky Road, sir."

"Hap?"

"Mint chocolate chip. You, sir?"

"Jamoca almond fudge."

"That doesn't mean anything," I say. "Lots of people like vanilla."

"Insurance salesmen, financial advisers, bankers, vanilla, vanilla, vanilla," Boomer says.

I look down at my feet. Rich's favorite ice cream is vanilla. We order it at our favorite shop, MooTime Creamery, on Coronado Island, where they make their ice cream from scratch. Granted, we're always asked by the folks behind the counter what we want to mix with it—candy, nuts, cookies, fruit—receiving curious looks when we answer that no, we're good with just vanilla, thank you.

Ouch! Bump! Pothole. I'm lifted and bounced on the wheel well, and I scrabble to grab the sides of the truck. *Bump!* Another one. *Bump! Ow!* Stupid truck.

Boomer grins, his face glowing, just as it did when we flew in to the airport. His attention has shifted now to the mountains, and begrudgingly I can see why he would smile at this. The Sierra Nevada on one side, the White Mountains on the other, Bishop sits smack in the middle of the Owens River Valley with a perfect view to both.

The change in scenery from Fallon to this place—located thirty miles southeast of Mount Morrison, where we did our rescue yesterday—is striking. The vertical relief of the Sierra Nevada stuns, peaks rising ten thousand feet above the valley floor. Only the steepest, craggiest formations of black granite poke out from the creamy layer of new snow that now coats the range—a spectacular sight in anyone's book.

The local Chamber of Commerce boasts that Bishop is a "small town with a big backyard." That just about sums it up, although in the mountaineering community, it's a world-renowned backyard. Climbers, skiers, and mountaineers travel from across the globe to play in the mountains near Bishop, which is one of the reasons our search and rescue unit keeps so busy.

But today's flight isn't about searching or rescuing. Rather, we fly

to return accumulated rescue gear—that's Boomer's excuse, anyway—
to the Mono County SAR Team. And, oh, we just happen to be
meeting them at one of their favorite hangouts.

"Behold," Boomer says with a flourish. "Schat's Bakkerÿ!"

The driver pulls into the parking lot next to a building with a
Dutch/Swiss façade, brick walls, and a steeply slanted roof, checked
in blue and gray. Our crew tumbles out the back of the truck, and
Boomer strides ahead. On the way to the front door, we pass floor-to-
ceiling glass windows displaying a bounty of souvenirs that would
give any gift shop in the Netherlands a run for its money. Shelves
upon shelves of Dutch kitsch—most of it Delft pottery, the signature
Dutch blue-and-white earthenware—featuring cows and windmills,
clocks and kettles, coffee mugs, and kissing-couple figurines.

Boomer holds the door open for me and the rest of our crew as we
enter the establishment that has won the hearts and minds of Longhorn crew members for as long as the squadron has been in existence.

Mr. Schat, you had me at hello.

I stop in the doorway, bombarded with the mouthwatering smells
of freshly baked bread, pastries, rolls, assorted cookies, candies, and
cakes. To my left, an entire room—almost as big as my apartment—
devoted entirely to bread. Dozens of baker's racks, crammed side by
side, showcase hundreds of hot-out-of-the-oven loaves. In front of
me, happy coffee-drinking, pastry-eating patrons crowd the central
seating area. And surrounding this, more baker's racks, these stuffed
with pound cakes, homemade Dutch candies, preserves, and honey.
Along the back wall, a long countertop with glass display cabinets
houses strudel, cinnamon buns, and a bazillion varieties of doughnuts. Even the ceiling is crowded, hung with Dutch wooden clogs of
all sizes and colors.

The shop hums, workers moving racks into position on the floor,
bakers shuttling dough into the back ovens, customers massing near
the counters, and engaged diners partaking of thick glazed doughnuts that look so light and fresh they could float.

The Mono County SAR crew gives us a wave, motioning us over to
their spot in the far corner. We squeeze through the packed dining

area to get to them, and one man puts out his hand, a hand coated in confectioner's sugar, to Boomer, giving a firm handshake.

"How are you, Jack?" Boomer says.

"Just looking forward to our Morrison debrief," Jack says with a wink.

"Ah, good man. A consummate professional. We'll take care of that *debrief* here in just a moment. But, strudel comes first."

"Would this be Lieutenant Malone?" Jack asks, standing.

"It is, sir," I say, offering my hand. "And it's just Alison. Nice to finally meet you in person."

And it is nice. Jack's one of those people you instantly like, but you're not sure why. He's the head of the Mono County Search and Rescue Team, but also one of Boomer's best friends. I've never met the fifty-something man personally, only having heard his voice on the radio, but from what I understand, he possesses a legendary mountaineering résumé.

I jump, startled, when a dog with cream-colored fur and golden, floppy ears pokes out from his hiding place under the table. I'm still shaking Jack's hand when the dog begins to sniff my fingers, before offering a warm lick.

"Well, hello there," I say, giving the dog a scratch behind the ears.

"His name is Mojo," Jack says.

I smile, remembering my own Labrador retriever, a gift for my fifth birthday. My mom thought he'd be good company for me after my dad left. Protect me. Maybe even help to heal a broken heart. I bring my other hand to Mojo's head and give him a thorough pet while Boomer continues his greetings.

"Walt," Boomer says, offering his hand to Walt Hillerman, Mono County's assistant SAR coordinator. "You're lookin' good, my friend."

Walt is the oldest member of the team—in his early seventies— and as hearty as they come. Tall and wiry, just like Beanie and Hap, he wears faded jeans, nicked-up cowboy boots, and a red-checked flannel shirt.

"And you, sir," Walt says. "Did you bring the gear?"

"It's waiting for you at the airport."

"'Bout time you returned that," Jack says.

"You know the drill. I needed to collect enough so I'd have an excuse to fly out here."

"Well, go grab some food, and then get back here," Jack says. "We need some serious conversation about how the Kings obliterated the Lakers on Friday."

"Preseason, sir. Preseason," Boomer says.

"Oh, no. The home team is *on* this year!"

"The home team might not be the home team anymore!"

"No way. The good people of Sacramento would never let it happen," Jack says.

"Just sayin'," Boomer says. He looks back to us. "Okay, we need food."

I give Mojo one last pet before he ducks under the table and curls at Jack's feet.

Boomer takes the lead, moving between multiple display stands to the far back counter, Hap and Beanie in his wake. I linger behind, looking up and down the baker's racks, knowing we'll have plenty of room in the aircraft if I want to purchase a few things to take with me. I remember the handheld shopping baskets stacked at the entry and turn to score one.

"Oh!" I say, bumping into a customer leaving the bread room. The man wields two brown-paper shopping bags held high, one cradled in each arm. "Excuse me! I'm sorr—"

He lowers his arms, and a smile broadens across his tanned face, weather lines radiating above his ruddy cheeks.

Good god but he's handsome.

Keen blue eyes, framed by slightly ruffled, surfer blond hair, regard me curiously . . . studiously . . . knowingly.

"Rescue Seven, by chance?" he says.

What? How would he—? Oh! Tall, broad-shouldered, lean, early thirties . . . and wearing a bright yellow North Face jacket.

"Whiskey One?"

The smile that was wide to start stretches further, his eyes crystalline, shiny. His hand shoots out from underneath a shopping bag. "Will Cavanaugh."

Strong handshake. No surprise.

"Alison Malone."

He nods, releasing my hand, and I straighten, trying to absorb the energy that surrounds this man. *A lot* of energy . . .

"Was that you on the controls yesterday?" he asks.

"It was. And you were the one looking like Spiderman?"

"I don't know about Spiderman. Just had to get to them quickly, you know?"

"I don't think I've ever seen anything like that in my life," I say.

"Guess that makes two of us."

"What?"

"You. Your flying. I've never seen a pilot hold a hover that still. I don't think you moved an inch."

"Well, we were pretty lucky with the winds yesterday."

"Uh . . . I think it was more than that."

"Will!" Boomer says, retracing his steps down the row of baker's racks. He puts out his chubby hand, which Will shakes. "I see you've met my protégé here."

"Indeed," Will says. "Obviously Boomer-trained."

"Obviously. She's got the stick and rudder skills, no doubt about it. Still working on her head, though," he says, pointing to his temple.

I roll my eyes. Damn. I've got to stop doing that.

"So when'd you get back?" Boomer asks.

"Just a week ago."

"What was it this time? Ama Dablam? K2?"

"Annapurna."

"Big?"

"Yeah, pretty big."

"I'm sure it was epic. All your trips are. But man, you've lost weight."

Will shrugs.

"Well, it just so happens that we're *debriefing* here today," Boomer says, pointing to the group.

"That's what I'm here for," Will says. "That and some bread." He motions to the bags he carries.

"Seriously, dude, you need some nourishment," Boomer says. "Add some doughnuts to that bread order, will ya?"

"That's the plan."

"That's what I'm talkin' about!" Boomer slaps Will on the shoulder before dodging and weaving through a throng of customers to return to the pastry counter.

"So you just flew in, then?" Will asks.

"Yeah, we're supposedly here to return your gear."

He laughs. A hearty laugh. "I think Boomer owns stock in this place. He usually schemes some way to get here. A lot of cross-country navigation flights, from what I understand."

That's exactly what Boomer would do. He's taken me on several cross-country navigation flights, *crucial* flights for my training and familiarization with the area, that always seem to arrive at a time coinciding with breakfast, lunch, or dinner, and in places like Tahoe City, South Lake Tahoe, Carson City, Reno. . . . He would *never* get away with this in the H-60 community. Never.

"So first time here?" Will says.

"Yeah. The selection is sort of overwhelming."

"I'd be happy to help, if you like."

"I think I'll take you up on that. Let me just grab a basket."

When I return, we move down the aisle toward the back counter, and Will points out his favorites. My hand reaches out at almost every suggestion—Dutch crumb coffee cake, artichoke spread, sheepherder bread, butter brickle, blueberry preserves . . .

"Ooh, this is Rich's favorite," I say, holding up a clear sack of plain dinner rolls, tied in cube-like knots.

"Rich?" Will asks.

"My fiancé. These dinner rolls are his favorite."

"Oh, congratulations. When's the big day?"

"May twentieth," I say, placing the rolls carefully in the basket. "Uh, Will, we're not even halfway, and this is already full."

"Well, you know you'll be back, especially if you're flying with that character," he says, inclining his head to Boomer. "Why don't you buy what you've got in the basket and take that home for later. And then, for breakfast, you should follow me to the doughnuts." He motions to the back counter, a substantial line of customers now between the doughnuts and us.

"Might as well get in line, then," I say, moving forward.

"So did you get any sleep last night?" he asks.

"No . . . no, not much."

"Me either. I can never sleep after rescues like those."

"Really? I was wondering about that when I was wide awake at two this morning."

He nods knowingly.

"I was thinking how stupid it was to not be able to sleep," I say. "But it seems to happen to me a lot."

"Well, yeah. Lots to process. It's like coming down from a super-high, all your engines firing, you're totally focused, the adrenaline, all of it. Yeah, not uncommon at all."

I exhale, relieved. "I'm glad I'm not the only one."

"No, you have plenty of company. And speaking of yesterday, I know I already mentioned it, but you were amazing. Seriously. The guys can't stop talking about it. They watched it all with binoculars and were pretty much blown away, which is a hard thing to do with this group."

"No, amazing is you climbing up an ice wall without a rope. Although, I shouldn't say amazing. I should say crazy. That's flat insane to climb without a rope."

"Who says?"

"Well, what if you fall?"

"You're worried about me falling? You, who's hovering just inches from a wall of rock?"

He pauses, while I consider it.

"I think I'll take my chances with an ice axe."

"Okay, point taken." I shift my basket to the other arm. "I don't know if you realize it, but the guys idolize you. You're all they could talk about once when we landed at the hospital."

"They're a great group. We do a lot of training together, so I've gotten to know them pretty well. Beanie, especially."

"Beanie . . . who's training to be a mountain guide. Wait, is that you? Are you training him?"

"I am. That's one of my day jobs. Guiding."

"Ma'am? Excuse me, ma'am? What would you like?" the women behind the counter says.

I look up, and we're at the front of the line. How did we get to the front?

"May I make a suggestion?" Will says.

"Yes, please."

"Since this is your first time, I'd stick with the basics, a classic."

"Which is?"

"The glazed doughnut. It's not fancy, but it's damn good."

"Glazed doughnut, please," I say to the woman.

"Make that two," Will says.

Since Will has both hands full with his bags of bread, I slide the basket farther up my forearm and take both plates offered. We snake through groups of undecided shoppers toward the cash register, arriving at the coffee-ordering station located just in front of it. "Coffee?" I ask.

"Definitely."

"Two coffees, please," I say. I place our doughnut plates on the counter, then bend over, fumbling through my flight suit pocket for my wallet.

"Please, let me," Will says, handing the cashier his credit card.

"Oh no, Will, you don't have to do that."

"My pleasure. Think of it as a thank-you from the guys you rescued yesterday. They're friends of mine, and they'd hit me over the head if I didn't buy you some breakfast for your trouble."

"But, I have all this," I say, indicating the basket of food treasures the cashier now bags for me.

"It's fine, really. And if it really bothers you, you can get the coffee next time."

"All right. Deal."

I turn to walk to our seats. "So they're okay, then? Your friends?"

"Yeah. The feeling's returned to Grant's legs. He was even walking around this morning. And Gale has a broken arm and a few scrapes. But they're both pretty lucky."

"That's the spirit, Alison!" Boomer says, admiring the large brown bag I hold in one arm, along with a doughnut plate in each hand. "Now you're talking!"

After depositing our bags of breads and goodies, Will returns with our coffees, taking the seat next to me. I turn my focus to a glazed doughnut sent straight from heaven and bring it to my mouth. My eyes widen, turning to Will, as I chew.

Smile lines crease from the sides of his eyes. "What do you think?" he asks.

"I think that's the best doughnut I've ever tasted," I say, wiping the crumbs from my lips.

"You know why?"

"Uh, because they make good doughnuts?"

"Well, yeah. But it's something else, too. It's what happens after you do something like you did yesterday."

I take a sip of coffee—my first, which means I can't blame the caffeine for the buzzing I feel. I look to Will. To the source. The energy is there.

"When you risk so much," he says, leaning forward. "When it requires all of your being to stay in the moment, to remain singularly focused, blocking out everything else, everything is heightened after that. The simple and the mundane aren't anymore. The next doughnut you eat, no matter where it is, is the best doughnut you've ever tasted."

I stare at Will, processing.

"See what you've done, Will?" Walt calls loudly from across the table. "You've stunned the poor girl. Too much philosophizin'. He tends to do that, you know. Gets all cerebral on ya. Now you just go on and ignore him and get to the business of eatin' your food."

I take another sip of coffee, glancing at Will over the Styrofoam cup's rim. "I think I know what you mean," I say, speaking in a low voice. "It's something I haven't been able to put into words since I've been here, but that's it. I feel 'heightened,' like you say. Just . . . up . . . or something."

"Exactly," Will says, blue eyes sparkling.

Beyond Will, I notice when Boomer pulls his vibrating pager from his waist belt. Glancing at the number, he picks up his cell phone that lies on the table and dials.

Watching this exchange, pager to cell phone, I remember when I first checked into the base operations office, and they handed me a pager. I thought it was a joke. People still use pagers? In Nevada, the answer is yes. Huge swaths of land remain in dead zones with no cell phone coverage, so to ensure our crews are always reachable no matter where we fly, we still carry pagers.

"Yep, yep, okay," Boomer says into the phone, checking his watch. "We'll be back at thirteen hundred. Have the team standing by at the hangar. Yeah, yeah, copy that."

Boomer looks up, holstering his phone. "Unexploded off-range ordnance near Bravo Nineteen," he says, referring to Bombing Range 19. "We need to pick up the EOD team and deliver 'em out there."

Will throws a curious look my way.

"It's part of our job," I explain. "We work with the explosive ordnance disposal team, when unexploded bombs land outside the range fence line."

"Sounds like they keep you busy out there."

"Yeah, working with the EOD team is just another thing we do."

"I'm embarrassed to say, I really don't know *what* you guys do. Seems strange to have a navy base in the middle of the desert," he says as he tears off a chunk of doughnut and pops it in his mouth.

"Yeah, I know. They have bombing ranges out there, and every carrier air wing—this is like sixty or seventy aircraft—has to come through Fallon to train before they go on deployment. We're just the search and rescue asset for them."

"But why Fallon of all places?"

"Wide-open desert. Wide-open skies. Nothing to run into, I think."

I stuff the last bit of doughnut into my mouth. Heaven. Just heaven.

"But we work with you guys *a lot*," Will says. "I mean, it seems like you're here more often than there."

"Yeah, the civilian SAR work is a bonus—a goodwill gesture to the community, basically. It just so happens, though, that eighty percent of our work is for civilian rescue."

"Lucky for us," he says, raising his coffee mug to clink against mine.

Boomer lifts the final piece of strudel to his lips, savoring the morsel. "Damn, that's good!"

"Need a ride back to the airport?" Jack says.

"As a matter of fact, we do," Boomer says.

"I've got my truck," Will offers. "I could fit two in the front, but two would have to ride in back."

Boomer gives me a purposeful glance. "Yes, Malone, *you* can ride in front."

"I'm not worried about me. I'm worried about the crew."

"As am I, which is why you will ride in the front. Just lookin' out for you, Vanilla."

Will raises his eyebrows. "Vanilla?"

"It's a long story," I say.

"Let me demonstrate," Boomer says.

Oh, no . . .

"Jack? What's your favorite ice cream?"

"Cookies 'n' cream."

"Walt?" Boomer asks, shifting his gaze one seat over.

"Chocolate chip."

"Kevin?"

"Coconut rum."

Kevin turns to his right as everyone now realizes Boomer is moving down the row.

"Thomas?"

"Butter pecan."

"And we already know Beanie's and Hap's," Boomer says, looking at our aircrewmen, who sit next in line. "Rocky Road and mint chocolate chip."

I sit back, wiping my hands across my face. Follow the rules. Boring. Vanilla.

"And you, Mr. Cavanaugh, what is *your* favorite flavor of ice cream?" Boomer asks with relish.

Will looks to me first before shifting his eyes back to Boomer. "Vanilla."

I sit up a little straighter.

"You've gotta be shittin' me," Boomer says.

"Why, what's wrong with vanilla?" Will asks.

"Oh, criminy," Boomer says, pushing himself up from the table. "Let's get outta here."

The group begins to rise, chairs scraping against the floor as they're pushed back. I lean in to Will. "Thank you," I say.

"Anytime."

5

"Longhorn Seven, Fallon Tower, you're cleared to the south, over."

"Fallon Tower, Longhorn Seven, roger," I say.

I follow Highway 95 south to Bravo 19—we call our bombing ranges Bravo for short—using our call sign "Longhorn" instead of "Rescue." It's a subtle difference, but to air traffic controllers, a big one. When you use the title Rescue, while engaged in activities relating to a rescue, the rules change. Suddenly, you're cleared *direct* to practically anywhere you need to go. Complicated entrance and exit patterns to airfields are waived. Airspace restrictions, altitude and noise limits, fall by the wayside. All of this performed with an unspoken urgency, so the rescue aircraft can get to its destination in the quickest possible manner.

This afternoon's mission is not urgent, or "rescue urgent," I should say. In fact, transporting the EOD team to the site of an unexploded thousand-pound bomb falls on the routine side of our SAR unit's day-to-day life here in Fallon.

In stark contrast to yesterday, we fly over mostly flat pastureland, and into a bombing range located sixteen miles southeast of Fallon, comprising low-lying alkali flats, scrub, and sage. The Blow Sand

Mountains run diagonally across the upper right corner of this rectangular range, rising about seven hundred feet from the valley floor.

Flying across the center of the range, we pass fifteen light armored vehicles in the helicopter strafing area, four tank targets, two forward air control platforms, and, just as you might imagine on a practice-bombing range, a large, round bull's-eye target—known as the bull—dead in the center, formed by three concentric circles, the length of two football fields. The target is lighted for night missions, one of the most dangerous evolutions the jet pilots fly, due to the mountainous terrain here.

"Do you have the fence line in sight?" the EOD officer asks.

"I have it," I say.

"The bomb is two hundred yards east."

I slow down, moving over the sloping, rocky terrain that defines the foothills of the Blow Sands, and the EOD officer points out the site. Yep, the unexploded bomb is most definitely out of bounds, and in a precarious spot.

"We're not gonna be able to land," I say. "Are you good if we one-skid it?"

"Yeah," the EOD officer says, "if you could just help us unload the gear."

"No problem, sir," Beanie says.

"How about that large, flat rock right there?" I ask Boomer.

"Perfect," he says.

And then he sits back, looking overpleased, as I make my approach.

"Yep," he says. "One-skids are a great maneuver when you have no place to land. We have these slick ski-like things called skids under the aircraft. If we can get close enough, our passengers can embark and debark the aircraft, just like climbing a set of stairs. It's fast *and* efficient." He looks at me pointedly. "You can't do *that* in an H-Sixty."

I look away so he can't see my face—don't want to give him the satisfaction of knowing I agree with him—as I pull into a hover.

"Men are exiting the skids, ma'am," Beanie calls. "Steady right there. I'm goin' up hot mic, while I unload."

The huffing and puffing is loud in my ears as Beanie hauls equipment and duffel bags out the cabin door.

"All right, ma'am," he says, breathing heavily. "That's the last of it. Men are clear. We're clear to go."

"Copy," I say, pulling collective, lifting, and accelerating away.

"Longhorn Seven, EOD Eleven, recommend at least one mile clearance while we defuse, over."

"One mile, copy," I say, before switching to our internal radio. "Sir, did you want to return to the helipad?"

"Helipad? Come on, Malone, we've been through this before. Why not right there?" Boomer says, pointing to a stretch of desert flats below us.

"It's not navy property, sir."

He turns in his cockpit seat. "Malone, seriously. Think. Outside. The. Box. We're in the conduct of official military business, a mission that's critical to the safety of civilians, and we need to be in a position to see our guys in case they need our help. *Capisce?*"

I let out a huff. "Yes, sir."

Beanie calls me in to an easy flat landing, a good mile away from the EOD team, who we're still able to see once we've touched down.

"Might as well shut down and save some fuel," Boomer says.

"Shut down? Out here? But—" I say.

"But what?"

"But you don't have a fireguard. I mean, for the restart. You don't—"

"And . . ."

"Sir, this goes against everything I've been taught. It goes against *this* very manual," I say, lifting my H-1 pocket checklist and waving it in the air. "No matter the aircraft, no matter where you're stationed, a person acting as a fireguard and in the possession of fire-extinguishing equipment is *required* to be posted prior to an engine start. Just so you know."

He laughs, a deep belly laugh, one that seems to go with his six-foot-two, 250-pound frame. Or maybe he's up to 260. Regardless, it's up there. "Well, you're in a new schoolroom now. New teacher, new rules. Get used to it."

What do I do? Roll my eyes, of course.

"Cutting throttles," I say.

As I do, Boomer reaches up with his ungloved hand and kills the battery switch. The aircraft rocks from side to side, as the rotors slow, until it comes to a silent stop. I pull my helmet off with a loud exhale.

"You gonna live, Vanilla?"

"No," I sigh.

I look out over sand and sagebrush that stretches for as far as the eye can see, as Boomer, Beanie, and Hap bounce out of the aircraft. They meet in front of the bird, laughing and yukking it up, not a care in the world.

No. No, I'm not sure I'll make it.

6

"Remember the pocket doors I ordered for the entrance to the laundry room and the pantry?" Rich says. "The contractor is scheduled to come in tomorrow to install them."

"That's great," I say, sitting at the kitchen table, absently stirring my rapidly cooling oatmeal.

I glance at the clock. 0620. Ten minutes until I need to leave to brief for my flight, which is avalanche training today. I was thrilled when Rich called at 0530, knowing we'd have almost a full hour to talk. To catch up. To vent . . .

In these fifty minutes, I've learned not only about the pocket doors, but about the drywall guys he contracted to enlarge a nook area in the living room so he can fit in a larger flat screen, the deposit he put down for the wedding reception, a new fixed annuity that guarantees interest rates as high as 3.65 percent, and the honeymoon package he's working on with the travel agent, which includes hiring a sailboat captain to tour us around the Bahamas. He's even arranged for a guided snorkeling trip.

"I've also chartered a private fishing boat for deep-sea fishing," he says. "You don't even have to do anything. They rig the lines, put the bait on the hooks, and clean the fish after you catch them."

"That's . . . wow, yeah, that's great."

I put down my spoon, and reach for my mug of coffee, the mug my mom bought me when I was twelve. I had fallen off the balance beam midroutine at the gymnastics regional championships that year and missed qualifying for finals. So she bought me a pep-me-up gift—a motivational cat poster, but on a mug. This poor cat is hanging by its front paws, clinging—barely—to a thin metal bar. Underneath, the caption says, *Hang in there, baby.*

"I know that might sound like a lot," Rich says, "but I was thinking of it as a honeymoon with an adventure theme. I thought you'd like it. You know, something different."

"Oh, yeah, guided tours . . . of so many different things. For sure, Rich. Thanks. It sounds spectacular."

I need to call Celia back. Oh, and damn it, I need to call my mom, too. . . .

"Is it all right? Are you sure?"

"Yeah, really. You're putting so much thought into this. It's great."

"So how about you?" he asks at 0625.

"Oh, just . . ."

"I'm sorry," he says. "God, I've been shooting my mouth off this whole time. I just wanted to make sure I kept you in the loop on everything."

"No, that's fine. You're right. It's nice to be back up to speed."

"Well, we'll have more time to talk when I visit, right? Only three more weeks. Actually, less than three weeks."

"Yeah, I'm really looking forward to it. I just . . ."

I look at the mug in my hand, staring at the cat.

He hangs there, wide-eyed, little paws straining to hold on to the bar, at the limit, about to fall . . .

"What's up?" Rich asks.

"Well, just lots of things," I say, looking at my watch. Not enough time . . . crap. *Just say it, Ali. Get it out there. Something . . .* "I can't sleep, the rules are crazy up here, actually, not crazy, there *are* no rules, and the stuff we're doing is risky as hell, and I feel like I'm standing on the edge of a cliff, and it's like I can't come down, and I'm in danger of falling the whole time, but it's terrible and wonderful at the same time, and I just—"

"Whoa, whoa, whoa! Hold on, Ali. Hold on."

I breathe in deeply, then release the air in one giant *whoosh*.

"So wait. What's going *on*?"

"I don't know. I just . . . I don't know."

"Okay, so let's just think about this. We know Commander Bigelow's working on getting you transferred early. And then you can—wait, what did you just say? Wonderful?"

"What?"

"Wonderful. Just now. You said it was terrible and wonderful at the same time."

"I did?" I pick up my spoon and begin rolling it through my fingers, under and over, under and over, watching it travel down to the pinky, and then rolling it back toward my thumb—a nervous habit picked up in flight school. "See, I can't even think straight."

"Well, when's the last time you talked with Commander Bigelow? Maybe he's got an update for you. If he can make it happen, you can get back to San Diego. To some stability . . . which I think you need."

"I do need some stability. I really do. He left a voice mail a few days ago. Said he was making progress. Sounded optimistic."

"Well, you should be optimistic, too, then."

I start stirring again, not able to muster up anything even remotely close to optimism. A weird silence stretches the seconds.

"You seem so anxious," he says finally. "I don't think I've ever heard it this bad before."

"I'm sorry," I say, putting my spoon down, now fidgeting with my flight suit zipper. "It's not as bad as I'm making it out. I'm not even sure what I'm saying."

"You sure?"

"Yeah, I'm sure. Really." I look up at the clock. 0630. "Rich, I'm sorry, I have to go." I rise from the table, pouring my uneaten oatmeal down the drain. "I'll try to call tonight."

"Well, in the meantime, just try to relax. We'll figure it out, okay?"

"Okay," I say.

I hang up, wishing I could believe it.

7

"Lieutenant Malone? Lieutenant Malone?" Will says, waving his hand.

I tune in as the aircrewmen chuckle.

"Are we drifting, Vanilla?" Boomer says.

"No, no. I'm sorry. What was that?"

Will stands on a mountain slope, which is covered in three feet of snow, on the grounds of the Marine Corps Mountain Warfare Training Center, located high in the Sierra. He's training fifteen members of our SAR team, along with a platoon of thirty marines, on the basics of avalanche rescue. I never knew this about Will, since he was gone during my first months here, but he is *the* go-to guy for anything mountaineering-related at this base.

"I asked, what are the three modes of use on your avalanche transceiver?"

"Uh . . . ," I say, clearing my throat.

My brain has not been present today. I forgot to call Celia back, for one. My phone call with Rich this morning was . . . okay, but not okay. And then, I didn't call my mom, either. I make it a point to call her every Sunday, at a minimum. But we spent all morning in Bishop yesterday, and flew with the EOD team all afternoon, and I collapsed when I got home, not waking up until two a.m.—I tell you, like clockwork—and then it was too late to call her.

"Off, transmit, and receive," I say.

I pull the answer out of who knows where, and Will knows it. If eyes could laugh, I'd swear that's what his are doing. He starts toward me. "I'd like you to switch your transceiver to the transmit mode."

Oh, boy. Please let this device be intuitive.

I look down. Thank god. Easy-to-read labels.

I turn the dial to transmit, but when I look up, Will has moved to stand just in front of me, so close his breath wafts across my forehead. He switches the dial on his transceiver to receive, then extends his arm so his transceiver almost touches mine—to ensure it's my signal he's recognizing.

Beep . . . beep . . . beep . . . beep. His unit picks up the audio signal my transceiver is producing.

He raises his eyes to meet mine, and his mouth curls upward ever so slightly. "Yours checks good."

He moves away to test the rest of the group's transceivers, continuing his instructions to the class as he goes. "Your transceivers are now emitting a pulsed radio signal, just like the skier's would. . . ."

But my thoughts linger in the moment just before. I look down toward my buried mountaineering boots, my ski pants disappearing into snow that comes up to my knees. That energy. That crazy, intense energy. It was here. And now it's gone.

Beep . . . beep . . . beep . . . beep.

"What if the avalanche is happening, and you're watching it?" Will asks.

Well-spoken, intelligent, humorous. Will is all of these things. As he moves from person to person, testing each transceiver, instructing, joking, laughing, I find myself furrowing my brow, trying to nail down his most obvious trait, something difficult to define. So I listen—mostly—as he transitions from the steps for transceiver usage to quizzing the group on what we covered this morning.

"If you're in a safe place, watch the victim, and note their last known position," Beanie says.

"Outstanding! Now, Lieutenant Melley, what goes along with watching the victim?"

Clark Melley is the only other aircraft commander in our group. The blond-haired, blue-eyed, should-be-on-a-recruiting-poster-somewhere Texas A&M grad is an H-60 transfer, like me. And also like me, he's none too thrilled about being stationed in Fallon, far happier flying off an aircraft carrier. So we've clicked, routinely commiserating about the unfairness of it all.

"Look for visual clues sticking out of the snow, like a glove or something," Clark says.

"Very good!" Will says. "Remember—and I've seen this several times—the gear you see on the snow could still be connected to the victim, like a hand in a glove. It's easy to jump right to the avalanche transceiver and the search patterns we'll cover today and miss the obvious signs of the location of a buried victim."

My brain ticks and spins, mulling over that elusive quality of Will's. That *je ne sais quoi*. Innate leadership? Definitely. But something else . . . Charisma? Yes . . . Yes, I think that's it. A magnet that draws people to follow. I'm sure this comes in handy in his position as a mountain guide, and it's probably another reason our aircrewmen think so highly of him. I suspect it's also the source of that energy I felt earlier. I steal a glance side to side at my squadron mates, as they look on, riveted.

". . . with the exception of Lieutenant Malone," Will says. My head snaps up; I heard my name, but not the instructions before it.

He looks at me with a hint of mischief in his eyes.

Not only did I not hear what he just asked me to do, but I sort of checked out on this entire last bit.

"Please switch your transceiver to receive mode," he says.

Uh-oh. Will just called on the kid in class who wasn't listening. So embarrassing. And so not me.

Clark, who's standing next to me, discreetly points to the dial, showing me where to turn it.

"Thanks," I say out of the corner of my mouth.

The transceiver lights up and begins beeping.

"Okay, find the buried transceiver," Will says.

I look at him, confused, because he still holds his transceiver in his hand . . . and it's turned off.

"But you—"

"I buried one earlier," he says.

Oh, shit.

A light blinks on the left side of my transceiver display. I hesitate, glancing up at Will, who is clearly enjoying the fact that I have no idea what I'm doing.

Following my gut, I pivot to the left. The light shifts into the center position, indicated by an arrow. Okay, arrows usually mean follow. I step forward and the distance number on the display begins to drop—8 meters, 7 meters, 6, 5 . . . Will falls in beside me, the beeps pinging faster and louder, 4, 3, 2, 1. The lighted arrow starts to flash, and the beeps are the loudest they've been.

"Very good," Will says, like praising a six-year-old for picking up her laundry and throwing it in the hamper.

"As you approach the victim," Will calls back to the group, "the beeps will grow louder and more frequent and the lights will flash. At this point, we begin the pinpoint phase of the search."

Will holds up what looks like a tent pole—a collapsible aluminum set of rods connected by an elastic string—and quickly snaps them together, one into the other, in a series, until he holds a long, slender pole, half an inch in diameter and ten feet in length.

He hands me the pole, reciting the directions at the same time. I punch the pole through the snow in intervals, until I feel a soft thud. The pole indicates something two feet below.

"I think I found it," I say. I wonder now if Will placed the transceiver in a backpack or wrapped it in something, due to the softness I feel.

"When you strike something," Will says, "leave the pole in place."

To me, he says, "Nice job." And then to the group, "We'll go over shoveling procedures for extricating the victim later. For now, let's break off in groups of two. One of you will hide your transceiver, and the other will find it. Spread out well to give yourselves room."

When everyone pairs off, I'm the odd man out.

"I, um . . . ," I say, pointing.

"That's okay," Will says. "You can stick with me."

Something shifts—weirdly, warmly, wonderfully—in my stomach. What the heck?

Our group scatters, and it's not long before the slope and surrounding forest are inundated with beeps on this unseasonably mild autumn day—temperatures even warmer than yesterday.

Will walks among our group to observe, and I follow.

"You called me out," I say.

"Just trying to gain your attention, that's all."

"I was paying attention . . . mostly."

Beep . . . beep . . . beep . . . beep. The sounds grow louder as transceivers are switched to receive, one after another.

"Can I ask you something?" I say.

"Shoot."

"Is vanilla really your favorite flavor?"

The question brings him to a stop. "Is that what you were thinking about?"

"No . . . I mean, it wasn't then, but it was earlier."

"Does it matter?"

"No. I was just curious."

"How about a definite maybe."

"I knew you didn't like vanilla."

"I never said that."

Beep . . . beep . . . BEEP . . . BEEP . . . The volume increases as the searchers home in on their targets.

"Did you get a chance to try any of the food you bought from Schat's?" he asks, starting to walk again.

"I did. The sheepherder bread with the artichoke spread."

"And . . . ?"

"It was pretty good."

"*Pretty* good?"

I look up, meeting his eyes—alight, happy, bursting with . . . *energy.*

"Okay, it was the best bread I've ever tasted. Like ever. Like out-of-this-world ever."

BEEP . . . BEEP . . . BEEP . . . "Found it!" BEEP . . . BEEP . . . "Got it!" BEEP . . . BEEP . . . "Got this one!"

"Guys!" Will shouts. "Go ahead and switch places when you find it, so you both have a turn at searching!"

He looks to me. "I know, right?"

What a simple thing. A piece of bread. We're gushing about a piece of bread. Rich sounded like this, well, sort of, when he told me about the interest rate he secured for the annuity. *"Can you believe that, Ali? A fixed interest rate like that is unheard of!"* But he should be excited, shouldn't he? It's what he does. What he's good at. I have flat zero financial sense, so I leave all of it to him. Maybe that's why I didn't react in quite the same way.

Beep . . . beep . . . BEEP . . . BEEP . . . The second man in each pairing is narrowing the distance to his find.

"Since I live forty-five minutes from Bishop, I buy several loaves—well, you saw—and freeze them." Will turns and heads to our group's clustered pile of backpacks and equipment. "It tastes just as good when you thaw it and warm it later."

"I'll have to remember that," I say, my steps heavier now and taking far more effort, due to the mushy snow—snow that feels like we're walking through mashed potatoes, courtesy of the warm afternoon sun. "Forty-five minutes from Bishop? Where do you live?"

"June Lake. It's just north of here."

I stop in my—literal—tracks. "You *live* in June Lake?"

"Uh-huh."

"We . . . we flew over it two days ago! On the way back from Mount Morrison. It's one of the most beautiful places I've ever seen! I mean, one of *the* most beautiful places I've *ever* seen."

"It is pretty special. Out of the way. Quiet."

"And jaw-droppingly gorgeous. You are so lucky."

BEEP . . . BEEP . . . BEEP . . . "Score!" BEEP . . . BEEP . . . "Got it!"

"All right, guys, come on back!" Will shouts. He raises his arms,

waving everyone to him, as we finish walking—slogging—the remaining distance to our gear.

Our group straggles back—while the marines run—and transceivers are turned off as everyone clusters around Will.

"Okay, you've found your victim, you've placed your avalanche pole
at the site, and now you have to dig the victim out," Will says, leaning
over and pulling his shovel out of the snow. "This is by far the most
time-consuming aspect of any avalanche rescue. Shoveling just a
cubic meter of snow is going to take you at least ten minutes, probably
more, and it's exhausting work. If you're working in teams, you'll
want to rotate out to help reduce fatigue."

As Will talks, he demonstrates, purposely using incorrect shoveling techniques, followed by correct ones. He moves like an athlete
would, coordinated, sure, strong. I tell myself not to look, and yet, I
keep looking. I try not to notice, but keep noticing. Not the shoveling
techniques, but him. The way his muscles move in his forearms, striated and lean. The way his wicked technical T-shirt clings to his
back. Everything connected and tight. Of course, he *should* look
this way. Any mountain guide would.

"So we're going to do some digging practice here first," Will says.
"Just spread out and pick a spot."

Everyone moves out while Will looks at his watch. "Okay, begin!"

I put my shovel to the snow, but Will stops me. "Would you mind
helping me out?" He motions to the spot I found earlier, still marked
with the avalanche pole. "I need to get my backpack and since you're
digging anyway . . ."

His grin is a wide one.

"Remind me never to get on your bad side."

I move to the spot and start digging. Five minutes into it, a runnel
of sweat trickles down my hairline. Maybe it's the sun's intensity at
high altitude, maybe it's dehydration, or maybe it's just that shoveling
snow like this is just plain hard work, but I'm huffing.

Shovel in. Scoop up. Snow to the side. Shovel in. Scoop up. Snow
to the side.

The minutes tick. . . . Shovel in. Scoop up. Snow to the side.

My arms are getting heavy. Crap. Shovel in. Scoop up. Snow to the side. I'm even in relatively good shape. I run. I do yoga. But this?

Shovel in. Scoop up. Snow to the side.

I glance at my watch, now ten minutes in, and admit that this little "getting-a-feel-for-it" exercise is kicking my ass. I peek around, wondering if anyone else might be tiring like I am. I'm relieved to see several others wiping their brows, some bending at the knees to rest.

I resume digging, catching Will in my peripheral vision. There's so much movement around us, but he stands stock-still, only moving his head as he looks over his charges. His scan includes me, and it almost pulls me up short because—and I'm probably just imagining it—it seems that he's staring. Although, I am looking for *his* backpack, which probably explains it. But still . . .

Self-consciously, I look myself over. My jog bra is visible through my supposedly moisture-wicking, yet sweat-soaked shirt, but that's nothing. My upper arms glisten with perspiration, and my hair has come a bit loose from its tie, but no big deal. Hmm. Everything seems okay. I chance a quick peek once more as I drive my shovel into the snow. He stands tall, arms crossed, but I catch it when he looks away.

When I start digging again—and this is strange—the task no longer seems as difficult. The shovel strokes come with less effort, and I don't seem to be breathing as hard. I imagine Will, full to overflowing with his energy supply, transferring just a bit to me, enough to get the job done.

Shovel in. Scoop up. Snow to the side. Over and over. A rhythm. A tempo. A happy, blissful groove.

The pit widens. Shovel in. Scoop up. Snow to the side.

My breathing is steady now, hard, but steady, and my muscles ache, but in good way. Good . . . This feels *good*. Snow flicking in bits across my torso. The smell of pine. The sun resting in an azure, cloudless sky. Deeper and deeper, I begin to disappear into the snow, as I shovel it in piles around me.

Shovel in. Scoop up. Snow to the side.

I smile when my shovel stroke finally reveals a snow-encrusted black strap. Dropping to my knees, I use my hands like a dog digging up a bone to pull the snow away. Finally, bright blue material surfaces. I grasp the backpack, give a good yank, and pull it clear. Got it!

Proudly, from the position on my knees, I raise it up to show Will. He smiles, walking toward me.

"Nice job!" he says, jumping into the pit and kneeling next to me.

"Thanks," I say, working to catch my breath. "You weren't kidding about the hard work."

"Good thing you're in shape. It's lot rougher for those who aren't," he says, motioning to the many who have stopped, shovels hanging in their hands. Not the marines, of course.

Standing, he offers me a hand, and pulls me up. Such strength. I sensed it with his handshake the first day I met him, and again now, popping to a stand without effort.

"Thanks. You saved me some work having to dig that up later," he says.

"You're welcome . . . I think."

Beep . . . beep . . . beep . . . beep . . . beep . . .

"What's that?" I ask, looking at the backpack in my hand.

He reaches for it. "Here, I'll show you."

Pulling the zipper open, he removes a fluorescent orange bit of electronics that looks much like the avalanche transceiver strapped to my chest.

"Is that an avalanche transceiver?"

"It is, but it's a prototype unit Jack's been working on."

"Jack? You mean, Mono County SAR Jack?"

"Yep. It adds a GPS feature with an SOS button—that's this here—to the avalanche beacon. Right now, beacons and GPS units are separate."

"So why is it beeping?"

"Because Jack just transmitted an SOS signal. He carries the other unit. We practice like this all the time."

"But I thought your unit was in transmit mode. I mean, it was just producing a signal that I followed and found."

"Yes, but the GPS portion works separately and on a different frequency. It's sort of like a cell phone in that it's always ready to receive a call. Jack can punch the SOS button on his unit and transmit the signal anywhere in the world to my unit via satellite. This way, if he's in trouble, he has a way of letting me know where he is."

"So why not just use that as an avalanche beacon?"

"Because first, you have to hit the button to transmit. If you're in an avalanche, more than likely, you won't be in a position to push a button. That's why you turn on your avalanche beacon ahead of time, so it can continually transmit. And second, the GPS unit isn't designed for small, local searches. You just wouldn't have the fine degree of accuracy necessary."

"I see. So how far away is he right now?"

Will shows me the unit. "When we're talking small distances like this, it's hard to know for sure because of the range of error, how many satellite signals we're picking up, that kind of thing, but he's probably within a quarter mile."

"Or closer," I say, pointing to the creamy white Labrador that streaks across the snow. Mojo wears a red vest with the word "RESCUE" printed in white across it, tongue lolling, ears flapping as he sprints to us.

Will drops to one knee. "Come here, boy!"

Mojo almost tackles Will with an all-body hug and a lick to the face. "Hey, you," Will says, scratching him well behind the ears. "Where's Jack, then?"

Will stands, searching for Jack, as Mojo turns his attention to me.

"Hi, Mojo!" I say, patting my thighs. "Don't you look official in your vest!" Mojo stands on his hind legs, placing his paws on my legs, a happy grin playing across his face. "He's a rescue dog?"

"One of the best. He's here to give a demonstration on the effectiveness of using an air-scenting dog for avalanche search. And this guy's incredible. He's found avalanche victims buried as deep as fifteen feet!" Will turns and gives him another pet. "Yep, you rock the rescue mojo, don't you, buddy?"

Mojo drops to all fours and gives a little bark.

"There you are!" Will says.

Jack approaches, holding an orange unit identical to Will's.

"Did you get it?" Jack asks.

"I did."

"That was four hundred yards," Jack says.

"Sweet," Will says. "That's actually pretty close to what I was showing."

"Hey, Will!" Boomer shouts from about ten yards away. He leans on his shovel, chest heaving, sweat dripping down the sides of his face. A red face that glows brighter than his flight suit—tough to out-glow a rescue-orange flight suit—which he insisted on wearing, even though everyone else changed into ski pants. "Are we good then? I think you've proved your point on the difficulty with shoveling."

"Yes, sir, you're good!"

We return to the group, Mojo bounding in front of us, his bright red vest a beacon against the white. Will then continues his training, including a demonstration by Mojo, who, in a blinding turn of speed, accurately locates Will's buried ski glove in about twenty seconds.

Through it all, I wonder if transceiver training raises your aware-ness altogether, about any number of things. For example, if you had asked me at any given moment where Will stood, I could have told you. Behind me, ten feet. To my left, twenty feet. Upslope five yards.

On the flight home, I try to remember if I was able to do that with anyone else. Did I know where Boomer was without looking? Actu-ally, I did. But that's a *big* presence! I laugh to myself as we transition from the high mountains to flat desert, from swirling snow to stead-fast sage, from animated winter to sedate brown reality.

8

I struggle to extricate myself from the covers when I hear the ringing. In a groggy stupor, I finally free one hand and reach for the phone.

"Hello?" I say, my voice crackly.

"Ali?" Rich says. "Did I wake you up?"

"No . . . no. I just closed my eyes for a second."

I glance at the clock. Eight thirty p.m. I didn't realize I'd fallen asleep.

"So how are you?" he asks.

"Good, good." I push myself up. "It was a, uh, long day. But now I'm good. Yeah."

"Did you get my message about the office?"

"I did. That's . . . wow, yeah, that's great news."

I made it a point to listen to Rich's message before I dropped, exhausted, into bed after avalanche training. He's still riding high after his recent promotion.

"So yeah, I moved into my new office today. We're talkin' tenth floor, a sweet view of the harbor . . ."

Maybe it's that I'm still a little foggy, just waking up and all, but as Rich goes into detail about his promotion and new office, my visions of San Diego Harbor begin to morph, the twinkle lights transforming into pine trees, the bay into a glacial lake, skyscrapers to mountain peaks.

". . . my feet are up on the ottoman now."

"What . . . ?" I say.

"You know, an ottoman. The thing you put your feet on when you watch TV."

"I know, but what about it again?"

"The leather sectional and ottoman I ordered came in. They delivered them to the condo this afternoon, and they are *sweet*."

"Oh . . . okay."

"Uh, Ali? Is something wrong?"

"No, no. Everything's great. Just a little tired, that's all."

"Well, what'd you do today?"

I breathe in deeply, sinking a bit into the protection of the covers. "We went to the Marine Corps Mountain Warfare Training Center. I learned how to use an avalanche transceiver."

"So how was it?"

"It was good. I learned a lot about skiers in the back country, why it's important to have avalanche-rescue skills, how to find victims . . ."

"You know, I don't get it. Why would someone put themselves in a situation like that in the first place?"

"What do you mean?"

"Like why would you need to go into the back country to ski, when you have a perfectly good ski resort right there? It's patrolled, it's safe, you don't have to worry about avalanches, you've got food, a warm lodge. I just don't get it."

"Um . . . yeah. I don't know. I guess you're right."

"So you never told me about the rescue you had a couple days ago. You said it was a tricky one."

Ah . . . Thank you, Rich. Thank you!

I sit up straight, very much awake now.

"It was. The most difficult one yet . . ." The story comes gushing out in one impossibly long run-on sentence. Good lord, have I breathed?

"Whoa, whoa, whoa," he says. "Back up. So this was where again?"

"Mount Morrison."

"And the guys were doing what? Climbing a wall of ice?"

"Yeah, they were in the Death Couloir—"

"The *Death* Couloir?"

"Yeah, and they—"

"Seriously?"

"Seriously what?"

"They were climbing something called the Death Couloir," he states flatly.

"Well . . . yeah. It's just a nickname. The real name is Mendenhall Couloir. Anyway, they . . ."

And I find myself repeating much of what I've already said. Although, the air seems a bit strained this time. Maybe it's that I don't hear any "uh-huhs" or words of acknowledgment in the background like the first time.

"Rich, are you there?"

"I'm here."

My shoulders relax. "I don't know why, but it feels better telling someone." I realize I haven't spoken about the Mount Morrison rescue with *anyone* yet, not in detail like this. It's like all that pent-up tension I felt right after the rescue has blessedly been released. "Thanks for listening."

I wait for a response. And wait.

"Rich . . . ?"

"Yeah."

"I said, thanks. You know, for listening."

"I know. . . . But it sort of pisses me off, Ali."

"What . . . ?" I ask, my breath stolen.

"I mean, you're risking your life here. What you did was incredible—super, ridiculously incredible—but my fiancée is risking her life for guys who are climbing a mountain and for what? To get to the top? Like what's the point? When you guys do air evacs for car-accident victims, I get it. When you pick up one of your pilots who's had to eject, I get it. But most of the time, it's wackos like this who ski out of bounds, climb up rock, ice, whatever—up *death* couloirs—and for what? Early death wish, what?"

"Uh . . . I don't . . . I don't know."

Familiar faces flit through my vision. The members of our aircrew, the Mono County SAR Team, the climbers we've plucked from cliffs, the hikers we've found who were lost in the forest, and the injured back country skiers we've rescued from deep ravines. In all of them, under the folds of their well-worn jackets and gloves, harnesses and hats, I've seen a spark, a brightness, a curiosity about life and the next horizon.

And for every one of these faces, I see Rich's friends at the anniversary party, cocktails in hand, dressed in custom-tailored suits, discussing so-and-so conglomerate's latest acquisition, or capitalizing on such-and-such short sale. Deep conversations on the merits of Cadillac versus Lexus. Men and women on top of the world, who sit at computers, and with a few well-timed keystrokes, move markets.

The members of the SAR team aren't on top of the world. They're in it. Of it.

"Ali? Ali, are you there?"

"What?"

"I thought we got cut off," he says. "But anyway, you get what I mean. I just want you back in one piece. I worry about you, you know?"

I flush with an unexpected warmth. "You do?"

"Of course I do. I love you, remember?"

My heart swells. "Thanks. I think I just needed to hear that."

"So, seventeen days, right?"

"Yeah. I can't wait."

"Me either. So you're okay then? I mean, you were pretty spun-up this morning, and with the rescue you described, I can see why. But are you good now?"

"Yeah, that was just . . . I don't know what that was," I say, the last word stretched out of proportion by the yawn I can't stifle. "But I'm good now. I'm talking to you, and it's good."

"You sound exhausted. Maybe I should let you get back to bed."

"No, really. I'm"—*yawn*—"good."

"I think we should say good night, Ali," he says with a light laugh. "You need your beauty sleep."

"Okay, maybe so. But Rich, I love you. I want you to know that, okay?"

"Love you, too, Ali. Talk soon."

I hit END and lean back heavily against the headboard, our conversation turning in my head, niggling . . . something. Maybe it's not our conversation at all. *You still haven't called your mom or Celia.* That's probably it. I sit up. Cider time.

"Hello?" my mom says, answering out of breath.

"Mom? Did you just run to the phone?"

I sit in the kitchen, a steaming mug—my cat-poster mug—of cider in hand. At least it's only nine p.m., not the middle of the night this time.

"Hi, honey. Yeah, I was in the backyard."

Tending to the larkspur. She doesn't have to say it, but that's what she was doing. She keeps a veritable forest of the plant in the backyard. The flower petals, arranged in loose vertical groupings at the upper end of the main stalks, bloom in a wide spectrum of colors from white to pink to light plum, before delving into the deep lavenders and velvety blues that dominate the yard.

Never mind that it's dark now. She's got dozens of those little solar garden lights to illuminate whatever she's doing. And she's always doing *something* back there. Probably because this is my mom's one connection to her first husband, my biological father. The one who left us when she was twenty-four years old.

Getting her to talk about him has been a fruitless endeavor. "Nick is your father and that's the end of it" is how any conversation about my father usually ends. Nick Malone was a good stepfather—she called him father, I called him Nick—and a good husband, before he was hit by a drunk driver and killed five years ago. He sold insurance, provided us with a nice home and a steady paycheck. I never wanted for anything.

Only once, in an unintended slip, did I learn something about my real father. I was eleven, and Mom was adding another row of larkspur—a new hybrid that would bloom lavender with a midnight-blue center. I sat next to her in the dirt, watching closely, idly floating through another stress-free summer vacation. She mumbled it, almost like she was talking to herself. "Your father would love this new color. It's his favorite flower. . . ."

Later, I asked Nick about it. "I didn't know you liked larkspur."

"What's a larkspur?" he responded.

And so, I observed. When Mom seemed melancholy, she would invariably wander out to the backyard, sit on the rod-iron bench that overlooked her garden, pull up her knees, and wrap her arms around them. I would watch her breathe deeply and close her eyes. In my child mind, I thought she just enjoyed sitting among the flowers. But my adult mind realizes she was sitting with my father.

Only recently, since Mom started seeing Dr. Grant, have I considered that maybe her depression has nothing to do with Nick, and everything to do with my biological father. After all, she sat with "him," in the garden, all those years, well before Nick died. But she didn't seem as depressed then. Although, truth be told, she wasn't particularly happy, either. But it wasn't like now.

"Sorry I didn't call on Sunday," I say.

"That's okay, honey. I have no shortage of people checking up on me."

I can "hear" the roll of her eyes loud and clear.

"Hi, Ali!" Celia says in the background.

"Oh, good!" I say. "Tell Celia I want to talk with her after I get off with you."

"Gonna gossip about me, huh?" Her question is lighthearted. Nice to hear that, actually.

"No, we aren't!" Celia calls. "Candice, why don't you put Ali on speaker, so we can all hear? No secrets that way."

The background noise increases—hum of the refrigerator, whir of the heater—when my mom switches the phone to speaker.

"I'm trying to convince your mom to do Thanksgiving at the lodge this year," Celia says. "What do you think? Could you make that work?"

"I think I have duty then," I say. "But I'll see what I can do."

"I don't know . . . ," Mom says, the trepidation oozing.

While I carry fond memories of our Thanksgiving get-togethers at the lodge, for my mom I don't think they were so pleasant. She never overtly said she didn't like going there, but when we did, she hunkered down inside, rarely leaving our cabin.

I do know she enjoyed our time with Grandpa Alther, but after he passed away, we stopped going. I was thirteen at the time. And in the years after, come the holidays, when we would normally pack up and make the drive to Walker Canyon, she seemed downright relieved she didn't have to do it. She was never a fan of the outdoors, so maybe that was it.

"Really, Candice, it would be nice," Celia says. "I have some work to do there, anyway, and Roberto has asked for time off for the holidays. It'd be perfect."

"Roberto should get the caretaker of the century award," I say. "Seriously, when was the last time he had a vacation?"

"Exactly," Celia says.

"I'll think about it," my mom says. "But no promises."

"So is everything *else* going okay?" I ask.

"You know, Ali, you can just ask me directly how my therapy sessions are going."

"Okay, how are your therapy sessions going?"

"Better. Actually, a lot better."

Whoa. I haven't heard *that* before.

"So that's . . . good," I say.

"It is. So tell your aunt she doesn't need to keep coming over to check up on me. The water's not gonna boil any faster, know what I mean?"

Mom laughs then, and I almost fall out of my seat. I'm sort of afraid to say anything else, lest I upset the apple cart.

Tie it up quick, Ali. End on a good note.

"So, um, I'll call you when I figure out Thanksgiving," I say. "Sound good?"

"Sounds like a plan," Celia says. "And Ali, we're better than I thought, so no need to call me back."

"See, I knew you were talking behind my back," my mom says.

"Hey, it's all good, Sis," Celia says. "You know we love you."

"Yeah, right," she says.

9

"Keep the bubbles going. That's it."

Clark's voice warbles, since my head is underwater. I float in the shallow end of the indoor swimming pool located on base, learning how to relax in the water. Which, apparently, is impossible for me.

"Let your wrists go limp," Clark says. He reaches for my hands and gently shakes my fingers. Yikes, they were stiff. Like rigor mortis stiff. "Wiggle your fingers. There you go."

Clark swam competitively at Texas A&M, so he's been helping me with my swimming, which I've struggled with since forever. I was a land animal through and through, growing up a gymnast, until I became too tall, and was gently encouraged to leave the sport. As a result, I didn't see much pool time as a kid, nor as a teenager, which means my stroke basically sucks. I *barely* passed the swim tests at the Academy, same in flight school—a struggling member of the sub squad in both places.

But I'm tired of fighting the water, so I've finally decided to do something about it.

Although that's easier said than done.

Exhaling my last bit of air, I stand, push my hair out of my eyes, and lift my goggles.

"Okay, that was better," he says. "But this time, we're gonna focus on the head and neck. Remind me, what's the number-one rule in swimming?" He offers a playful smile, as this is the one hundredth time we've gone over this, and yet I still have issues with it.

"Release the head," I say. "And relax."

"Good. Let's try it again."

I swear, Clark is the most patient and encouraging person I think I've ever met.

I pull my goggles over my eyes, inhale, and flop over, letting my arms and legs hang. I wiggle my fingers, realizing they've already tensed. *Cripe* . . .

"All right, now let the tension go in your neck. No wrinkles!"

Aghh! I'm doing it again.

Head up and looking forward? Tension. Which you can see by the crunched-up wrinkles in the skin on the back of the neck. Head down and looking below? Relaxation. Smooth skin, no wrinkles.

"There you go," he says, in a manner so soothing I'm sure he could coax me to sleep if he wanted. "Let the tension go. Let the water support you."

I think I'm letting the tension go, until he tries to move my head. He's met with sound resistance. Same with the shoulders. He moves them around—yep, they were shrugged up nice and tight, too. *Geez* . . .

I focus on relaxing, letting my muscles go limp, blowing my little bubbles. In the background, I hear the delighted screeches of kids, giggling as they slosh down the three-meter-high circular slide that empties into the diving well. For families stationed in such an out-of-the-way place, the pool is a godsend. And in the unpredictable weather we see here in the high desert, it's doubly so.

Although, in the week since we completed our avalanche transceiver training in sunny sixty-degree weather in Mammoth Lakes, the weather has only continued to warm. Perhaps we can delay full-on winter just that little bit longer.

"Way better, Alison," Clark says.

I blow out the last of my air and stand again.

Clark and I both turn to look when the interior door to the pool opens and several men in flight suits stream through. Ten? Twelve? The man in front wears captain insignia. The line of men stretches out behind him, but three lieutenant cronies remain close, all of them joining the captain in snide laugher.

". . . just make sure you keep your eyes in the boat," the captain says. "Fuckin' faggots everywhere in the ranks now."

With a whoosh, the locker room shuts behind them.

I whip my head around, wondering if anyone else in the pool area heard that. They must have, it echoes so much in here.

"What a—" I say.

"Yeah. Hammer is exactly that."

"Hammer?"

"The air wing commander."

"*That's* the air wing commander?" I turn to him, mouth open. "*That* guy? Are you ser—"

He confirms with a nod.

"How can he say stuff like that?"

"He says that and *a lot* more."

"But—"

"He's my boss, remember? Trust me. I know."

"DAD!" The shouts are a chorus from across the pool, aimed at one of the men in flight suits, who has just moved beyond the interior door. "Dad, watch!" a boy, maybe four years old, shouts before flinging himself down the slide, squealing all the way. Two older girls, I'm guessing six and eight, with wet pigtails and pink Hello Kitty swimsuits, scramble up the ladder next.

The dad is accompanied by another pilot, one I recognize—Shane "Snoopy" Forester, a Naval Academy classmate and an old friend. He was here just a few months ago, acting as a liaison for the air wing in preparation for their arrival this week.

"Alison!" Snoopy says. He leaves his friend and walks over to Clark and me.

"Snoopy!" I say. "When did you get in?"

Snoopy wears his flight suit, including a patch on his sleeve from the USS *Carl Vinson*. The dad who watches his kids has the same patch, and Clark wears one on his flight suit, too. I know Clark is happy to see his old friends from the *Vinson* again. If he was offered a ticket out of Fallon to return with this group to the carrier, he'd take it in a minute.

"Just yesterday," Snoopy says. "So how are you?"

"Better lately, thanks."

Clark raises his eyebrows. He knows all too well my feelings about being stationed here, feelings that match his. But I can only shrug, just as surprised that those words left my mouth.

"Dad! Watch me! Watch me!" The Hello Kitty–clad little girls have positioned themselves at the top of the slide.

"I'm watching!" the dad calls.

"Wheeeeeeeeee!" Splash!

"They're so small. And so comfortable . . . ," I say wistfully.

"Hey, you're getting better," Clark says with an encouraging nudge. "You've made huge improvements since we started."

"I am a work in progress, true."

"Are you ready to swim?" Snoopy asks Clark. "I have to brief in an hour, so . . ." Snoopy holds a Navy swim bag, a former competitive swimmer, like Clark.

"You go ahead," I say to Clark. "I said I'd help the guys with their training today, and it looks like they're about ready."

In the lap area of the pool, our rescue swimmers are finishing their swim workout. They have to pass a laundry list of swim tests to keep their qualifications current, and swimming laps in a certain time is just one of them. After their workout, they're scheduled for rescue-litter training, doing an open-water rescue scenario. They asked if I'd pose as their victim, which, since my only job is to float, is something I felt capable of helping them with.

"All right," Clark says. "We'll schedule another session soon, okay? Remember, you did good today."

"Yeah, right. But thanks, anyway."

"See ya, Alison," Snoopy says.

Clark climbs out, and as he and Snoopy walk toward the locker room, I turn my attention to the father in the flight suit, laughing as he walks toward his kids in the diving area, and who's tackled upon arrival. I don't know why, but the whole scene triggers something weird. A twang.

I've always thought I would have kids, but I've never *felt* like having them. And maybe that's not even what I'm feeling now. Perhaps it's that this week has been one of phone calls and texts and planning for the wedding. A wedding, which leads to a honeymoon, which leads to . . .

Kids . . . What would our kids look like? Rich, with fair skin and black hair, and me, olive-skinned with varying shades of red hair mixed with strands of brown. And what would they do? Baseball? Football? Gymnastics? I can't picture it. I can't picture it at all. I close my eyes a moment, waiting for an image. . . . Is that the twang? Is it so far out of reach, I can't even imagine it?

Or is it that thoughts about kids always lead to guesswork about my father. Would his grandkids look like him? Do I? Unfortunately, the images I keep are hazy at best. I just wasn't old enough to remember him. And my mother hasn't been any help. She rid the house of anything that reminded her of him—photos, clothing, memorabilia. If any of it still exists, she's got it locked up somewhere, because I've never seen it.

As a result, I've grown up with this, I don't know, void, a missing piece of myself. At a loss when putting together that school project about my family tree. Left wondering why my skin is so much darker than my mother's. Like something taken from me . . .

"Okay, ma'am. We're done!" Beanie calls from across the pool. "Ready to play victim?"

I dog-paddle to get to them, arriving as they lower the rescue litter into the water. They're going to practice loading me in and strapping me to the contraption.

"Just float facedown for us, ma'am," Beanie says. "We're doing unconscious victim, so go totally limp, all right? You don't have to do anything."

Beanie has no idea that for me, "not doing anything" actually requires an enormous amount of effort.

I push off toward the center of the pool, let my body go limp—at least, I think it's limp—and float there, trying like the devil to relax. But I stop myself right there. I'm *trying* to relax. Which means I'm *doing* something. *Alison, come on!* You *just* relax. There's no action required. Just let go and relax, for god's sake.

I need to blow my bubbles.

That's it. Just focus on the bubbles. . . .

But then Beanie shakes my shoulders and arms, pulling me up.

"The pagers!" he says.

Boom. Relaxing practice over.

I pull off my goggles and make for the edge of the pool as our pagers beep and vibrate in a clamoring harmony, a racket made far louder by the echoing in this high-ceilinged natatorium.

Hap gets to the side first, leaps out, and checks the screen. "All eights!" he says. The code for civilian rescue.

We fly out of the water and race to put on our flight suits and boots. Within a minute, we're sprinting out of the building. And as our group spills out into the warmest afternoon I can remember, the door slams resolutely shut behind us.

10

"Sir, I don't see how we can do this," I say to Boomer. He keeps the controls as we fly south, while I run the performance numbers. "We're going high, and it's too hot."

"How high again?" Boomer asks.

"North Palisade Peak is over fourteen thousand feet, sir," Beanie says. "And with what the sheriff is describing—climber with a head injury in a bergschrund—it's gotta be U-Notch or V-Notch. We're talkin' thirteen thousand feet, if that's the case."

"What's a bergschrund?" I ask.

"It's a crevasse, ma'am," Beanie says. "But a special kind, formed when glacial ice separates from the back wall of a cirque."

I may not have ever heard the term "bergschrund," but I do remember the word "cirque" from a past training lecture. A wide, bowl-shaped area, carved by a glacier, that underlies a ring of mountain peaks above it.

"Thanks, Beanie," I say. "But I have a feeling we're not gonna get to see it, because it's *seventy-five* degrees down here. Granted, it'll be cooler at altitude, but not by much."

"Shit," Boomer says. "Did you account for the loss in weight by removing the doors? We can do that when we land at the airport."

"I didn't. Stand by."

I go back to the aircraft performance charts, checking how much power we'll have available and how much we'll need to effect the rescue. The higher the altitude and the warmer the temperature, the less power you have. So if we need to pick guys from a peak at thirteen thousand feet on a sixty-something-degree day, we might have to lose weight first by dropping off one of our crewmen, throwing out some equipment, or even dumping fuel to be light enough to do it.

I fly through the calculations, surprising myself with the speed of doing it the old-fashioned way—using a pencil, a calculator, charts, and a scratch piece of paper on my knee board. In the H-60, a computer did it for us.

"No, sir, even with the doors off, we won't have enough power."

Boomer doesn't look convinced. And when we finally land at Bishop Airport, I can see he hasn't given up. "Let's have a little powwow with the ground team. I'm sure we can figure out a way to do this."

We step inside the airport operations building, and Walt, the assistant Mono County SAR coordinator, is there to meet us. He's surrounded by the Mono County SAR Team, most of whom I recognize. But there's one member in particular who's missing.

Try as I might, I can't explain the sinking feeling that weighs on me when I see that Will isn't here. But that's not the only thing I sense. This group is restless. Looking closer at Walt, I see that he shares the same worried expression as the rest.

Normally, no matter how dire the situation, the group maintains a certain levity, a lightness. But the room is thick with tension, no joking or smiles today.

"Boomer, Alison," Walt says as we approach. No friendly banter or handshake.

Now that the men are moving to the side, I see they're standing around a center table, a map spread across it.

"The victim fell into a bergschrund right here," Walt says, getting straight to the point, using his pencil to tap on the location.

Wait a second. If Will's not here . . . Something squirms inside. No . . .

". . . at the base of V-Notch on Palisade Glacier. A hiking party—four of our team members—saw him fall. They called and—"

Walt looks up, and the rest of the SAR team members turn, as Will strides into the room.

A wave of relief washes over me as he pushes through the crowd, a mountaineering backpack slung over one shoulder. I could swear someone just turned the lights up a little higher, everything brighter, crisper.

"What do we have?" Will asks. His eyes dart from Walt's to ours to the others'. "Wait, what is it?"

"It's, uh," Walt says, swallowing. "It's Jack."

The restless room goes still, just as Will goes still. It's several long seconds before he speaks.

"What happened?" Will says.

"He fell into the 'schrund below V-Notch," Walt says. "Thomas and Kevin are up there. They were camping at the foot of the glacier with Tawny and Kelly. Saw it happen. They're hiking up to it now, but they don't have the right gear."

Will turns to Boomer. "Can you fly me up there?"

"That's the million-dollar question. I've got the guys taking the doors off now. The charts say no, but uh . . ." He turns to me. His eyes narrow, his face screwing up, as he thinks. "Yeah . . . it just might work."

"What might work?" I ask.

"Do you have the charts with you?"

I nod, raising my hands to show him.

"Redo the calculations, this time with only three people in the aircraft."

"Three?"

He nods.

"But that's you, me, and Beanie. What about Will? What about the victim? We'd need power for five, and we don't have enough for four. Even if we don't take Beanie, that still leaves four of us when we bring the victim in. We can't—"

"We go single-piloted," Boomer says. "Will rides in front, Beanie in the back. Will can load the victim, but stay on the ground after. Sound good, Will?" Boomer asks, turning.

"Yeah, I'm good with that. Either I can hike out, or you can come back for me."

Amazing he can sound so nonchalant about what Beanie said would be a half-day hike-out.

"Okay, let me run the numbers," I say, plopping the charts on the table.

I lower my head, but look up just as fast. "Will you be bringing your gear?" I ask, motioning to the pack.

"Twenty pounds," he says.

I plot the points on the graph carefully, double-checking the temperatures at the higher altitude, using a straightedge to ensure I'm reading the correct number. "Damn," I say under my breath. Then, louder. "Still not light enough."

A collective sigh resonates in the room, heads turning to me, to Boomer, to Will.

"What weight did you use for the pilot?" Boomer asks.

"Two-sixty, right, sir?"

"That'd be correct," Boomer says, standing taller, his mid-section popping out just that bit further. "But let's try it with one-thirty."

"One-thirty? But you're not—"

"No, *I'm* not. But *you* are."

"What?" It takes a moment for the words to sink in. The meaning. Oh, no. No way.

"But I'm not an aircraft commander yet. I can't even sign for this aircraft, let alone take it up and fly it by myself."

"Who says? That's a paperwork drill, anyway. You're as qualified as you need to be."

"But *you* signed for the aircraft, sir. We can't do this."

"I signed for the aircraft, which means I'm responsible for the safety of it and its crew. There's nothing anywhere that says I need to be the one flying or even physically *in* the aircraft to ensure everyone's safe."

"I think it's implied, sir. You know, that the pilot who signed for the aircraft would be *in* it."

Boomer puts his hands on his hips. "Implied, but not specifically stated," he says, triumphant.

"But . . . you can't . . ." I look around for help, but it's clear. I stand on my own.

The longer I hesitate, the worse it gets, the collective energy in this room now directed solely at me.

"Is it possible?" Will asks, looking directly at me. "I mean, weight-wise. That's all I want to know." He remains collected and calm, his voice steady and smooth, but his eyes communicate something else entirely.

"I . . . well . . . okay, let me run it with the new weight."

I lower my head again, performing the calculations with me as the sole pilot. I bite my lip when I see that Boomer's hunch is right.

"It's possible," I say, looking up.

"Will you do it?" Will asks.

Crystal-blue eyes and a steady gaze communicate an underlying plea as clearly as if he were speaking aloud: *Please. Please, help me.*

I glance at Boomer. He remains unwavering. Permission granted.

Turning back to Will, I hold his gaze for a long moment . . . and nod.

11

Will moves past me toward the door, and as I pull the charts together, Boomer taps me on the arm. "You got this, Vanilla."

I can only shake my head, to which Boomer responds by gripping my shoulder and giving it a good squeeze.

He follows me outside, barking directions at Hap and Beanie, who have just finished removing the doors. Beanie then moves to assist Will, who has climbed into the left seat, handing him a helmet and helping him plug in his internal radio cord.

"Your radio switch is there," I say to Will, "at your feet. Just step on it to talk."

I've got the bird turning in less than a minute, and just a short sixty seconds after that, we're airborne. Will points the way to an area he knows by heart, a transit that should take less than ten minutes.

I notice that Will fiddles with his chest harness. On it, he carries a utility knife, a Leatherman, a radio, and a flashlight, all attached in easy-to-access pockets. In addition, the strap houses his fluorescent orange transceiver unit, which he now removes. He turns dials, flips switches, and then I hear a solid tone—loud enough to be heard over the noise of the transmission and rotor blades.

"What's that tone?"

"A test signal, to see if the unit's working properly."

"Are you looking for a signal from Jack?"

"Yeah, but I'm not getting anything."

"But I thought the range was—"

"It's not a range problem." He looks down at the screen again, then turns to meet my eyes. "He just has to be able to push the SOS button."

The despondency in his expression is clear. Jack would have to be conscious or physically able to push the button to transmit the SOS signal. So if he hasn't pushed it . . .

Will searches my eyes for a moment, then moves back to planning. "Have you been here before?" Will asks, tucking the unit away in his chest strap.

"No."

"The slope angle of V-Notch runs about fifty degrees toward the bottom of the couloir, so I don't know how close you'll be able to get to let me off."

"What do you think, Beanie?" I ask.

"It'd be too steep to land, ma'am," Beanie says. "This is one-skid all the way."

"There it is," Will says, pointing.

A grand, wide bowl of snow, circumscribed by towering black granite peaks, looms before us. Several tunnels of snow cut through the black, most of them half the length of the Death Couloir on Mount Morrison, but much, much higher in elevation. I spy the one that distinctly looks like a "V."

As we close the distance, flying over the bottom of the cirque, which lies above the tree line, the edge of a turquoise glacial lake peeks from the snow. The terrain around it is relatively flat—rocky, but flat—and free of snow.

"I've got a person on the ground, three o'clock," Beanie calls. "I think it's Kelly."

A hiker wearing a fluorescent pink technical T-shirt and sporting a long red ponytail waves at us, two tents in place about twenty yards behind her.

"That must be Thomas, Tawny, and Kevin up the slope then," Will says. I look forward and up the vast expanse of snow to the three tiny figures nearing the top.

"The couloir they're approaching, that one on the left, that's V-Notch," Will says, confirming my earlier guess.

"At least you'll have help getting everything rigged," Beanie says.

"Yeah, no doubt," Will says.

"What will you do?" I ask.

"Once I'm on the ground, I'll have to climb up the side of the 'schrund. I have no idea how high or steep it's running now, so we'll have to see when I get there. When I get to the top, to the opening of the crevasse, I'll rappel down and get Jack secured. Then, I'll climb back up and rig a Z-pulley to haul him out. I can load him in the litter once he's out."

"I'll get the litter rigged and ready in the back," Beanie says.

"How long does it take to rig the pulley system?" I ask.

"Hard to say. Twenty minutes?"

I glance at the fuel gauge. "We might have to land and shut down to save fuel," I say, not believing those words just came out of my mouth.

"I'll be quick."

Our helicopter is now dwarfed by the surrounding summits, a tiny speck of orange against a colossal massif. As the group on the ground comes into clearer focus, I see that they're wearing technical T-shirts only, no jackets—another confirmation of the warm temperatures. The outside-air temperature gauge reads eighteen degrees Celsius, or sixty-five degrees Fahrenheit—a veritable scorcher at thirteen thousand feet.

And then, a fourth figure. Small, coated in cream-colored fur, he would have blended into his surroundings perfectly if not for his bright red vest. Mojo races back and forth animatedly in front of the group, urging them upward.

I see it then. The bergschrund. A gaping chasm running the length of the base of the couloir, and not just along V-Notch, but along U-Notch couloir next to it. The walls of the bergschrund that lead to the crevasse opening on top look almost vertical, covered in gray ice, even overhanging in places. "Formidable" would be an understatement.

"She's yawning, all right," Will says.

"Yawning?"

"The 'schrund. As it gets warmer, the glacier recedes, pulling farther from the rock, widening the mouth of the crevasse. Like it's yawning."

It would be easy to gawk at the crevasse, so broad and menacing, but I shift my focus to the gauges, performing an in-flight assessment, just as Boomer taught me. I note the power we're using now, all the while thinking about the power we'll need to hover, not knowing if we'll have enough. On paper, yes. But at the actual rescue site, with all the variables of wind and weather, you just never know. Although, I will say, the winds have been kind so far. Before we passed the tree line, the pines below remained still, and the glacial lake was straight as a mirror.

"I need to pull into a hover here, guys, just to check the power," I say, approaching the bergschrund from the side, flying parallel to it, but still one hundred feet above it.

As I reduce speed, the controls feel mushy, like they did on Mount Morrison, only worse. I ever-so-gradually pull into a hover, swallowing hard as the rotors begin to slow. Not enough to trigger an audible alarm, but close. I dump the nose to gain airspeed.

"Based on the power we were pulling just now, we should be okay in a low hover. Right on the limit, but doable," I say, accelerating and circling left, setting up my approach for a one-skid about fifty yards downslope of the bergschrund.

"See where it levels somewhat, Beanie?" I say.

"Got it, ma'am."

Above us, Mojo darts about at the base of the bergschrund, no doubt sensing his owner, but unable to see or reach him.

"Will, could you help me out, please?" I ask. "See the gauge on the upper right corner of your instrument panel? If you could call out that number for me as we make our way down, it would be a huge help. It tells the amount of power we're using, basically."

"You got it. Looks like it's reading forty-five percent."

"Yep. And if you look on the gauge below it, there's a needle with an 'r' on it. That's for rotor speed."

"It reads one hundred percent," he says.

"And hopefully it'll stay that way," I say. "We've only got ninety-two percent power available, and the charts say we'll need eighty-nine to hover. Based on what it looked like in the high hover, it's gonna be close."

"Easy forward forty," Beanie calls as we move steadily forward on a shallow glide slope, adding power in the most minute amounts to control the rate of descent.

"Passing forty knots," Wills says. "Sixty-four percent."

"Easy forward thirty," Beanie calls. "Easy forward twenty."

"Seventy-eight percent," Will says. "Eighty, eighty-two, eighty-four . . ."

My stomach tightens when we pass the go/no-go point, that place where if the aircraft doesn't have enough power to hover—a sudden downdraft would do it—we would drop to the ground, not high enough anymore to nose over and gain airspeed and without the power to stop our descent. In this case, because of the slope angle, there would be no landing, just an uncontrollable tipping and subsequent roll, actions that would prove catastrophic.

My hands squeeze the controls, and I curse myself for wearing my gloves again, my fingers slipping inside. *Stubborn much?*

"Easy forward fifteen, easy forward ten . . . ," Beanie calls.

"Eighty-nine, ninety, ninety-one, ninety-two . . . ," Will says.

Crap! Keep it steady, Ali!

"The rotor speed is dropping. It's at ninety-eight," Will says.

"Easy forward five . . . ," Beanie calls.

"You're holding at ninety-two percent. Rotor speed's now at ninety-six."

Crap . . . crap, crap, crap.

"Four, three, two, one, steady right there, ma'am."

"Ninety-two percent power, ninety-four on the rotor speed," Will says.

The rotor-speed alarm would have sounded at ninety-two. Of course, I shouldn't be anywhere *near* ninety-two.

I *cannot* believe I'm doing this. *So* far beyond any acceptable standard of responsible flying.

Out the open door to my right, the tip-path plane of the rotors presents a blur of movement, the group of three standing just above it, at the base of the bergschrund. Mojo stills now, bracing against the onslaught of the rotor wash. "You're clear to go," I say to Will. "If you could step out as gently as possible, that would be a great help."

He unhooks his helmet from the radio system and steps out through the center console.

"Nice and steady, ma'am," Beanie says. "Lookin' good. We need to come down about three feet. Easy down three, easy down two, easy down one, steady. Steady right there. Man's at the door. He's on the skids. . . ."

Beanie doesn't have to tell me when Will steps off. Even though he did so with care, the subtle dip in the aircraft told me the moment he left.

"Man is out," Beanie confirms. "I have a thumbs-up. Stand by. Grabbing the litter. Okay, I have the litter. Handing it down. He's got it."

Will crouches, backpack over one shoulder, and drags the litter in the snow behind him to clear the rotor arc.

"All right, ma'am, he's clear. You're clear to go."

Easing the nose down, dropping left at the same time, we begin to accelerate, using the slope to our advantage as we speed downward.

I look at the fuel gauge. "Beanie, I think we're gonna have to land to save gas."

"Roger that, ma'am. I don't think we'll have to shut down, though," he says, peeking through the cockpit passage to look at the fuel gauge. "We could just idle and still be fine, right?"

"Agreed," I say. And because we screamed down the cirque, in only seconds we're flying over the eastern tip of the glacial lake. Beanie calls me down over the rocky landing site, and we steady into a hover about a foot off the ground.

"Ma'am, it's a little more uneven than I thought."

"I can see that, yeah. Guess we'll have to look for a place further downslope."

"I don't think that'll be necessary. Let me jump out. I think I can build up the rocks under the skids, and we should be good. Just hold it steady here."

"You're gonna do what?"

"SAR-flying fun fact. If you don't have a level platform for landing, just make your own!"

Beanie jumps out of the bird, and starts picking up boulders and shoving them under the right skid. He walks farther away, finds the sizes of rocks he needs, returns, and continues to build until satisfied. Then, moving beyond the rotor arc, he signals me downward. I feel the skids crunch as I lower onto the rocks, but there's no shifting, no slipping. I lower the collective all the way, settling firmly on Beanie's platform. Crazy.

Beanie waits for my nod, then ducks under the rotor arc and returns to the aircraft cabin. Once connected to the radio, he says, "Ma'am, I'm gonna go talk to Kelly."

I look up, seeing Kelly and the tents about fifty yards away.

"I'll let her know what we're doin'. Be right back."

Beanie leaves the rotor arc once more, making a precarious walk over the large stones that litter the base of the cirque.

And here I remain. . . .

There are out-of-body experiences, and then there are *out-of-body* experiences. I sit perched in a bright orange helicopter on a platform of rocks at the base of a glacial cirque with a direct view into the Owens River Valley over eight thousand feet below. In a word, electrifying.

My senses heightened, every molecule awake, I feel bouncy in my seat. I peer across the empty left cockpit seat, ducking so I can see upslope. The bergschrund is one thousand vertical feet above me. One tiny dog and four tiny humans scuttle about in the snow, but one of those humans is already higher than the rest. Will is easy to pick out, climbing in his yellow jacket and neon-orange gloves—the same clothing he wore on Mount Morrison, minus the thick insulating base layers he needed on that bitterly cold day.

I imagine him scaling this wall of ice with single-minded focus and concentration, reaching the top, and peering over the edge into the blackness below. Self-assured, self-reliant. In charge.

And I have the most bizarre thought—a vision, actually.

I stand at the rail of a fishing boat in the Bahamas, a boat heavy with the smell of diesel fuel, salt, sunscreen, and fish parts. I stand there as someone baits my hook. . . .

I catch myself, having just laughed out loud. Someone is going to bait my hook . . . then put my pole in the water before handing it to me. I will catch a fish, reel it in; Rich will take my picture, post it on several social-media outlets; I will hand the pole back to the deckhand, and he will clean my catch. I don't have to touch anything except the pole, do anything except stand and reel, and of course, smile for the camera. A true fishing experience, all neatly packaged and presented to the world as if we'd done it ourselves. Yep, me and Rich, the adventurers.

"Rescue Seven, Whiskey One, I'm at the victim. Estimate fifteen minutes, over."

"Copy, Whiskey One."

Conflicting thoughts, thick enough to touch, battle in my brain over the next ten minutes. And in all of them, Will is there. In some way, shape, or form, he's there.

Beanie waves to grab my attention from outside the rotor arc. I nod, and he runs under.

"Rescue Seven, Whiskey One, victim is out of the crevasse, unresponsive, head injury, securing him in the litter now."

"Rescue Seven copies." I switch to the internal radio, rolling up the throttles at the same time. "Ready to do this, Beanie?"

"Ready, ma'am. You're clear to lift."

I do a quick scan of the gauges, and everything looks good. I start to pull up, but stop.

"Ma'am?" Beanie says.

"Stand by," I say. "I just need to do something first."

I remove my left hand from the collective, bring my hand to my mouth, and pull my glove off with my teeth. I then use this hand to steady the cyclic while I remove the other glove in the same manner.

When I regrip the controls, the sensation is a strange one, like standing on the beach naked or something. I've only *ever* worn gloves. I don't think I've actually felt the controls before. Can that be possible? I flex my fingers, stretching them, before curling them around the controls again. I take a deep, satisfied breath.

"Okay, Beanie, I'm ready now."

12

I hover near the spot where I first dropped Will, watching out my window as he and his friends pass the litter to Beanie in the main cabin. Jack wears a green jacket, his red helmet still on his head, yet smashed on one side.

Pain masks Will's face as he steps back, a pain that stabs through me just the same. He stands with Mojo, who's pressed firmly against his leg. Mojo seems oblivious to the whine of the engines, the steady whop of the rotors, the erratic wind, and the swirling snow particles kicked up by the rotor wash that beat his tiny face.

Like a son letting go of his father, Will looks into the main cabin one last time before shifting his gaze back to me. *Take care of him.*

Dejected, he turns, and follows his friends out from under the rotor arc.

"Okay, ma'am, you're clear to slide left," Beanie says.

"Copy, sliding left."

I move away from the slope, allowing myself a glance at the gauges once safely clear. One hundred percent rotor speed. Eighty-nine percent power. Eighty-nine . . .

I've got three percent to spare.

I turn my head back to the right, meeting Will's eyes as he stands motionless in the snow. It turns out, all the while I was saving fuel, I was burning a little, too. Perhaps enough to accommodate the weight of one more person and a sixty-five-pound dog . . . maybe.

Another look into Will's eyes, and the decision is made.

"Beanie, I'm gonna slide back. I think we have the power to take Will and Mojo."

"Roger that, ma'am, clear to slide right."

"Whiskey One, Rescue Seven," I say as I move the controls to the right.

Will raises the radio to his mouth—another of those weird out-of-body moments, me hovering, yet looking directly into his eyes, as I talk to him.

"Rescue Seven, go ahead."

"We can take you, Will. We have the power. You and Mojo."

His eyes widen, communicating that same thank-you I saw at the Bishop airport when I said I'd fly.

"Steady right there, ma'am. Callin' 'em in."

Will then drops to one knee, an arm around Mojo, and gives a command while motioning him toward the aircraft. Mojo bounds away, leaping into the main cabin, and Will follows right behind him.

"Man's stepping onto the skids," Beanie says.

The aircraft dips, and I shift my eyes quickly to the torque gauge. Ninety-two percent. Rotor speed, ninety-seven. *Oh, boy . . .*

"Beanie, I'm gonna have to skim the surface here, until we hit translational lift. We don't quite have full power now."

"Roger that, ma'am."

I coax the aircraft forward and left—gently, gently, slowly, slowly, moving downslope. The aircraft begins to accelerate, and my muscles relax just that little bit when I feel the telltale bump indicating we've hit translational lift, the extra boost you get from obtaining forward airspeed while still low to the ground—a cushion of air that lifts and speeds you on your way.

"There we go, ma'am. Sweet," Beanie says, feeling it, too.

As before, we drop away from the mountain, and plunge toward the valley.

"Will, are you up?" I ask.

"I'm up."

"Bishop or Mammoth Hospital?"

"Mammoth would be better, if we have the fuel."

"Barely, but yeah," I say, scanning the low-fuel lights that began to flicker just a few minutes ago.

"Can we radio the hospital to give them a heads-up?" Will says.

"Absolutely."

"Okay, stand by."

Beanie and Will put Jack on oxygen first and take his vitals before Will relays the information to me, which I, in turn, relay to the hospital. I note that Will speaks in a detached way, remote. I'm sure he's had to go on autopilot, shutting down the emotions for his friend, to get through this. How gut-wrenchingly difficult.

The helicopter moves in slow motion, that infuriatingly laggard, stuck-in-maple-syrup pace, when a medevac victim needs to be at the hospital *now*, and a twenty-minute transit becomes a lifetime.

The exhale I release when we finally settle onto the deck of the helipad—the one on the roof of Mammoth Hospital—is a big one. The medical team awaits, and Beanie and Will slide the litter directly onto the stretcher, which is immediately rolled away. Will follows, and Mojo trots along behind him.

"Ma'am, I'm goin' in with them," Beanie says. "I'll call Boomer and figure out the logistics of where to meet up."

"I'll be here," I say.

And so I shut down, feeling the aircraft rock from side to side as the rotors slow, wondering for the life of me who the hell was flying just now.

13

"Alison?"

My eyes blink open as someone touches my leg.

"Will," I say, groggily.

"I'm sorry, I didn't realize you were asleep."

"No, don't be. I can't believe I actually nodded off."

I rub my eyes, yawning in the process, as Will stands sedately in front of me. It takes a moment to recollect where I am and why. I sit up, still in the middle of the helicopter cabin, right where I lay down when Will and Beanie went inside the hospital earlier. My phone is still in my hand. I tried to call Rich, but he didn't answer.

"Where's Mojo?" I ask, realizing as soon as the question is out of my mouth that I've just asked about Jack's dog before asking about Jack.

"In the waiting room. Wouldn't leave."

"They let him stay there?"

"Everyone here knows Mojo. Kind of a local hero. Has the run of the place, if you ask me." Will allows a light laugh before his tired expression returns.

"Would you like to sit?" I ask, motioning to the space next to me.

He nods, and lowers himself to the cabin floor. I thought I felt tired, but Will looks flat exhausted.

I'm thankful that all the doors have been removed from the aircraft, which allows for the exact-perfect-temperature, lazy autumn breeze to drift through the cabin. Aspen trees blaze in gold, their rounded leaves shimmering, producing a whispered tinkling, like a thousand dainty wind chimes.

The seats remain flipped up, just as they were earlier to make room for the litter, so Will scoots back against a pile of equipment bags, which are nestled near the cockpit passageway in the center of the cabin. I lean back against the opposite bulkhead.

"I want to thank you," he says, pulling his knees up and wrapping his arms loosely around them. "I know it was a big decision for you to fly today, but especially in this case, I want you to know how much I appreciate it."

"You're welcome." I decide he doesn't need to know how much I'm still struggling with that decision. "How is he?"

"They've sedated him, and they're taking him for a head scan. So we'll just have to wait," he says, hanging his head.

"Will, I'm so sorry. You and Jack seem very close."

Will draws in a deep breath, holding it for several seconds, before releasing it in a long, slow exhale.

"He's my best friend. . . . Actually, more than that. Like a father."

Exactly what I sensed during the rescue.

"Did you find out what happened?"

"Based on what Thomas and Kevin saw, he was climbing V-Notch, just like he does every year. He's more than capable. They think it might have been rockfall that caused him to slip."

"Should he have been climbing alone like that?"

"Depends on the route and the conditions, I suppose. But there's a risk no matter what you do." Will pulls a metal carabiner from the handle of an equipment bag, and mindlessly begins opening and closing the gate.

"But he's so accomplished."

"Yeah. That's one thing you learn early in this business. No guarantees, not even for the best."

I pull my water bottle from my helmet bag and offer it to him. "Water?"

He hooks the carabiner back on the equipment bag, then takes the bottle and, several long gulps later, hands it back. "Thanks. Thirstier than I thought."

"I should think so, with what you had to do today." I take a quick drink, then hand the bottle back to him.

Rather than drink this time, he spins the bottle in his hands, while looking out the cabin and into the forest—an absent stare, his expression wrapped in a patchwork quilt of worry. I'm sure that as he turns over the events of the day in his mind, it will only get worse. Maybe talking would help. I know it helps for me.

I take a chance, trying to sound upbeat. "Have you known Jack long?"

"Sixteen years."

"How did you meet?"

He takes another drink before answering. "Are you sure you want to hear this?" he says, wiping his mouth on his sleeve. A glimmer of a smile actually escapes from him, which piques my interest even more.

"Yeah, I wanna hear."

"Okay, you asked for it." He shifts to face me more directly. "When I was fifteen, I was with my family on vacation in Yosemite. I had read about rock climbers and mountaineers, studied everything there was to study, watched videos, you name it. I knew this was what I wanted to do. But uh, my father had different ideas.

"He was Special Forces, Army, and after he got out, he built his fortune as an arms dealer. His whole life was guns—*is* guns—buying, selling, collecting, shooting, hunting. So it became my life, too. Gun shows, shooting ranges, competitions, hunting trips. He traveled around the world, and often I went with him. Hell, you show me any weapon—rifle, pistol, shotgun, no matter the manufacturer or the country—and I'll tell you anything you want to know about it. *Anything*. I'll take it apart, put it together, clean it, fire it. I was forced to learn it all. To learn the trade, so to speak."

He pauses. "Have I bored you yet?"

I sit, rapt. "Absolutely not." I shove the coiled climbing rope that lies in front of me into the far corner, and stretch my legs straight, my toes touching the base of the hoisting mechanism.

"We even have a guesthouse in the backyard that he converted into a gun vault. It houses an arsenal." He shakes his head, letting out a frustrated sigh. "Anyway, it was a *given* I would cut my teeth in the military, follow in his footsteps. But it was never what I wanted. And he never heard me. . . ." Will pauses again, dropping his eyes. He focuses on the carabiner that he's just plucked off the equipment bag a second time, opening the gate, closing it, opening, closing. Click. Click. Click. Click.

"When I finally got up the nerve to tell him I wanted nothing to do with the military or his guns or any of it, that it was the outdoors I loved, the climbing, the mountains, he erupted, which is putting it mildly."

I pull my feet in toward me again, crossing my legs, completely absorbed.

"I almost fell over when he announced we were going to Yosemite for vacation that summer," he says, looking up. "I thought, finally, he's acknowledging what I'd like to do. Maybe offering an olive branch. But when we got there, I realized he had no idea this was rock-climbing Mecca. In his eyes, it was just a camping trip. So I took matters into my own hands, snuck off, and hiked my way to Lembert Dome. I didn't even know the name of it at the time. I just knew I wanted to climb it. So up I went.

"It seemed innocuous enough, big and rounded, but as I climbed, I slowly drifted left, the rock getting steeper and steeper. My foot slipped, and on this slab, there's just nothing to grab on to. I was able to get pressure back on my foot, press into the rock, but then I froze. I was over two hundred feet above the ground, not able to move up or down. I clung there for hours, watching the sun drop. My muscles ached, my calves cramped. I thought, what an idiot. The shortest climbing career ever recorded."

The wind swirls, sending golden aspen leaves spinning into the cabin. I grab one by the stem and begin twirling it between my fingers.

"Normally, this dome is crawling with climbers, but on that day, it was blistering hot, and I had no one to yell to. Then I heard a voice above me telling me not to move, which, of course, wasn't a problem," he says, chuckling. "A man rappelled down, so smooth, so confident. 'Need some help?' he asked. I'll never forget the smile on his face. 'My name's Jack,' he said. 'Hang on just a second. I'll get you hooked up and we can get you down from here. Sound good?'

"He was never judgmental, never spoke down to me. He offered me a ride back to the campground and delivered me to my parents, who had just called the rangers to report I was missing. So there I was, having just experienced the scariest moment of my life, happier than I'd ever been to be in the company of my father, and you know what he did? He lit into me like I'd stolen something. All in front of Jack, too."

He stops, pressing his lips, also taking the opportunity to stretch his legs straight. He crosses his feet where mine used to be, near the hoist. "I'll never forget what Jack said to me after my father stormed off. He said, 'Will, I just want you to know that the route you tried is normally a three-pitch climb, done with ropes, gear, and rock-climbing shoes. But you . . . you did it with nothing more than sneakers and guts. And, just so you know, you were at the crux of that climb. One more move, and it would have been free sailing to the top. The fact that you even attempted it shows the spirit of a great climber. If you ever want to learn how, give me a call,' he said, and he handed me his business card before leaving.

"I was banished to my tent for the rest of the trip, but once inside, I pulled out his card. It said he was a guide at the Yosemite Moun-taineering School."

Will suddenly blinks out of his memories, focusing on me. "And yeah, that's about it."

"What happened next?"

"The short story is that I graduated high school early, left home, and traveled back to Yosemite. I called Jack, he took me under his wing, and the rest is history."

"Sixteen years, huh?"

"Yeah. He taught me everything, got me a job at the mountaineering school, and we became climbing partners. I've been around the world and back again with him, and he's always been there for me. When I broke my leg in a freak fall, he stayed in my hospital room. He's rescued me on more than one occasion, I'm embarrassed to admit. But that's the thing with him. He's just always been there."

"That's an incredible story," I say, with a deep pang of remorse.

My father was never there. And it's not just that he missed my birthdays or gymnastics meets or school plays. There wasn't any support at all. Nothing monetary. No child support. No gifts. Nothing.

Add to this, no photos, no images, no memories. I can't remember what my father looked like. And this lack of imagery, this . . . just lack . . . has only grown more profound as I've gotten older. I remember feeling this so acutely as I stumbled into my teenage years, that age when we search for our identities, separate and independent from our parents. Except, I never had that starting point with my father. That baseline.

Sure, I asked for pictures. Sure, I thought about searching for him, but those quests always started and stopped with my mother, whose pain of recollection always stopped me in my tracks. I couldn't hurt her more than she'd already been hurt.

I swallow. "Jack sounds like an incredible guy."

"He is. He really is. I know if he wakes up—*when* he wakes up—he'll want to thank the pilot personally, who was gutsy enough to fly up to get him."

I look down to my lap. Gutsy? No.

"Can I tell you a secret?" I say.

"Of course."

The cell phone at his waist vibrates. He glances at the screen, then shuts it off, returning his attention to me. "Sorry. Go ahead."

"I uh, I wasn't gutsy. I was nervous as hell. Even scared."

"You'd never know it."

"Ha. At least I fooled one person. But I have to say, after today, I imagine that doughnut would taste pretty good right now."

He surprises me—and himself, I think—when he breaks into laughter, and I can't help but join him.

"You could eat anything in this hospital café right now and it would be gourmet fare, trust me!" he says.

Oh, that feels good! Letting the pressure out, the tension, all of it. Sharing it with someone who understands. Who was right there with me, doing something equally scary, equally gutsy.

His eyes return to mine, holding there, and our laughter slips into silence.

"You are . . . amazing," he says, his voice low.

Maybe it's that I'm tired or that he's tired, I don't know, but neither of us seems to have the energy to look away.

"You're amazing, too," I say, and all the while, strange curly-Q things wind around my insides. Something new. Something foreign. Something I've never felt before.

The door to the helipad slams open. "Hello, children!" Boomer trumpets. "Trading stories of your heroics?"

The spell broken, Will and I look away.

"God damn, Vanilla! I'm gonna have to find another name for you. Beanie gave me the skinny. Told me everything."

"Sir, it wasn't—"

"The hell it wasn't!"

"See?" Will says, smiling at me.

"And good news for *you*, sir," Boomer says to Will. "Jack, that son of a gun, is awake."

"What?"

"Passed the docs on the way up here," Boomer says.

Anxious, thrilled, Will looks set to spring. He starts to move past me, but stops. "Thank you," he says. His eyes hold mine for several long seconds, before he jumps out of the cabin and bolts to the rooftop door.

14

Boomer accelerates on the snow-covered, four-wheel-drive-only road, winding deeper into the Owens River Valley. It's been a week since Jack's rescue on North Palisade Peak, and the weather has undergone yet another radical change. The outside air temperature is back to single digits, and heavy snow has fallen for the last several days, finally tapering to a stop early this morning.

We've just finished a full day of training at the Mammoth Lakes airport with the Mono County SAR Team. And now? I'm crammed into a vehicle, driving to I-still-have-no-idea-where. *Another* bumpy truck ride with Boomer. But at least I'm *inside* the cab this time. I sit next to Tito Vasquez—one of two new pilots who checked into the squadron last week. He's given me several quizzical looks during this drive, none too sure about this next bit of "training" Boomer has planned for us.

And because Boomer borrowed a truck with an extended cab, in the seat right behind us we're joined by Danny Davis, new pilot number two. Both Danny and Tito have come from East Coast H-60 squadrons, and believe it or not, look even more out of place than I did when I arrived.

Just stand by, guys. Stand by. . . .

Next to Danny in the backseat, Hap and Beanie. And squished at the end, Petty Officer Mike "Sky" Simmons, another of our rock-solid crew chiefs. At five feet, five inches tall, Sky is our basketball team's phenom point guard, quick as a whip, and with a forty-inch vertical to boot.

Sky, Hap, and Beanie have been regaling Tito and Danny with the highlights from the Mount Morrison rescue. I've been watching our new pilots, and their mouths have remained open for most of the re-counting.

"Damn, I just wish I was there!" Sky says.

"I don't know, Sky," I say. "It was pretty risky."

"Risky?" Sky says. "Nah, ma'am, no way. That was one *sexy* rescue scenario. I'm jealous as hell I wasn't there!"

Sexy? That description positively never entered my mind.

Rounding another set of hills—we moved out of view of the high-way miles ago—Boomer slows, and I see the steam. It rises in plumes from various spots on the ground that remain conspicuously absent of snow.

A few cars are already here—Will's blue truck is one—and Boomer pulls over, just as the other vehicles in our caravan do.

"We're here!" Boomer announces.

"Where?" I ask.

"The hot springs!"

"Hot springs?"

Prior to briefing, Boomer told us to wear our swimsuits under our flight gear, but without telling us why. I've dreaded this moment all day, thinking surely he's cooked up some crazy polar-bearing, let's-jump-in-a-frozen-lake kind of deal. So I'm beyond happy as I look through the rising steam to . . . Will?

And not just Will. Will in swim trunks. A man sculpted like an honest-to-goodness, no-I'm-not-exaggerating Renaissance statue.

Oh . . . my.

Boomer flies out of the truck and has his flight suit pulled down to his waist before Tito and I even open the door. "Look out, I'm comin' through!" he says, stripping off the last of his clothes. Which is when I realize that Boomer will probably take up an entire hot spring on his own. Fortunately, there are several to choose from.

"They're all running about a hundred and five degrees," Will says, walking up to me. "So you can have your pick."

The rest of the group swarms around us, removing their clothing, kicking off their shoes, but Will looks only at me, that overpowering energy directed in only one place. And I'm reacting, flushed from head to toe.

"Come on," he says, grinning, before disappearing into the steam again.

I remove my flight suit and boots, instantly shivering in the sub-ten-degree temperatures. But . . . what's this? I stand on glossy black, bare rocks, and they're not cold. Actually, they're quite warm.

"Well, get in, Vanilla!" Boomer says. He's already fully submerged, head lying back on the rock rim. And there's room for others—he picked one of the largest springs.

I dip my toe in, gently lowering myself, oohing and aahing all the way.

"Tell me this is not fine," Boomer says, peeking one eye open.

"Yes, this is very fine."

He gives a forceful "harrumph."

"But, sir, how is this training again?"

He speaks with his eyes closed. "As potential rescuers, we must be intimately familiar with this terrain. Someone could get scalded out here, and we would need to know how to find them expeditiously. As someone who believes in careful preparation, I'm sure you can appreciate the importance of the matter."

As I give Boomer the requisite roll of the eyes, Will steps in next to me. "Mind if I sit here?"

"No . . . no, not at all," I say.

"So what do you think?" he asks.

Holy *crap*. I *can't* think.

"This is great," I say, my voice squeaking. Oh, god. Not squeaking!

Okay, Ali. Head together. "How do you guys know about this place?" I say, proud that I delivered a clear, coherent sentence.

"Locals' secret."

"Just glad you let us in on it," Boomer says, eyes remaining closed. He's the picture of bliss, arms behind his head now.

"Is there room for us?"

I look up, thankful for the distraction, as Kevin and Thomas drop in, followed closely by two women. I recognize one of them—Kelly, the hiker with the pink shirt and ponytail.

Freckle-faced, like Beanie, and with that red hair I remember, she slides in and sits next to me. I take advantage, and shift, hopefully discreetly, away from Will, and turn to her.

"Hi," I say. "Kelly, isn't it?"

She nods.

"I'm Alison. I saw you on Palisade Glacier."

"Hi," she says, putting out her hand. "Nice to meet you, officially." She points a thumb to her left. "This is my husband, Kevin." Then she points across from us. "And Thomas and Tawny."

I remember Kevin and Thomas from Schat's Bakkerÿ and, of course, from the rescue.

"Nice to meet you all," I say. "It's a good thing you guys were up there when Jack fell."

"It was an even better thing you were flying that day," Kelly says. "You rocked that rescue, girlfriend."

I smile, inside, outside, everywhere. How genuinely nice of her to say that.

"Girl power, yeah?" Tawny says. She gives me a fist bump as Thomas slips his arm around her and pulls her close.

Kevin shifts his position to sit nearer Kelly, and she moves over to give him room, forcing me to slide right. I'm able to stop before running into Will, but I have to turn my body toward him to avoid contact. We may as well be touching, though. There's only half an inch between us, if that.

"So will you be coming to the party?" Will asks.

"What party?"

"My bad," Boomer says, sitting up a bit. "Will invited us to a party at Jack's house to celebrate Jack's release from the hospital. The Mono County SAR Team is going, and he's invited us, too."

"When?" I ask.

"Friday," Boomer says.

My heart sinks. Sinks . . . ? Rich is coming on Friday. Okay, so this isn't right. I've been looking forward to Rich's visit for weeks.

". . . and has been at home resting since," Will says.

"I'm sorry, what was that?"

"Drifting again, Vanilla?" Boomer says, chuckling.

"I said, he was released from the hospital two days after the accident and has been at home resting since. The doctors can't believe his rate of recovery." Will shifts slightly to face me, which thankfully brings more separation. "He can't wait to thank you, by the way. Will you be coming, then?"

"Um, no," I say. "I won't be able to make it, unfortunately."

"I see. Well, some other time then."

He leans back against the edge of the spring at the same time Kelly scooches over, and wham, Will and I are pressed together. My leg flush against his. Our arms touching, too.

But what causes me to freeze, causes him to freeze, is that his hand now rests on top of mine—something inadvertent, yes, but unmistakably intimate. Much different than just being smashed up next to someone in a crowded place.

He looks down at me, and under that steady gaze, my heart beats faster.

I don't look away, either, and a sizzling jolt of *something* zings straight through me. *Holy shit . . .*

I pull my hand out from under his, bringing it to my lap, trying to cover up whatever that "exchange" was. And it *was* an exchange. A heated one. And that *something* that zipped through me, remains. Humming, burning . . .

Okay, Ali. This is ridiculous. Get it together.

"So, how did these get here?" I ask, sweeping my arm around to indicate the hot springs.

Will clears his throat, then obligingly launches into a discussion of the geology of the area, the system of lava domes that surrounds us, how Mammoth Mountain was created by a series of eruptions fifty-six thousand years ago, and the hydrothermal activity that still occurs below us.

But his geology lesson is lost on me as I attempt to recover. To reconcile what's happening here. Which ultimately leads to thinking about Rich.

I consider my phone calls with him, the ones I've had since moving here that have left me . . . wanting? Hollow? Something?

It will be good to see him. I need to see him. It's been two months since we were together last. And I know absence is supposed to make the heart grow fonder, but it doesn't seem like the phone calls, the e-mails, the texts are enough. Which must explain why, when I spend just a few minutes with Will, I'm full to exploding. It must be a physical nearness thing. And we are indeed near right now.

I start fanning myself.

"Too hot?" Will asks.

"Yeah, I'm uh, I'm not sure what's going on. Normally, I'm fine in a hot tub."

"Here, let me show you another spring. The ones around the corner are cooler than these." He stands, climbing out of the pool, and lowers his hand to me, which I take.

He may as well have touched me with a lightning rod.

He pulls me up and out, and we stand there, steam swirling around us, obscuring the fact that our hands remain together a moment longer than necessary. The air that was like an icebox minutes ago, doesn't sting anymore. He finally lets my hand drop before turning to lead me to the cooler pools.

Yes, cooler. *You need to cool off, Ali!*

"Try this one," he says, pointing to a spring in the far corner, roomy enough for at least eight people. He walks with sure footing over an uneven spread of rocks and sagebrush, and steps in, moving across to the other side. "It runs more around a hundred here."

He watches me get in. And by watching, I mean, *really* watching. Not hiding that he's looking.

I step in, sitting opposite him. "This is much better. Thanks. I don't know what that was."

"Just wait, I bet we have the whole group over here in a few minutes."

I think of the zap I received when he took my hand to help me out of the other pool, and that same charge is here, the water, electric.

Will dunks underwater, running his hands across his hair, like you do when shampooing. When he surfaces, he shakes his head from side to side. "Poor man's bathtub," he says, grinning. "We come here often after climbing."

"I can see why." I pry my eyes away from him to take in my surroundings. The White Mountains rise in front of me, the snowcapped Sierra behind.

"You know the best time to come, though?" he asks.

I shake my head.

"At night. It's a star show unlike any other."

"I can imagine."

No light pollution out here. Probably much like the starry nights I viewed when on a ship on deployment in my last command. A ship . . . a navy ship . . . on deployment. I couldn't be farther from that world right now.

I continue to look around, feeling his eyes on me. God, I feel it.

"Boomer says you're unhappy here," he says.

The shock that registers is genuine. But his statement shouldn't shock at all, because it's true. I mean, it was true.

Is true.

Was true.

"You never seem unhappy to me," he says. "So I find that curious."

"When did he tell you this?"

"At the hospital. I wanted to let him know how much I appreciated him and you and the crew going the extra mile to get Jack and that you were a natural at this. That's when he told me. Said you even wanted to leave. Is that true?"

My mouth opens. Stays there. "Well . . . yeah. That's true," I say, suddenly not wanting it to be true.

"Why would you want to leave?"

"Well, I . . . I . . ." All those ironclad reasons for an early transfer seem to evaporate before I can give them voice. Looking into Will's eyes, I can't seem to find a single one.

"Maybe you could rethink it," he says.

The laughs and conversation grow louder as people begin to emerge from around the bend.

"See, what did I tell you?" he says.

Once again, spell broken.

Beanie, Hap, and Sky jump in next to us—actually jump, splashing all of us.

I take this as an opportunity to duck away, and I submerge. Once underwater, I do the motions like Will did, shampooing my hair, and it feels *divine*. The mineral water is soft, and when I surface, smoothing my hair back, the strands are slipperier than normal.

"That feels so good," I say, erupting into a smile. "Guys, we should definitely do this more often."

"Hell, you don't have to sell me," Sky says.

"Looks like it's good for you, too, ma'am," Beanie says. "I don't think I've ever seen you smile so much."

I flush right to the roots as Will looks on, beaming.

"Nah, it's not the hot springs. It's probably because her fiancé's comin' to visit," Hap says.

How did Hap remember that? I put in for leave *weeks* ago.

The light dims on Will's face, almost imperceptibly, but it's there. And to be truthful, my internal lighting systems just flickered, as well.

"Is that why you can't come to the party?" Will asks.

"No . . . I mean . . ."

"You're welcome to bring him," Will says, noticeably swallowing. "The invitation's open to both of you."

"Thanks," I say, something withering inside. "That's really thoughtful of you."

He smiles, a sad smile, before standing and hopping out of the pool. He walks away without looking back.

I watch him go, while at the same time, envisioning Rich striding through the airport to greet me.

I duck underwater again as my insides twist, facing the monumental task of righting a listing ship.

15

Please pick up, Mom. Please. I need to talk.

At home in my apartment, tucked in a bathrobe, and nursing a mug of apple cider, I blow my nose again into a tissue. I was supposed to have left two hours ago to pick Rich up at the airport, but he called and canceled.

"I know it's lousy timing, but Brian needs me at a work retreat in Santa Barbara," Rich said. "I can't not go."

Knowing Rich's I-don't-take-no-for-an-answer boss, Brian, I can understand. But this time I don't want to understand. It's the fifth time he's canceled a trip to see me. The *fifth*. On the previous *four* occasions, I flew back to San Diego instead.

"But I can come next weekend and stay even longer," Rich said. "Or you could always come here."

My pouty self put my foot down on principle. I want *him* to come *here*. I want him to see this place, so he can make sense of it. So he'll know what the heck I'm talking about when I call.

I hung up the phone in a daze, undressed, took a shower, and curled up in my bathrobe. The few tears I've shed have been born from frustration mostly, and have done more to piss me off than anything else, because now my nose is clogged.

"Hello?" my mom says.

"Hi, Mom. It's me. Do you have time to talk?"

"Yes, honey, of course. What's wrong?"

How do moms *do* that? Amazing how they know.

"Rich canceled his trip to see me."

"But you were supposed to pick him up today."

"Supposed to . . . He got pulled into a last-minute work retreat."

I draw my legs up, sitting crisscross-applesauce, just like I did as a kid, when I would sit close to my mom on the couch to talk.

"Oh . . . well, that's not his fault."

It's exactly what I expected her to say. No matter the issue or the complaint, she has staunchly defended him. Not that I've had much to complain about. Rich is hardworking, successful, he treats me nicely. It's all been there. But no matter how great the guy, I think all girls still want assurances that the man they've chosen to marry is indeed the right one. Am I making the right choice? So I've asked my mom and she's always been ready with the "yes" before I've even finished asking the question.

She's met him on two occasions and they've gotten along just fine. "Smart choice, Ali," she said. "Smart choice." It's what she always says. But I've always wondered, does "smart" equal "right"?

"Ali? Ali, honey, are you there?"

"I'm here."

"What's the matter?"

"Mom, did you love Nick?"

"What? Of course I did."

A defensive answer to a subject I haven't broached with her in ages. A practiced response that always begins with a question—*What?*—spoken with strident incredulity. As in, *How could you ask such a thing?* Followed by a decidedly vehement *Of course I do*, or *Of course I did*, depending on when I ask. Answers rendered with finality to prevent further questioning.

Sometimes I'll push it, selfishly asking the follow-on question, knowing the hurt to her that will inevitably result. Most times, though, to spare her this, I back off. But this time, I have to know. I *need* an answer. I need confirmation.

"Did you love *my* father? My *real* father?"

"Nick was your father."

Boom. Standard. Pavlovian.

"Mom, please. Please, for once don't say that."

"Ali, I don't—"

"Please don't say you don't want to talk about it. Please, can you just answer me this? Just this once. I'm about to *marry* Rich. And if he can cancel on me like this—*again*—maybe he's just like my father. Maybe he's capable of leaving, too."

No answer, no answer . . .

"I'm not asking for much, Mom. I just want to know if you loved him. That's all."

Her breathing slows, and after an interminable silence, there's an unmistakable hitch. "Yes."

Whoa. She actually confirmed it. What I've known in my heart, because she sat with "him" all those years in her garden of larkspur, but something she's never openly admitted.

"But after he left? You still—?"

"I've never stopped loving him."

"But . . . how?" I ask, a knot lodging in my throat. "He left us, Mom. He *left* us." I reach my unsteady hand to the end table to deposit my cup of cider before it spills. "*Why* did he leave? Was it someone else? Was it—"

"No, it wasn't someone else. He loved me equally as much, if not more."

"But . . . I've spent my entire life hating this man for what he did to us. To you."

"You don't understand, Alison."

"But it doesn't make sense!"

I pop to a stand. Years of frustration, so many unanswered questions, and finally, finally, my mom has opened the door. Just a crack. But when I see the opening, I can't help it. I burst through. Why? Why leave? For what? And does it matter anyway? How could you leave a young mother—especially one you loved—and her four-year-old? How? What was so pressing? Did they have an argument? Did he ever come back? Has she talked to him since? Did he ever ask about me? "Why?" I say, my voice finally kicking in. "Why would he leave? That bastard! Why—"

"Alison!" she shouts, stopping my ranting cold. "Don't ever speak about him in that manner! Ever!"

The laser-sharp rebuke thunders in my ears.

"He was a good man, Alison. A good man . . ." She has to stop to compose herself, and frankly, I'm doing the same. Because she never told me anything, I've had to fill in the blanks, concocting tales of a vile person, so callous he would abandon his wife and child when he was needed most.

Needed most . . .

My mom married Nick just eighteen months later. . . .

"I . . . I'm sorry," I say softly. "I didn't . . ."

I can almost see her standing taller, pulling back her shoulders. "You're making too big an issue about Rich. Taking it too personally. He's just doing what he needs to do. Nothing more."

"Um . . . yeah. Yeah, I guess."

"I have to go, Ali."

I choke down the sob that swells in my throat.

"Remember, honey, I love you. More than anything in this world, I love you."

Somehow, I manage an "I love you" in return, before she hangs up.

No! We were just getting started!

I slump down to the couch, my head pounding, beyond frustrated. Finally, my mom opened up, talking about what I've so desperately wanted to discuss since forever, and then wham, she shut it down.

My fault for pushing it, though. Damn it.

But then . . . Whoa.

It dawns on me that I've just witnessed an unmistakable break-through. Maybe the therapy's working after all, because this is the most my mom has ever opened up about my father.

I place my hands on the sides of my head, holding it still, while her revelations ping against the sides of my skull.

She loved my father. Loves him still. And this *good* man loved her.

I don't understand. I don't understand it at all.

He's just doing what he needs to do. Nothing more.

My mother's words re-form in my mind, communicating a message—perhaps intended, perhaps not. *I did what I had to do. Nothing more.*

And then I start to see things—stalks of larkspur growing up through the carpeting and peeking through cracks in the walls. Me, sitting, just like my mom . . .

And just like that, I'm dressed and driving to June Lake. To Jack's house.

16

I drive past June Mountain Ski Resort, then turn off the main road, and follow a twisty, snowy lane upward. I'm ushered along by rows of stick-bare aspen, bony sentinels directing me forward, every turn bringing another house into view, cabins quietly tucked into the mountainside forest and invisible from the main street. I move at a crawl, looking for mailboxes, searching for the right address, while passing trucks rigged with snowplow shovels on their bumpers, all jammed into the slimmest of pullouts.

Finally, I emerge into an open cul-de-sac, where at least twenty cars are parked front-to-back. A nearly hidden driveway leads downward through the trees and out of view. The airport manager's truck we used in Bishop is parked here, too. Yep, right place.

I park, step out, then follow tire tracks down the meandering drive, the snow crunching softly under my feet. Heavy-laden boughs of pine arch overhead, pencil-thin icicles dangling from the branches. I shove my hands deeper in my jacket pockets as I drop out of view of the street.

Low rumbles of laughter break the silence as I round the last corner. Here the driveway widens, revealing a nestled log cabin, the windows glowing a warm and welcoming gold. It's so embedded and tucked in, the house looks as if it's part of the forest itself. Exactly the home I would have pictured for Jack. Will's truck is parked outside the garage, right next to cars I recognize as belonging to Boomer and Hap.

I turn down the front walkway, one that has been shoveled, snow piled high to either side, to the entry alcove, which is dominated by oversized wooden double doors. The heavy brass knocker resonates with a deep bass thud.

I clench and unclench my fists in my pockets, wondering for the hundredth time if I should have come here. The correct answer is no.

I mean, what are you doing, Alison? Like, what is this? Would you have come to this party if Will wasn't going to be here? No, you would have given it a miss, because you were feeling lousy and not in the mood to see anyone. But you did come, and you know the reason why. . . .

The door opens with a *whump*. Will stands in the entryway, beer in hand, wearing a startled yet genuinely pleased expression. It's something I have to latch on to, though, before he slides down an invisible shield. *Whump.* Just like the door.

"Alison . . . ? I wasn't expecting you."

"I wanted to call, but I didn't have your number." I look up, down, around, anywhere but into his eyes, nerves running helter-skelter. "So anyway, is it still okay?"

"Of course," he says, looking discreetly over my shoulder and then to the sides. "So, where's Rich?" he asks breezily.

"He . . . he had to cancel his trip."

"Oh, I see."

The silence stretches. And stretches.

"Um . . . so may I come in?"

He jumps slightly, putting out his hand. "Oh, god! Sorry! Yes!" he says, stepping back to let me walk through the entry. He snaps to, moving past the awkwardness. "Can I take your jacket?"

I shrug out of my jacket and hand it to him. As he opens the entryway closet, my head turns upward to the triangular-shaped ceiling, ribbed with good old-fashioned cedar logs, a framed skylight in the center.

A whirl of fur circles my legs, and Mojo gives a healthy yip as his tail beats the air. I crouch, taking his head in my hands. "Hey, boy, how are you? Didn't recognize you without your vest!"

He answers with a quick lick to my face before bounding away.

I rise to face Will, who stands, arms crossed, a look of wonder on his face. "That's new," he says.

"What's new?"

"Mojo coming to greet someone at the door tonight. He's been sticking like glue to Jack since the accident and hasn't left his side since the party started. Interesting that he felt your arrival important enough to merit a personal welcome."

"Maybe it's that I used to have a Lab, too. Probably senses it. Anyway, I want to apologize for not letting you know I was coming ahead of time. For just showing up on your doorstep like this."

"Nonsense, I invited you. But may I give you my number? You know, just so you have it . . . for something like tonight, I mean."

I add Will's number to my phone, but when I look up, my breath catches. In front of me, a recessed central living room, one easily as large as my entire apartment, walled on all sides by glass. I turn to look behind me—modest entryway—then back to something not so modest. Is there such a thing as a log *mansion*? My god. That's what this is. All of it hidden.

Beyond the glass walls, a balcony sweeps on all sides. I spot some of my squadron mates outside, drinking and laughing with the Mono County guys. They don't appear to be fazed by the cold, although it does look like heating lamps are spaced across the balcony at intervals. I do a quick scan of the living room—close to thirty people here. Many in standing groups, some sitting on the rust-colored leather couches, and a few lounging by the hearth next to the oversized fireplace.

To the left is a large open kitchen with a granite countertop running about fifteen feet long, every barstool along its length occupied. A potluck feast stretches across the counter—a mishmash of offerings— and a large stockpot steams on the stove, hot chili spilling down the sides.

Country music plays lightly in the background from unseen speakers. I scrunch up my brow, trying to recollect. I know this voice. . . .

"What is it?" Will asks.

I point to the air. "This song. Who sings this?"

"This? You mean Randy Travis?"

I nod.

"You don't know Randy Travis?"

"No. I mean, yes. Sort of . . . well, no."

His cheeks move like he wants to smile, but he stops before you could officially call it one.

"'Better Class of Losers' is one of the more well-known country tunes out there."

"I've heard it before. I have. Really. I just didn't know who sang it."

It *is* true. I *have* heard this song before. In our aircraft—grrr—but also at the Safeway grocery store in Fallon. Country music is the only thing they play, and in the few short months I've been here, I've learned many of the songs, singing along—which, of course, I would never admit to Boomer—but never knowing the artists. And now that I know who it is, I certainly recognize Randy Travis's voice.

"Do you like it?"

"Yeah, I do."

"I mean country music. In general."

"Well . . . I'm kind of new to it."

"Ah. Well, it grows on you," he says, his eyes lingering. The invisible shield cracks just a bit, and something flares deep in my stomach.

Thankfully, he blinks. "Can I get you something to drink?"

"Yes, please."

He places his hand lightly on my back, steering me to the left, in the direction of the kitchen. It's only for a moment, his touch, but my back goes tingly, a sensation that quickly spreads—arms, legs, hands, feet.

We walk down three wooden steps, each at least ten feet in length, running across the breadth of the entryway to the level of the living room. And by the time we step off the bottom stair, a span of maybe four seconds top to bottom, the invisible shield is gone.

"What would you like?" he asks as we enter the kitchen.

"How about what you're having?"

"Coming up."

He opens the door to the refrigerator side of the wide stainless-steel refrigerator-freezer just as Thomas walks up behind him. "Any ice cream left, bro?"

"I knew *you'd* be coming, so yeah, I stocked up," Will says. He opens the door to the freezer side, pulling out one of several half-gallon containers of ice cream, this one butter pecan.

"Your favorite, right?" I say to Thomas.

"You know it!" he says, spinning away.

I peer into the voluminous freezer, spying at least ten other containers.

"Chocolate chip?" I say, motioning to the one, two, three, four containers of the flavor.

He grins. "Yes . . . ?"

"That's your favorite, isn't it."

"Used to be," he says, grinning.

He closes the freezer door and pokes his head into the refrigerator side.

"Hey, our favorite pilot!" I turn to see Tawny sitting at the kitchen counter. Kelly is next to her—

And then it registers. *What did he just say?*

Tawny reaches out and gives me another fist bump.

"Hey, guys," I say, flustered.

"So what'd you think of the hot springs?" Kelly asks.

Besides having my insides turned to liquid, because I was sitting next to Will? "They were great. Really great."

I start a bit when Will moves to my side, nudging me as he proffers a bottle of Corona. I take it, trying to ignore the all-over body buzz when he doesn't move away, his arm lightly touching mine.

I have to focus hard to remember what Kelly and I were just talking about. Were we talking about anything? Oh yes, hot springs.

"We go there a lot after climbing," Kelly says.

"Those springs, in particular, are the best, because only the locals know about them," Tawny adds.

"Kelly and Tawny are two of the best climbers around here," Will says. "Freakily good, actually."

"I don't doubt it," I say, eyeing their toned arms.

"Have you shown her around yet?" Kelly asks Will. "The views are to die for," she says, turning to me.

"I haven't," Will says. "But perhaps we should go rectify that."

Again, the touch is gentle, to the small of my back, as we move forward. His hand is there, and then it's gone, but the sensation lingers.

Arriving at a sliding glass door in the corner, he reaches around me to open it, and we step out to the balcony, to a stunning panoramic view.

"This is . . . utterly breathtaking."

He looks down at me, beaming. "You like it?"

"How could I not?" I say, walking along the railing. I stop, pointing to a mountain that looks as if it tipped over and spilled, while still in liquid form, before hardening suddenly. "What's that peak?"

"That's Carson Peak."

"Oh, yeah. I remember seeing it on the map when we flew by here. And what's that cabin right there?" I motion to a partially cleared area downslope of the house—a small cottage, tucked away in the back.

"That's Jack's guesthouse. I'm staying there now."

I raise my bottle, taking another drink, letting my gaze drift over the cottage before shifting it to Carson Peak and the surrounding forest draped in white. "How long have you lived in June Lake?"

"About five years now, on and off."

"On and off?"

"Yeah, finding a place to settle—actually, just settling, in general—is tough for me."

"Do you think you'll stay? Like is this the place you'll be twenty years from now?"

He takes a long draw from his drink, licking his lips when finishing.

"Truthfully, I don't know where I'll be in twenty years. I don't even know where I'll be *next* year. Hell, I could be dead tomorrow."

My hand flies to my heart. "Please, don't . . ."

We need something else to talk about. I look side to side. "What about the lake?" I ask. "Can you see it from here?"

"From the other side of the house you can. We just have to walk back the way we came."

He turns, leading me the other way, past the glass door and to the balcony area that wraps around the house to the east. It's only quick glances here and there, but I notice the smooth finish on the railing, the intricately carved eaves above us, the way the door sealed as Will closed it on the way out. Vast attention to detail, solidly built, quality all the way. I've only seen a portion of the house, but it had to have cost Jack a fortune.

"There it is!" I say.

Because the sun is angled low, June Lake throws off colors of burnt orange and rust. And the clarity . . . clear as crystal. I think back to the first time I saw the lake, now almost three weeks ago, a view from a helicopter.

"It's nice to look at the lake while stationary," I say.

He raises his eyebrows.

"I mean, seeing it from the air is great and all, but this way, you get to savor it."

"I know exactly what you mean."

I would have bet money that nothing could have drawn my attention from the lake, but Will's eyes burn into the side of my face. I raise my eyes to his, held here, out of view of the rest of the partygoers.

"I'm glad you could make it," he says, his voice low.

"Me, too."

He takes a sip from his bottle, his last. A long look follows.

"This isn't going to come out right," Will says finally. "In fact, it's rude as hell, but fuck it, I'm gonna say it anyway. I'm not sorry Rich had to cancel."

I lower my eyes, looking intently at the Corona label and those little yellow dragons, or whatever they are, fanning their wings.

"I, uh . . ." What the heck do I say? But then I think of what Will and I have been through together in the little time we've known each other, and there just isn't room for coy behavior. For communication barriers.

I return my gaze to him, taking an extra deep breath in the process. "Will, I'm confused. I'm really confused right now. This thing . . . this . . ." I move my hand back and forth between us. "I don't know what this is or if it's a thing at all or—"

His eyes remain on mine as he reaches out, slowly, and gently touches my hand. Tremors roll through me as his fingers travel lightly over mine, but then—I suck in my breath—his fingers move through mine, our hands lacing together. He brushes his thumb delicately against my palm.

"Do you feel that?" he asks.

"I feel it everywhere," I say, my voice shaking just that bit.

"I do, too. I don't know what it is either, but . . ."

I swallow. "It's so strong."

"Yeah. It is." Slowly, he releases his fingers and slides them out of my grasp.

I look down at my hand, invisible sparks shooting hither and thither.

"Would you like to head inside?" he asks. "I think I need another beer."

I tip my bottle back, draining it. "I think I do, too."

17

Will pulls two more beers from the refrigerator, hands one to me, and gives my bottle a soft clink.

I take a good swallow, composing myself, looking around the room in the process. "Will, I can't believe I haven't asked you this yet, but where's Jack? And Boomer, for that matter? I saw his truck when I walked in."

"They're all downstairs."

"There's a downstairs? You mean there's more than this?"

"Yeah. The house is built on a slope, so you can't see it from the driveway. Under the balcony are two more levels. My guess is they're playing pool. Jack's nuts about it. Wanna go check?"

"Yeah, definitely."

Off to the side, in an alcove I hadn't noticed before, a stairwell drops to the lower level. I pass several framed photos—spectacular landscapes, Will and Jack standing in the foreground of most of them.

I stop mid-landing. "Is this Jack?" I point to a photo where Will poses with a man sporting a deeply tanned face, and raccoon eyes—the white circles that form around your eyes when you get sunburned wearing ski goggles.

"Yeah, that's him."

I don't know why I stop. Maybe it's just this photo. Maybe it's all of them collectively. Will and Jack out in the world. In nature. Tanned. Or sunburned, in Jack's case.

"This is the mirror opposite of my upbringing—of my life, in general," I say, pointing to the photos.

"How so?"

"I was *the* indoor girl."

"*You?* Really?"

"Yeah. My mom shuttled me from one indoor activity to another, no sunscreen, glasses, or goggles required."

Although I did have a pair of old ski goggles once, when I was in kindergarten. I don't remember how I got them, but I figure I must have nabbed them from a girlfriend's house on a playdate. I didn't know what they were for, until I asked my mother, who told me, then promptly took them away. She seemed pretty upset at the time, and now I understand why. I can only imagine her embarrassment, having to return the property her daughter had lifted. Anyhow, that was the closest I ever got to skiing.

"Pretty bizarre that I rescue skiers and climbers now, when I could never have even fathomed skiing or climbing period."

"Is that you, Vanilla?" I hear Boomer, uh, boom.

We turn down the stairs and drop into a rec room of sorts, smaller than the living room, but with the same windowed walls—ones that now frame a brilliant sunset, the clouds turning all shades of cotton-candy pink and crimson. A billiard table occupies the far back corner of the room, around which Boomer, Jack, and Beanie hover, pool sticks in hand. Mojo is curled near a smaller fireplace, lifting his head only for a moment before nuzzling it back under his leg.

"Ah, so it is!" Boomer says loudly. "Here she is, Jack."

Jack leans his stick against the table and walks, gingerly, to me. His head has been shaved, clearing the way for a row of stitches—make that staples—across the left side of his scalp.

"Alison!" he says, moving past the hand I've offered and wrapping me in an embrace.

"Jack, good to see you, again."

"Well, finally!" He pulls back, hands on my shoulders. "I owe you a helluva thank-you!"

"You're welcome. Beanie helped, too, of course," I say with a nod to my lanky crew chief.

"Oh, yes. I've heard about everything. Thanked him, too!"

Rough scratches mark Jack's face, the left side having gotten the worst of it. His skin glows red on that side, like a horrible case of road rash. I point to the staples. "Nice souvenir you've got there."

"I think I could have done without it, but yes," he says, grinning.

"Nah, he looks better that way," Boomer says, laughing far too hard at his own joke.

Jack ignores him. "You guys keep playing. I need to speak to this one." He turns to me. "Mind if we sit down? I'm recovering well and all that, but standing for long periods is still a bit of a chore."

He leads Will and me to a couch and chairs positioned against one of the windows. Mojo rises from his spot, checks in with his owner with a quick brush against the leg, then reassumes his position near the fireplace. Jack sits on one end of the couch while I take the other. Will sits in the chair next to me.

"Alison," he says, "the docs told me in no uncertain terms that if you hadn't airlifted me out of there, I wouldn't be alive today. So, thanks. Needless to say, I owe you one."

"You don't—" I start to respond, but he appears to have moved on, as he looks me over in a studious way.

"You know what Will said to me that day I met you in Schat's Bakkerÿ?" he asks.

I shake my head.

"Later that night, he said to me, 'She's beautiful, don't you think?'" Jack lets his gaze slide to Will for a moment before returning it to me. "But I don't know. I think he was understating the matter."

Will's tanned face flushes cherry red.

"You said that?" I ask, embarrassed, flattered, shaken, all of the above.

"Well, I may have mentioned it." He then looks to Jack. "Thanks a lot."

"You know you can count on me, my friend."

"Hey, Will!" The shout comes from above. Kevin pokes his head over the stair banister. "Man, you have any more of the Jägermeister?"

"I do," Will says. "It's in the storeroom." He puts his beer on the coffee table as he stands. "Excuse me," he says, before bounding up the stairs.

"So what do you think of him?" Jack says.

"Uh . . ." The question catches me completely off guard.

"He told me you're engaged. Is that right?"

"I am. But he did? He told you that?"

"Well, he talks about you so damn much, I asked why he hadn't asked you out yet."

"He talks about me?"

"Never heard anything like it from him. I've known him for a long time, too."

"Sixteen years," I say. "He told me."

"So what do you think of him? You never answered that."

"You never gave me a chance."

"Ah, you're right. I don't think I did. But I'm giving you the chance now," he says with a smile.

"Well . . . he's . . . ," I say, rubbing my now sweaty hands together. "I've never met anyone like him."

"And . . ."

"And . . . I like being with him. I'm in a very good place when I'm with him."

"But you're engaged."

I nod.

"Bit of a pickle, isn't it?"

Normally, I'd think a conversation like this might be a tad out of line. Heck, *I'm* not even sure what's going on, let alone discussing it with a stranger. But oddly, he doesn't feel like a stranger at all.

"It is." I start to take a drink from my beer bottle, but notice Jack doesn't have anything. "I'm sorry. Can I get you anything? Something to drink? Some water, maybe?"

"No, I'm good, thanks," he says, sinking back into the couch. He wears the same weathered lines as Will, but they sag a bit more, the skin around his eyes puffy, his body clearly exhausted. "Considerate of you to ask."

"Tired?" I say.

"Perceptive, too." He goes into study mode again, and I imagine him ticking off a list of personality traits, wondering when he'll hit on the not-so-good ones. Maybe I should just go ahead and tell him to get that part over with.

"And stubborn," I say. "Really stubborn."

Jack breaks into a wide smile, his beautifully straight, white teeth lighting up his olive-skinned yet wrecked face. "Stubborn, huh?"

"And I'm a terrible swimmer. A lousy bowler. A bit obsessive. Actually, a lot obsessive. And a control freak. That goes with the obsessive part. And, Jack," I say, leaning forward. "I'm a horrible, deceptive, rotten fiancée."

"How so?"

"How so?" I place my bottle on the table next to Will's. "Because I'm engaged and . . . and I shouldn't be feeling what I'm feeling . . . with Will, I mean."

How am I speaking like this? I've met this man only once before, and now, five minutes into our second conversation ever, I'm spilling like I'd spill to my mother. It's the alcohol. *But you haven't even finished two beers.* I push the bottle farther away, anyway.

"Why not?" he asks.

"What do you mean? I'm engaged, that's why not."

"That's your head talking. Not your heart."

I sit back, staring. "Are you always this forward?"

"Only if it concerns Will."

Again, the pang. What a father would do for his child. Looking out for him. Loving him. And Jack isn't even Will's real father.

"It's obvious, you know," he says.

"What's obvious?"

"I've seen you and Will together for exactly three minutes tonight, and there's something very special there. Don't ask me how I know, but it's unmistakable."

"So are you gonna play or what?" Boomer calls out to Jack.

Rather than answer Boomer, Jack looks to me. "I suspect you've had enough of me," he says, rising. "I hope you can forgive me. The forwardness and all. I just want what's best for Will." He smiles, a comforting smile, before turning.

As he walks away, I hear it when he says under his breath, "And, truthfully . . . I think he's found it."

Jack, Boomer, and Beanie continue their game, and even though Jack is well older than both of them, he's easily in the best shape of the three. Granted, he's injured and moving slowly, but like Will, the muscles in his arms are lean and taut and he moves in a graceful, purposeful way. The longer I watch, the more the differences become pronounced. With Boomer and Beanie, there's a lot of "extra" going on. With Jack, every movement seems planned, so as not to disturb the air around him.

I'm stirred from my observations as my phone vibrates in my pocket. The letters on the preview pane seem larger than usual. It's a text from Rich.

I wanted to tell you again how sorry I am for having to cancel. Trust me, I was just as disappointed. I'm done for the night, so call if you get the chance. I can't wait to see you next week! Love you!

I stare at the message, reading it through again and again, my heart sinking lower and lower. I am indeed a horrible fiancée. A horrible person, in general. I put the phone on the table, lean forward, elbows on my knees, and cradle my forehead in my hands. I stare some more. Between the lines, I read, "I'm sure you're sitting at home alone now. Missing me. Thinking about me. Anticipating my visit even more. Just like a fiancée should . . ."

When I finally look up, Will is standing there, watching. How long has he been there?

"Everything okay?" he asks.

And Jack thought *I* was perceptive . . .

"Yeah, it is. I, um, I have to get going," I say, standing.

"Are you sure? You haven't even eaten anything."

"Yeah, I'm sure." I slide my phone into my pocket and turn for the stairs. Will follows. At the top, he moves ahead of me to the entryway closet to open it and retrieve my jacket.

"Would you like to take anything with you? Some water? Food? You have a long drive."

"No, thanks," I say, threading my arms through the sleeves. "I'm good."

He opens the door for me, and I step out, met with a rush of cold.

"Can I walk you to your car?" he asks.

I notice he doesn't put on a jacket to walk outside, quick to follow. We move through the grand arch of pine boughs, the only sound the hollow crunch of snow from our footfalls, exaggerating the uncomfortable silence between us. Reaching my car, he steps in front of me, opening the driver's-side door.

"I hope everything's all right."

"It's fine. I just have to go."

I move past him, toward the front seat, but stop before getting in. Even with my back to him, I *feel* him.

"Alison, I meant what I said tonight on the balcony."

I freeze.

Our interaction on the balcony replays. That look in his eyes, his fingers slipping through mine, my reaction. God, my physical reaction.

I pinch my eyes shut, Rich's text so vivid. *I can't wait to see you next week! Love you!*

Gathering myself, I turn to face him. "I'm engaged, Will. What happened . . . well, it shouldn't have happened."

"But it did."

"It won't anymore," I say, as sternly as I can muster.

He stares. I stare. It's cold. He's in short sleeves. Not a goose bump.

"But you *felt* it," he says. "I felt it. Why would you—"

"That doesn't mean anything. Physical attractions happen. It doesn't mean you have to act on them."

"It's more than that, and you know it."

His eyes hold mine, communicating a connection I can't acknowl-edge.

"This can't happen, Will. I'm sorry."

I drop into my seat, and turn on the ignition.

He steps back, closing the door, and remains there, unmoving, as I disappear down the drive.

18

"Longhorn Seven, Fallon Tower, you're cleared to the east, over."

"Fallon Tower, Longhorn Seven, roger," I say.

I follow Highway 50, passing over a dry lake bed baked with salt so white you could easily mistake it for snow. In front of me, the Sand Mountain Recreation Area, a haven for off-road enthusiasts. The sand dunes glare, much like the alkali flats, peppered with dirt bikes, sand rails, and quads, popping, careening, carving tracks upways, sideways, and crossways through the sand in the early-morning sun. It's a workday, Monday, but you'd never know it based on the number of RVs and trucks parked out here, like a mini off-road city.

I glance up at the outside-air temperature gauge. Sixty degrees Fahrenheit.

Just three nights ago, I needed four-wheel drive to grind my way through June Lake in multiple feet of snow and in subfreezing temperatures. And Will stood in that snow, so still, eyes uneasy, as I drove away. . . .

I've tried not to think about that, focusing on Rich instead. I called him, talked with him, as I drove home from the party, and again the next day. But it's no use. Will is *in* my head. He's in there, and I can't seem to push him out.

"I can't believe I'm gonna do this," Snoopy says. "What the hell was I thinking?"

I saw Snoopy last at the Fallon swimming pool, almost two weeks ago, the day after he arrived for his air wing's training. Today, he rides in the cockpit in the left seat. He was appointed as the investigative officer for a noise complaint—sonic boom—so I've been tasked to fly him to Cold Springs Station, a restaurant, hotel, and RV park located about fifty miles east of Fallon, to interview the complainant and other witnesses. It's my first flight as an aircraft commander in the H-1; I completed my check flight just one week ago.

My first flight as an aircraft commander, and I'm about to do something so far outside the rules . . .

Snoopy—somehow—convinced me to do a trade with him. When he was here last time, he flew me to San Diego in a two-seater F/A-18—my first and only Hornet ride—for a search-and-rescue model manager conference. He asked if I'd let him fly the Huey if he let me fly the jet. Surely, I thought, this cannot be allowed. But on that blue-sky day at 26,500 feet, I took the controls of an F/A-18, never admitting to him that it was one of the biggest thrills of my twenty-eight-year-old life.

"So, are you ready, then?" I ask.

"No," Snoopy says, laughing. "And Beanie, not a word of this to *anyone*, got it?"

"My lips are zipped, sir."

"Okay, you've got the controls," I say.

I take my hands and feet off the controls, and the nose immediately whips to the right. My feet fly to the rudder pedals to stop the yaw.

I look left. Snoopy has his feet on the floor. He must have pulled up on the collective or something to make the nose yaw like that, but he definitely wasn't in a position to correct it.

"Uh, Shane, you need to have your feet on the rudder pedals."

"Ah," he says. He places his feet on the pedals, and I remove mine. The bird is a little wobbly, but straighter now.

"We don't really use the rudder pedals," he explains, referring to flying the F/A-18. "Once in flight, I mean."

"I can see that," I say, trying to keep a straight face.

What a trooper. This guy's an extraordinary F/A-18 pilot, a bazillion hours under his belt, but he's never flown a helicopter. For a jet jock, flying a helicopter should be easy-peasy, right? Yeah, that's what he bragged about in the brief.

I stifle the giggles as he wrestles with the controls, the aircraft slipping and dipping like it's teetering on a Bosu ball.

"Shit! Okay, so I take back everything I said in the brief," he says, gripping the controls like he's about to yank them from the fuselage. "And I apologize *forever* for laughing after your Hornet ride."

On that flight, Snoopy let me have the controls for most of the straight-and-level parts both ways. However, once we arrived at the training ranges in Fallon, he took the controls back, so he could "show me what the aircraft can do."

Now, I hadn't done aerobatics in a fixed-wing aircraft since flight school. Barrel rolls, aileron rolls, loops, all of that was ancient history for me. I had forgotten most of it . . . and so had my stomach. I cringe, even now, thinking of it. The worst part of the whole thing was asking him for the airsickness bag. I remember looking up, watching his head tipped back in laughter. I didn't get sick in the plane—couldn't give him the satisfaction—but I did get sick on the drive home. Had to pull over and empty the contents of my stomach on the side of the road in a cow pasture.

The day after, I was a good girl. I ponied up and admitted it—to more good-natured, raucous laughter, of course.

"I think you're getting the hang of it," I say as the aircraft begins to smooth. I knew it wouldn't take long for him.

"I've had night carrier landings that were easier than this."

"I highly doubt that," I say, knowing a night carrier landing would be infinitely more difficult.

As Snoopy gets a handle on things, I have yet another out-of-body experience, that thing that happens to me on a regular basis since coming to Fallon. Two months ago, when I agreed to the trade, I never thought I'd have to go through with it on my end. First, in what circumstance would I ever be flying with Snoopy? And second, this was *me.* Give someone who has never flown a helicopter the controls on a flight? Me?

But now, post–Mount Morrison, post–North Palisade Peak, this does little to register on the "extreme" meter.

Which sort of blows my mind.

Snoopy rolls the aircraft to the left, entering a narrow, gently sloping valley that splits two north-south-running mountain ranges, ten-thousand-foot peaks on either side. I'm reminded of the Sierra, because these mountains—at their summits, anyway—remain coated with snow, even on this warm mid-November day in the middle of the high desert.

"So what's next for you after this deployment?" I ask.

"Grad school. I'm going to Monterey to get my master's. Then a department head tour, and then, hopefully, my XO and CO tours."

A man with a plan. Just like Rich. Just like me. Yeah, I've thought about that, too, since I last saw Will. "I don't even know where I'll be *next* year," Will said on the balcony.

See, this isn't a fairy tale, Alison. He has no long-term plans. Will might be in your head, but this is reality we're talking about. . . .

"There it is, Shane," I say, pointing out the RV park. "One o'clock, four miles."

"Got it. So are you ready to take the controls back?"

"You mean you don't want to try to land?"

"Are you *crazy?*" Snoopy says.

"Just kidding. I've got the controls."

I land about one hundred yards from the RV park and shut down—yes, I shut down. I remind Beanie that he doesn't have to mention that part to Boomer.

Beanie accompanies Snoopy, but I remain, "guarding" the helicopter. I'm glad for the alone time, as it gives me an opportunity to phone my mother again. Her voice-mail greeting over the weekend said she was "off hiking." This new activity cropped up after she started her therapy sessions, and when I speak to her after one of these outings, she breathes life again. Energetic, positive, vibrant.

I wait for some time before calling, mulling over how to approach this conversation. During the last call, she admitted she *still* loves my real father, has always loved him, *and* that he was a good man. But *why* did he leave? Finally, I pull out my phone, relieved to see I have two antenna bars.

"South Land Park Realty, Candice Malone speaking," my mom answers, all business.

"Mom?"

"Oh, it's you. The caller ID didn't show for some reason. Sorry, honey. I was expecting a call from the title company."

"That's okay. So how was hiking this weekend?"

"Oh," she says, and I hear it when she plops into her high-backed leather office chair, the one that lets out a large *whoosh* every time you sit in it. "It was a dream, Ali. Just a dream. Sequoia National Park was resplendent! The trees were on fire. Quaking aspen, god, the yellows and golds! The maples, the oaks, red and orange! It takes your breath away, it really does."

I lean back in the helicopter cabin, propping my head against the rescue litter, and offer a silent thank-you to Celia and Dr. Grant for helping my mom get to this place—a good place.

But it's a *new* place, too. She never liked the outdoors before now, and when I was growing up, she was pragmatic with a capital "P." Why would you go on vacation when you could stay home and relax just fine, saving money in the process. And traveling somewhere to look at *leaves?* The very notion would have been preposterous.

"It was just like the Pyrenees. God, the colors in autumn there!"

"Wait. The Pyrenees? When were you in the Pyrenees?"

"Oh . . ." Her voice falls, enthusiasm evaporating into the ether. "It was before you were born."

"But . . . you never told me that. I thought you hadn't traveled. That you—"

"That was a long time ago," she says with finality. Topic shuttered.

"Um . . . that sounds amazing. . . ."

The prolonged silence is awkward. Like our conversation on Friday. She must know I'll want to follow up on what we talked about, and now that she's just hinted at the past again, that's exactly where my brain goes. I'm about to bring it up—which she senses—so she dodges.

"Have you found out anything about Thanksgiving?" she asks. "Will you be able to come to the lodge?"

That's weird. She's must be pretty desperate to keep me off the subject of my father, if she's bringing up the lodge.

"Um, no. No, I'm sorry. I haven't had a chance to ask. But um, the lodge . . . you're okay with that?"

"I think so," she says. "I think so. . . ."

Wow. She's okay with it. Going to the lodge. That's new.

I breathe in, set to speak, ready to broach the subject of our last phone call, and darn it if she doesn't sense it again. She launches another preemptive strike.

"Have you spoken with Rich this weekend?"

Okay, later.

"I did. Twice." My left hand reaches for the zipper on the pant leg of my flight suit. I zip and unzip, zip and unzip. "He seemed really sorry."

"Of course he is. I'm sure you two will have a great time this weekend."

Zip, unzip. Zip, unzip.

"Mom, can we—"

"Will you tour him around Reno?"

"No . . . no, I don't think so. I'd rather show him the mountains."

"The mountains? You?"

A comment like this from me probably surprises her as much as her comment about hiking surprised me. Given the option—a tour of the city or a trip to the wilderness—in the past, I would have chosen the city every time.

"Well, yeah," I say. "We fly to them a lot. And they're really something. High. Rugged. Snowy."

"I'd have bet money you'd have preferred dinner in a penthouse restaurant with a view."

"Well . . . that would be nice, too, I guess."

"I'm sure Rich would like that."

"Probably . . . yeah . . . so, Mom, I really need to talk . . . that last phone call—"

"Alison. Please. I need time."

"But . . . but, Mom. You can't leave me hanging like that! *Why?* Why did he leave?"

It wouldn't surprise me if a tumbleweed blew by in this moment of strained silence. It would fit, though. The helicopter cabin frames a view like a picture window—a desert so still, so remote, hawks lazily riding the updrafts above the staunchly rugged foothills of the Desatoya Mountains. And there is no sound here. Like literally, no sound. No cars. No humming of motors or generators. No conversation. No birdcall. The wind in my ears is about all that registers. And oddly, I find it overwhelmingly beautiful.

"He loved you so much," she whispers.

I jump to attention. *What did she just say? What—?*

The statement is so out-of-the-blue, so shocking, I almost drop the phone.

"What? What did you—? How could he—"

"You should know that, Alison. It's something I should have told you a long time ago. But at the time . . . well, at the time, I couldn't afford to think that way."

"Mom . . ." My eyes glass up and my throat chokes with . . . hope . . . frustration . . . irritation? "Why? Why didn't you tell me? This would have been nice to know," I say, not able to keep the anger out of my voice. As a kid, it's natural to blame yourself. You're the reason a parent would leave, right? Too much trouble. Too much whining. Too much crying, needy, needy, needy.

But you can't walk away from your kid. You just can't. Not if you love her. So since he did walk away, I assumed he didn't love me. Hated me even.

"I was selfish," she says. "So much was my fault. I didn't want to hurt anymore. Better to just shut him out."

I stand, unable to keep my place, leaping out of the cabin onto the barren desert floor. How is this conversation happening? Out-of-body experience? Are you kidding?

"Oh, Ali, that's the other line. I have to get this."

"No! No, Mom. I need to talk with you!"

"I'm not ready yet, Alison. I don't want to hide this anymore, but I need time. Do you understand? Please, I need time."

I stumble, catching myself before I faceplant. *Ali, think about what she's saying. She's not refusing to talk about it. There's still an opening here.* I blow away my anger in a long, exaggerated exhale.

"I understand," I say.

"I love you, honey. We'll talk soon." Click. And she's gone.

I hit END, and my hand drops to my side. Hamster mode kicks in, and I begin doing circles around the aircraft. I'm walking around a helicopter in the middle of freaking nowhere surrounded by dirt and dust and sage and . . . my father loved me.

Oh, god. I bend over, hands on my knees. It's what I've wanted to believe. I've wanted it so badly. . . .

"We're back!" Beanie calls.

I look up, world still spinning. Snoopy and Beanie are walking toward me.

I stand upright and drag myself back into the cockpit, donning my helmet and sliding the visor down so they can't see my watering eyes.

"He loved you . . ."

Why, if it's something I've wanted so badly, does it hurt so much?

19

"Next, I'll demonstrate how to use the figure-eight knot to secure a rope to a climber's harness," Will says. "I just need a volunteer."

Now almost a week since Jack's party, it hasn't gotten any easier—Will still fixed in my thoughts. But I've worked to get my mind right, to focus on reality. I've decided that, yes, I can acknowledge my physical attraction to Will, but I don't have to act on it. How could I possibly jeopardize what I have with Rich for some passing fancy?

But then this came up. Rock-climbing training. Led by Will. And we've had a rough start this morning. . . .

"Alison would love to volunteer!" Jack pipes up.

"No. She wouldn't," Will says flatly.

What? Sure, Will wasn't satisfied with the outcome of our last conversation, but to have him answer for me . . . ?

"*Yes.* She would," I say, stepping forward.

Our aircrewmen shuffle their feet. Tito and Danny clear their throats. Kelly, Tawny, and the rest turn their heads, looking at the sky, the dirt.

I step closer, right in front of him. "I'm ready."

Will holds my eyes a moment longer—not happy—before getting back to the business of training. It doesn't take long to figure out why

Jack so readily offered me up as a volunteer, because Will has to stand so close to demonstrate what he was talking about.

He threads the rope through my harness—*yank*—then rethreads the rope through the figure-eight pattern—*yank* and *yank*—never meeting my eyes as he speaks to the group.

"After you tie the figure-eight," Will says, stepping away, "you're set to climb."

Will picks up the other end of the rope, runs it through the belay device on his harness, and pulls in the slack.

"You're on belay," he says. No inflection. Nothing.

"I am? Wait! How am I first?" I ask, turning to Jack, to my aircrewmen.

"Well, you're tied in, ma'am," Beanie says. "Only makes sense."

Jack offers a too-cheery smile.

"Thanks a lot," I say, with a scowl in his direction. It only makes him smile wider.

"After I say, 'You're on belay,' you say, 'Climbing,'" Will reminds.

Will did cover all of this, the proper communication phrases between climber and belayer, and I actually did pay attention. I just didn't think I'd be *first*.

"Climbing," I say.

"Climb on."

I face the granite slab and look fifty feet up to the top, where the anchor system holds the rope in place. Schoolhouse Rock is supposed to be the beginner area on Donner Summit, but you could have fooled me.

Oh, boy.

"You've got this, Alison," Jack says. "Remember, keep the weight on your feet."

I study the rock, with its microscopic indentations, where I'm supposed to place my feet, then look at my running shoes, which seem to grow in front of my eyes, as large and bulbous as Mickey Mouse's. No way this is going to work.

I chance a quick peek at Kelly, who wears slim, rubber-soled, sticky-bottomed rock shoes, understanding registering in a flash of the need for proper gear.

Clark leans in next to me. "You know the deal," he says in his comforting way. "Relax, and you'll be fine."

Deep breath.

Will must sense my nervousness, because he adjusts the tension on the rope, a reassuring gesture to let me know he's got me. I'm not going far, if I slip.

And so, I start up. Reaching for handholds, placing my feet with care, slowly, surely, not wanting to do anything rash or spastic, especially not in front of an audience. Jack offers hints—put this hand here, stand on that nub there, pull your hips into the rock, and up I go. Every reach, every step, every movement is performed with greater confidence the higher I climb. I am concentrated. Focused. Only the next hold. Only the next placement. Up and up and up.

What a bizarre, crazy, wonderful thing. Muscles enervated, small beads of sweat trickling at my neck, loose strands of hair lifted by a crisp, soft breeze, eyes wide, looking for the next hold, stretching, flexing, breathing, exhilarating—and in one of those fast-forward, time-warp moments, my hand touches the carabiner that anchors the rope at the top.

To my right, Donner Lake glistens turquoise in the midmorning sun, and ten miles beyond is the deep sapphire blue of Lake Tahoe. I breathe it in, the scents, the sights, the silence, filling my lungs, filling my soul. And in one long, satisfied exhale, I'm able to purge the stresses and tension of the morning, feeling fresh and new.

Will's voice startles.

"Ready to take?" Will says.

Take? Wait a second—

"Lean back! Let the rope take your weight!"

Lean back?

He covered this earlier—get to the top, lean back, make an L shape with your body, straighten your legs, plant your feet on the rock, and let go of the rope. But now, fifty feet above the ground, the instructions don't seem that simple anymore.

My forearms tighten, my fingers squeezing harder on their holds, secure in my perch.

"Alison, lean back!"

I look down, meeting Will's tiny eyes. I feel the rope tighten as he pulls it in. "I've got you!"

Will's voice is no longer so remote. Clearly, he's concerned.

I start to lean back, but stop. I can't let go. There's no control in this. I look below me, lowering my foot. Maybe I can just climb down?

"Alison, I've got you! You have to lean back!"

My calves, tiring from where I cling, begin to quiver. My fingers are numb, heavy. I can't hold here. Shit!

"He's got you, Alison!" Clark yells up. "You have to relax and lean back! You can do it!"

I feel the last bit of strength ebbing from my fingers. Please let there be another way. I look down again. *Just start down-climbing, Alison!* But it's too late, my fingers start to slip off the rock. Out of options, I grab on to the rope.

"That's it! Now lean back!" Will says.

Squeezing my eyes shut, I lean back, at the mercy of Will and the rope, yet still clinging to it for all I'm worth.

"Let go of the rope!"

Let go? Every molecule in me screams, *No!*

"Let go, Alison! You gotta let go!"

I stare fixedly at the twisted nylon strands, a blue and yellow mix. *Will has done this a thousand times. The rope will hold. It'll hold, Alison. You have to trust him.*

I close my eyes as he lowers me, surely only moments away from plunging to my demise. But as my feet touch bottom, the switch flips, and the exhilaration returns. I've cheated death! Every over-the-top emotion I felt at the top washes over me in a torrent. I put my hands to my face. Yes, that's a smile I'm feeling. A big one.

"Off belay," Will says.

Bursting and bubbling, a five-year-old at Disneyland, I turn to Will. "That was awesome! I want to go again!"

The look in his eyes rocks me to the core—something so deep, so sad—like he's had the rug pulled out from under him.

"You should probably let the others have a turn first, though, don't you think?" Jack says, completely upbeat.

"Yeah, no hoggin', ma'am," Sky says.

I clear my throat. "Um, yeah. I mean, after everyone else, of course."

Clark arrives with a fist bump. "Nice work."

"Thanks," I say.

As Clark walks away, I look down at the knot, unsure how to proceed. Undo the whole thing? Untie it partway for the next person? "Now, how do I—?"

"Like this," Will says, moving close. He begins to unthread the rope from its twisted figure-eight configuration, but unlike earlier, no yanking this time.

"Have you ever climbed before?" he asks.

"No, never."

Will looks to Jack, and they shake their heads.

"What is it?" I say.

"You're just . . ." He lowers his head, and pulls the rope through and out of my harness, leaving the skeleton of the figure-eight knot still twisted into the rope.

"What?" I ask.

He hesitates, focusing on the knot, pulling it out a bit to loosen it.

"A natural."

"I am? But with what I just— With the down part—"

"You are." He returns his gaze to me, and just for an instant, his eyes burn a line straight through my soul.

My breath catches. *Holy shit.*

Will breaks away, quickly turning his head. "Okay, who's next?"

Under a cobalt-blue sky and in "balmy" fifty-degree temperatures, members of our aircrew and the SAR team rotate through, and we climb for most of the day. I've found the "up" part of climbing to be exciting, energizing, and flat-out thrilling. But the "down" part? *That's* going to take some getting used to.

Will has belayed me several times this afternoon, and I've tried to keep that emotional distance, but the tension that strained our interactions this morning is gone. Probably because it's been hard to hide the joy I feel when climbing. Hard not to share it. Especially seeing the spark in Will's eyes when he lowers me to the ground after I've finished a route. The spark he tries to hide. The spark I pretend not to notice.

Jack has belayed me several times, too, but now we enjoy a break, sitting under the shade of a Jeffrey pine. I know the tree is a Jeffrey pine because Jack just told me. Tree trivia seems to be his thing, and I've learned more about these coniferous evergreens in the last few minutes than I thought I'd ever want to learn.

"Did you know Jeffrey pines can live to be five hundred years old?" Jack says.

"I had no idea."

"They're strong trees, too. The roots penetrate deep." He points to the more mature trees upslope of where we sit, ones that must be at least 150 feet tall. "The root systems for trees like those are massive. You'll find roots two inches in diameter more than eighty feet from the trunk."

"No wonder they live for five hundred years."

"Yep. It's one hearty tree. Even better, they smell good." He opens his hand, showing me what he's holding.

"What are these?"

"Jeffrey pine needles. I just crushed 'em up. Go ahead. Smell."

I bring my nose to his palm and take a whiff, a pleased smile spreading across my face. "It's like . . . vanilla? Can that be right?"

"Yeah. Or they can smell like apples or even butterscotch. I can't get enough of this smell."

He dumps the needles into my palm. "You keep these. They're great for tea, you know."

"Thanks. I'll have to try that." I take another smell, a lingering inhale, before storing the needles in my pocket, then return my attention to Kelly, who climbs with Tawny belaying. Will was right. He said they were freakily good, but I would call it something else. Grace in motion.

When they switch places, Tawny rigs the rope in a way I haven't seen before, adding foot loops. She instructs several of our crewmen who gather around her as she begins to ascend using the rope only, not touching the rock.

"What's she doing?" I ask, watching as Tawny holds the handles to what look like carabiners that she slides up the rope.

"She's using mechanical ascenders," Jack says. "But we just call them by their brand name, Jumars. They have a cam inside that allows them to slide in one direction, but if you pull in the other direction, they clamp down on the rope. Those foot loops are called aiders. You attach them to each Jumar. When you slide the Jumar up, the foot loop is raised as well, so it's like steeping up a ladder. You'd use this kind of setup for aid climbing."

"Aid climbing?"

"When you need aid to get through a section of rock that's not climbable—like a smooth face with nothing to hold on to."

"I see," I say, craning my head upward.

"So what do you think?" Jack says. "One more climb?"

"Sure, I'll do one more."

We rise and move to the granite slab, where five ropes are now anchored, so several people can climb at once. Will has just lowered Tito on the rope next to the one we approach.

"Off belay," Will says. "Great climb, man."

Jack rests his hands on his hips, which causes me to pause. I look at him closely. Hmm. A woolen cap covers his shaved head, and the redness and swelling on his face are considerably reduced since the accident two weeks ago. But he looks a bit drawn.

"Jack, are you okay?" I say.

"Doin' your perceptive thing again, huh?"

I notice that Will observes Jack, too.

"As much as I hate to admit it, I'm not quite at full strength yet. I'm just tiring out sooner than I'm used to."

"That's okay," Will says. "I'll belay her."

"Yeah, Jack. Why don't you sit down. I'll do this quick and be done."

I know how to tie in myself now, so I attach the figure-eight knot, and I'm off. The experience is exhilarating, as it has been all day, but this particular climb is by far the most challenging. By the time I reach the top, I'm a shaky, worn-out mess, my forearms and fingers done.

"Take!" I shout.

"I've got you!" Will says.

I pinch my eyes tight—as I've done every time I've been lowered today—while leaning back.

Relax, relax, relax.

This time, though, I'm not clinging desperately to the rope. I can't. With this last effort, my arms dangle, spent and useless, at my sides.

I land gently, opening my eyes. "I can't even feel my arms."

"Good climb," Will says.

Clark approaches and hands his harness to Jack. "Just wanted to let you know I'm taking off."

I look beyond Clark to where Snoopy stands near the side of the road. Hand held high, he offers a friendly wave.

"The guy's flown over Lake Tahoe a million times, but never driven around it," Clark says.

"Well, enjoy your time as a tour guide," I say. "Just don't let him con you into any trades!"

He laughs out loud, remembering, I'm sure, the story about me losing my lunch in a cow pasture.

Clark walks away, but then—"Hey, where's everyone going?" I ask, looking at Beanie, whose backpack is slung over his shoulder.

"We have a date with dinner and the margaritas at Rosie's in Tahoe City," Beanie says. "Wanna come?" I notice that Danny, Tito, Sky, and Hap have gathered their gear, too.

Is it dinnertime already? To my left, the sun hovers at the horizon, the last rays of the day splashing across the high-altitude granite. Holy crap. Completely lost track of the time.

"Um . . . no. Thanks, Beanie. Not today, but thanks."

"Later, man," Jack says to Will. "See ya, Alison." Mojo circles a couple of times, offering his good-byes, before scampering down the path.

It happens so fast. The group that was milling about just minutes ago—Kelly, Tawny, the rest of the Mono County guys—is gone, leaving only Will and me, just as the sun drops behind Donner Pass. Oh, no.

I go to untie myself from the harness, but now my fingers don't work anymore. I stand, helpless, looking between the figure-eight knot and my hands that tremble with fatigue.

"Will? I can't work the knot. My fingers are just—"

"They should be," he says, reaching down to untie the rope for me. "You only climbed a five ten just now."

"What does that mean?"

"It means it's a route not normally done by a beginner."

"Really?"

He tugs at the rope, pulling it from my harness.

"Yeah, really."

"You know, Will, I really like this."

He meets my eyes just briefly before returning his attention to the rope. I take a seat on a nearby boulder and begin unlacing the rock shoes that Kelly let me borrow. Thank goodness, as they make all the difference.

"When I walked off the mat at the final gymnastics meet of my career at the ripe old age of thirteen, I had to do a lot of soul searching, wondering why I'd spent so many hours in the gym and for what."

He stops and looks directly at me.

"But now, fifteen years later, I'm putting those skills to use for the first time, and it's the most empowering thing I've felt since I can remember."

"You were a gymnast?"

"I was."

"No wonder."

"No wonder, what?"

"No wonder you're so good on the rocks. Strong, graceful . . . you have it all." His voice noticeably falls at the end, his cheeks flushing as he averts his eyes.

But the way he said it—god, my insides are going to mush.

Ali, don't. Don't do this.

"So, did Rich ever reschedule his visit?" he asks.

He grasps the climbing rope, yanking it, hand over hand, bringing it down from the anchor above.

That's right, Ali. Remember him? Rich? Your fiancé. Let's remind ourselves about that. Why are you marrying him? He's the extrovert to your introvert, so you balance. He makes friends easily and is a great conversationalist. He's smart—a business degree from Stanford, an MBA from Harvard—and a hard worker. He does well with his company, is financially stable, he's happy with himself, happy with you, content with his life. Bottom line, unlike your father, he's not going anywhere.

"He's coming in two days. On Saturday."

He stills, then begins pulling on the rope, harder this time.

"Well, I'm glad I got to watch you climb today. It'll give me something to think about when I leave," he says.

Yank of the rope. *Yank. Yank.*

"Leave?" My head snaps up. "What do you mean, leave?"

"For my next trip." *Yank.*

"When?"

"Monday."

"Where?" Bullet-point questions matching frantic emotions I shouldn't even have.

"Rope!" he says loudly, a standard call made by rock climbers for safety. I can see why when the rope comes skittering down as it slips out of the metal bolt that once held it secure at the top of the rock, to land in a heavy heap at the bottom. "Patagonia. It's the beginning of the summer climbing season in South America."

"How long?"

He coils the rope now, while I remain stock-still in shock.

"I don't know. A month? Two? I get antsy if I stay in one place too long."

"Two *months?* But you just got back."

"I know."

"Was this planned?"

"No. But I usually don't care to plan. I just do it. Just go."

He finishes tying the rope, then shoves it forcefully into his pack. He hoists his climbing sling, racked with a wide array of colored nuts, cams, slings, carabiners, and Jumars, and stuffs this in next.

I stare, several paralyzing seconds, before I'm able to look down to my shoes to finish unlacing them.

He's leaving. . . .

"Some water before we walk down?" he asks—detached, a guide to his client—holding his bottle out to me.

"Sure." I take several generous swigs. He kneels next to me when I offer the bottle back, drinking well, too.

"So, when are you leaving, again?" I ask, pulling off one shoe, then the other, mind still reeling.

"Monday night. And twenty hours later, I'll be touching down in Buenos Aires."

"Monday?" I whisper.

He nods.

"Monday . . . ," I repeat, my heart in a vise.

Physical attraction or not, my heart shouldn't be in a vise.

Will resumes buckling the top flap of his pack, cinching it down with several firm yanks. The yanking again. "We'd better get down before it gets much darker," he says, slinging his pack over his shoulders.

I hurry to put my running shoes back on and stuff Kelly's shoes in my backpack. He starts to move, but I touch his arm from behind, stopping him. He remains looking away, so I don't force it. I talk to his back. "Will . . . thank you for the climbing today, for everything. I haven't had this much fun in . . . actually, I don't remember when."

"You're welcome," he says, quickly turning down the trail.

My car is parked well down the road, but to get there, I have to pass Will's truck, which is parked in the dirt pullout at the base of the slab. When I catch up with him, he's opening the tailgate and throwing in his pack. But then, he just stands there, hands on hips, looking into the back of his truck.

It's hard not to stare. He cuts such a strong figure. Broad shoulders and a well-muscled back. He even wears a loose technical T-shirt, and yet, you can still see the firm musculature underneath. And his hands? They're real. Nicked and scarred, not manicured and neat. Tight waist. Sturdy legs. Scuffed, dirty hiking boots. I let my eyes drift up to his head. He's had a haircut recently, neat and trim around the back, a little longer through the top, still bleachy blond. He furiously works his jaw muscles, which is when I realize how rigid the rest of him really is.

I start to turn away toward my car, trying to be quiet, thinking I can slip away without him noticing.

"Do you have fun with Rich?" he asks.

The question jars me to a stop midstep.

He spins around to face me, but it's several long seconds before I can find the words.

"It's not Rich," I say. "It's me."

"You didn't seem to have any problem having fun today."

"But that's because I was—" I stop myself before I say "with you."

"Was what?"

"Rock climbing," I say, attempting to keep my expression even. "It was new. Something different, and, uh, yeah . . ."

"I see," he says, folding his arms.

I look away, focusing on my car, which is parked about a quarter mile below us on the switchbacked road to Donner Summit.

"So this is it?" Will says. "You haven't thought at all about how you've felt when we've been together? At Jack's house? At the hot springs? Hell, *any* time we've been together?"

"I'm sorry about what I did on the balcony," I say, returning my gaze to him. "I never should have held your hand like that. And I shouldn't be feeling *anything*."

"Shouldn't, but are."

A silent, yet booming, exclamation point, hitting exactly on the problem.

But he's leaving. Up and gone! Just like someone else . . .

"No," I say. "I'm engaged to Rich. We're getting married in May. I'm happy. And that's it."

He unfolds his arms, standing taller. And while repositioning, has also moved closer.

"You missed something," he says.

I step back. "What do you mean?"

"In that list just now—engaged, getting married, happy—those are big-ticket items. I'd think you'd have included the word 'love' in there somewhere, just to hammer down the point."

I shake my head, backing away. I don't have a response for this.

" 'I'm engaged, I love Rich, we're getting married.' Is that what you meant to say?" he asks. "Or was that an intentional omission?"

I continue moving my head from side to side, three yards away now and continuing to move backward.

"You're leaving," I say. "You're leaving on Monday."

"What does that have to do with anything? You're avoiding my question."

Five yards . . . backing away. "I can't do this. I can't."

I turn and run.

20

As I drive home on Interstate 80, light shines upward from beyond the foothills of the Sierra, like something from a UFO movie. Tucked out of sight, Reno burns with its trademark 24/7 energy, only forty minutes separating the casinos, the neon, and the artificial from the mountains, the rugged, the real of Donner Lake.

I would have said five minutes, though. My mind has kicked into overdrive since I left Will, his question turning somersaults, battering my brain. "Do you have fun with Rich?" "Do you have *fun* with Rich?" "Do you have fun with *Rich?*" The accent drops in different places depending on which piece of the question I'm attempting to untangle.

Do we have fun . . . ?

We have a nice time together.

It's a yes-or-no question, Ali.

Well, how do you define "fun"?

Oh, Christ! Might as well ask what the definition of "is" is. Is that the game we're playing?

No.

Fun is something that provides mirth or amusement. It's whimsical, even frivolous.

I'm not frivolous.

That's an understatement.

So what was that today, then?

I don't know. You tell me.

I stare into the lights of downtown Reno. The lights. *Light . . .*

Climbing today was light. Unburdened. Free.

My life, in general, has not been. And this has been of my own doing. My father's abandonment has been my excuse. Nobody loves you, boo hoo, can't have fun, can't be happy. But if you're not happy, you can't get hurt, not the real kind of hurt.

Since my father left my mom and me, I've employed Self-Defense 101—you are neither high nor low. Allow yourself to get too high and you get hurt. Simple.

Using the hands-free on the steering wheel, I make the call to my mom.

"Hello?" Celia answers.

"Celia? I thought I dialed Mom's number."

"You did. She ran out to buy us a bottle of wine, bless her, but she left her phone. But when I saw the caller ID . . ."

"Actually, I'm glad you picked up. Have you . . . I was just wondering . . . has my mom started opening up with you at all? About anything?"

"She has. Finally."

"Are we allowed to compare notes?"

Celia chuckles. "Ali, honey, I don't know. But what I do know is that I've learned more about your mother over the last month and a half than I've known in a lifetime. God, I feel like *I'm* the one who needs the therapist. Where *was* I when she was going through all this with your father? When she needed someone the most?"

"You were in medical school, doing your internship, your residency, setting up a new practice, beginning your life in New York. You can't beat yourself up over that."

A heavy sigh resonates on the other end. "I was so out-of-touch. So self-absorbed."

"You weren't self-absorbed! You were *absorbed* in medical school! You had to be."

"Right. Wanna know how I found out about your birth? It was by accident. By *accident*. I hit Candice's number on speed dial by accident! I mean, what the hell? I had her number programmed on the speed dial, but did I ever bother to punch the damn button? Some older sister."

"You *are* some older sister. Let me tell you, Celia, you've made a huge difference in her life since you moved back."

"But it's not like I came back for *her*. It was for Dad. He was gonna lose the lodge, if I didn't come back."

"Regardless, you came back. And when you did, you connected with her again. Brought her to the lodge for Thanksgivings. And then when you hired Roberto to look after the place, you could have gone back to New York, but you didn't. You opened your practice in Sacramento to be near her."

"And you," she says. "Please don't forget, I did it to be near you, too."

"Okay, me, too. And then, you were there for her after Nick died. And of course, now, you're closer than ever."

"But I'm just getting to *know* her. How could I not know that this sadness she's carried since forever—and you know the sadness I mean—"

"Yeah, I know."

". . . is due to a breakup that happened twenty-five years ago!"

"Actually, I just realized that myself. So has she talked to you about him? My father? Anything?"

"She loved him. Still does. Deeply so."

"I know. I mean, now I do."

"Lisa—Dr. Grant—says Candice is breaking new ground every time they meet. She's getting out, she's just . . . it's been amazing. She reports to me now, like a kid telling her mom how her day at school was."

"So you learned that my father loved me, too."

"He did. She talks about that a lot, you know."

"But what was he *like?* What did he *look* like? What—?"

"I'm so sorry, Ali. I don't know. She hasn't told me much yet—that area's really raw. And it blows my mind that I can't tell you what he looked like. I know you've asked me in the past and my excuses were pretty lame. The truth is I have no idea. I know just as much as you do, probably less, at this point."

"Well, she *is* bringing wine home with her . . . ," I say.

"True. And she had a productive session with Lisa today—that's what she said before she left—so yeah, we'll see."

A door slams in the background.

"She just walked in," Celia says. "Oh, before I forget, were you able to switch your duty? I *really* want to make Thanksgiving work at the lodge. I don't know why, but it seems important to your mom. It's important for her to go there, I think."

"Oh, I wondered where I'd left my phone," I hear my mom say. "Who are you talking to, Cee?"

"It's Ali. We're talking about Thanksgiving."

"Sure you were," she says. Paper rustles in the background. Wine out of the bag?

The phone clicks to speaker. Refrigerator door opens, closes. "You're on speaker, Ali," Celia says. "Weren't we talking about Thanksgiving?"

"We were. And no, I haven't been able to get my duty switched yet. I'm gonna hit up one of our new pilots, Danny, on Monday. I'm pretty optimistic."

"Excellent," Celia says. "All right, I'm switching off the speaker and giving the phone to your mom. I've hogged it long enough."

"Okay, bye, Celia."

"I'm going back to the bedroom, Cee," I hear my mom say. "I need to get out of these clothes."

"Okay, I'll fire up the grill," Celia says. "Here, take the phone."

"Hi, honey," my mom says.

"Hi, Mom."

"I'm glad you called. I've been thinking about you a lot today, and I think we need a visit. Just you and me. And soon."

A visit. Which could mean a talk. Which could mean more information about my father. I would want to see my mom anyway, of course, but with her revelations of late, it can't happen soon enough.

"Yeah, definitely. When were you thinking?"

"How about this weekend?"

Shoot, shoot, shoot. "Mom, Rich is coming this weekend. Remember?"

"Oh . . . that's right. How could I forget?"

"Well, how about next weekend?" I ask.

"I'll make that work. We need to talk."

"Mom, I desperately want to talk. I have so much to ask. There's so much—"

"I know, I know. But Ali, remember, honey, I need to take this slow. I'm working through a lot, and I'm getting there. But just . . . slow."

"Okay . . ."

God, so many things to ask. About my father. About what the heck I'm feeling right now with—

"Mom, can I ask you just one thing right now, though?"

I can feel her bracing on the other end.

"Did you know . . . I mean, did you have any idea he might leave? Was it sudden or was it . . . ?"

"It wasn't a surprise, no."

Not a surprise . . .

"Why not?" I voice with restraint. Only two words leave my mouth, but it takes all of my willpower to stop there. In my head, the questions continue. *Had he talked about leaving? Was there a disagreement? Did you wake up one morning and he was gone? Or did he tell you in advance—*

And with a suddenness that leaves me near queasy, I realize that not only has Will told me he's leaving, I probably won't see him again before he departs for South America. I'll be spending the weekend with Rich, and then Will leaves on Monday.

He's leaving.

". . . Your father wasn't much for staying in one place. He liked to roam. To explore. If he was home for too long, he would get—what's the word . . . ?"

"Antsy?" It pops out of my mouth, no thought required.

"Yes! Antsy."

You see, Ali. You can't go there.

21

Mushroom-shaped, bulbous clouds build up behind me, shifting into ominously darker shades of gray. I have a close-up view from my perch on Basin Mountain, elevation 13,240 feet. Actually, I'm not that high. I'm positioned on "the Notch," located at the upper end of Basin Couloir, which is probably closer to twelve thousand feet.

I enjoy a rather grand view from my position high in the Sierra, including the Bishop airport—tantalizingly close, and yet impossibly out of reach.

I was playing victim for training purposes with Clark and Danny—no issues with power at this altitude today, since it's so cold—and they dropped me here with the intention of returning in less than five minutes to effect my "rescue." But a sudden loss of oil pressure in the number-one engine changed all that. They were forced to depart to make an emergency landing at the Bishop airport.

So now I'm waiting for Boomer, Tito, and the crew of Longhorn 06 to come retrieve me. Fortunately, I brought a small backpack containing a fleece sweater, a windproof shell, and a fleece ski hat. I donned them as soon as Longhorn 07 departed, knowing that my pickup would be delayed. It's probably in the low twenties up here, and Longhorn 06 is still an hour away—they're coming all the way from Fallon.

Stranded up here, I realize I'm going to be late picking Rich up at the airport. Why? Because today is Monday, and we had *this* conversation on Saturday.

"What do you mean, you can't come?" I asked, throwing my hands in the air.

"I know how it sounds," Rich said. "But Monday. I can be there on Monday."

"But I'll be working on Monday. I . . . I cleared this whole weekend for you."

"It's lousy timing, but it's just a few days, and it's beyond worth it."

"Why? What's so important?"

"We're finally closing on that deal I told you about. The investors are flying in tomorrow. Ali, this is huge. We're talking a multimillion-dollar deal here."

"But—"

"There's no way I can't be here for this. We've worked this deal for two years."

I stared, appalled, at the grooves I'd just cut into my wooden kitchen table with a paring knife. I'd been cutting apple slices during our conversation, popping them into my mouth at intervals, but once the subject turned to another postponement of Rich's visit, my knife turned its attentions to the wood grain, carving checker patterns among discarded apple seeds.

"When I get there on Monday, I'll take you out to celebrate," he said. "Wherever you want, okay?"

That conversation happened just an hour before I was to leave for the airport to pick him up. I had felt so guilty about pulling myself from the duty schedule, just when the air wing's op tempo was picking up, just when Stage Three training was getting under way.

If there's ever a week during the course of an air wing's training when the SAR team might be needed, it's this one. The exercises flown in the last stage are always the trickiest and most complex, involving almost every aircraft they bring. They're also the most dangerous, because they're flown at night.

But it was going to be worth it. A weekend alone with my fiancé was absolutely going to be worth it. . . .

Thankfully, the air wing's exercises have progressed like a dream over the weekend. But for me, I've been left to replay my conversation with Rich, just as I've done countless times this afternoon, while the wind picks up, the temperature noticeably dropping.

An hour in these conditions would be doable—not comfortable, but doable—on most days, but the mountain has other ideas. I know I need to leave this exposed position and move lower.

I start the hike down the snow-filled couloir—a wide thirty-degree swath that runs close to two thousand vertical feet. It's the easiest way down this mountain, by far, but as I sink into knee-deep snow, a creeping disquiet moves through me. The only protective layers of clothing between the lower half of my body and the snow are a single base layer of polypropylene long underwear, my flight suit, a pair of socks, and steel-toed flight boots.

"Longhorn Six, Longhorn Ground, over," I say, speaking into my handheld radio.

"Longhorn Ground, Longhorn Six, go ahead," Boomer says.

"Longhorn Six, I had to leave the Notch. The weather's not looking too good up here and I couldn't stay. I'm climbing down the couloir now. Just plan on finding me lower down, over."

"Roger that. We're fifty minutes out."

I trudge my way through the snow in switchback fashion, gritting my teeth against the cold as the snow finds its way into my socks and boots. And while the polypropylene base layer I wear is moisture-wicking, my flight suit is not. But that's okay, because the sky directly above me remains clear, and my ride is only fifty minutes away. I can do this.

Distances can be deceiving in the mountains. I falsely believed I could descend the length of this couloir to the shelter of the extra-large boulders at its base in thirty minutes, maybe forty minutes tops. That was two hours ago.

If I had to guess, I'd say I've made it three-quarters of the way down. I can't say for certain where I am, because the visibility has been reduced to zero. Ten minutes after I started my descent, my worst fears were realized, as the darkening storm moved over the summit of Basin Mountain, swallowing it whole. God, the speed of it. The enormity. The winds turned on in earnest—thirty miles per hour? forty?—and the clouds let go, snow pummeling the mountain, pummeling me.

A helicopter rescue? Out of the question. According to Boomer, when they arrived in the area, what I had thought to be a local weather phenomenon, affecting the high mountains only, had in fact moved into the valley. Boomer even had to fly an instrument approach to get into the Bishop airport, due to the low ceilings and accompanying low visibility. The "good" news is that our maintenance guys repaired the oil line on Longhorn 07, which now sits side by side with Longhorn 06, neither able to fly in whiteout conditions.

I always thought that flying on a pitch-black, moonless night would be one of the most disorienting things I could ever experience. I'm proved wrong in the blinding snow that whips frontways, sideways, backways, up, down, and around. Wholly vertigo-inducing, I'm reduced to crawl speed, guessing where to step next, knowing I can't stop in the open, always hedging to the left—where I think is left, anyway—to the rocky border of the couloir for some shelter from the wind.

From the waist down, I'm so wet and cold it hurts. My muscles throb from the shivering and my feet and hands sting. I shove my pained hands under my armpits, cursing the fact that I wear a flight suit and boots. I'm dressed this way because when pilots act as victims, a routine scenario is for the aircraft commander to remain in the helicopter while the copilots rotate through, one doing the flying while the other waits for pickup. Bottom line, we're all dressed for flying.

We are *not* dressed for hours of exposure in a snowstorm. I thought I had done my due diligence in bringing an extra fleece, a hat, and a jacket shell in a backpack, but I never could have anticipated this. *Where the hell was this storm in our weather brief!* I may as well not be wearing shoes at all, the steel in my boots voraciously hoarding the cold, the pain akin to stepping on shards of glass.

The shivering started in earnest forty-five minutes ago. Whether this is the reason for my loss of coordination, or if it's my brain function deteriorating in the throes of hypothermia, I don't know. But I've fallen several times, losing both my pack and my hat somewhere along the way. Somehow, I've managed to hang on to my radio, which is a miracle, since my flight gloves are soaked through, and my hands *burn* with cold. God, they burn.

The alarm runs thick, because I know I'm in trouble. Desperate trouble.

I tuck my head, pinching my eyes closed to shield them from the snow that slaps my face, while keeping my ear to the radio.

I've been privy to a few intermittent calls, the key word being "intermittent." Maybe it's storm interference? Or maybe it's my wet radio—I've dropped it how many times? Whatever the reason, from what I gather, Boomer knows I'm in trouble, too.

"Mono . . . SAR, Rescue Six . . . affirm. She . . . Basin . . . hours. Way to get . . . some . . . for her?"

I'm lucid enough to recognize that Boomer is using the call sign Rescue rather than Longhorn. And yeah, that's probably right, too.

"Rescue Six . . . Mono County copies. Going . . . impossible . . . whiteout."

I try to answer, pressing the radio switch with my wrist, since my fingers are useless. I hear the momentary static of the keying sound, so it seems to be working, but I receive no response to my calls.

I continue blundering downward. Snow clings to my exposed neck, my hair now frozen into hard plates. I shield my eyes with one hand while keeping the other one "warm" under my armpit, rotating every thirty seconds or so. The exposed hand suffers a sustained piercing, the wind slicing straight through the soaked fabric of my flight gloves.

Add to this, my legs aren't working right anymore. Numb from the waist down, I move my feet, not really knowing if they're doing what

I'm asking them to, particularly since I can't see a damned thing. I could walk straight off the side of this mountain and never know it.

An icy gust pounds into my chest, and I stumble once again, plunging headfirst into the snow, my legs flipping over the top of me in a clunky somersault that leaves me head down, feet upslope . . . I think. I push myself up, completely disoriented. Right? Left? Up? Down? My only recourse is to begin walking, feeling for that downward pull of gravity, the steps taking longer if I'm tracking downhill.

My foot slams into solid rock, a jarring shock to the knee, but a welcome one. I put my hands out, feeling for the rock wall, scooching along its sides to find any relief from the wind. My hand slips around a corner, finding a space between a fallen boulder and the rock wall lining the couloir. I drop into a tiny ball and back into the corner. It's not great, but it's better than where I was—in terms of exposure, anyway.

The sounds are a different story. The wind takes voice—a tenacious roar in the opening in front of me, a high-pitched caterwauling through the cracks in the rock above. I pull my knees more tightly to my chest, tucking my face as best I can into the collar of my jacket, all of me shaking.

And I think, *What just happened?* How did I get to be here—in what I would now classify as dire straits—in so short a time and without warning?

My jaw aches with the effort of clamping down so my teeth won't chatter. All my muscles ache, actually—contracting and shuddering in spasms in an involuntary effort to keep my body warm. It crosses my mind, just briefly, how ridiculous this is going to play out in the local news—search and rescue team member dies of hypothermia during SAR training.

Slowly, although I no longer have a reliable sense of time, the notion of dying from hypothermia takes solid root, as the shakes begin to subside and my mouth widens into a yawn. Oh, no. This is how it happens, right? Didn't I learn about this? In the late stages of hypothermia, the victim becomes tired. All they want to do is sleep. My hand moves shakily to cover my mouth when the next yawn comes.

It's all happening so fast, and yet, it's not.

I'm dying.

Shit, Ali. You're in a life-or-death situation here, and you're utterly helpless.

This is a jarring thought, because I've always been able to take care of myself. I've made it a point of pride not to have to rely on anyone, so it should be no different now. Except that I don't have the faintest idea what to do.

This is the point in the story when the hero comes to the rescue, right? God, how embarrassing.

But I don't need a hero. I need a miracle.

22

Will carries me. . . . At least, I think it's Will. A balaclava covers his face, no skin exposed. The hood of a yellow ski jacket is cinched tight over his head. I peer into goggle lenses tinted gold, comforted by the familiar blue eyes behind them. He is speaking; I see the lips moving behind his mask. But this dream is soundless. I close my eyes, strangely at peace.

"Come on, Alison! Talk to me!"

Warm, moist air rushes over my face. My mouth seeks the source, my head turning. I breathe in deeply. Ahhhhh. Like drinking in the sun. I inhale again, the heated air moving over my palate, warming my throat.

"Alison! Hey! You can't go to sleep on me, Alison! Come on. Wake up!"

My eyelashes are heavy, frozen, but the unknown thermal source works to thaw them. I bring my hand to my eyes, fumbling, pulling, trying to draw them open.

"That's it, Alison. That's it."

The voice is warm, too. Like the air over my face. My left eye springs open, freed from the cold's frosty hold, followed by the right eye.

I've awakened into a dream. Will's face hovers just above me, his mouth open. I hungrily suck in the precious hot air contained in his exhalations, and my lungs fill with the life-giving warmth.

"Will?"

A strong arm lifts me to a sitting position, hugging me close, but my head lolls backward. I only want to lie down. My body slackens.

"Alison, stay with me! Come on, stay with me!"

A hand—the dream-Will's hand?—moves across my face, fingers pulling at my eyelids.

I blink, opening my eyes, coming eyelash-to-eyelash with the dream-Will, another rush of warm air across my lips.

"Look, we have a fire," the dream-Will says. "You're going to warm up here in just a second. But I need you to wake up."

"Is it you?" I ask. "Are you real?"

"Yes. It's Will. It's me. I'm here, okay?"

"Will . . ."

I raise my hand to touch his face. The stubble across his chin and jaw confirms it. He's real. He's here.

He loosens his hold just briefly, turning and reaching for something.

"Here, you need to drink this."

He raises a thermos cup to my lips. Warm liquid dribbles into my mouth, spills a bit, drips down my face. Sugar . . .

"That's it," he says. "This'll work miracles, if we can just get it in you. Keep drinking, Alison."

I take a sip. And another. Warm sugar water.

"Do you think you can hold it?" he asks.

I wrap my fingers around the cup, bringing it to my lips. Without warning, the shivering starts again, my body racked by a series of uncontrollable spasms. I cough, sputtering, spraying Will's face.

"Sorry," I say, as he takes the cup from me.

His mouth spreads into a smile. "Hey, I'd much rather have you awake and spitting up on me than unconscious."

He brings his hand to my face, wiping the spill.

"This is pathetic," I say, looking at my trembling hands.

"I'm sure if you could control it, you would. So don't beat yourself up. Especially not with what you've been through today."

He positions the cup at my mouth for another try, and even though we miss a little, I get most of it down. Like manna from heaven, it melts in my throat, warming me from the inside out.

Releasing his grip, Will reaches for the thermos to refill the cup, and I bring my hands to my throbbing head. As the shaking that started so violently begins to ebb—the sugar elixir working its magic—I scan my surroundings, trying to figure out where I am.

Granite walls behind me, to the sides, and above. I sit in a rounded alcove, sand and rocks covering the floor. The space is large enough that Will would have room to lie across the width of it, and if he stood upright . . . well, I think he'd have *just* enough clearance. In front of me, a tunnel in the rock, about fifteen feet in length and four feet across. The opening at the far end is a blur of white as snow blows sideways across it.

To my right, an archway in the stone, leading to another tunnel, which terminates in a rounded cavern, like an anteroom to the main chamber. Will has propped his skis and a pair of snowshoes there, along with his backpack. Above his equipment, he's placed a battery-powered lantern on a tiny ledge jutting from the rock itself.

Moving my focus back to the tunnel, I see that a fire burns in a ring of stones about five feet in front of me, the concentrated flames heating our tiny space, providing adequate light, as well.

A foreign, hollow keening rises and falls in sporadic intervals, but then, a familiar sound. A yip and a bark. Mojo nuzzles into my chest, rapping his tail against the dirt.

"Hey, you," I say. "Where did you come from?"

"Wait just a minute there, big guy," Will says, shooing Mojo away. "You'll get your turn."

Having refilled the cup, he hands it to me, steam escaping the top, and I wrap my now-steadier fingers around it, guiding the flow myself. I take several lengthy swallows while he looks on, attentive, watchful.

The tunnel starts to spin a bit. Overcome by a rush of dizziness, I set down my drink. I bring my hands to my head again, squeezing my temples, trying to shake away the cobwebs.

Will places a steady hand on my back. "Are you okay?"

"Yes. I just . . . Where are we?"

"A mine tunnel."

"A mine . . . ?"

"We're at the bottom of Basin Couloir. This is an old mine tunnel we use for bivouacking."

As if suddenly realizing his nearness, he pulls his hand from my back and scooches away, clearing his throat. "Uh, yeah. So it's a good thing this place is here."

He jumps to an almost-stand—he has to duck just slightly, so his head won't hit the rock above—and moves under the archway. Bending over, he gathers wood from a pile, and returns to add a few pieces at a time to the ample fire. Mojo sits at attention, watching the proceedings.

I take further stock of my situation. I wear my base-layer shirt and leggings, topped with an extra-large, extra-puffy down jacket. I wiggle my toes, although I can't see them, tucked as they are in a plush, down-filled sleeping bag. It's the first time I've felt my feet in hours. Next to me, my boots lie discarded on the sandy floor, wet socks and gloves strewn next to them. My flight suit also lies on the floor in a crumpled heap, covering my leather jacket, and next to them are my fleece sweater and jacket shell.

Will's gaze follows to where I've been looking. "I had to get the wet stuff off in a hurry."

I reach up to my head, now cognizant of the wool hat there, and I pull it off to look.

"That's mine," he says. "When I found you, you didn't have a hat."

"Oh." I know I had a hat at one point. . . .

Then I remember. "I lost it . . . when I was hiking down the couloir. There was a storm. . . . I was stuck in the snow."

"Yeah. I found you about fifty yards above here." Next to Will, Mojo relaxes his position, dropping to his stomach, but his head remains up, alert. "Actually, Mojo found you. You'd fallen asleep next to a boulder."

I replace the hat, tugging it well over my ears. "What time is it?"

He glances at his watch. "Five in the afternoon."

The mental math takes longer than it usually would, but I finally figure it out. "Two hours . . . The last time I looked at my watch, it was three p.m."

"You were lucky. Really lucky." He points to my fingers. "No frost-bite."

I look down at my hands, pink, warm, and a bit swollen, turning them back and forth. "How did you find me?"

"They radioed that you'd begun climbing down the couloir, so we started at the bottom and worked our way up."

My head moves back and forth in disbelief. "How did you do it? I couldn't see anything. I was completely disoriented."

"Well, this area is my home turf, if you will. I used to live in Bishop before moving to June Lake. And then, when we got close, Mojo ran directly to you."

I hug the sleeping bag a little tighter around me. Between the bag and my jacket—his jacket—I'm swaddled in a veritable cocoon of in-sulating, fluffy down.

"How are you feeling now?" he asks, depositing the last of the wood in the fire.

"Much better. Thank you." I pull the collar of his down jacket higher up my neck, so it moves over my nose and mouth, feeling, smelling, sensing . . . him.

What a difference in his demeanor since our last tense words on Donner Summit. His guard is down, unmitigated concern overriding everything else.

I watch as he pokes at the fire with a long stick, remaining crouched on the opposite side. "With that drink I made you, the sugar goes right to the bloodstream."

"I feel it," I say, my mouth warming into a contented smile.

My eyes drift to his backpack, noting the luggage tag attached. Luggage tag . . .

"Wait," I say, the fog lifting further. "How are you here? I thought . . ."

"I was on my way to the airport when I heard them talking about you on the scanner."

"You were on the way to the airport. . . . Hold on, did you miss your flight?"

He nods.

"You missed your flight. . . ."

He watches me closely, and though my body fights to stay upright from exhaustion, my muscles sore from all the shivering, I can't seem to look away from him. And I remember this same worried face so close to mine when I regained consciousness.

"May I ask you something?" I say.

"Shoot."

"When I was waking up just now . . . I don't know, maybe I was a bit delirious, but it felt like you were . . . well, like you were breathing into me." I lower my head, realizing how ridiculous the notion sounds when spoken out loud, but that's what it felt like.

"I was."

I look up. "You were?"

"There are different names for it—rebreathing, inhalation rewarming. It's a technique used for warming a victim of hypothermia."

"Oh," I say, heartened by the thought of Will's breath, his energy, channeled directly into me. "Have you ever had to do that before?"

"No," he says, a small laugh escaping. "You're the first."

"Well, just in case you're interested in feedback, it worked quite well."

He smiles, our eyes lingering. And this is several times now in a very short span of time that we've stopped like this.

Many seconds later, he shakes himself out of it, rising again, this time busying himself with hanging my wet clothes. Rewinding, I imagine what it must have been like for him carrying me all that way through the snow, finding the mine tunnel, laying me on the floor—someone who was frozen and unconscious—and then struggling to get my clothes off, stuffing me in a sleeping bag, boiling water, and finally, having to coax me to wake up.

But now that the urgency has eased, he goes about organizing— first my clothes, hanging them to dry, then adjusting his equipment, all to make more room.

Mojo seems to sense this. Tension dissipating. Emergency over. He pads across to me, stepping over the sleeping bag, circling around, and settles his warm furry self right up next to me.

I bend down, encircling him with my arms. "Thank you for finding me," I whisper into his ear.

"Are you hungry?" Will asks. "I brought some ready-to-eat meals. And they'll be hot, which you need." He opens his pack, pulling out four vacuum-sealed bags. "You have your choice of beef Stroganoff, lasagna, chicken with mashed potatoes, or chicken teriyaki with rice."

"They all sound good to me, but how about the Stroganoff?"

"All right, comin' up." He turns his attention to a portable propane ministove that he's placed near the "antechamber." He adjusts the flame, setting a pot of water to boil.

"Come here, boy," Will says to Mojo. He opens a pouch of some-thing meaty, and Mojo leaves me—with haste—to dive in. Yeah, I guess he would be pretty hungry, poor guy.

"I thought Mojo was Jack's dog," I say. "But he seems to respond just as well to you as to Jack."

"That's because he's well trained. A quality search dog can work with anyone."

"Really?"

"Well, yeah. It's important for them to be able to respond to any handler. Like if their owner gets injured, the dog can be taken by someone else."

"I see."

"Jack had him at the airport today when I arrived, so we decided he should come with me."

Our heads snap up at the same time. A howl of wind, a siren wail, screams across the tunnel entrance, standing my hair on end. I pull my knees further into my chest, burrowing into the warmth of the sleeping bag.

"This storm's a mean one," he says, laughing lightly. "You sure know how to pick 'em."

"I'm just wondering where this storm was in our weather brief. I don't recall anything forecasted that was even remotely close to this."

"Welcome to the high mountains," he says, ripping the tab across the beef Stroganoff packet. He pulls on the zip-seal closure, spreading the pouch open wide, and places it next to him, removing the now-boiling pot of water and pouring it directly into the beef Stroganoff pouch.

"Here," he says. He places the bag next to me and hands me a heavy-duty plastic spoon. "You have to let it sit for about three minutes and then it'll be ready to eat."

"Does this really taste like beef Stroganoff?"

"Not exactly. But when you're cold and hungry and stuck high on a mountain, it usually tastes pretty darn good, regardless."

"Like the doughnut."

"Like the doughnut," he says, nodding his grinned approval. "You're catching on."

23

Will's fire, in its ring of stones, burns undisturbed. The wind howls outside, and yet the gusts are unable to penetrate this protected space.

"I wish I'd caught on sooner with this storm," I say. "I didn't realize how quickly things could change. I've read about mountain weather. Studied it. But the experience of it is something altogether different."

"Yeah, mountain weather's a whole different animal." He rips the top from the teriyaki chicken pouch, then opens the top zippered pocket on his backpack to retrieve a second spoon.

"Truthfully," I say, looking at the floor, "I'm embarrassed. Like really embarrassed for getting myself into this situation. I normally don't . . . I mean, I normally handle things."

"What? You have no reason to be embarrassed. You did the best you could given the circumstances."

"But—"

"It happens to the best of us, Alison. No one's immune."

"I guess. . . ."

"Besides, you can't hog the hero attention all the time."

He pulls the pot of boiling water off the stove and pours it into his dinner pouch. "Yours is probably ready," he says.

"That's okay, I'll wait for you."

"You almost died of hypothermia, and you're worried about manners? Incredible," he mumbles.

I adjust my position within the layers of my sleeping bag, sitting cross-legged, and lean my arms on my thighs, clasping my hands together. Myriad thoughts cross my mind, meandering here, curving there, until I have a jarring one.

"What is it?" Will says.

Am I that transparent? Indeed, I was thinking about a troubling problem, a difficult one on so many levels.

"I'm fine. I, uh . . . I just remembered something."

"And that is . . . ?"

"Rich."

His face falls.

"He was supposed to fly in today."

"I thought he was supposed to come on Saturday," Will says, busying himself with his dinner pack. He opens it, stirring the contents.

"He had to postpone . . . again."

Will's ears perk up. "Why?"

"He needed to close some deal. Very important." I open my own dinner pouch and stir, putting my nose in the path of the escaping steam. Actually smells delicious. "Millions of dollars. 'I can't not be there.' That's what he said."

"But he's here now?"

"Yes, or I think he should be. I was supposed to pick him up this afternoon. He has no idea where I am."

Will blows on his first spoonful of rice to cool it. "I can radio the guys. Have them contact him. I called in earlier to say I'd found you, but that was it."

"Could you, please?"

He lowers his spoon without tasting, I supply him with Rich's phone number, and he makes the radio call. He strives to keep a neutral tone, an expressionless face, but he's having difficulty.

"Copy," Will says. "Yeah, that's what I figured. We can get her out in the morning."

The radio crackles again as the mic is keyed from the other end.

"Both birds will be here," Jack says. "They're stuck, too. So we'll remain on standby at the airport, and we'll contact you at say . . . first light?"

"Sounds good," Will says.

"You take care up there."

"Thanks, Jack. We will."

After replacing the radio in his chest harness, Will picks up his dinner pack, stirs it a bit, and begins to eat, while Mojo sniffs and explores the circumference of our cave-like space.

"Thank you," I say.

"Anytime," he replies without looking.

"So we're staying the night, then?"

"Yeah," he says, focusing on his spoon. "It's dark now and obviously the storm's still insane. Best to see what we have when the sun rises."

He resumes eating, and I take my first bite. "Wow, this really *is* good."

He acknowledges me with a small smile, but concentrates on his food.

How awful this must be for him, knowing I'm thinking about Rich, but making the radio call all the same, and doing so without hesitation.

"Will, may I ask you another question?"

"Sure."

"It's personal."

He lowers his spoon, bringing his eyes up to meet mine.

"Have you ever . . ."

I stop myself right there. Stupid question. Awful question. *Why the hell would you want to know that, Alison? And why bring it up? What purpose could it possibly serve?*

"Forget it," I say. "I'm sorry. I just . . . forget I said anything."

He brings his fingers to either side of his chin, rubbing the stubble there. "I'm not gonna let you off that easy. What did you want to know?"

"It's none of my business. Please, forget it."

"You said it was personal. And . . . hell, there's no sense in hiding it. I want you to know me . . . personally. Just like I'd like to know you. So, I'd like to answer your question."

The firelight flickers red and gold in his eyes. A glistening spectacle. And a mesmerizing one. I know the eyes are the window to the soul, but I'm not just looking in; I'm being pulled in. And I want to know . . . "Have you ever . . . had someone special? I mean . . . well, you know what I mean."

The wind's steady roar fills the "quiet" between my question and his answer.

"No, not special in the way that you mean."

"How is that *possible?*"

Did I just say that?

"Excuse me?"

"You're just . . ." And then—what the hell—my mouth runneth over. "There's so much about you. . . . You're giving and kind and . . . and you canceled an international flight just to come rescue someone. I mean, who does that?"

"I didn't cancel an international flight to rescue just anyone. I did it because it was you."

I try to pull in my next breath, like someone who's had the wind knocked out of them, and it just doesn't come.

"You asked if I've ever had someone special. The answer is no . . . not until now, that is. But unfortunately, she's taken."

He searches my eyes for a long moment, then returns his attention to his dinner. But rather than take another bite, he zips it closed, and stands, moving to his backpack. He pulls out a fleece sweater, some ski pants, and a silver space blanket, spreads the blanket near the wall, then rolls the pants and sweater together to make a pillow.

"Can I get you anything else?" he asks.

I haven't moved in all the time he was arranging his bed, and I can't seem to do it now, either, my brain still stuck on what he said before.

"Alison?"

I move my head slightly in the negative, so he turns, and drops to his blanket.

"You don't have a sleeping bag," I say.

"That's okay. I'm good."

He lies down, turning away from me, and rests his head on his makeshift pillow.

Any appetite I may have had vanishes. I draw the seal on the pouch closed and put it aside, then look across the fire to Will's form. He lies so exposed. He's dressed in his mountaineering gear, but still. The sleeping bag rustles as I adjust my position. He's given me all of his things. . . .

I stand—having enough clearance above—feeling a bit more wobbly than I would have expected. I remove Will's down jacket and cross the sandy floor on stockinged feet—his socks, too big by half—and kneel next to him. I place his jacket over the top of him like a blanket, and he shivers, startled, I think.

He cranes his head around as I remain kneeling. "Will you take this at least? I'm warm now."

I say this as the wind rails outside, but I really am warm, next to the fire, next to him. He says nothing, so I decide it's best to return to my spot across the fire. I slide into his sleeping bag, zip it up all the way, but roll to face him. His back turned to me, I watch him breathe. Slow. Rhythmic. He doesn't wear a hat—it's on me. Always me. Always me first. He even put down his spoon before taking his first bite of food to make a radio call for me.

"Will?"

"Yes," he says, not turning to look.

"Rich has never canceled a flight for me."

His body stills. Many long moments later, he rolls to face me, meeting my eyes.

"In fact, he's never canceled anything for me. Not that that's a requirement to prove you love someone, but just sometimes . . . well, it would be nice to know you were the higher priority."

He shifts, propping his head in his hand, his bent elbow on the floor. "Remember what you told me on the balcony? You said you were confused?"

I nod.

"I was wondering if you still felt that way."

Invisible lines of energy arc across the fire, cinching the molecules in the air, surely closing the distance between us. All of me hums, on the receiving end of a plaintive yet powerful gaze.

I burrow a bit further into the sleeping bag. I don't *want* to be confused. I want to be objective. Practical. Make the correct decision, so I don't get burned like my mom. Not only that—and maybe even more importantly—I want to do what's *right*. After all, I made a promise to someone. A solemn promise.

Will waits patiently for an answer. . . .

I owe him the truth.

I owe myself the truth.

"Yes," I say. "Very much so."

24

Sunlight splays across the sandy floor, illuminating the granite walls inside the cave entrance. And just outside, a solitary figure stands, holding a thermos cup in his hand. Somehow, Will has cleared his sleeping place, packed it, and made something hot to drink, all without disturbing my sleep.

I stretch within the warm confines of my sleeping bag, the surrounding air colder this morning, as Will has not made a fire. The movement jostles Mojo, who lies curled up and pressed against my back. He sits up, shaking himself, before trotting to Will and offering a nudged greeting.

I push myself up, adjust the wool hat on my head, unzip the sleeping bag, and stand. Mojo senses the opening and returns quickly to nestle in the vacated warm spot.

As I approach Will from behind, he remains unmoving, a chiseled statue, surveying the mountainscape. I duck a little to move under the roof of the stone entrance, but when I rise, I see what holds him motionless.

Fresh snow stretches for miles, brilliant against the velvet blue sky. Will has been busy shoveling this morning, too, clearing space outside our "doorstep," allowing us to see over what must be at least five feet of new snow. It settles, deep and creamy, splendidly undisturbed, all the way to the valley floor, over six thousand feet below.

"Magnificent . . . ," I say.

He turns, looking down to me. "Quite a sight."

"I've never seen anything like this."

He smiles, happy, I think, that I'm appreciating the view like he is.

"Would you like some coffee?" he asks, offering his cup.

"Maybe just a sip, sure."

"We have a decision to make," he says. "Either we can hike down or we can call the helicopter in."

"I'd rather not involve the bird," I say, handing back the cup. "How long a hike is it?"

"Well, with you using the snowshoes, probably about an hour, maybe an hour and a half. And that's just to where my truck is parked. Then we'd have to drive into town. That's another forty-five minutes to an hour."

"I'm okay with it," I say.

The radio crackles. "Whiskey One, Mono County Sheriff, over." It's the distinctive slow drawl of Walt Hillerman.

Will pulls the radio from his chest strap. "Mono County, Whiskey One, go ahead."

"Good mornin', lad," Walt says.

"Good morning to you, Walt."

"Uh, Will, we have a bit of a situation down here."

Will and I look at each other briefly before he responds.

"Go ahead," Will says.

"Lieutenant Malone's fiancé is here at the airport, and he's been raisin' a bit of a scene."

Will stiffens.

"And, uh, that's actually putting it mildly," Walt adds.

I put my head in my hands.

"He's demanding that the helicopter take off to get her. Boomer's here, but he wants to hear from you how you want to proceed."

"Whiskey One copies. Stand by."

"Oh, god . . . ," I mutter. If there's one thing about Rich, he's used to getting his way. It's probably why he's so successful. Although normally he does it with a smile on his face, greasing the skids, smooth as silk. So it comes as a bit of a shock that he's raising a scene. Definitely not his style. But then a queer part of me thinks—and likes the fact—that maybe it's because of me. Maybe he's *that* worried.

"What would you like to do?" Will asks, the annoyance clear.

"I don't want to waste government funds on a helicopter flight that's not necessary. If you say we can hike out, I'd like to hike out."

"Mono County, Whiskey One, Lieutenant Malone would like to hike out, over," he reports with a clear touch of satisfaction.

"Whiskey One, Mono County copies. I'll relay that."

"I'll apologize to Walt and everyone later," I say.

"Walt, I estimate about noon," Will says.

"Copy that, Will."

Will returns the radio to its holder and ducks into the tunnel. "Would you like some breakfast before we head out?"

"If you have something easy."

He turns to his pack, unzipping the top pocket, searching.

In the meantime, I remove Will's socks, exchanging them for my own, and don my now-dry flight suit and boots.

"Granola bar?" he says, digging out two of them.

"Perfect."

We sit on the floor, eating our bars and sharing his coffee in companionable silence, and I'm altogether content. I don't have the urge to *do* anything or *go* anywhere. Which, of course, doesn't make sense, since my fiancé is waiting for me at the airport.

Will doesn't seem all that pressed for time, either. But, surely, he's worried about his trip, his missed flight, making new arrangements.

His trip . . .

It still blows my mind that he canceled his flight for me.

"I don't think I've officially thanked you yet," I say.

"Not necessary," he says with a dismissive wave.

"It *is* necessary. You went *way* out of your way. So thank you."

He shrugs mildly.

"Will you be able to get another flight?"

"There's another one on Saturday. Just haven't decided if that's the one I want to take." He sips his coffee, taking his time swallowing. "Hell, the sponsors are probably so pissed, they won't want me anymore, anyway," he says, setting down the cup.

"Sponsors . . . ? What are you talking about?"

He pulls his knees up, loosely wrapping his arms around them. "I wasn't exactly truthful with you when we were rock climbing on Donner Summit."

"What do you mean?"

"That bit about not planning. That I just up and go. I mean, sometimes that's the case, but this trip wasn't one of those spontaneous ones. Not totally."

"Why weren't you truthful?"

"Because I was frustrated. Well, you remember. I threw a tantrum. It was stupid."

"So the trip *was* planned, then."

"Everything was set, I just hadn't fully committed to going, what with you—well, never mind. Anyway, a lot of money was on the line for this one. A first ascent. A documentary. A magazine spread. The whole deal."

"Oh, no," I say, my hands flying to my open mouth. "Oh, please don't tell me you gave up an opportunity like that for me. Please don't say it."

"Okay, I won't say it."

I stand, turning away quickly, my eyes burning.

"Besides, all that matters is you're okay," he says.

The knife in my gut twists, and I have to lean over, hands on my knees, to steady myself.

"Alison?" He flies to my side, placing a hand on my back. "Are you all right?"

I straighten, turning away, so he won't see me wipe my face. "I'm fine. I'm fine. . . ."

But then he's in front of me. "What is it?" he asks.

"It's nothing, it's—"

"What's this, then?" He brings his finger to my cheek, wiping the single tear that got away.

He stands so close. Too close.

"Confused?" he asks softly.

I nod, slowly, honestly, my eyes never leaving his.

Ali, Rich is at the airport. He's waiting for you. . . .

I have to clench my fists when I say, "We should probably go."

It's a long moment—an eternity—his eyes holding mine, his body inches away. He lets his finger drift down the side of my face, delicately brushing the skin, before removing his hand. "If that's what you want."

My fingernails dig into my palms. "It is," I whisper. And I step away.

I busy myself with my snowshoes, fiddle with my clothing, retie my boots, doing anything to avoid eye contact with Will, unless absolutely necessary, as we prepare to depart.

"Here, take this," he says, handing me the bright orange combination avalanche transceiver/GPS unit. "The avalanche danger will be extreme following such a large snowfall with such high winds."

I buckle the straps to secure it and turn the dial to transmit, relieved that Will has shifted into guide mode.

"We'll cross the couloir one at a time," he says. "I'll go first. Wait until I signal, then move across fast. Got it?"

Facing the immediate threat of avalanche danger, I shove all other concerns to the back burner, and concentrate on a safe crossing.

We do it quickly, and begin our downward trek.

On the way, I inhale deeply—filling my lungs with that post-storm, crackly-clean air. Calming. Cleansing. I focus on these cleansing breaths as we make quick time down the mountain, him on skis, me on snowshoes. Will leads, tramping down the snow and laying a trail for me to follow, while Mojo brings up the rear.

Ninety minutes after starting, we arrive at his truck, which is buried above the level of the wheel wells. We free the truck after about twenty minutes of digging, and the subsequent one-hour drive is completed in silence, the air between us strained, stiff.

And now, as we turn onto the long single-lane road that leads to the airport, I squirm in my seat, wondering what scene we'll find upon arrival. I chance a peek at Will, who bristles with unease. Mojo senses it—he fidgets, as well—and I put my arm around him, more for my comfort than his, I think.

We make the final left-hand turn into the airport . . . and it's so much worse than I expected. Like the scene from a fully functioning command and control center in the midst of a natural disaster, police cars, fire engines, several sheriff's vehicles, and an ambulance all crowd the parking lot. Beyond, on the tarmac, the bright orange airframes of Longhorn 06 and Longhorn 07.

"Oh, no. This can't be for me. . . ."

"We would have heard it on the radio otherwise," Wills says grimly.

Rich has rallied an entire legion of rescue forces on my behalf, it appears.

I give Will one last look, then open my door and step out. Mojo runs ahead, making a beeline for Jack, who stands with Boomer, our pilots and aircrew, and a crowd of sheriff's personnel, including many SAR team members I recognize. I pick out Kelly and Kevin, Thomas and Tawny. Walt, too.

Will and I walk together for about twenty yards, and then I see Rich jogging toward me. He wears an Armani pin-striped suit, totally out of place here. But this is how he dresses when he takes charge. Worry and relief, intertwined, are etched on his face as he pulls me into his arms.

"Ali, are you okay?" he asks, holding me tightly. It's many moments before he pulls back, hands on my shoulders, looking me over. "I was so worried."

"Yes, yes, I'm fine."

I look over my shoulder, intending to tell Rich who it was that searched for me and ensured my safety, but my heart shudders when I meet Will's gaze.

His face is a mask of anguish. I only get a quick glimpse before he turns and starts jogging back to his truck.

186 / Anne A. Wilson

"Will, wait!" I say, calling after him. "Rich, that's Will Cavanaugh. He's the one who found me and stayed with me."

Rich leaves my side and runs after Will, meeting him at the door of his truck. From a distance, I can't hear what's being said, but I see it when Rich, who stands several inches shy of Will's height, extends his hand.

Will takes it, but then suddenly, violently, Will pulls his hand back. I let out a strangled gasp, shocked at his reaction. Based on body language alone—Will's hands move in a flurry—the words they speak are far from friendly. Will ends the "conversation" by jumping in his car and slamming the door shut. Ignition on. Gun the engine. Wheels slipping and spinning, he jerks the truck around, finds traction, and screams out of the parking lot.

Rich throws up his hands and stalks back to me.

"Ungrateful son of a bitch!" Rich says.

"What? How is he—? What happened?"

"That was a one-hundred-dollar bill for Christ's sake!" he says, pointing a shaking finger at the snow being kicked up in Will's wake. "That fucker tore up a one-hundred-dollar bill!"

My body turns to stone. "Wait a minute. . . . You gave him . . . you gave him *money?*"

"Most guides would appreciate a tip. Jesus Christ! What the hell is his problem!"

In all the time I've known him, I've never seen Rich lose his cool. But what he just did to Will . . . Like a hired hand. He couldn't have delivered a more degrading insult.

"I can't believe you did that," I say, backing away.

Rich's face goes white. "Wait, Alison, what is it?"

"How could you do that?"

"Do what? Ali, I thought it was the right thing," he says, scrambling. "I was just trying to show my appreciation." He looks up, suddenly aware of the growing number of sheriff's personnel and navy aircrewmen who observe his display with grim expressions. Kelly and Tawny, in particular, issue glares of disapproval.

"Ali, please, I'm sorry. You have no idea how worried I've been. I showed up at the airport, and you weren't there. I called your cell. No answer. I called the base, and oh yes, your fiancée is trapped in the high mountains in a blinding snowstorm, and we can't get to her. Jesus God, I didn't know what to do! So I'm calling the commanding officer, the sheriff, your squadron, anyone I can think of to mobilize and get you back. Please," he says, reaching out his hands to me. "I'll call Will back. I'll apologize. I'll do whatever you want."

Jack stands rigid, fuming. Next to him, Boomer mirrors Jack's stance, hands set firmly on his hips. Both stare daggers at Rich.

"Let's just go," I say.

I give a quick thanks to Walt, Jack, Boomer, and company, promising to debrief later. For now, I just want to escape the awkwardness. Rich points out his rental car on the opposite end of the parking lot, so I turn and sprint-walk, anxious to just get there and go. I realize I've left Rich behind when I hear him breathing hard, jogging to catch up.

When he reaches me, he takes my hand, but I find myself looking over my shoulder at the dusty white plume that obscures Will's truck as he accelerates away.

25

We decided to start over.

Yesterday was a wash. Rich drove me back to Fallon, and we spent the rest of the afternoon and evening in my apartment. Which is unfortunate. The only thing I'd wanted to do with him, since he told me he was coming to visit, was show him around the area. But yesterday, I didn't have the heart for it, trying as I was to reconcile his behavior. In the end, we agreed that he didn't handle it well. It was due not only to the worry he carried for me, but also the fact that he felt so helpless, something foreign to him.

He was humbled, no doubt about it, and sincere in his apologies. So, new day, new start. I decided to drive to the hot springs first, thinking I might as well begin with the best thing.

My spirits lift when I see that Rich has turned his head sideways, to the Sierra, as we drive farther south, the highway affording a spectacular view of the range. At the base of the foothills, snow-covered pastures spread for miles, cattle rummaging for grass, horses clustered for warmth.

"You know, I still don't get it," he says.

"What's that?"

"The climbing thing. I mean, these mountains are fantastic and all, but I just don't get the allure of climbing up a vertical face."

My heart sinks. I stretch my hands on the steering wheel, still scratched and scarred from the rocks at Donner Summit. . . .

"I went rock climbing," I say.

"What?"

His phone vibrates and he retrieves it from the chest pocket of his pullover fleece jacket.

"I climbed last week for SAR training. It was actually fun."

He pulls his eyes from his phone to look at me. "Really?"

"Yeah, really."

"Hmm," he says, looking down again. "Oh, good, my car's gonna be ready on Monday."

"Is something wrong with your car?"

"No, I bought a new one. I was gonna surprise you. I dropped some serious nickel for a Lexus, and it has *everything.* Like even a roadside-assistance plan. If you ever get a flat, or you're stranded *anywhere,* they'll come out and get you. It's an incredible deal."

"Yeah . . . that sounds pretty good."

"*Pretty* good? Ali, come one, it's *awesome!*"

"Okay, awesome."

"But you wanna know the *really* great news?"

"What's that?"

"I'm this close to closing a deal for a bigger condo for us. Same building, but penthouse this time." He turns to me proudly.

"Penthouse?"

"The views are . . . To. Die. For."

"But the place you have now is fine. And what about the contractors, all the work you're having done?"

"Oh, they'll still complete the work. I'll just sell it when they're finished. And anyway, it's a great investment," he says, tapping away at his phone again.

"Rich—"

"Ho . . . Hold on," he says, raising his finger. His phone vibrates again and he looks at the screen. "Let me just answer this one quick."

I reach over and switch on the radio. Hitting the scanner, my finger hovers over the preselect button. The channels scroll through . . .

classical, jazz, alternative rock . . . There! I press the button for three seconds, ensuring the channel is now permanently programmed.

Rich looks over to me during his conversation, turning his hands up and mouthing, "What's this?" And his expression? Like he just drank sour milk.

"It's country music."

"Since when do you listen to country music?" he asks, holding his hand over the phone.

"Since . . . I don't know. Just since I've been here."

He gives me a funny look before returning his focus to his phone call. And me? I have to bite my cheek to keep from smiling when the next song starts. Who else but Randy Travis, singing the song I heard at Jack's house, "Better Class of Losers." I listen to the lyrics closely, vaguely aware that I'm nodding. Randy begins his lament about socializing with the uppity-ups in the penthouse suite, before making the choice to hang out with more down-to-earth folks.

Rich's hand shoots out to grasp the handle above the passenger door, as I turn onto the four-wheel-drive-only road, my 4Runner bumping and jumping.

"Whoa!" he shouts. "What? No, dude, not you. Listen, I'll call you back. Right. Yeah later."

He fumbles to stuff his phone back in his pocket, but finally gets it in.

"Are you sure you know where you're going?" he asks, now hanging on to the handle with both hands.

"Yes. I've been here before. And trust me, it's worth it."

As I navigate to the springs, I revel in the sight of fresh snow from Monday's storm, blanketing the rocks, the sage, and a weathered wooden fence. Other than a few animal tracks—tiny paw prints disappearing into unknown hiding places—there's no indication that anything has moved out here since Monday.

But the sky is unsettled. Today—unlike yesterday, which carried that post-storm stillness and a clear sky—the clouds have moved in again. And they look different somehow. Alien. Horse-tailed, iron gray, and thick. But the disquieting thing is their speed. Slow and methodical, this new weather system crosses the Sierra like a storm god pulling a veil over the Owens River Valley.

I push away the ominous feelings, berating myself for being so melodramatic, and focus on the hot springs instead. "See! You can see them there."

"How did you ever learn about this?"

"A local," I say, clearing my throat, "showed us. Our entire crew came, along with the search-and-rescue guys from Mono County."

Rich looks ahead and to the sides. "Where are the . . . I don't see any buildings or facilities."

"There aren't any. These are just natural springs. It makes it better, too."

I glance at Rich, observing him taking in his new surroundings, filled with a strange exuberance, something I haven't felt in what seems like forever with him. Finally, *finally*, he will understand.

I pull to the side of the road, thrilled that it's just the two of us. I had worried we might have company.

"So this is it!" I say, opening my door, and stepping out.

I meet Rich on his side. "What do you think?"

"Well, I've never seen anything like this before." He pulls his jacket tighter around him.

"You have a choice," I say, removing my jacket, and lifting my fleece sweater, then shirt, over my head. "One hundred five degrees here or one hundred degrees over there."

"How are you doing that? It's flippin' freezing out here!"

"No, it's not that bad, really. Especially once you get in," I say, removing my boots, followed by my mountaineering pants. I stand now, clothed in only my swimsuit, next to Rich, who hasn't moved.

"Well, I'm not waiting. I'm going to the one-hundred-degree pool." I open the back hatch of the truck, throw my clothes in, and make a beeline for the spring.

I was shocked by the cold two weeks ago, so it seems natural for Rich to react the same way when he finally takes his shirt off. I hear him, though I can't see him, from behind the snow-covered mounds of earth. "Shit, that's cold!"

His voice grows louder as he nears. "Shit! Ow!" The rocks rumble as they move beneath him. "Shit, shit, shit, this is cold!" he says, rounding the bend.

I smile as he approaches, unsteady in his bare feet, knowing his grimace will morph into a relaxed smile once he slides into the water.

"Almost there," I say. "The water is *so* nice!"

"Do they treat it out here or anything?" he asks, head down, stepping carefully here, cautiously there.

"Do they what?"

"You know, treat the water? For whatever, bacteria?"

"Uh, no, I don't think so. These are natural, so . . . But it's fine. Look," I say, ducking under.

"If you say so," he says, before finally stepping in. "Oh . . . that *is* nice."

"Told you," I say, proudly.

Rich slips lower, the water rising to his neck as he leans back against the rock. We sit across from each other, so it's easy to observe him. Just like last night, I feel like I'm getting to know him all over again. Fine black hair, trimmed neatly, slightly rounded face, smooth, pale skin—a victim of far too many office hours indoors—wide-set brown/black eyes, and a jaw that sits just this side of an underbite. Most would say he's nice-looking, but I'd have to add that it all seems to work better when he's in a suit. He just has that put-together look when he's well dressed.

"What do you think?" I raise my arms in the air and motion to the view. "Is this place incredible or what?"

"It's nice, yeah," he says with not quite the amount of enthusiasm I was hoping for.

"Soooo, this is it." I sweep my arms around in a wide arc. "This is where we fly all the time. Remember the rescue on Mount Morrison? You can see it from here," I say, pointing. "And then, Palisade Glacier, well, you can't see it from here. It's further south. And there's—"

He finds my hand underwater, pulls me toward him, and his mouth is on mine. It happens so fast—my head was turned—I never saw it coming. Our lips move together in an odd way—this getting-reacquainted period that feels a little off—but it's more aggressive on his end, and I find myself leaning back.

"Whoa," I say, pulling away for air.

"I have definitely missed that," he says.

"Uh, yeah," I say, smoothing back my hair.

Last night, it was the same. This weirdness, going through the motions, like sharing a bed with a stranger. It was familiar, yet it was mechanical . . . I guess. But then, I don't know how it's supposed to feel when you haven't seen someone in so long.

When I was gone for my long deployments overseas, I hadn't met Rich yet. No one to miss or come home to. These last ten weeks have been the longest stretch so far for us, and I'll be the first to admit that this readjustment period is lasting longer than I would have thought. But of course, with what happened yesterday morning . . .

"Did you know on Bimini Island—you know, in the Bahamas— they have a natural spring?" he says. "It's not hot like this, but they advertise it as *the* Fountain of Youth, *and* it's totally gorgeous. I've already hired a guide to take us there—in kayaks! It's gonna be great."

"You've packed in quite a bit for our honeymoon."

"Well, once you get going . . . There's just so much to do down there."

"Yeah—"

"And it's *warm*," he says as he scans the snowy landscape. "I cannot *wait* to hit the beaches there."

Maybe I'm imagining it, but he seems sort of done here. "Did you want to stay here longer or go on or . . . ?"

"Sure, what's next?"

"I wanted to show you Mount Morrison up close, and then, drive down to Bishop—"

At the mention of the town, his expression takes a turn south.

"Just to go to the bakery, the one I've been telling you about."

"Oh. Okay."

He rises and steps out, moving out of my sight, while I remain in the spring, a little stunned. I know he would prefer not to have any reminders of what happened in Bishop, but I did want him to experience

Schat's Bakkerÿ, having raved about it yesterday. And then, I guess I thought he would have liked to hang out at the springs a while longer.

I duck my head underwater, and stay there, running my fingers through my hair, feeling how slippery and smooth it is, the water chock-full of healthy minerals. Surfacing, I remember someone else who "washed" his hair, and that someone was not concerned about bacteria or facilities.

By the time I reach the car, Rich is clothed and sitting in the passenger seat. His head is down, and he scrolls through something on his cell phone.

I pass him, moving to the back of the car, then stop, turning a circle. I do so in my suit and bare feet, not bothered at the moment by the cold. Of course, with what I experienced Monday, this is tame by comparison.

Around me, the mountains are—to borrow a word my mom used—resplendent. The Sierra Nevada and the White Mountains, both blanketed in snow, just like the valley. A black hawk with a red tail soars overhead, its wingspan pushing four feet, at least. The bird is resolutely unfazed by the striated black and gray clouds that threaten, dropping lower by the minute. And it is blessedly quiet.

I shudder, reacting to the artificial clicking noises that stab the silence as Rich taps on his phone. It's the thirteenth time he's checked his phone since we left Fallon three hours ago. Not that I'm counting.

I peel down my wet swimsuit, wondering about my own habits with a phone. Do I check it that often? Maybe I do.

I dry myself and dress, then walk to the passenger door and open it.

"Did you wanna see Mount Morrison?" I ask. "We could drive there. . . ."

He finishes tapping. Slots the phone back in his pocket.

"Or . . . I could just point out stuff. I just wanted to show you, you know, the site of that rescue I told you about."

"The Death Couloir," he says. He opens the door wider and slides out. "I remember that."

"Yes," I say, straightening. "So that's it, that black corridor of snow."

I point to the couloir, which is once again hidden in shadow by the steep rock surrounding it. "See the ice wall on the bottom part? That's where the climbers were stuck."

"That is seriously steep." He brings his hand over his eyes and squints. "And you hovered there?"

"Yeah."

"Most impressive, Alison Malone-soon-to-be-Gordon," he says with a grin.

He puts his hand on my elbow, turning me away from the mountain, before pulling out his phone and stretching out his arm. "Selfie with the Death Couloir!" He aims the phone and snaps.

I look over his shoulder as he checks the screen. In the photo, his smile is bright, mine a little awkward, the couloir cutting a sharp, shadowed line between us in the background.

"So, anyway, when we got there, we—" I start.

"Hold on a sec, I wanna post this on Instagram."

"Oh . . . okay." While his head is down, I stare at the couloir, seeing it as clearly as I saw it that day, a bright yellow jacket moving steadily upward, methodical, sure.

Yes, I admit it; I did slip once in the days after the party at Jack's house. I searched for Will on Facebook, Twitter, and Instagram, thinking surely he had photos posted of his exploits. But—and maybe I shouldn't be surprised—I came up empty. Will is so modest and self-deprecating, one would never guess what he's accomplished. Which, based on the pictures I saw on Jack's wall, would amount to an impressive mountaineering résumé.

"Okay, the photo's up," Rich says, reseating himself. "So what's next?"

"Did you want to see anything else here? Maybe take a walk or something?"

"Nah, I think I'm good."

I bite my lip. "Okay."

I close his door and shuffle to the back of the car, my eyes stinging. *He's so not into this.* I plop myself in the cargo area, letting my legs dangle over the tailgate, and wipe my eyes. *But how can you* not *be into this? Look at this place!* I peek up at the hawk again, still floating in the updrafts overhead. *That's the problem, Ali. He's not even looking.*

When I shove my hands into my jacket pockets, my fingers move across a scattering of pointed pine needles. How this elicits a smile, I'll never know, but I pull them out, and breathe in their glorious Jeffrey pine scent—more like butterscotch this time. I sit for a good five minutes, completely uninterrupted, by the way, taking deep, pine-infused breaths, composing myself.

The light dims as the alien clouds continue to drop, pressing ever lower into the valley. But my eyes continue to be drawn upward, especially now that the first dollop-sized raindrops—*rain?*—begin to plunk on the roof.

I shove the needles in my pocket, close the back door, and rush to the driver's seat.

"Ready to go?" I ask.

"Yeah," he says without looking up. Tap. Tap. Tap. "Whatever you want."

I buckle myself in. Turn the key.

Plunk. Plunk. Plunk.

I check the temperature display. Forty degrees. No wonder.

Tap. Tap. Tap.

Plunk. Plunk. Plunk.

Tap. Tap. Tap.

"Rich, can I ask you something?"

"Of course."

"Where do you see us in twenty years?"

He stops, lowering the phone, an invisible vacuum sucking the air from the front seat.

"What do you mean? You're sounding all serious."

"Well, I was just wondering, do you think we'll still be in San Diego? Will you be doing the same job?"

"I *hope* I'm doing the same job. Two more promotions, and I'm a partner! And why would I want to live anywhere but San Diego? The weather's great. It works perfectly for you, and we'd be livin' large."

His head turns down, but mine turns up. To the Sierra. My vision blurs, replaced by a memory. A mountain buried in white. A mine tunnel.

Two days ago, two souls spent the night tucked inside a mountain. And one of them has no future plans.

26

Beep. "You've reached Will Cavanaugh. Sorry I missed your call. Please leave a message, and I'll get back to you as soon as I can. Thanks." Beep.

"Will . . . this is Alison. I just . . . well, I just wanted to apologize for . . . I'm sorry about what happened with Rich. He was wrong to do that and I just—"

"Alison?" Will says, picking up.

"Will! You answered!"

"I thought I probably should," he says, the words distinctly distant. "I'm leaving on Saturday at noon. I just wanted you to know."

"Oh." It hits me with the force of a blunt object, although it shouldn't, because he told me this. He said there was another flight on Saturday. "Well . . . when will you be back?"

"I don't know yet."

"You don't . . ."

"I have to go. Take care, all right?"

"I . . . okay . . ." The phone clicks and he's gone.

I sit on my covered balcony, still in my pajamas, observing night give way to day, the sun not yet having peeked over the horizon. Rain continues to fall, just as it did yesterday, when I called Will after dropping Rich off at the airport.

By the time I arrived home, I felt sick, raw, and wrong. I ran a hot bath and stayed there until the water grew cold, my future life flashing before my eyes. And the really hard thing is that it's a good life. Mrs. Richard Gordon is going to live comfortably, no surprises, with someone who treats her well, doesn't take unnecessary risks, and is committed to a lifelong, stable partner 'til death do us part.

Lifting my cat-poster mug to my lips, I blow across the surface of newly steeped tea, made from the Jeffrey pine needles Jack gave me.

Currently, not a breath of wind stirs the rain. It cascades in sheets, heavy enough that flight ops for the carrier air wing were canceled last night. The plan is to resume this evening *if* the storm lightens. Whatever system this is with the alien clouds hasn't budged since it arrived, and it's been raining without letup ever since.

I take a warming sip of tea, smiling as I swallow. Remembering when Jack gave the needles to me. Remembering Will—

My cell rings. It should be my mom. We were talking just a moment ago, when her phone started acting up, so she was going to hang up and call me from her land line.

"Hi, Mom."

"Hi, honey. Sorry about that. I don't know what's going on with my phone, but anyway, where were we?"

"I had to take Danny's duty over the weekend in order to get Thanksgiving off, so I won't be able to see you then."

"Oh . . . Well, that's okay," she says.

The words gnaw. It's not okay. I wanted alone time with her. I really did.

"Cee's been bugging me to go with her to the lodge early, anyway," my mom says. "She's leaving tomorrow, so I'll just go ahead and go with her. And actually, this will be great. We'll have everything ready for you this way. And when you get here, you and I can sneak off for some alone time. How does that sound?"

So upbeat. Maybe Celia's right about the lodge. My mom really seems to want to go back.

"It sounds fine," I say.

"Really?"

"Yeah . . . yeah, really. That'd be great."

"Are you okay? You don't sound right."

"I'm all right."

"Ali . . . ," she says, waiting.

"What?"

"What's the matter? You just had three days with Rich. You should be bouncing off the walls."

Bouncing? Definitely not.

"It was a good visit."

"Just good?"

"Well, it was—Mom, am I doing the right thing?"

"What?"

"Am I doing the right thing, marrying Rich?"

"Of course you are. How many times do you need reassurances?"

"But that's just the thing. Why do I need reassurance? I should just know, right? Isn't that how it's supposed to work?"

"Not necessarily," she says, her voice lowering, the words ringing false almost as soon as they're spoken. "No one can see the future, Ali, so I think we're all a bit timid when stepping into something like this. It's only normal."

"But what if I'm wrong? What if Rich isn't the one for me?"

"Nonsense," she says. "He's a good man. He'll treat you well, give you a nice home. It's a smart choice, Ali."

Smart . . . I blow on the smooth surface of my tea, ripples forming, shuddering, disappearing.

"Mom, do you think he loves me?"

"Of course he does. It's obvious." She answers without hesitation, in her standard, no-nonsense way, as she does whenever Rich is the topic of discussion.

"Do you think I love *him?*"

"What? You're asking me?"

I stand, slip my feet into my clogs, and walk through the sliding patio doors, returning to the warmth of the living room. "Well, I just . . ."

"I think you love him enough."

What? I almost trip, because I stop so suddenly.

"Enough? What does *that* mean?"

"Ali, we should probably save this conversation until I see you in person."

"No!" I say, startling myself with the emphatic volume. "What are you saying? Enough? Enough what?"

I start pacing in the protracted silence. Why do I always pace with my mother? This can't be normal. But she's not answering. She's holding something back. What?

"Mom, please answer me. Enough? What do you mean?"

Wait. Wait. Pace. Pace.

"Mom!" I shout, the frustration boiling over. "Enough what—"

Her response is rendered too quietly. "Enough for your marriage to work, but not enough that he can break you."

My throat constricts, as if she's reached her hand through the phone and clamped her fingers around it.

That's it. I look furtively around my living room. That's it! Nick couldn't hurt my mom. . . . She never let him in. Not to that deepest place.

As a couple, they treated each other with respect, consideration, all the niceties—they coexisted well. However, it was her reaction when he died that seemed really off. She grieved, yes, but she moved on. Just like that.

But my mother has not moved on from my father, wallowing in her garden of larkspur, suffering, broken.

She knows Rich poses no danger. He can't hurt me. Why? Because I only love him *enough*. Somehow, she knows this, and therefore, it's a *smart* choice.

But is this true? Do I love Rich just enough or do I *really* love him?

Or do I love him at all . . . ?

"Alison? Are you there?"

"I'm here," I say dully.

"I'm sorry. I shouldn't have said that. I'm sure you love Rich just fine. It's not my place to suppose anything about your feelings for him. It was uncalled-for, and I'm sorry."

"But I asked you," I say, pacing my way into the kitchen. I place my mug in the sink and lean heavily on the counter. "No, I yelled at you. I'm sorry, Mom. I didn't mean to raise my voice."

I wish she were here. So badly, I wish she were here, and we could sit together and talk into the night.

"It's okay, honey. But can I ask you something?"

"Sure," I say, twirling a strand of hair, now that my mug hand is free.

"Is there something else you're worried about? Something you're not telling me?"

No way. She couldn't know. But a mother's intuition . . . ? Still, no. But crap. She's right. There is something else. A big else.

"Yes," I say quietly.

"Would you like to talk about it?"

"Um . . ." Oh, boy. I walk uneasily into the living room, lowering myself to the couch, and take a deep, steadying breath. "Well, I met someone here."

I hear it when the breath rushes out of her. "I thought as much."

"You did?"

"Based on our last few conversations, yes."

"Oh . . ."

"Do you want to tell me about him?"

"Well, Will . . . His name is Will. He's . . ."

"He's what?"

"Mom," I say, my eyes glistening. "He could break me."

27

Beep! Beep! Beep! Beep!

"What the—?" I scramble to sit up.

Beep! Beep! Beep! Beep!

I lean over and switch on the lamp, fumbling for my pager, which bounces, vibrating, across the nightstand.

A straight row of "1"s. Military SAR.

Glancing at the clock—0030—I tumble out of bed, wiping the sleep from my eyes. Okay. What day is it? I stumble to the bathroom and splash water on my face. Friday. No wait. It's just after midnight. It's early Saturday morning.

I almost trip and kill myself trying to insert my leg into my flight suit, balance not quite there yet. Saturday . . . Saturday.

Boots. Tie the boots. Grab the phone. Saturday . . . I remember. The air wing's final week of flight ops. They're flying tonight, because the weather finally cooperated, the rain easing and even stopping sometimes throughout the course of the evening—the tail end of the weather system with the alien clouds. It's their largest-scale, everybody-is-airborne party, the most difficult flying yet. Oh, no . . .

I punch the speed dial for Base Operations. "Lieutenant Malone," I say when the petty officer answers.

"Ma'am, we have an F/A-Eighteen down. The skipper wants to speak with you personally on this one."

"Does he want me to call him?"

"No, ma'am. He's right here. Hold on."

I climb into my car and fasten the seat belt.

"Alison," Captain Woodrow says. "A Hornet went down in Bravo Nineteen. We don't know if the pilot ejected. Hammer's in the air. He's assumed on-scene command. The rest of the exercise has been canceled. All aircraft are returning to base."

Hammer . . . the air wing commander. The jerk from the pool.

"Roger that, sir."

"Everyone's monitoring Guard," he says, referring to the dedicated emergency frequency on the radio used by all aircraft for search-and-rescue efforts. "Everyone on the ground, every pilot flying tonight. They're all listening."

"Understand, sir."

"When I ask for a status, remember the code."

"Copy. Will do, sir."

No one but a coroner can officially pronounce someone dead, so if we find a person where the outcome is obvious, we speak in code on the radio. This way, we're not officially saying anything, but everyone involved will know the score.

I speed to the hangar, pulling in just as Clark arrives.

This will be the first time I've flown with Clark where he will act as the copilot, while I sign for the bird as the aircraft commander.

"What do we have?" Clark says as we jog through the security gate, the sentry waving us through.

"A Hornet's down. Bravo Nineteen."

Clark's gait changes, just slightly, his body stiffening. Although I don't dwell on this, because Hap and Beanie sprint by us, throwing their gear into the bird, and start undoing the tie-downs.

"Beanie!" I call. "Rig the Nightsun!"

"On it!"

The Nightsun is a searchlight rated at forty million candlepower, a light so intense it could start a fire if you turned it on inside.

We're airborne in thirteen minutes from the time of the pager alert, Clark flying, heading south along Highway 95, the radios buzzing nonstop with chatter. Captain Woodrow was right. *Everyone* is up this frequency, but Hammer is leading the chorus, flying overhead in his E-2 aircraft, using his aircraft's call sign, Seahawk One.

Good lord. He's barking commands, issuing orders, and frankly, choking the airwaves with unnecessary directions . . . and unfounded criticisms.

"Where the fuck is the goddamn SAR helo? This is fuckin' unsat!"

Which is ridiculous, as I've reported our status at least three different times to Fallon Tower, which is up this same frequency.

Deep, calming breath. "Seahawk One, Rescue Seven, on site, commencing search, stand by."

"Well it's about goddamn time! Last known coordinates . . ." I block out the ranting and check the aircraft's last known position according to Hammer with what Fallon Tower gave us earlier—a conversation Hammer should have heard. Whatever. He finishes speaking, thankfully, yet nervous energy continues to bleed into our aircraft via the radios—jets reporting in, returning to base, others put into holding, still others given altitudes and headings to keep everyone separate and safe.

But I'm nervous for another reason. I remember the rising terrain on either side of Bravo 19 from when we delivered the EOD team here just four weeks ago. Yes, we're searching for a downed aircraft, but it's all too easy to get so focused on this that you lose situational awareness, forgetting that you, too, fly in mountainous terrain.

At least it's not raining—for the moment, anyway.

Flying over the range, Clark tracks east, then west, moving south all the while, like tracing rungs on a ladder. At the same time, Beanie has the Nightsun trained on the landscape, giving us fair warning as the Blow Sand Mountains loom in front of us each time we track east.

"Rescue Seven, Range Ops," Captain Woodrow says.

"Range Ops, go ahead," I say.

"Anything yet?"

"Negative, sir."

Our search continues, while dozens of aircraft from the air wing circle, hold, return, land—the radio chatter constant. The beam from the Nightsun sweeps forward and aft, side to side, as we move along at a crawl.

"Ma'am, did they say who we're lookin' for?" Hap asks.

"No, not specifically."

Back and forth we sweep. I say a silent, fervent prayer—several, actually—that this pilot will be okay. That he or she ejected safely and is just waiting for a ride home.

"I've got something, two o'clock!" Hap reports.

"Clark, slow down," I say.

"Debris field," Beanie says. "This is it."

Another prayer . . . Please . . .

We make another pass, and my heart sinks. We only need to fly by once to know that the pilot didn't make it. Still, we need to confirm.

Clark makes a cautious approach to land, but the pucker factor is high, due to the uneven, rising terrain. Hap and Beanie relay ground clearances until, finally, the skids settle, albeit at an angle, since we're on a rise.

Beanie shines the Nightsun in the direction of the crash site, to an area of concentrated wreckage. The tail fin sticks up prominently, the wings still close to what used to be the airframe. A wheel here, twisted metal there.

"Okay, Clark, I'll take the controls while you and Hap confirm."

Clark remains unmoving, staring ahead, his hands rigid on the controls.

"Clark? Clark, I've got the controls."

Nothing.

"Hey, Clark," I say, leaning over and touching his shoulder.

He turns his head and looks at me with the oddest expression, like he's . . . scared?

I lift the microphone away from my face and speak to him directly, so the aircrew won't hear. "Are you okay?"

Almost imperceptibly, he shakes his head.

"Would you like me to go instead?" I ask, again not using the radio.

He nods.

"Okay," I say, with a squeeze to his arm. Granted, no one wants this job, but Clark's reluctance surprises me. "We'll be right back."

His head moves—just barely—in acknowledgment.

"Hap, let's go," I say.

"Roger that, ma'am."

I step out my door, my stomach churning. I so don't want to see this.

Moving oh so carefully across the rocky, slippery terrain, I put my hand to my mouth to stifle a cough. The smell of burning rubber chokes the air, and smoke drifts upward, wraithlike in the watery, chill night.

Our boots scrape against loose rocks as we move upward, now stepping over and around chunks of metal. Beanie moves the Nightsun ahead of us, illuminating the front section of the aircraft. The cockpit is sunken, awkwardly low, into the airframe, the canopy missing.

I swallow hard when the reflective tape from the back of the pilot's helmet glows red. He's still strapped in. I can see it from here, just ten yards away. We continue forward, every step heavier than the last. Something sticks out of the cockpit, like a tree branch, curled and gnarled, the flight suit sleeve missing, an arm charred through, fingers splayed sideways.

And then something that stops me cold. Snoopy. The little cartoon figure cut from red reflective tape now comes into focus on the back of the pilot's helmet.

No. It can't be. *No, no, no!*

I will myself forward, those few extra leaden steps, to confirm by looking at the name tag on the flight suit. It reads too clearly amid the charred material around it. SHANE FORESTER LT USN.

I bend over, hands on knees. "Oh, Jesus."

"Ma'am? Are you all right?"

"Hap, just do it, and let's get outta here."

Hap moves past me, to a sight that will be seared into his memory and mine for the rest of our lives, putting his hand on a burnt, broken neck to confirm no pulse.

The smell suffocates. Burning rubber. Composite metals. I turn,

Hap on my heels, and we do a combination walk-jog to get back to the aircraft, moving stupidly fast, almost falling multiple times. Shane . . .

The acid rises. *Hold on, Ali. Hold on. Not now.*

I strap into my seat. "Are you okay to fly?" I ask Clark, another question without using the mic, so the crew can't hear.

He looks at me. Swallows. "Who?"

I close my eyes. Squeeze. Open them. "Snoopy."

Clark deflates before my eyes. He continues to hold the controls as his shoulders slump and his elbows sag, dropping to the back of his seat as if he lacks the strength to hold himself upright. He turns to me, looks into my eyes, holds them, holds them, like he's clinging to a lifeline. His eyes water into glass, haunted, anguished . . . vulnerable.

Snoopy and Clark were close. God, now that I think about it, they were *always* together. At the last planning meeting with the commanding officer, before the air wing arrived. At the swimming pool. At Donner Summit. And then all those other times, like when Shane came to Fallon for his liaison work. Clark and Shane at the commissary. Clark and Shane running. At Burger King. At the bookstore. At that crappy, run-down casino that still allows smoking but makes the best apple turnovers on earth. Best friends, probably. Assigned to the same aircraft carrier. Clark miserable when Shane had to leave. Always wanting to go back to H-60s. To the *Carl Vinson.*

But the look in his eyes . . . his soul shredding. The husband who's been told his wife has died on the operating table. The wife who answers the door to the casualty assistance calls officer, there to inform her of her husband's death, killed in action. "I'm sorry to inform you . . ." and she misses the rest, because she crumples to the floor. The person who has just lost their lifelong partner—

I pull in a sharp breath. Oh no.

Oh no, oh no, oh no.

Partners. They were . . .

I lift the microphone away from my lips. "You were together. You and Shane. I . . . I had no idea."

He stares. I stare. A million heartbeats.

"I . . . ," he stutters. "I don't know what you're talking about."

"What? But you were— What do you—?"

Wait a minute. . . .

I don't think he wants me to know. I don't think he wants anyone . . . oh, good god . . . Hammer. The air wing commander. His *boss.*

". . . just make sure you keep your eyes in the boat," Hammer said. *"Fuckin' faggots everywhere in the ranks now."*

"Clark, I won't tell," I say in a rush. "I mean, if that's what you're worried about. I won't—"

He swallows hard. Robot voice. "Nothing to tell." He turns his head forward, hands so firmly gripped on the controls, I feel sure he could rip them from their moorings if he wanted.

I touch his arm. "I'm sorry. I'm so sorr—"

He shakes me off. Breathes deeply. Lips tight. Cheeks taut.

"Ready to lift?" he asks, keying the mic.

"Set in back, sir," Beanie says.

I observe Clark for a long moment, watching his controlled, measured breathing. His hands are steady—strained and white, ready to crack the controls, but steady.

"Okay, let's get outta here," I say, using the mic switch again.

He lifts, returning to the highway, while I put my hand to my chest, questioning my ability to speak, the pain acute—for me, yes, but far worse for Clark.

I check him again. Flying professionally, competently, compartmentalizing what's destroying him on the inside. A searing reminder that I, too, have a job to do. A radio call I dread to make.

Range Operations is monitoring the guard frequency . . . along with an entire base, an entire air wing.

"Range Ops, Rescue Seven, RTB," I say, using shorthand for "return to base."

"Rescue Seven, Range Ops, what's your status, over?" Captain Woodrow asks.

God help me. I press my lips together, swallowing, swallowing, my throat sore from the effort.

"No joy," I finally push out.

The guard frequency becomes a tomb—not one sound from Hammer or anyone else for the full ten minutes of our return flight to base.

As I drive home—it's now four in the morning—I have the nightmare déjà vu moment from hell, pulling over to the side of the road, to the same pasture I visited after Shane flew me in his F/A-18. I vomit, as I did then, but this time I can't seem to stop, retching when there's nothing left to throw up. The despair brings me to my knees. On hands and feet, I rock back and forth, trying to get my breath back, numb from the inside out.

And the rain starts to fall again.

28

"He hit his tail, Rich, while pulling up," I say, still drowning in disbelief. The words are coming out, but it's like someone else is saying them.

I cried myself out at the side of the road in the middle of the night, returning home a miserable, frozen shell. I know I'm not supposed to let it in. I normally don't. My defenses are usually up, just like they are for the rest of our team. Morbid gallows humor gets us through sometimes, but mostly, we detach.

I've been at the command for just over five months now, and this is death number four, up close and personal. The first? An F-5 pilot attempted to recover from an unrecoverable flat spin. Too late, he ejected, upside down, two hundred feet above the ground. We found him on a hillside, thrown away from the wreckage, his body leaning against a tree. From behind, he appeared to be resting, just back from the barber, his hair freshly cut. That sliver of hope rose. *He's okay. He must be.* Until our crewman pulled back on his shoulder to check his pulse, and his face fell apart, caved in like a jack-o'-lantern three weeks past Halloween.

I saw this, my physical body present. But in my mind, it registered just on the periphery, like a black-and-white horror movie, disconnected from all feeling. Same with deaths number two and three, a civilian glider pilot we found in the Sierra and a car-accident victim who took her last breath in our aircraft on the way to the hospital.

But Snoopy—Shane—bright eyes, quick, intelligent, humble, so ridiculously highly trained, and such a gifted flyer. Of course, we'll have to wait for the results of the mishap investigation, but when I contacted the base prior to calling Rich, the talk among those in the know centered around how fast the barometric pressure was changing, also suspect altimeter readings, and possible instrument failure. Bottom line, they felt Snoopy had done everything right. And that's the hardest part for me to reconcile.

Apparently, it's also hard for someone else—Rich.

"That doesn't mean he did something wrong," I say.

The conversation took a strange turn earlier, Rich's questions about the accident ringing far more like accusations, and I find myself defending Snoopy.

"All I'm saying, Alison, is you can't take this so hard," he says, trying to cheer me up but failing in a very big way. "This is on him. If he'd done everything right, as you say he did, he wouldn't have crashed. That's just the fact of it."

"How can you be so flippant?" I say, my voice rising.

"Whoa, whoa! Ali, don't get angry. You're making way too much of this."

"Am I? 'That's just the fact of it'? You're sitting in your penthouse condominium in San Diego with your feet up on an ottoman watching reality TV on your eighty-inch flat screen and have the audacity to say, 'If he'd done everything right, he wouldn't have crashed'? Who the hell do you think you are?"

"Ali! Wait! Don't do this! I'm sorry, okay? I'm sorry. I didn't mean it."

"You have no comprehension of this, do you?"

"No, that's not it. This is a tragedy. It's awful. Of course you should be affected. It's just . . . well, it's just that you've always handled it before."

"But I've told you about him, Rich. We've talked about Snoopy. I flew with him. Knew him. We were joking around just a week ago."

"Ali, please. Look, I'm sorry. I'm sorry, all right?"

I take a moment to breathe, to corral my emotions, knowing deep inside that something has just irrevocably shifted in our relationship, something that, like a flat spin, will not be recoverable.

He doesn't understand. Can't. Here's a man whose biggest worry revolves around the roadside-assistance plan for his Lexus. *"It runs out at the forty-eight-month point, one of those items in small print, but I think they have a deal with Triple A where you can get a membership at a discount to keep the coverage after the four-year mark,"* he said during *this* very phone call. Yes, this is how our conversation started this morning. I listened to his "woes" in a state of suspended animation. This minutia. This trivial, insignificant, meaningless, of-no-account, worthless, unimportant blather.

And after, he asked how I was doing.

"I have to go," I say.

"You're hanging up mad. Please don't."

I'm about to respond with something positively rude, but I stop myself. I'm not blameless here. I joined the navy for security, as crazy as that sounds. Advice from Grandpa Alther, who enjoyed a successful, thirty-year navy career. He forever espoused the built-in support system found in the military. Something that couldn't be yanked out from under you.

So by the time I had made the decision to enter the military, everything about it seemed safe and familiar—guaranteed housing, health care, a paycheck, all the "guarantees" my mother and I lacked when my father left us. And within that context, I've locked myself in a supposedly impenetrable cocoon—life insurance, savings accounts, a stock portfolio, a 401K, annuities, mutual funds, and yes, even an AAA membership. Protected. Secure.

Flat tire? Covered. Dead battery? Got that, too. Extended warranty on the car? It goes without saying. Wrapping myself in security blankets, just like Rich.

When we met a year and a half ago, Rich and I matched. We were planners. Organized. The next fifty years of our lives laid out before us. *Just* do this, and such and such will happen. Got it wired. No problem. That's *just* the fact of it.

But Snoopy had plans, too. He was on top of it. In charge. In control. And in love . . . And yet, his life was snuffed out in a millisecond. I've always felt I was in control—until I got to Fallon, that is, now tiptoeing on a knife edge, barely splitting the difference between sliding on the blade and slicing myself with it.

And that same realization—in control one minute, out of it the next—occurred while I was hugging a rock face on Donner Summit. *"Let go, Alison! You gotta let go!"* That's what Will said, someone who knows all too well that control is an illusion. That things don't always turn out the way you'd like. That bad things happen to good people, prepared people. No rhyme or reason. Stuff just happens. Hell, it happened to me on Basin Mountain.

And in an electric moment of clarity, the truth sinks in. Really sinks in. That thing that's been knocking deep in my gut for weeks, but that I now know with certainty—I'm talking to the wrong person.

"Ali, are you there?"

"I'm here."

"Is everything okay? I mean, we're okay, right?"

I take a deep breath. Hold it.

"No, Rich. We're not okay."

29

My eyes flick to the dashboard clock—1105. *No!* I'm not going to make it!

I speed west on Interstate 80, assuming Will is still at the airport, but not knowing for certain.

I tried to call him before leaving, but—no surprise—was transferred to voice mail. Even if he could have answered, I doubt he would have.

You have to try, Ali. At least try.

I rub my eyes, still bloodshot after the *two-hour* conversation I had with Rich. It was the breakup conversation I hadn't planned on having—the ending of our engagement—and it was torturous.

I tried to convey—with difficulty, because Rich wouldn't hear it—that this was not his fault. Yes, I was upset with him, with how he handled Shane's death. But that wasn't the reason for breaking our engagement. It was just the smack in the head for me. The wake-up call that so many other things were wrong with our relationship. That our pairing just wasn't right, wasn't meant to be.

He's still a smart, engaging, successful man. He hasn't changed . . . nor will he. *I* have changed, and I can't go back to that place where Rich dwells in his small circle of stale comfort.

Rain spatters against the windshield. Spat. Spat. Spat. My brain muddied. Thick. Tired.

I wind through a curvy swath of low foothills that leads into Reno, noting the dirt and slush piled high to the sides of the road. Another weather system settled in today. Back-to-back warm fronts. And the rain that started falling early this morning continues, only heavier now.

I grip the steering wheel firmly, focusing on the slippery road ahead, but my gaze keeps drifting to my bare left ring finger.

I envision the jeweler's box housing my engagement ring sitting forlornly on my nightstand at home. Prior to Rich's visit, I hadn't worn the ring since October nineteenth, a date that just so happened to correspond with the rescue on Mount Morrison and my first introduction to a certain Will Cavanaugh.

Day to day, I'd explained it away. I was flying—of course, no wearing it then—or I was exhausted, having come home late, or tired, having woken up early, or I was going to be swimming that day. Any number of excuses. So when Rich and I finally returned to my apartment after the Basin Mountain "adventure," I had to rush into the bedroom, blow the dust off the box before Rich could see, open it, and put the ring back on my finger.

I should have seen it all along, this sign, written in the tea leaves, like so many others. After Rich left Thursday, I pulled the ring off my finger and stowed it in the box—presumably, so it wouldn't slip off while I showered that morning. And there it's stayed. . . .

I told Rich I'd send it back to him, but he wouldn't hear of it. Said it was mine. His promise to me . . .

I grab a tissue. Damn it.

That conversation was so hard. I hurt him, plain and simple. I tried to explain I wasn't the right one for him, but he wouldn't accept it. And as we talked, I realized I was on the devil end of the worst, most horribly clichéd kind of breakup conversation there is. *There's nothing wrong with you. It's just me.* Those words actually came out of my mouth! And the more I talked, the more I built him up, listing everything that is nice and funny and sweet about him, how another girl is going to be so lucky. All of that. I said *all* of that! To which he re-sponded, "And that's not enough?"

I pull another tissue from the box.

Damn, damn, damn.

Another glance at the clock—*1120!*

Please let me make it! Please still be there, Will!

The rain pounds, a muted roar across the roof, almost loud enough to drown out the sound of the ringing. . . .

Ringing!

The phone lying on the passenger seat glows. It's Will.

"Hello?" I say.

"Alison? Is that you?"

"Yes! Will, I really need to talk with you."

In the background, the sounds of people shuffling, suitcases roll-ing, bells and dings, flight announcements on the PA system.

"Alison, I'm at the airport. I'm going to be stepping on a plane here in about twenty minutes."

"I know. I'm driving to the airport now."

"What?"

"I really . . . I just need to . . . Will, a friend of mine was killed in an F/A-Eighteen last night. We did the search. I saw him—" I say, choking on the words.

"Oh, Jesus. Where are you now?"

"Just entering Reno. I think I can be there in ten minutes."

"Okay, I'll meet you in the main lobby, by the slot machines. Do you know where that is?"

"I know it. I'll be there soon. Thank you, Will."

I rush from the parking garage, outside to the crosswalk, using a run-walk to move across the slippery concrete to the terminal. Water runs over my hair and drips across my face as I race through the double doors that slide open to the lobby, maneuvering through what looks like the floor of a casino, slot machines flashing and ringing.

He stands just outside Peet's Coffee and Tea, hands in the pockets of his gray mountaineering pants, wearing a loose technical T-shirt, untucked, topped by a thin microfleece jacket. His boarding pass is shoved in his back pocket, and he carries a small leather carry-on bag, slung over his shoulder. His eyes latch on to mine, brimming with empathy and understanding, but something else, too. Something that sends my heart racing.

As much as I don't want them to, my eyes begin to water. My hands move to my face, covering my mouth, and I feel the sobs collecting in my throat. It's Snoopy, but it's Will, too. Facing him, missing him, needing him.

He doesn't hesitate, stepping forward and wrapping his arms around me. My breaths come in hitches, my shoulders shaking as the tears come. He squeezes tighter, running a comforting hand across the back of my head. And that energy that is uniquely his envelops me.

I've never been held by him, not like this, so I didn't know what to expect. But it's different, much different, from how it was with Rich. I *fit* here. Part of it is physical. Rich stands just an inch taller than me, whereas Will has me by about five inches—six-one, six-two?—so my head fits perfectly in the crook of his neck. And chemically? My systems are wired to him, my body molecules standing at attention and shouting, *"This is the one!"* As much as I tried to convince myself otherwise with Rich, there's just no comparison. I knew it the first time I ran into Will in the bakery, the first day I met him.

He doesn't rush, doesn't check his watch, doesn't do anything but comfort. I'm in his arms, and god, it feels right. But then I have a devastating thought. He's probably five minutes away from saying, "See you in a few months." And not only that, I've just put him on the spot. What if he's just being nice right now? What if he's written me off already? Probably. Would make sense.

I pull back just slightly, but he keeps his arms loosely wrapped around my neck. "Will," I say, lifting my hands to my eyes to wipe them. "I'm sorry. I know this is lousy timing. I know you're leaving. But Rich doesn't understand. He can't understand. I just need to talk . . . to *you*."

"Passenger William Cavanaugh, please proceed to Gate C-Ten for boarding," the voice calls over the PA system. "This is the third call for passenger William Cavanaugh. Please proceed to Gate C-Ten."

He brings a tentative hand to my face, sweeping a tear-soaked strand of hair away from my cheek. "Are you saying what I think you're saying?"

"I broke my engagement with Rich. I'm saying I need you, Will. Only you. I know that now."

He swallows, his hand still flush across the side of my face, his fingers gently caressing my skin.

"Passenger William Cavanaugh, This is your final boarding call. Please proceed to Gate C-Ten."

"Your flight . . ."

"Come on." He takes my hand, lacing his fingers through mine, and I swear I'm going to fly. We whisk around the counter to the United Airlines desk, where he flags down an agent.

"My name is Will Cavanaugh. I'm supposed to be on Flight Ten-Sixty, final destination Buenos Aires. Is it possible to take my bags off the flight? I have to reschedule."

"Let me see what I can do," the agent responds, lifting the telephone receiver.

"Will, are you sure? I didn't mean for you to do this. I didn't know what to do. I just needed to see you, that's all. To let you know—"

He squeezes my hand. "Shhh," he says, putting a finger to his lips.

"Yes, Mr. Cavanaugh, we can do that for you. They're taking your bags off now. You can retrieve them in baggage claim."

"Thank you."

Wrapping his fingers more firmly through mine, he leads me away from the ticket counter, past the lobby entrance, and around the corner to a deserted baggage claim.

"You canceled your flight," I say, still in disbelief as he takes my other hand and turns to face me. "This is twice now. Will, you can't—"

"I was only leaving because of you. I couldn't stay. Not with what I was feeling."

He cups a hand under my chin, letting his thumb skim across my lips, holding there, searching my eyes. He smiles then, and with a look to melt the soul, leans down to kiss me. It's all I can do to stand as his mouth sinks into mine and the world around us disappears. His other hand reaches to my face, cradling it, holding me in the most protective way, even as his kiss deepens.

Who knows how long we stay like this? Who cares? But he does pull back just slightly, breathlessly. "I've wanted to do that for so long."

I smile, the tears brimming.

His hands remain at the sides of my face, holding my head as he stares into my eyes. "Although, as many times as I envisioned kissing you, it was never in an airport baggage claim," he says with a small laugh. "Probably the all-time worst place to share a first kiss."

"It could have been on the moon and I wouldn't have cared."

His fingers comb back through my hair and he shakes his head. "I was supposed to be sitting alone on a plane right now."

"I know." But then my face falls. "I'm just sorry it took something like . . . well, like what happened to make me realize how stubborn I was being."

He draws away, letting his hands drop to find mine again. "I'm so sorry about your friend. So very sorry."

I move my fingers through his, soaking in the reassuring pressure of his hands. "Shane was so capable, Will. So . . ." So everything. Shouldn't have died. Bottom line.

"I know," he says.

And that was all anyone ever needed to say.

30

"Turn right here," Will says.

Feather-light snowflakes drift through the headlight beams as I turn in to what appears to be a near-impenetrable wall of evergreens. But then the slimmest of openings is revealed, and a hidden road becomes visible, one without tire tracks, just untouched snow. With the increase in elevation from Reno to June Lake, the rain morphed into sleet, and finally to a quiet snow, the temperature hovering just above freezing.

"This isn't the way to your house," I say. "Or is it a back way or something?"

"You'll see."

I drive cautiously on this narrow route that winds and falls, noticeably dropping in elevation. Granted, it's dark now, but I don't see any signs of houses—no driveways or mailboxes—just forest. What I do see are the pinpoint silver twinkles of stars that peek through open slivers of unseen clouds. And I think, how wondrous to experience both the stars and the falling snow in the same moment.

Five minutes after we turn from the main road, Will directs me to park in a small clearing. He removes one of his North Face duffel bags from the back, opens it, and removes a small headlamp. He straps this to his forehead, then slings the duffel over his shoulders, wearing it like a backpack.

"Come on," he says, holding out his hand.

I'm glad I've worn my hiking boots, as we tromp off in the snow, following the narrow beam from Will's light. We negotiate what feels like a stairway, each step marked with a soft powder crunch, then exit the clearing and turn onto a forest trail, not even wide enough to accommodate us side by side. We thread our way through a stand of bare-branched aspen, and a short minute later emerge into a second clearing, one ringed with stately pines. Shifting ribbons of steam rise from a pool of water in the middle.

"Is this—?"

He smiles.

The pool is part of a larger creek that disappears into the forest on either side, visible because of the steam that floats in sheets above it. Gurgling water spills into the depression in front of us before shooting through a tapered channel, then continuing downward and out of view. This particular pool has human touches, lined with rocks around the sides, flat ones, like patio tiles.

"I thought you might like to see this . . . you know, at night," he says, slipping the duffel bag off his shoulders and letting it drop to the ground.

"The star show . . ." I lift my gaze from the water to the sky, remembering his comment when we soaked in the hot springs near the Mammoth Lakes airport.

"But you need to see it as it was meant to be seen," he says, switching off his headlamp.

Instantly, we're wrapped in the blackest black, a no-moon-night-over-the-ocean black. I squeeze his hand, because now I can't see *at all*.

Except for above, that is. The clouds have parted like curtains. Absent the moon's reflective shine and without any artificial light to wash out the view, the sky shimmers, awash in silver. And maybe it's that we're at altitude, the air thinner, less pollution, but there's a thickness to the starlight, a saturating sense of wonder, possibility.

"Spectacular, isn't it?" he says.

I look up to the sound of his voice, unable to make out his features. "It sort of takes your breath away."

His hand finds the back of my head, he pulls me to him, and lips so warm press down on mine. His kiss is sensuous, like an ache, the only two people on the planet. Snowflakes alight—pat, pat, pat—on my nose and cheeks, but melt away on contact, my skin rushing with warmth.

He pulls the zipper on my jacket, the sleeves roll off my arms, and he tosses it aside.

"Are we . . . out here?" I ask.

It's snowing. It's thirty degrees.

"Nope," he says, shrugging off his own jacket. He follows by lifting his shirt up and over his head. I can't see his chest, but my hands find it, moving over its wide contours. My fingers move at will, exploring, gliding over the washboard abdomen I remember from our first trip to the hot springs.

"Or are we—?"

His hands move to my hips, gathering my shirt, and pulling upward. Somehow he finds the hook to my bra, and that falls next.

I'm about to complete my question when he fits his mouth over mine, and the words die on my tongue—probably because his wraps so wondrously around mine. Snowflakes drop, pitter patter, across my back, but his warm hands smooth over them, gliding down to the dip in my waist. Any thought of the cold evaporates as his fingers slip under the waistband of my pants and circle to the sides, finding my hips.

His fingers stay there, sliding along my hip bones, back and forth in that narrow groove. I press into him, and his hands move lower, every touch searing, sending a burn so deep—

"Will, this is torture!"

His deep laugh fills the night air. "You like that, then."

"I can't even . . . I can't even think—"

"That's the idea," he says, hands now on my pants, unbuttoning them, zipper coming down . . .

"I know we're supposed to go slow," I say. "But, this time—"

I almost laugh out loud at the absurdity, realizing I've lived a sex-by-the-numbers existence until now. You do this, then this, next step, next step . . . Like my entire life up to this point.

He doesn't answer as he removes my boots, then socks—ooh, the rocks are hot, like they were at the springs near Mammoth Lakes. His hands return to my waist, and he pulls my pants down. Down, down, down, and off.

"Will . . . ," I start, but then I hear the gentle *swish, swish* as he removes the rest of his clothes.

"Just wait," he whispers.

He must have kneeled, because now his hands glide up my legs and move over my torso. A kiss to my navel. Another just above. His lips press gently against my abdomen, one slow kiss after another, moving sensually upward, until his fingers smooth over my breasts which swell and harden under his touch.

"Oh god, Will—"

He finds my mouth again, and his lips press hard against mine. A guttural sound issues from the back of his throat, his kiss deepening, just as the clouds knit together, closing our picture window to the stars.

I'm pummeled with sensory overload. The wholesome fragrance of him, like earth and pine. The sound of his breath washing across my cheeks, echoing, roaring in my ears. His slow-beating heart pounding as if it were in my own chest. Every touch heightened, every sensation amplified in the all-consuming darkness.

I thought we'd move into the water. I'm sure Will thought the same. A romantic interlude in a hot spring? What could be better? But as the heat explodes between us, my body molded to his . . . it's too much. The notion of a dip in the spring quickly goes by the wayside as he lowers me to the flat rocks next to the pool, where the sensory overload bumps up one more notch—my backside warm like butter, my front rippling with goose bumps as snowflakes dot across my skin.

"Ooh, it's cold!" I say with a shiver.

"It won't be in just a second."

I hear him move away. The zip of a zipper. The ripping of paper.

A condom. Thank god he has one.

He moves over me, his body weight settling. Instant warmth.

And in this blackest of black, there's nothing to cling to visually, fostering an intense connection to the warm-blooded being who hovers over me, now in me, all of him, becoming all of me. We move as one, no more holding back, and soar into oblivion.

The clouds pull apart to allow another peek at the cosmos, the stars winking their approval. My head presses firmly into Will's chest, his arm wrapped securely around me, one side of my brain absorbed in the forever of the universe, the other trying to decide if I'm hot or cold.

I burrow my head further, and Will responds by extending his other arm across me and pulling me close for a light kiss on the forehead.

"Cold?" he asks.

"I can't decide, but I think you're tipping the scales toward warmer than colder."

"We can go, if you want."

"No, no. I could stay here all night. Just like this."

"Really?"

"Yeah, really."

"You know . . . ," he says, shifting. "We *could* stay here, and we wouldn't have to be completely exposed like this. I have my tent in my pack. A sleeping bag, too."

"I guess you would, wouldn't you? For your trip . . ."

"So what do you think?"

"I don't know. I've never slept in a tent before."

I don't need any illumination to know he wears an incredulous look on his face.

"You've *never* been in a tent before?"

"I was an indoor girl, remember?"

"That still does not compute with me."

"Well, yeah. The closest I got to the outdoors was my aunt Celia's lodge on the Walker River. I thought it was so rugged, staying in a *cabin*."

I feel his head shaking as his chin brushes the top of my head. "Just gimme a couple minutes."

A light rummaging sound, and then the light is near-blinding when he twists on his headlamp.

"Here," he says, handing me my clothes. "We can get dressed first, then put everything together."

He dresses quickly, then begins to pull things out of his North Face bag. This is followed by the clinking of metal as he snaps aluminum poles together and lays them across the yellow nylon material he has spread on the ground.

I don my clothes, pulling on my boots last, not bothering with the laces. But at least I'm covered now. "May I help you?"

"Sure, you can thread these poles through the loops there," he says. "They run diagonally and insert into the straps at the ends."

I oblige, sliding the poles crossways and snapping them into the grommets built into the webbing at each corner. But when I stand back, the tent promptly collapses, twisting awkwardly in the middle.

"Uh, Will, I think I missed something."

He tries to stifle the laugh, but it escapes anyway. "These are supposed to cross in the center. Like this." He talks as he works to undo my mess. "Easy mistake."

"Sorry."

"Hey, it's how we learn, right?"

"Well, you've done a fine job of scrambling my brain tonight, just so you know."

"Good," he says, chuckling.

Will works on the last pole—click, click, click—snapping the final section into place. "This one's for the entry, and then we should be all set." He slides it through the loops, and the material bends, forming an arched entryway.

He turns back to his duffel and removes a sleeping bag, the one from Basin Mountain. Releasing it from its stuff sack, he rolls it out inside the tent.

"There we go," he says, wiping his hands.

"Home away from home," I say.

He turns to me, arms dropping, the oddest expression crossing his face.

"What is it?" I ask.

He approaches me, taking both my hands in his. "This *is* home. I mean, it's home for a lot of the year, depending on where I am in the world." He shifts his feet. Stalling? Nervous? "But that's not exactly right, either. Truthfully, home is wherever I am at the moment. I don't have—"

"Stop," I say, squeezing his hands. "I guess I'm home, then."

31

I open my eyes to a tent suffused in light. Naked and blissfully warm in my sleeping bag, I stare at the yellow dome above me. The haze of sleep lifts, and I'm flooded with memories of a singularly transcendent night with Will.

Will . . .

Smiling, I peek out from my downy enclosure, my nose and ears nipped in greeting by the chill morning air.

I search for my clothes, which lie haphazardly discarded in the corner, and dress within the warm confines of my sleeping bag. I rub my eyes—teeth, too, using my finger as a toothbrush—and swipe the hair away from my face. Unzipping the front flap of the tent, I step out to a most glorious sight.

A tough little fire leaps in yellows and reds, crackling and snapping, emitting a woody, tangy odor, like cedar. Next to it, a healthy blanket of steam hides the hot spring that bubbles beneath, all of this surrounded by the now fully visible lofty pines, layered in white, sixty, seventy, eighty feet high. A thin layer of snow coats the ground, and the clouds hang heavy—another morning without sun, a sun that has been absent for more than a week. And in the middle of it all, one Will Cavanaugh, perched on a log next to the fire, wool hat on his head, stubble on his face, pulling a coffeepot from its stone resting platform and pouring a cup.

"Coffee?" he asks.

"Are you kidding?"

He moves over to give me room, and I take my place next to him. Reaching for the cup, I bring it under my chin, the steam washing over my face.

"Thank you."

"Anytime."

I take a cautious first sip, blowing first, not expecting the delicious flavor of . . . "Mint?" I ask.

He smiles, pleased. "You like it?"

"Very much," I say, taking another drink. "But how did you—?"

"Added it to the coffee grounds. Great for the flavor, don't you think?"

I nod, sipping. "I've only tried it with tea, but this is great in coffee. I had no idea."

He watches me, a playful look on his face. "You know, for an indoor girl, you seem to take to the outdoor life pretty easily."

"Tent skills aside, yeah, I think I could warm to this," I say, leaning into him. "What can I say? The snow, the trees, the stars. It made what we shared last night . . ."

I'm unable to finish, because I don't know that I'll ever have the words to describe it. And not just what happened by the spring. We shared the same sleeping bag, so . . . The lovemaking was slower then, but every bit as intense. I find his eyes, and here they hold, steam from my cup curling softly between us.

"That was . . . beyond anything I could have ever imagined," he says.

"And beyond the best birthday present I could have ever imagined," I say.

"What's this? It's your birthday?"

"Actually, no. It's tomorrow. But close enough."

He leans in, brushing his lips softly against mine. "Happy birthday."

"Thank you," I say, drawing back with a smile.

We sip our coffee, our shoulders pressed together, and soak in the warmth of the fire. I'm so utterly content, I let my eyes shutter closed.

"Do you think you can stay over tomorrow?" he asks. "We could celebrate."

"I have duty, unfortunately."

"You're standing duty on your birthday?"

"Gotta love the navy. Isn't the first time. Won't be the last."

"Well, we're gonna need a makeup day for sure."

I open my eyes and turn to him. "I'm all for that, especially if it's like . . . well, what it's been like the last twenty-four hours."

"I'm sure I can arrange that," he says, skimming his hand across my cheek.

"So where are we, by the way?" I say, looking up, around.

"I guess we never got to that, did we?"

"Uh, no," I say, with a small laugh. "So is this another locals-only hot spring?"

"Actually, no. This is private property."

"Oh. Are we trespassing then?"

"You think *I* would trespass?"

"Well . . . yeah, for a sweet hot spring like this?"

"True," he says, with a wink.

Are these words really leaving my mouth? Condoning trespassing? Talking about it in fun? I think I can officially say I've been unmade since coming to Fallon. But the weird part is, I like this new Alison far better. She's not as hard on herself. Doesn't sweat the small stuff. She tries new things. Takes chances. Even ventures on the occasional rogue criminal outing.

"Although, this time, it's legit," he says.

"Why, did you get permission or something?"

"Well, yeah, I guess you could say that. I own the property, so I gave myself permission."

"You *own* this?"

"You look shocked! Is that so far-fetched?"

"Well, I just thought, you know," I say, pointing to his tent. "Your said this was your home . . . and then, you live with Jack . . . and it's okay, it's totally okay. I don't care where you live. This tent life is pretty awesome, if you ask me."

"You think so?"

"Yeah, I really do. And I meant what I said last night. My home is with you, wherever that might be at the time." I look down to the half-full coffee mug in my hand, knowing I have spoken the heartfelt truth. I remember the same contentment in the mine tunnel in Basin Mountain. No urge to go or do. I couldn't pinpoint the reason at the time, but now I know. It was him. He was there, and I was with him. And so I was content. I was home.

"Although, I have to admit, I'm glad you weren't trespassing. If we're living in a tent on *your* property, I'll breathe easier."

He looks at me for some time. "You really don't mind this, do you?"

I shake my head. "I was warm last night. We have food and water and . . . coffee," I say, lifting my mug in a small caffeine salute. "I'm not sure what you do long-term about bathroom facilities, but other than that . . ." I shrug my shoulders, bringing the cup to my lips for another sip.

Rich would be aghast at this conversation. He has all the comforts, and I don't think he could imagine living without them. And for most of my twenty-eight years on this earth, *I* couldn't have imagined living without them. But the more that's stripped from me, the longer I do without, the more liberating it becomes. Like the dull pencil run through the automatic sharpener, I've become honed, tightened, balanced. Everything is clearer. More present. More real. Will is real. What we share is real.

"I'm glad that you say that, but, uh, the tent thing. You don't have to worry about that. The tent is just for trips. I'm staying with Jack, so you won't have to be subjected to this too much."

"Subjected? Far from it. This is amazing, every bit of it. It's just a bonus that you get to live at Jack's."

"No," he says, tipping his coffee cup back, draining it. "I said, I'm *staying* with Jack. I don't live there."

"Okay, so I'm confused."

He stands, offering me his hand. "Care to talk a walk? I think I can help with your confusion."

He steps into the forest, not on any path that I can discern, but a decidedly upward trek. We zig twenty or so steps one way, zag twenty or so steps another, weaving through pines mixed with aspen, back and forth, snow deeper here—crunch, crunch, crunch of the boots—our exhalations floating away in icy puffs as we make our way up.

I glance behind us, Will's tent and my car already out of view. The only indicators of where we just stood are the smoke from the fire and steam from the hot spring. Up and up, the trees begin to thin, and then, as if growing out of the forest itself, sturdy stilts rise solidly in front of us, spaced at ten-foot intervals, supporting a patio made of diagonally running slats of wood. Hiking further, I see the house attached to the patio. The second level is wrapped in glass, like Jack's house. Then a third level. More glass. I look behind us again. The house's location affords sweeping views above the trees to the high mountains and a lake I don't recognize. My hand moves to my mouth, my breath catching in my throat.

"Would you like to see inside?" he asks.

"What is this?"

"My house," he says, unable to contain his grin.

"This . . . this is . . . like Jack's . . ."

"It should be. I designed both of them."

I turn, dropping his hand, stunned. "You . . . designed . . . Jack's . . . house?"

"And his guesthouse, where I'm staying now, while this one is finished."

My mouth opens wide and stays open, but Will playfully reaches for my jaw, and closes it.

"Did you *build* this?" I say, waving my hand at the elegant—yes, another—log mansion. "Like actually build it? Or—"

"I designed it and then headed up the team that built it. That's what I do for a living, besides guiding, that is. Jack and I are part owners of a construction company that designs and builds homes."

"I had no . . ." I finish the sentence with a shake of the head, incredulous.

"So do you want to see it?"

"Yes, I want to see it!"

He leads me to the front entry, through the broad double doors, and we enter the foyer. As in Jack's home, my eyes are drawn to the far glass wall and a panoramic alpine view that leaves me speechless.

"What do you think?"

I step down one, two, three, four stairs, one more than in Jack's home, moving forward through a living room empty of furniture to the windows. "I don't even know what to say. This is extraordinary. Just extraordinary."

"Jack agreed to let me design his house first, so I could try out ideas for this one. Sort of my guinea pig."

"That was awfully big of him."

"Yeah, he reminds me all the time how he stepped up, that I owe him, blah, blah, blah."

"You two have the most amazing relationship. . . ."

And this time I can honestly say my sentiment comes without wistfulness. Jack is part of Will's life, which means he's now a part of mine. And Jack acts . . . well, fatherly. Our relationship is already a good one, and now I can look forward to it becoming even closer.

"Yeah, it's pretty special," he says, opening the door to the balcony.

We step out, which is really like stepping in—into the forest, that is.

"You know," Will says. "I've told you about my parents, about my relationship with Jack. But how about you? Mother? Father?"

I move to the wooden railing and place my hands there, sliding my fingers along the smooth finish.

"My mom and I are pretty close. We've had to be." My voice drops along with my head. As I stare at the railing, it dawns on me that Will doesn't know about my father yet. Doesn't realize that the girl he first kissed in an airport baggage claim carries—oh god, are you kidding me?—baggage.

"What is it?"

I look up. A steadying breath. "My father left us, when I was four years old."

"Oh, boy."

"So I should warn you, you're dealing with someone who has some serious security issues."

He pulls me around to face him, wrapping his arms around my shoulders. "Consider me warned," he says, then kisses me gently on the forehead. "So how did you and your mom get along after he left?"

"We did okay. Mom remarried a year and a half later. Nick was nice, he provided for us well. He died five years ago in a car accident."

"I'm sorry."

"I'd been out of the house for many years when it happened, and we were never that close. But what I just learned—and we're talking only within the last two weeks here—is that my mom still loves my real father, has loved him all along. I always thought she hated him for leaving us. I know I did . . . still do."

Poor Will. He had no idea he was signing up for something like this.

"Has it changed the way you feel about him? The fact that your mother still loves him?"

"I don't know yet. I still can't see under what circumstance you would leave your wife to fend for herself and her four-year-old, not to mention leaving the four-year-old herself. I don't know that I can ever forgive him for that."

I look beyond Will, to a lake that peeks through the forest, one muted gray by the low clouds. It's some time before I return my gaze to him.

"I have to admit, when you first told me about your relationship with Jack, I felt a little jealous. And then meeting him . . . I just wish I'd had that."

"Well, I know it's not much consolation, but going forward, you *will* have that," he says. "Jack thinks the world of you."

A smile slips across my face.

"In fact, I can't wait to tell him. You know, about us."

"Where does Jack live? From here, I mean."

"Over the ridge, to the west."

"So what's this lake then?" I ask, grateful that the snow is holding off long enough to allow a view like this. Although, it's grown steadily warmer this morning. If the clouds decided to let loose now, I suspect we'd get rain, not snow.

"That's Silver Lake. A little more tucked-away, just like this house."

"*Why* aren't you living here?"

"I probably could, but we're still finishing up some things." He turns, puts his arm around my shoulder, and leads me back inside.

"But you were going to leave . . . for months. How do you do this between trips?"

"My crew and I work on it, chunks at a time, on a not-to-interfere basis with our other jobs. This house has been a work in progress for over four years now."

"Wait," I say, turning to face him. "That's not going to change . . . is it?" I say it more as a statement than a question, a lump forming in my throat. "You're going to be leaving . . . on trips . . . antsy."

He reaches forward, taking both of my hands in his. "Alison, about the antsy thing. I said that out of frustration. I said a lot of things out of frustration that day. I do take trips for the purposes of guiding, but I have a lot more leeway now. Our construction business does well enough that I don't *have* to leave. But, then again, I've never had a reason to stay." He leans in, pressing his cheek to mine, a light kiss on the ear. "Until now, that is."

32

"It's really getting warm," I say, pulling the hood of my jacket up to shield my head from the rain.

"Can you grab that last bag?" Will asks. "I think we can make it one trip, then."

I pull the last grocery bag from the back of my truck, and, arms full, shuffle through the entrance to Jack's guest cottage.

"Just set it there," Will says, indicating the kitchen table.

I enter a breakfast nook surrounded by bay windows, and set the bags down. I'm treated to an intimate view of the forest, which slopes gently downward, eventually terminating on the shores of what I now know is June Lake's neighbor, Gull Lake.

"The thermometer's reading fifty-one," he says. "How's that for a weather swing?"

We were up to our ears in snow last week, winter-storm warnings, roads closed, the whole Basin Mountain debacle—twelve new feet of snow in that storm alone—followed by three days of "warm" rain from the alien clouds. And when the first rainstorm passed on Friday night, it did so just in time for one of the final air wing exercises, the one that took Snoopy's life.

There will be a memorial, of course. There always is . . .

Too many friends lost. Too young. Too early. Peacetime. Wartime. In training. On deployment. Losses that remain with you, permanently woven into your soul, stretching your heart and mind to the breaking point, until you're left questioning everything, and believing nothing.

I stare out the windows, a steady patter of rain and slush sliding off the roof, landing with hollow *whumps*.

"I don't think I've ever experienced such crazy weather in my life," I say, turning back to the table and joining Will in unpacking the food.

"I know. I always chalk it up to life in the high mountains, but I think I'd have to agree with you. This is unusual even for here."

He moves to the refrigerator, opening it, and I pass him a carton of eggs, a gallon of milk—the basics. Will had emptied his refrigerator, thinking he'd be gone for several weeks, so we stopped at the general store and loaded up on supplies.

"I think pancakes are definitely in order," he says, pointing to the box of Bisquick and a heaping carton of blueberries.

"Sounds perfect." I remove the maple syrup from the last bag and set it on the counter. Behind me, the cupboards bang and glass clinks as Will removes bowls, pans, and spoons and begins his pancake preparations. "Would you like some help?" I ask.

"No, thanks. I've got this. But you're welcome to look around, if you like."

From the kitchen, I move into the adjacent living room—yet another space built with a wall of glass. "This seems to be your signature design item," I say, pointing to the floor-to-ceiling windows.

The kitchen and living area here, unlike the ones in the house he built for Jack, are separated by a wall, bringing a far more intimate feeling to the cottage. Snug, and yet open, owing to the windows.

He peers around the corner. "Yeah, I can't bear to wall that off." He looks reverently to the forest, touches of green now showing through the white. "Originally, the glass was Jack's idea, and once we tried it, well, now I can't do it any other way."

I then look to the worn—but in a good way—leather couches

encircling a wood-burning fireplace. Large, hard-backed picture books are stacked on an oversized square coffee table console in the middle. I pick up the hefty one on top, titled *The Mont Blanc Massif.* Leafing through the pages, I see it's written in French.

Replacing the book, I glance to the wall that separates the kitchen from the living room—the wall opposite the fireplace—with its built-in bookshelves, positively crammed with reading material. "You have *so* many books."

"We get snowed in a lot, so yeah," he says, calling from the kitchen. I hear the sizzle as the first dollop of pancake batter hits the griddle.

It's then that I notice that he doesn't have a television. Not in this room, anyway. I wonder if he has one at all. . . .

I wander into the master bedroom and flip on the light switch. Two lamps, placed on nightstands on either side of a quaint double bed, flicker on. A carved wooden headboard anchors the bed, which is covered in a forest-green quilted down comforter. With a mild hint of resin in the air, the room breathes life and warmth.

Draped at the foot of the bed, a crocheted red throw provides a splash of rustic color, and a matching wooden armoire and dresser complete the simple furnishings. Unlike the outside walls of the kitchen and living room, the outside wall here is solid, constructed with dense, sturdy wood and only a small curtained window to let in light. In the low glow of the lamps, the space is the definition of cozy.

I start when Will sneaks up behind me, sliding his hands around my waist. "Your pancakes are ready," he says, nuzzling his face into my neck.

"This room . . ."

"What about it?"

"It's so . . . homey."

He moves around to face me, placing his hands lightly on my waist. "More than the tent?" he asks, grinning.

I nod. "More than the tent."

His eyes, dilated now in the relative dimness, settle on mine, and the grin slips from his face.

"What is it?"

"I was wondering if it's too early to say what I'm feeling for you. I've heard the 'L' word can send women running for the hills."

"I'm not going anywhere, Will."

He reaches for my hand and pulls me to sit next to him on the bed.

"I've never said it to a woman before," he says, looking at our hands, bringing them to rest on his leg. "And I always wondered if I would know. But there's no question of it."

"This is going to sound awful, but I *have* said it. The only difference is I *didn't* know. Not until now."

He continues looking down, but I see it when he flinches.

"I'm sorry. I shouldn't have said that."

"No, it's not that at all. How could I expect any different? You were engaged. . . ."

He looks up. "I never told you how it made me feel that day when we came off Basin Mountain. When we got to the airport, and he took you in his arms . . ." Will winces again, a glimpse of the very same anguish I saw that day in Bishop. "I've been physically hurt plenty of times in my life, but I've never felt pain like that. Ever. Like being sliced from the inside. And I knew I shouldn't feel that way. It wasn't my right. You had pledged yourself to him and—"

I reach my hand to his face, placing my palm against his cheek. "I love you, Will Cavanaugh. My heart only has room for one, and it's you. Only you."

He covers my hand with his, drawing it over his chest, holding it there, his steady heartbeat reverberating through my fingers.

"I love you, Alison Malone," he says, letting the words hang in the resin-scented air. "It feels good to say that out loud." He presses my hand against his chest then curls his fingers around mine. "But even better is hearing it from you. That's what I realized, when I was standing at the airport in Bishop. It wouldn't have mattered what I was feeling for you if it wasn't reciprocated. And I didn't think it was at the time. It was a . . . despair—that's the only word for it—unlike anything I've ever experienced."

I squeeze his hand, and lean forward, gently touching my lips to his. "You don't have to worry about that anymore. Okay?"

"Okay," he whispers.

"So, um, how about those pancakes?"

The smile I was hoping for appears. "Coming right up."

33

Will places the stack of pancakes on the kitchen table, and I follow with the butter dish and syrup. We make coffee, too—a complete breakfast—even though it's now approaching three in the afternoon.

The snow continues to melt, sloughing over the roof's edge, cascading in a slow-motion sort of quasi rain while the real rain falls steadily everywhere else. On the ground, the once-smooth layer of white is now pocked with deformations, narrow rivulets running through it like capillaries, carrying the snowmelt into the forest, and ultimately to Gull Lake below.

"Better late than never," Will says, seating himself. *"Bon appétit!"*

We're just spreading the butter when we hear the knocks on the door.

"Excuse me," he says, rising.

I can't see the front door from where I sit, but I hear a light swishing when it opens.

"What are you doing here?" Jack asks.

"Uh, change of plans," Will says. "Come on in."

A jacket is shrugged off, probably finding a place on one of the coat pegs that hang adjacent to the door. The voices grow louder as Jack and Will near the kitchen, preceded by the scuttle of paws against hardwood. Mojo races around the corner—a blur of wet fur—and practically tackles me in my chair.

"I didn't recognize the car in front," Jack says, "so I thought I'd better come check—" They round the corner, and Jack jumps backward, running into Will.

"Well, I'll be . . . ," Jack says, once steady.

"Would you like to join us?" Will asks.

"Be happy to," Jack says, pulling out a chair. "Mojo, give the girl some space." He reaches for Mojo's collar and gives a gentle tug. The dog drops down, but remains staunchly beside me.

Jack sits, pivots to me, and stares with a shit-eating grin on his face. "Soooo, just stopping by or . . . ?"

"That doesn't sound like your normal forward self," I say.

"True enough. Let me rephrase that. Have you both pulled your heads out of your assess and realized you're in love with each other?" Jack picks up two pancakes from the main stack and drops them on his plate, then goes about his preparations, adding butter and syrup.

"There's the Jack we know and love," Will says. "I probably would have put it a little more delicately than that, but that's the gist of it, yes."

I place my hand over Jack's arm. "You were right," I say softly.

He tries to hide it, but the emotion wells, and he looks away, joking and gesturing to cover it up. But I saw.

"So, I reckon you'll be staying put for a while then, William?"

"I will indeed," Will says, seating himself.

"But what about the documentary?" I ask. "The magazine?"

"My heart wouldn't be into it. Not now. There'll be other opportunities, so don't worry about that."

"He's right. You two need quality time," Jack says, mouth close to full. "Damn, these pancakes are good! I should drop by more often."

"You know you're always welcome," Will says.

"Hey wait! That means you'll be here for Thanksgiving! Any plans yet?" Jack says, turning to me.

"We, uh, hadn't gotten around to discussing that," I say.

"Let's not smother her, Jack. We just . . . well, you know."

"I'm not smothering. I'm just asking if you two would like to join me for Thanksgiving, that's all."

"Well," I say, looking between the two. "I would love to, except that I've already made plans with my mother. She's driving over—"

"She's invited, too, of course," Jack says.

"Alison, don't feel like you have to do this. Jack can be a little—"

"A little what, William?"

"It's fine, Will. I'm sure she'd love to come."

As I say this, my brain makes the leap to planning mode, suddenly contemplating holiday logistics—dinner with one side of the family, dessert with the other—*those* kinds of logistics. *What am I doing?*

I can't accept an invitation like this. I can't speak for my mom. And what about Celia?

But I want my mom to meet Will. To meet Will's family. And the lodge is only a little more than an hour's drive north of here, so . . .

Call it rushed, but since she's in the area, why not? It would be perfect. And I bet Celia would be game for it, too.

I look up. More rapping on the door.

"What the heck?" Will asks, rising again.

The door swishes. "Mr. Cavanaugh!" Boomer says.

Boomer?

Shake of a jacket, splatter of water on the hardwood floor, a swish as the jacket is hung on a peg.

"I was supposed to meet Jack, but no one—" He stops almost as suddenly as Jack did as he rounds the corner. "Vanilla?"

"Care for some pancakes?" Will asks, rolling his eyes. He has no idea how funny I find that.

"Hell, yeah, I want some pancakes!" Boomer drops into the seat next to me.

"Help yourself," Will says. "I'll whip up some more." Will returns to the refrigerator—more milk, more eggs, more blueberries—and starts to mix more batter.

"So is this . . . ?" Boomer asks, jerking a thumb in my direction, but looking at Jack.

"It is indeed," Jack says.

"God damn it." Boomer reaches into his back pocket and pulls out his billfold. He opens it, removes a twenty-dollar bill, and hands it to Jack.

Jack receives it, clearly delighted, snapping it taut a few times before sliding it into his wallet.

"What's this?" I ask.

"Just a little side wager," Jack says. "I knew you two would get together eventually."

"You made a bet on that?" I ask, turning on Boomer.

"Hey, don't look at me. That was all Jack."

"But you bet *against* us?" Oddly, I'm not concerned about the wager itself, but on which side Boomer fell.

"Well . . . yeah. But that was before I met your fiancé at the airport."

"Oh," I say. My face goes red. "I haven't had the chance to apologize to you about that. And to Walt and everyone else. He was just—"

"Yeah, I know. *Worried*," Boomer says. "But, Jesus . . ."

"This arrangement is infinitely more palatable," Jack says, moving a finger back and forth between Will and me. "Am I right?"

"Even though I'm twenty dollars poorer, yes, sir, you are correct."

"You're coming to Thanksgiving, right?" Jack says to Boomer.

"Wouldn't miss it."

"How many—?" I start.

Jack reads my mind. "Don't worry. It's just Boomer."

Whew. Because a Thanksgiving with the entire SAR team, while wonderful, would be a bit much for my mom to walk into.

Will returns to the table and refills the empty platter of pancakes. "Care for some coffee?"

"Please," Boomer says.

"Yeah, me, too," Jack says.

"Comin' up."

"So, Boomer, why are you here?" I ask.

"We're meeting a bunch of the guys in Mammoth to play pool. Where, by the way, I fully intend on winning my money back." He directs a pointed look at Jack.

"In your dreams, man."

As Jack and Boomer banter, and Will serves coffee, something way deep down starts to niggle. A warning flag. This is too good.

And I realize I've let myself drift too far from Self-Defense 101. I know all too well that the universe exists in balance, the highs equaling the lows. And this moment is very high. Too high. Which would require an equalizing moment, something equivalently low. But then, the event that preceded this was abysmally low. Snoopy . . .

So maybe the universe has indeed had its say, and the balance is intact.

". . . just like you acted in Spain," Will says. "Your birthday, remember? Your mother—"

"Do not bring my mother into this!" Jack says, pealing with laughter.

"Wait. Speaking of birthdays . . ." Will stops and turns to Boomer. "Any chance you could tweak the duty schedule tomorrow? It's Alison's birthday. I wanted to see if I could keep her for one more day."

"Well now, Vanilla, how bad do you want the day off? It's me you'd be trading with."

"You would take my duty?"

"I could . . . you know, for the right price."

"How about twenty?"

"Done."

"Jack, can I borrow twenty dollars?" I ask.

Boomer snaps his open palm in front of Jack. "Love her."

"May I remind you, Alison, that he bet *against* you," Jack says, leaning over and pulling his wallet out of his pocket.

"Don't worry," I say. "I'll pay you back."

"So back to *your* birthday, Jack," Will says.

"Do we really need to revisit this? Like right now?" Jack says, dropping his wallet on the table.

"I think it's a grand time to revisit it," Boomer says. He turns to me. "I love this story."

"Rule number one," Will says, laughing. "Never raise the ire of Magdalena!"

Jack throws up his hands, and Boomer shakes in laughter.

"Who was Magdalena, again?" I ask.

"Jack's mother," Will says. "All Spanish passion and fury!"

"To this day!" Jack adds. "And she's—what now?—eighty years old!"

"Where's she from?" I say. Something spatters about in my ears. I look out the window. The rain makes the same sound. That must be it.

"Spain," Jack answers. "She—"

"She could probably chase you into that tunnel today!" Wills says, his chair tipping backward as he clutches his hands to his stomach, embracing a belly-aching laugh.

"No, I mean, what city?"

"Bielsa," Jack says. "It's in the Pyrenees."

"The Pyrenees . . ." I whisper.

Spatter, spatter, spatter.

Will, Boomer, and Jack continue with their bantering, their well-timed guffaws, snorts of laughter—a whimsical din that swirls and surrounds the kitchen table—while I recede from the conversation, whisked out as swiftly as an ebbing tide.

I ease myself into the back of my chair, and I look at Jack. Really look.

No . . .

No, that's ridiculous.

". . . never forget her face!" Will says. "Running . . ." He's laughing so hard, he's having trouble finishing the sentence. ". . . with a stick!" He pushes his chair away from the table, stands and wags a finger. "¡Vas a ver cuando lo agarre!" Will says, in a high-pitched voice and a perfect Spanish accent, before dropping into his chair again, his chest heaving, while he wipes at unruly tears.

Boomer and Jack are doubled over, all three of them now howling. Always the bantering between them . . .

"Oh, no. The home team is on this year!" Jack said.

"The home team might not be the home team anymore!" Boomer said.

"No way. The good people of Sacramento would never let it happen," Jack said.

The home team . . . Sacramento . . .

No . . . No way.

Jack looks in my direction. Once. Twice. Realization dawning that I'm staring.

"Alison?" he says, attempting to catch his breath. "Looks like you've tasted something you'd rather spit up than swallow."

Boomer and Will turn their mirthful gazes to me, the snorts and chuckles still escaping.

"You're from Sacramento," I say, not asking, but stating.

"I lived there for a time, yeah. How'd you know that?"

"Where?"

Jack looks at Boomer and Will, puzzled. "You mean, where exactly in Sacramento?"

"Yes."

The three observe me curiously, like a zoo animal behind bars. Laughter dying away . . .

"I lived in a neighborhood called South Land Park. Why?"

My body stills. The rain roars in my ears, drowning all other sounds, while the blood drains from my head.

No way. There's just no way. Think of the odds, Ali. There's just . . . and while one side of my brain pounces on all the reasons this chain of thought is preposterous, the other side absorbs Jack's darker olive skin color . . . the one that matches mine. The teardrop-shaped, upturned brown eyes . . . brown eyes that peer into my same brown eyes.

And what is it . . . what is it . . . ?

It's the eyes. The raccoon eyes . . . the photos in Jack's house . . . the ski goggles. That's it! That's what it was! In the other photos, the goggles were the same. They were the same brand as the ones I had in my toy box in kindergarten. . . . *Holy shit.*

"You were married," I say.

What are you doing, Alison?

"What's up with you, Vanilla?" Boomer says. "You're acting like the host on *This Is Your Life.*" He turns to Jack. "You're old enough, Jack! Ha! You remember that show."

Boomer laughs, but Jack does not.

"I don't know what—" Jack stutters.

"Married?" Will says. "Alison, Jack's never been married."

"What was her name?" I ask, my eyes not leaving Jack's.

"I . . . ," Jack starts. Blinks. Leans forward. Looking at me . . . like I look at him.

A seismic shift in his expression, one probably mirroring my own—a movie moment when the actor has just been shot in the chest—surprise, horror, incredulity, all wrapped into one.

"Alison?" Will says. "Alison, what's going on? Jack was never—"

"Candy," Jack says.

The world wobbles, the earth kicked off its axis.

"Holy shit," Jack says, leaning back. "It's your birthday tomorrow." His eyes flit back and forth, his brain working a million miles an hour. "*Your* birthday . . . November twenty-fourth . . ."

"I'm going to be—"

"Twenty-nine," he finishes.

Our gazes remain locked. In the periphery, a shrugging of shoulders and a shaking of heads from Boomer and Will.

"Alison? Jack? What's going on?" Will says, any trace of the conversation's earlier humor gone.

"You named your daughter Magdalena, after your mother," I say. My lip starts to quiver and Jack's olive-skinned, brown-eyed face goes blurry behind my watering eyes.

"Daughter?" Will says. "Jack? What's she talking about?" He turns to me. "What are you talking about?"

Jack pales, assuming the same still form as the statue that gapes at him.

"No . . . ," he whispers. "It just can't be."

"You called her Magpie."

Jack covers his mouth with a shaking hand.

"Jack . . . ?" Will says. "Please. What the hell is going on?"

I finally pull my eyes from Jack to look at Will. "He called me Magpie. A nickname for my given name, Magdalena. It's the only memory I have of my father."

34

The air is suffocating in its stillness. For seconds? Minutes? Jack, white as a sheet. Boomer, openmouthed. Will, mirroring Boomer. Me, a face wet with tears. Of joy, of sorrow, of pain, something lost, something found, regret, anger, elation. So tangled in opposing emotions, my body remains locked, my breaths coming short and shallow. Outside, the rain beats harder.

Boomer is the first to recover. "Screw the coffee. I'm breaking out the scotch."

"You know where it is," Will says, not taking his eyes from me.

Boomer rummages through a cabinet, but my eyes return to . . . my father. Jack.

"The name listed on my birth certificate for my father is Juan Gonzales Smith," I say.

Jack brings his shaking hands to his lap, holding his legs to try to quiet them. "Juan is Spanish for John," he says, his voice rough. "Jack is just a nickname."

"And Gonzales Smith?"

"My father was American. David Smith. My mother is Spanish. Magdalena Gonzales Alvarez."

Boomer returns, four short tumblers crimped in the fingers of one hand, a bottle of Johnnie Walker Red in the other.

"We didn't . . ." He speaks in a daze as Boomer pours and pushes glasses to each of us. "We didn't follow convention. Normally, *el nombre de mi madre*, my mother's name, would go last. But since my father was . . . he was sick . . ." He wraps his still-shaking fingers around the tumbler.

"Might as well drink up," Boomer says. "I think we could all use it."

I've had my fair share of alcoholic drinks at the highfalutin fancy parties I've attended with Rich, but only in politely sipped doses. I lift my glass, gulping the drink in one go. I wince as it burns hot down my throat, jarring me from the stillness.

I reach for Will's hand, which he readily gives, squeezing it tightly.

"But your name is . . . Magdalena Alison Gonzales Smith. Not Alison Malone," Jack says.

"Mom had my legal named changed. Malone was my stepfather's name."

"But Maggie. We called you Maggie."

The anger, the hurt, rears its head. "I suppose it was difficult for her to choke out your mother's name after you left us."

Boomer refills my glass. Jack's, too. He emptied it when I did.

"Why didn't you tell me this?" Will asks, staring at Jack.

Bits of incredulity, horror, flit across his face, and I realize this revelation is probably affecting him almost as much as it is me. Jack has been Will's father for all intents and purposes for over sixteen years. His best friend. His partner. Heck, his business partner. Will even designed and helped build his home for him. I think of all the days, weeks, and months these two have spent together on hikes to base camps, sleeping on portaledges on rock faces thousands of feet in the air, sitting next to each other on long overseas flights, and even visiting each other in their hospital beds. In all that time, amid every intimate, personal conversation, the topic obviously never came up. A skeleton of staggering proportions. I read it on Will's face as clearly as if he had spoken it. Deceived. Duped. Lied to.

Jack's face crumples. "I was so ashamed, Will. I made the biggest mistake of my life, when I left my family. I was only twenty-one when she was born," he says, eyes briefly drifting to me before returning to Will. "So goddamn young and immature. But I tried. I did. Candy said I needed to settle down. Get a real job. I had a responsibility now. I just . . . I couldn't do it. Me? In a suit and tie?"

"You called her Candy," I say. "No one has ever called her that."

He pinches his eyes shut, but the tears can't be stopped. "I loved her so much. God, more than my own life, I loved her." Shakily, he takes another drink. "We met in Yosemite. In Camp Four. She was one of the most talented climbers there."

"What?" I say, my breath leaving me. "No . . . she never . . . impossible."

"We were on the search and rescue team together. SAR was our life. She was so brave. Selfless."

My head moves back and forth. No . . .

"When we found out she was pregnant, we celebrated. So happy. You were such happy news. And when you were born . . . I'll never forget it. I thought to myself, nothing will ever top this moment in my life. Nothing."

He brings his hands to his face and wipes his eyes. "We moved to Sacramento from Yosemite. Time to be responsible. To provide for you. But I just . . . I couldn't switch gears. Your mom, she was amazing. She adapted. So strong. So reliant. Holy god, just like you." The tears rush this time, his shoulders heaving. He puts his head in his hands, sobbing.

I slump back in my chair, turning to Will, looking at the man I love with every fiber of my being. And I doubt I ever could have appreciated what Jack felt for my mother, had I not experienced it myself.

His voice shakes as he continues. "I got a job. I went to that office every day, nine to five, for four years. And finally, I told her, I can't do this anymore. I was sure I could make my way doing what I loved. What she loved. We could guide or go back to the SAR team . . . or something. But she put her foot down. Said we couldn't raise a child in a tent. We owed her more than that. Owed *you* more," he qualifies.

"I asked her to let me try. I had to try. She wouldn't hear of it. And so . . . so I left."

"Why didn't you come back?" I say sharply. "I'd say you've done just fine for yourself." I point in the direction of his grand house with a grand view. And then I think of the world travels with Will, expeditions here and trips there. He obviously wasn't hurting for money.

"I did."

"No, you didn't!" I say, my voice rising, the tears burning. "You never came back! You left us, and Mom had to work two jobs, while you were off traipsing around the world without a care! It's a wonder we ever crossed your mind at all!"

Throughout my rant, he moves his head from side to side in the negative. "No . . . no, it wasn't like that. I came back a year later. I told her, we can do this. I have a job with the mountaineering school. I'd worked all year to set it up. I was ready. But she'd already shut me out. Said I'd abandoned her. You. And later, when I tried to send money, gifts, they were always returned, unopened."

"But how can that be? She loved you! She's always loved you!"

"I wish that was the case. God, I wish that was so." He drinks again, thanks to Boomer, who has dutifully been refilling our glasses in the background, while moving his head back and forth as if he were following a tennis match.

"I came back one more time, about a year later. It was on your sixth birthday. You were having your party in Encanto Park. You wore a pink sundress with yellow flowers, white sandals, and yellow ribbons in your hair."

He stares out the window, remembering, while my tears join the steady downpour happening outside.

"And there was a man there, wearing a business suit, and he had his arm wrapped around your mother's waist—" The sobbing starts anew for him, and I turn immediately to Will, remembering what he told me about how he felt when Rich held me. For Jack, this must have been a hundred times worse.

"They . . . ," he continues, choking, sniffing, "they looked so happy. Then I watched him pick you up and swing you around, and I thought,

I can never get that back. Another guy is playing with my girl. He had my family . . . and it was all my fault.

"I could never speak of it, Will. Shame doesn't begin to cover it. But when I met you, I don't know what happened. A spark. Something. I thought, I have the chance to do this over. To make it right by someone else. To show that I care. That I could be responsible. Be the father I should have been to you," he says, looking at me tearfully.

His eyes then focus on his wallet, still on the table. He reaches for it. Opens it. Removes his driver's license, and then the photo behind it. "Here."

I take it, the white backing wrinkled, the corners softened, turn it over . . . and it's me. A girl of six, midtwirl on the green grass, on a sunny day, under a blue sky, in a pink sundress with yellow flowers.

"I took that photo that day, on your birthday. I've carried it with me ever since."

My eyes water anew. "You never forgot me. . . ."

He moves his head from side to side. "Never."

I lean my elbows on the table, head in my hands, clutching the photo, dizzy from drink and the truth, my life's one burning question having just been answered. But not in the way I expected. I've hated my father for so long, but I don't hate Jack. I also understand what he did and why. But most importantly, now I know that he never stopped loving us.

I give the photo to Jack, and he promptly returns it to his wallet. Tentatively, I reach my hand to Jack's and fold it in mine. "She still loves you," I say. "Nick Malone was a good man, but he wasn't her true love. He died five years ago."

"How can she possibly love me?"

"She has a garden," I say, gently squeezing his hand. "She's tended it well for the last twenty-five years and sits there often. I used to watch her, when I was little, wondering why she sat there alone all the time, looking so sad, crying sometimes. She only grew one variety of flower—larkspur."

At the mention of larkspur, Jack looks up.

"One day, I watched as she planted a new hybrid. She said, 'Your father would love this new color. It's his favorite flower.' I thought she was talking about Nick, but when I asked him, he said he'd never heard of larkspur. So I knew it was you she was talking about. Sitting with, day after day." I bring my other hand to surround his. "She loves you. There's no doubt in my mind."

Jack pushes his chair away and stands, leaning on the table for support. "I want to show you something."

He turns on unsteady legs and walks out of the kitchen. The swish of the door follows. Will, Boomer, and I look at each other before rising.

"Whoa," I say, grabbing on to Will for support. I blink rapidly, attempting to quell the spinning.

"Just hold on to me," Will says.

We shuffle through the front door, and Jack is already halfway up the narrow path that leads upward to the main house. He moves determinedly in the twilight, no jacket, rain beating on his slender form.

It's an effort for me to walk steadily, but Will helps me along, Boomer bringing up the rear. None of us wear jackets, our insulation provided by scotch only.

When we finally reach the top, we circle around the main house to the front, where Jack stands by the wooden double doors at the entry. He points to an engraved metal placard that I never noticed before. Based on its location, firmly seated in a long-bed planter running adjacent the front door, I realize it must have been covered in snow the last time I was here.

The placard is clear now, the snow having melted down its sides.

LARKSPUR.

I clutch at Will to keep from falling. He pulls me close, his arm securely around my waist.

"I named this for her. All of this is for her." He looks to Will. "When we designed this, I was thinking about what *she* would have wanted. We used to daydream about that, you know. We'd lie awake at night in our tent in Yosemite, dreaming of owning a real home in the mountains someday. She said she would want glass, windows everywhere, so she would still feel like she was outside, sleeping under the stars, as we were then."

Sleeping under the stars . . .

No wonder . . . No wonder she hated going to the lodge. To the outdoors. Anything that reminded her of him . . .

"Wait. That's it. You would have been to the lodge, then. In Walker Canyon," I say.

He nods.

"We went every year," I say. "Mom didn't want to, but she did it for Grandpa Alther. I knew she hated it, but I never knew why."

Jack wipes at the tears on face—a useless gesture as the rain pours on all of us. "I would—"

He has to stop to let a sob escape.

"I would hold you on my shoulders, like this." He puts his hands up, staring into a faraway memory. "And we'd walk along the river. You and me and your mom. And you wanted to know everything. Always questions. What's this? What's that?"

I strain to remember—why can't I remember?—but at the same time, now I know I had a father who cared. Who tried to teach me things.

Still holding on to Will for balance, I crouch down, reaching out to touch the sign. I stay there, my wobbly brain trying to assimilate. Emotionally, I don't think I could ever have imagined a more radically life-altering forty-eight hours.

I straighten again, receiving a steady assist from Will.

"She's gonna be blown away when she sees this," I say.

Jack blanches. "What? She won't see this."

"Yes, she will. You invited her for Thanksgiving, remember?"

35

The rain's steady drone continues this morning, just as it did last night. It was still dark when Boomer called to tell me that the other pilot scheduled for duty—Danny—called in sick, so I'm driving back to Fallon to stand duty as originally planned. Happy birthday to me.

But it has given me time to think. Due to the crazy string of events over the last two days, pitched from one emotional fire to the next, I haven't spoken once with my mother. But what to do? Call her? Tell her I've met Jack? Can I even speak of something of this magnitude on the phone with her? Wouldn't that kind of news have to be delivered in person?

But she can't walk into this blind, me waiting until the last minute to tell her. *Surprise! Guess who we're going to visit for Thanksgiving?*

I need my sounding board.

I dial Will's number, and he answers on the first ring.

"Alison! It's so good to hear your voice." Funny, that was my first thought upon hearing his. An instant energy infusion. "Where are you?"

"About thirty miles south of Fallon."

"What's the storm looking like where you are?"

"If anything, it seems to be getting worse. Why?"

"I've been listening to the scanner, while I've been driving around town inspecting our job sites. The rain's been nonstop since you left. Probably the heaviest I've ever seen."

"Are your sites okay?"

"So far, everything's holding up. But at lower elevations, the flooding . . . It's just not sounding good. I'd be willing to bet your services are going to be needed before too long."

"Oh," I say, looking side to side, up and down, at visibility that can't be more than a hundred yards. "You know, Will, I don't even think we could launch if we wanted to. The visibility's next to nothing."

"Well, I'm sure it'll be okay. Based on what I'm hearing, the county sheriffs have jumped on this early. So anyway, how are you?"

"Well, I'm stumbling over how and when to tell my mom what I've learned. She's with Celia now at the lodge, which is where I'm going to meet them for Thanksgiving. So do I call her and tell her on the phone? Wait and tell her in person . . . ?"

As I wait for Will's answer, I search either side of the highway for the mountains that I know are there, but that remain hidden by clouds that have practically settled to the desert floor. No way we could launch in this.

"Will . . . ?"

"Sorry, sorry," he says. But when I hear the crackle of the radio and the garbled voice of the dispatcher in the background, I realize he has one ear on the scanner. "Where did you say your mom was?"

"She's with my aunt Celia. At the lodge."

"In Walker Canyon, right?"

"Yes. Why?"

"I don't want to alarm you, but much of the talk on the scanner has been about the Walker River. So you haven't spoken with her?"

"No, I couldn't decide—"

"I think you might want to call her. If they're at the lodge, they should probably head for higher ground. The Mono County sheriff is already up in the area notifying everyone, so I'm sure it's okay, but probably worth a phone call."

"Okay. I'll let you—"

"Hold . . . hold on one sec, Alison."

I press the phone to my ear, trying to hear what's being said on Will's radio. Hard to know if it's the radio static or the drumming of rain on my roof that's making it so difficult.

"Whiskey One copies. Give me an hour, Jack. Alison? Are you there?"

"I'm here."

"Sorry about that. They're calling the SAR team out now."

"For what? Please don't tell me the Walker."

"No, it's for the town of Bridgeport. And actually, I don't think it's serious. Sounds like sandbag duty to me," he says with a chuckle. Which helps.

"Will, I . . ." I really don't have anything to say, the phone call to my mom far more pressing, but I don't want to hang up either.

"What is it?" he asks.

"Nothing. I just wish I didn't have duty. I wish we were together. I need more time with my sounding board."

"Your sounding board can always drive out to see you later. Maybe after I check out what's happening in Bridgeport, I can scoot over your way."

"Would you?"

"I would, and I will. How about that?"

"Thank you," I say, breathing a relieved sigh. "And um . . . well, I love you, Will."

"Alison, I wish I could describe what it feels like when you say that. It's like you're speaking to me from the inside or something."

"I'm glad you like it."

"Like it? I— Wait, uh, okay, wait. The radios are getting a little crazy now. I'll call you in a few hours, when I'm done, okay?"

"Sounds good."

"And Alison, I love you, too."

36

"Beanie, we haven't gotten any calls, have we?" I stand in front of the TV monitor, which is mounted in the ceiling corner of the SAR team's office, watching the breaking weather news.

After hanging up with Will, I phoned my mom, but was sent to voice mail. So I finished the drive home, ran up to my apartment, changed into my flight suit, and then checked in with Boomer at the hangar. Since I was originally supposed to be the aircraft commander on duty today, he returned the role to me, we preflighted the aircraft, and I signed for the bird—ready to go now, whenever we're called. If the weather lifts, that is.

I ran out briefly to try my mom again—Will, too, for that matter—without luck. So now I stand rooted in front of the TV, learning, processing. The unseasonably warm weather combined with what they're now calling a late-season tropical storm has brought rain, and snowmelt—from a heavier than normal snowpack, no less—and now flooding. The Truckee River near Reno. The Merced in Yosemite.

And the Walker.

"We did, actually," Beanie says.

"We did?"

"From Mono County. They called Base Ops. Said they might be needing our help. Wanted to know our status."

"Was it—?"

"They didn't mention the Walker View Lodge."

My shoulders drop, but only a little. I told Boomer earlier about my mom and Celia, and he said he'd pass word to the guys to keep an eye out for any news about the Walker River.

"They didn't set off the pagers," I say.

"Operations said it wasn't urgent. They just wanted to give us a heads-up that we might be needed when we get a weather window."

"Oh, okay. Did you call—"

"I just called weather," Boomer says. "Fifty-foot ceilings, practically nil on the vis."

I'm about to ask *why* they need us and exactly *where*, which is when I notice the frosted cupcake on my desk. A single candle has been placed in the center. A smile inches across my face.

"I know this isn't how you wanted to spend your birthday," Boomer says, "But, uh . . . happy birthday, anyway. From all of us."

I look up, and the rest of the guys have stopped what they were doing. They issue a chorus of birthday greetings, and my eyes water just that little bit.

"Thanks, guys. You're awesome."

And for a tiny moment, the world is a little brighter. Such a small gesture, but heartfelt, and so meaningful to me.

I lower myself to my desk chair, staring at my cupcake. My cat-poster mug sits next to it. I've dragged that silly mug to this office almost every day since I checked in to remind myself, *"Hang in there, baby!"* Stupid, but it actually helps.

"And while you eat that," Boomer says, "you can make some headway into that in-box of yours." He points to the stack of training folders, piled high on my desk, that need updating.

"Thanks a lot."

I pull the first one off the stack, open it, and find the evaluation sheet that was scribbled for Hap's latest check ride. Since notes are completed in flight, I have to enter the data into the computer after they return. But as I wait for the computer to boot up, I stare at the notes, the letters blurring.

I envision the Walker River, the one from my childhood memories, flowing gently in front of Guest Cabins Nine, Ten, and Eleven—the cabins closest to the water, the ones most requested, and reserved the farthest in advance. On a day like today, the guests would hunker down inside, and Mom and Celia would remain in the main lodge—after the animals had been taken care of, that is. If Roberto's not there, it would be Celia's job to ensure the horses were tucked away in the barn and out of the elements.

"Beanie?" I say, looking up. "Did they say anything else? Did Mono County say *where* they might need help?"

"Not exactly, but they have their command and control center set up in Coleville. So I'm guessing the help would be needed in that area."

Perspiration prickles across my skin. I swipe under my hairline, my hand coming away wet.

Okay, Ali, you need to calm down. That doesn't mean anything. They could be having problems anywhere *along the Walker. The river runs through more than just that canyon. We're talking hundreds of miles of waterway.*

But the command center is in Coleville. You know where Coleville is. . . .

I push my seat away from my desk, rise, and cross the room to the drinking fountain. Leaning over, I take a long drink, my brain turning, spinning. The river would have to widen by over forty yards in order to reach the first cabins. *Forty* yards. No, no way. And even if there was a chance of flooding near the lodge, sheriff's personnel would have notified everyone. So either way, it's fine.

I straighten, wiping my mouth on my flight suit sleeve. *Yes, it's fine.*

I step forward to return to my desk, and run straight into Clark, who has just entered through the door adjacent the fountain.

I haven't spoken with him since the accident. After we returned from the crash site and shut down, I wasn't exactly in the mood to hold a conversation, but neither was he, leaving hurriedly without saying anything. But it's clear he bears his grief alone. Bags under his eyes. Hair a mess. Flight suit looking like he pulled it out of the hamper.

We share a long look, until he finally opens the door and motions me out to the hallway. I follow him to the far end, out of earshot of our squadron mates.

"I, uh, I owe you an apology," he says. "I didn't mean . . . that night, I—"

"It's okay," I say.

"I also want to thank you. For what you did . . . for going off-mic . . . for your discretion."

Our eyes hold, the understanding passing between us, just as it did the night of the crash.

"Alison . . . ," he says, hands fidgeting, rolling over each other. "No one knows. No one can know. Not ever."

"I understand."

Those are the words that leave my mouth, but I *don't* understand. I don't understand why two people in love can't be treated like two people in love. Clark and Snoopy threatened no one. Both brilliant officers, skilled pilots, courageous, reliable, competent. I don't understand why, in this day and age, Clark still feels he has to hide. That his personal life would matter one iota to anyone else and that this would have any bearing whatsoever on his job performance.

I don't understand this.

But I *do* understand treating a fellow human being with respect and compassion. Like Clark, who stands in front of me, his lips pressed together, grief ripping him apart beneath the surface. A fellow human being, who has lost the love of his life.

"I'm so very sorry," I say. "Shane was my friend. I'm going to miss him dearly."

He squeezes his eyes shut, bringing his thumb and forefinger to the bridge of his nose.

"Ma'am? Sir?" Hap says, poking his head around the door. He holds his hand over his eyes, looking for us at the end of the hallway.

I peek around Clark, who keeps his back turned to Hap.

"Base Ops is on the phone," he says. "Mono County called again."

"Okay, we'll be right there," I say.

I turn back to Clark, placing my hand on his elbow. "Are you gonna be okay?"

He nods. "Yeah. Thanks." He wipes his face, takes a deep breath. "We'd better go."

He starts to walk away, but I stop him.

"Maybe some time, if you want, you could come over . . . you know, if you'd like to talk or . . ."

He nods, his lips curving upward, just a little. "Thanks. Yeah, I'd like that."

When we reenter the SAR office, Beanie is on the phone, nodding, responding in broken "uh-huhs" and "yeahs." His brows remain furrowed, and his expression doesn't change once he hangs up.

"That was operations," Beanie says. "Mono County called again. Said they've got a party of five trapped in Walker Canyon at the Walker View Lodge. The swiftwater rescue team is there, but—"

The ring tone signaling a call from my mom puts an abrupt end to Beanie's explanation. I scramble for the phone, fumbling as I take it out of my pocket.

"Mom?"

A clamoring racket fills my ears. A steady roar. And shouting. There's shouting. . . . What the—?

"Mom, is that you?"

"Alison? Ali . . . need and . . . rising . . . for . . . no time."

"Wait, what? Mom? Are you there?"

I put my hand to my other ear and smash the phone to my head.

"Mom? Mom, what's happening? Are you okay?"

". . . and . . . can't get . . . come . . ."

The connection dies.

I look to Boomer, the dread congealing, thickening, my body heavy with it. I move across the room to the window. Not good. This is not good.

"What is it?" he asks.

"That was my mom. I couldn't make everything out, but she's in trouble." I wipe the back of my neck again, thinking, thinking, staring at the tower. . . .

The tower! I can see the tower!

"Beanie! Call Weather. See what they're calling for ceiling and visibility."

"On it!"

"Hey, Alison," Boomer says quietly. He tugs gently on my arm, all calm, no hurry, directing me out of earshot of the others. "You're the aircraft commander today. If we launch, I have every confidence that you can remain objective and do this, but I also understand if you'd rather not take this flight. You can switch with Tito, if you want."

I note that Boomer's not quoting the squadron mandate, which dictates that personnel assigned to a flight who have a vested interest in a SAR scenario *shall* be replaced. But rather, he's giving me a choice.

"No. I want to do it." My eyes meet his without wavering. "I *can* do it."

"I know you can."

But his vote of confidence comes with an unspoken caution—*You need to keep your head.*

"Just wanted to make sure you were good with it," he says.

"I'm good, Boomer. Really."

Another rule broken . . . and I wouldn't have it any other way.

"Current ceiling one hundred feet," Beanie reports. "Visibility four hundred yards. Low clouds and rain expected to continue into the evening."

The phone rings again, but Boomer, Beanie, Hap, and I are already jogging toward the door that leads to the stairs and the hangar below.

"I'll get it!" Tito says, darting to the phone.

We're almost out the door when Tito calls out. "Hold up!"

He nods, phone pressed to his ear, then looks up.

"It's Base Ops. Mono County called again. They want to know our status."

"Why?" I ask.

"The situation's a bit more dire than initially reported. They've got their swiftwater rescue team out there, but four of *them* are now trapped, as well."

"Tell 'em we're launching ASAP!"

We turn and sprint for the stairs.

37

"Damn it," I mutter. I don't key the mic, but Boomer probably heard me anyway. We're only twenty minutes southwest of Fallon, and it's clear we won't be able to continue, not under visual flight rules, anyway.

The windshield wipers flick back and forth in a gallant effort to keep the cockpit glass clear. A wall of rain blocks our path, and we've been descending steadily to stay under the cloud ceiling, now flying only fifty feet above the ground. As we approach the town of Yerrington, Boomer and I both know that this small farming community lies in front of a long chain of hills that you wouldn't quite call mountains, but even at only a few hundred feet high, they're hills we can't see.

"Let's call back to Approach," Boomer suggests. "Maybe we could go another way."

I gnaw on the inside of my cheek, trying to quell the frustration, as Boomer switches the radio frequency.

"Fallon Approach, Rescue Seven, forty miles to the southwest, over," I say.

"Rescue Seven, Fallon Approach, go ahead."

"Approach, what's the weather looking like to the north? We need another way to Walker."

"Rescue Seven, Fallon Approach, ceilings are lifting to the north. Be advised, Rescue Six was just given takeoff clearance to Reno."

I look to Boomer, and I know he's thinking the same thing.

"Approach, Rescue Seven, can Rescue Six be diverted south?"

"Rescue Seven, Fallon Approach, negative. They're delivering blood for the hospitals. We can bring you northwest to Carson City. They're calling five-hundred-foot ceilings there. You could drop south then, and proceed visually to Walker."

"Rescue Seven copies."

I remain at the controls, turning the aircraft to the north, while Boomer busies himself with the aircraft performance charts.

Now under the control of Fallon Approach, we fly in and out of the clouds—most often in the clouds—to Carson City. Throughout, I replay the conversation with my mom, her alarmed tone particularly worrying. My mom is not one to panic, so for her to have sounded like that, something must be very wrong.

And what about Will? I don't think he's a member of the swiftwater rescue team . . . Although, wait. I have no idea. He very well could be.

My mind plods, thick with worry, and so does the time. Precious time. *We could drive faster than this. . . .*

"Rescue Seven, Mono County Sheriff, over." It's Walt.

And already, the worry moves up a rung. Normally, it would be Jack calling.

"Mono County Sheriff, Rescue Seven, go ahead."

"Rescue Seven, things are startin' to stack up out here. Request ETA, over."

"Mono County Sheriff, estimate—" I look to Boomer, who holds up two fingers followed by a zero sign. "Twenty minutes. What do we have, over?"

"We've got nine people trapped by rising floodwaters. Jack said you're familiar with the compound. Is that right?"

"That's affirm, Walt."

"You've got a family of three on the roof of Cabin Ten, two women on the roof of Cabin Eleven, and we've got three of our swiftwater rescue team members—Jack, Kevin, and Thomas—stuck on the detached garage, halfway between the highway and those cabins. Will's with them, so make that four men on the roof of the garage. The water's runnin' pretty fierce through there."

What? Water running between the outer cabins and the garage? I can't picture it. I can't picture it *at all*. That means the river has widened by at least forty yards, if it's surrounded the cabins, and if it's widened to the point that it surrounds the garage, that's another twenty. I know the distances exactly, having played countless games of hide-and-seek as a kid around those cabins, and in that very garage.

Not only has the river widened at least that far, it's running so fast that swiftwater rescue team members can't cross the gap.

Holy hell. What are we dealing with here?

I swallow, especially when I remember that Walt said "two women on the roof of Cabin Eleven." Mom and Celia. It has to be them. And Jack is out there. And Will . . .

"Rescue Seven copies. Anything else?"

"Be advised, there's a rope rigged from the main lodge to the outer cabins. Our guys tried to pull themselves across in a raft using the rope, but when they moved beyond the garage, the current was too great. They—Stand by."

Current was too great. Impossible . . .

I look at the fuel gauge, extrapolating, taking into account the headwinds and all the diverting, and realize we're going to arrive on-scene with less than an hour of fuel. Actually, way less. More like thirty-five minutes, forty if we're lucky.

"Rescue Seven," Walt says. "A new update for you. Jack's in the raft again. He's attempting to move across from the garage to the outer cabins."

He probably sees her. He sees my mom, and he's trying to get to her. . . .

"Mono County Sheriff, Rescue Seven copies. We're gonna need a fuel truck, over."

"Mono County Sheriff copies. I'll call for the truck."

We continue flying south, moving past the towns of Minden and Gardnerville, traversing wide, windswept pasturelands that butt against the eastern slopes of the Sierra, shrouded in a gray curtain of relentless rain, until we finally—*finally*—approach Topaz Lake, only ten minutes from Walker.

My eyes shift to the clock.

"What time did they say the sun sets?" I ask Boomer.

"Sixteen forty-five."

"Great."

We'll be pushing up against darkness, too.

"And the fuel . . . ," Boomer says.

"Yeah, I know. If they can't get a fuel truck, maybe Carson City Airport if we need to?"

"Yeah, they'd be closest."

We don't say anything more as we accelerate across the now-flooded ranch land south of Topaz Lake, finally passing the town of Coleville. Walker is just ahead, and less than a mile farther, Walker Canyon.

"Things aren't exactly stacked in our favor, are they?" I say.

"They never are . . . ," Boomer says with a resigned snigger.

The seconds stretch, rain streaking across the windshield, as we chase the remaining daylight to Walker Canyon . . . and to a scene I don't think I'm prepared to see.

38

"Rescue Seven, Mono County Sheriff, over."

"Mono County Sheriff, Rescue Seven, go ahead," I say.

"Rescue Seven, request ETA, over," Walt says, straining to keep the urgency out of his voice.

"Two minutes, over."

"Copy two minutes. Switch to ground frequency, one two three point six, for rescue coordination, over."

"Rescue Seven, wilco."

Depending on the nature of the rescue and the number of people involved, sometimes two frequencies are used—a "quiet" frequency, like the one we've been speaking on with Walt, and a "not-so-quiet" frequency that everyone involved on-scene can use.

Boomer leans over to enter the numbers on our second radio, and we know immediately that we're up the correct frequency, because the chatter is going a mile a minute.

". . . halfway across!" It's Jack, his words barely discernible over whatever's happening in the background. Crackling, garbling, roaring . . . that roaring again.

"Jack, this is *not* good!" Will's voice rises above a heavy, hollow thumping sound. And metal . . . screeching metal.

"Whiskey One, Mono County Sheriff, chopper's en route, ETA two minutes."

"Whiskey One copies," Will says. "Jack, the bird's here in two minutes! They can get them! Come back!"

"Guys, set in back?" I ask.

"All set, ma'am," Beanie says. "Hap has his harness on, and I'm ready on the hoist."

"Be ready for anything," I say.

I look at Boomer. "Can you take the controls?" I ask.

For a multifaceted, multiperson rescue like this one, it'll be far easier for Boomer to fly and me to coordinate.

"I've got the controls," he says.

"Walt, we're not in a good place here!" It's Kevin this time, shouting to be heard above the clamor in the background. "Water's undermining the building! Like really *not* in a good place!"

"Hang on, Kevin! The chopper's almost here!"

"Mono County, Whiskey One, is the helicopter up this freq yet?" Will says.

"Whiskey One, Rescue Seven, coming around the bend now. Stand—"

My breath is stolen.

We enter the canyon, where nature has unleashed its fury. The river arcs up and alongside the east wall of the canyon to our left, carving, gouging, dissolving, destroying. A muddy, brown, raging torrent, it carries massive chunks of debris—cars, propane tanks, trees, chewed-up pieces of wood, concrete, and metal fencing.

The Walker River—the normally gentle, slightly meandering trickle of a river—has consumed almost the entire width of the canyon. The flat to rolling terrain that normally separates the river on one side of the canyon and the highway on the other, a distance one hundred yards wide in places, is underwater.

To our right, a line of police cars, ambulances, and several volunteers' vehicles crowd the section of Highway 395 at the canyon's entrance that remains above water. Even with the poor visibility, I recognize Kelly's bright pink Patagonia guide jacket as she stands on the roof of a sheriff's van, looking through binoculars. Walt stands next to her, a radio in his hand.

Tawny, clutching a bullhorn and wearing the sky-blue jacket I remember from rock climbing at Donner Summit, stands on a small spit of land that remains above water about thirty yards in front of the cluster of vehicles. Continuing my scan further up-canyon, I see that entire chunks of the highway are gone.

But at the canyon entrance the highway remains intact, men and women scurrying about in rain jackets and ponchos, talking on radios, carrying ropes, and some just looking on at the one, two, three, four, five, six, seven structures remaining in the river's path.

Seven structures? There used to be fourteen or fifteen, easy. And they're gone. They're just . . . gone.

Crrrrrack! I jump in my seat, whipping my head around in response to a noise so loud it resonates above the thwack of the rotor blades. The barn—*No! Not the barn!*—pulls from its foundation and disintegrates into the torrent, the largest piece slamming into a tree downstream, shattering on impact. If the horses were in there, I didn't see them. I tell myself they're safe somewhere else, knowing it's probably a lie.

"Shit. This is serious," Beanie says.

And in an outright odd, slow-motion moment, a motor home lolls and bobs down the river, then is stopped in its forward progress by a cluster of trees that is almost totally submerged, one that has accumulated a car-sized pile of twigs and sticks and other detritus. I expect the motor home to move past, but there it remains, just downstream from . . . *Mom! There she is!*

Guest Cabins Ten and Eleven stand by themselves in the middle of the canyon, my mom and Celia on the roof of one, the family of three on the other. Cabin Nine is missing altogether. They're a full sixty yards from the highway, water on all sides. The family hunkers under a tarp of some sort, while my mom and Celia huddle in the corner of the roof, wearing yellow rain jackets.

Twenty yards closer to the highway, Kevin and Thomas, wearing neon-orange dry suits and white helmets, stand on the roof of the detached garage. Will is also there, probably the most visible person in the entire canyon due to his bright yellow North Face jacket, neon-orange gloves, and matching orange GPS unit, which is strapped to his chest. He is also topped with a white helmet.

And Jack. Dressed in a dry suit like Kevin and Thomas, but topped with a red helmet, he bobs in a raft, tossed and yanked in the water, moving hand over hand across the rope, which is attached to the main lodge at one end and a majestic Jeffrey pine near Cabin Eleven on the other. Because the main lodge is farther downstream than the cabins, the rope runs diagonally across the river—a distance of about seventy yards. The garage, where Will, Kevin, and Thomas have taken refuge, marks roughly the three-quarter point of the rope, and Jack is now a further ten yards from here, about halfway to Cabins Ten and Eleven.

I'm sure a sling connects the raft to the rope above, but I can't see it at the moment, not with the wind that snaps our helicopter sideways, and the rain that moves horizontally across the windshield, and the darkening skies as the unseen sun drops behind the walls of the canyon.

Due to the rolling nature of the terrain in this section of the canyon, four structures of the remaining seven stand taller than the others, like tiny islands—Cabins Ten and Eleven, the main lodge, and Cabin One. Of all the cabins, Cabin One is the largest, a two-story structure adjacent the main lodge.

Water crashes around the other remaining structures, just as it does around the garage—and thus Will, Kevin, and Thomas—closing in, set to swallow them.

"Rescue Seven, Whiskey—"

Kapow!

"Jack! Watch—" a voice yells on the radio.

The small aluminum equipment shed, the one next to where the barn used to be, the one I helped paint electric blue the summer I turned ten, shatters, catapulted by the ruddy surge directly into the rope that spans the width of the river, slicing it clean through.

"It's severed! The line's severed!" Will cries out.

I'm unable to follow the path of the snapped rope. All I know is that Jack has lost his tether, and is now being carried downstream.

It happens in an instant, the motor home twisting and corkscrewing away from the anchoring cluster of trees, just in time for Jack to slam into them.

"I can't see him!" Will shouts.

"I've got him!" Kelly says, viewing the scene with a better vantage point on top of the sheriff's van. "He's at your two o'clock, under the raft! Jack's under the raft!"

"Got him! I have him in sight!" Will says. "He's hung up in the trees. Jack! Are you up? Jack, do you copy?"

It's several agonizing seconds before he answers. "I'm up," Jack says, barely audibly. The roaring continues, like a house-sized vacuum cleaner.

"Boomer!" I say, pointing to where Will, Kevin, and Thomas huddle, the water ripping the siding from their perch. "The garage is coming apart!"

I recheck the situation at Cabins Ten and Eleven. The water is lower there, the structures more stable—for the moment, anyway. But the priority is absolutely these three men, followed by Jack.

"Let's go!" I say.

"Checking power," Boomer says. The wind wildly buffets the aircraft as Boomer checks the power required to hover.

We watch the gauges closely, and as suspected, the margins are slim.

"The winds aren't gonna make our lives easy today," Boomer says, accelerating forward. Our tail snaps left, right, left, right—"unsettling" would be an understatement—as we move toward the garage, reminding us that the only predictable thing about canyon winds is their unpredictability.

"Whiskey One, Rescue Seven, we're getting you first, then we'll get Jack."

"Whiskey One copies."

Boomer circles, and I look down and to my right, which allows me a direct view to Will. I wonder, briefly, why he doesn't wear a dry suit, while Kevin, Thomas, and Jack do. With all the talk of "warm" fronts and "tropical" storms, it's easy to forget that this flooded river is fueled primarily with snowmelt, resulting in icy, icy, frigid water. Add rain, with wind and temperatures that have now dropped into the mid-thirties, and without doubt these are winter conditions. Kevin, Thomas, and Jack are dressed for the possibility of immersion in this brutal cold, so I can only surmise that Will is not a regular member of the swiftwater rescue team, because if he was, he would have been outfitted similarly.

"The tree's not gonna let us in for a one-skid," I say to our crew, referring to the large cottonwood tree that butts up against the garage. "We're gonna have to hoist."

"Whiskey One, Rescue Seven, inbound," Boomer says. "Prepare for hoist, over."

"Whiskey One copies."

"All set, Beanie?" I ask.

"All set, ma'am. Recommend lowering Hap. He can hook up two guys at once, send 'em up, then we'll send the hoist back down for Hap and the remaining guy."

Stinging arctic air invades the aircraft as Beanie slides the door open, rain shooting inside and battering the back of my neck.

"Ma'am, they've got their harnesses on," Beanie says, leaning out. "This should go quick."

Beanie calls Boomer into position over the detached garage, and the sides are shaking. My god . . .

"Easy left two, easy left one. Nice and steady there, sir. Lowering Hap on the hoist . . . he's halfway . . . he's on the roof."

I sneak a peek at Boomer, so solid on the controls, even though the wind is trying its damnedest to jerk us around. My scan then moves to the gauges. The needles spike the moment Beanie begins to bring the two men up on the hoist.

"You're at ninety-four percent," I say.

"No, the winds are *not* helping," Boomer says.

We're at relatively low altitude, fifty-four hundred feet, and it's cold, but the winds . . . The downdrafts are killing us.

". . . halfway up," Beanie says. "Steady, they're at the door, bringing 'em in. Steady."

As Beanie lowers the hoist to retrieve Hap and the final man on the roof—Will, it turns out—we do a slow swing to the right, the nose pivoting to face the west canyon wall, which brings the main lodge and Cabin One into view out my right window.

We hover about thirty yards from these buildings now, and ten yards beyond this, water rushes over the surface of Highway 395.

"We're gonna be right at the limit on power when we bring these guys up," I say.

"Hoist's on the way down," Beanie calls.

"Which means we can't get Jack on this run," Boomer says.

"Steady," Beanie says. "Steady right there. First man is hooking up. . . ."

The nose swings left, seeking the wind, bringing Cabins Ten and Eleven into view again. My mom and Celia stand on the roof of Cabin Eleven, peering across the ten-yard gap to Cabin Ten, the churning water between the cabins making the space impassable. Like liquid fingers, the water reaches farther up the walls of Cabin Eleven, splashing, smacking, advancing. Without question, Cabin Eleven is in worse shape than Cabin Ten.

A giant Jeffrey pine and a similarly sized cottonwood tree stand adjacent Cabin Eleven, just upstream of it. At one point, the Jeffrey pine used to have the rope attached to it. My mom or Celia would have had to do the attaching, and now that I know my mom's background in climbing and in search and rescue, I bet it was her.

Oh, these familiar trees. We played around them as kids, but never climbed them, as the first branches were far too high. Jack said the Jeffrey pine is a hearty tree. I only hope it can outlast what's been unleashed here today.

I can't see Jack from this vantage point, but it's probably a coin toss as to who's in more imminent danger—my mom and Celia, or Jack. I shift my focus to the left, to Cabin Ten. A man and woman remain crowded under their tarp, the mother wrapping her arms around the bulge in her jacket. And while the water encroaches higher on the walls of Cabin Ten, it is relatively—emphasis on the word "relatively"—stable, for now.

"Both men are on the hoist," Beanie says.

Dip. Droop.

"You're at ninety-eight percent power," I say. "Ninety-eight on rotor speed." Of course, these are all rough averages, as the needles are bouncing all over the place. Up, then down, spike, then drop. Nightmare hovering conditions.

"Bringing 'em up . . . halfway up . . . ," Beanie calls.

"No way we can get Jack this trip," I tell Boomer.

"Agreed."

"Men are at the skids . . . ," Beanie says.

"Look to your twelve," I say to Boomer. "See the cabin on the right?" I point to the roof where my mom and Celia stand. "They don't have much time, but I don't think Jack does either."

". . . bringing 'em in," Beanie calls.

Boomer shifts his gaze out his left window. He would have a better view of Jack than I.

"Shit," Boomer says. "The raft's gone. He's half in the water, half in that pile of crap."

"Men are in! Clear to go!" Beanie says.

Boomer peels away to the left.

"Did you see that field at the entrance to the canyon?" I say. "It's just behind the police cars."

"Headed there now," Boomer says. I guess he noticed the patch of high ground, too. It's the closest place we have to land to drop off our passengers, or pax, for short.

A strong hand squeezes my shoulder. I turn as Will pokes his soggy head between the cockpit seats, and I allow myself a small moment to internalize and savor that yes, Will is safe. Thank god.

"Cabin Eleven isn't gonna hold much longer," Will says. "We could see it—hear it—just now." He shouts to be heard, because he doesn't wear a communications helmet.

"What about Jack?" I say.

Will leans farther into the cockpit, looking through the window. "Oh, boy. Not good."

I turn to look at Cabin Eleven. Over to Jack. Back to Cabin Eleven.

I look, and I look, and the vision that pops into my head is an absurd one. That stupid cat poster. *Cat poster?* What the hell?

But that crazy cat . . . hanging from a rope. It was hanging. . . .

"Okay," I say. "I think I know what we need to do."

39

"I'd say we have to get Jack first. Agreed?" I say.

Boomer and Will nod.

"But Cabin Eleven might not hold. We need to give my mom and Celia more time—give 'em someplace to go."

"What's your plan?" Will asks.

"Can you repeat what you did before? Can you shoot over another rope to Cabin Eleven?"

"Yeah. If I can get to the main lodge, I can shoot a line from there."

"We can get you there," Boomer says.

"I can aim for the roof, and they can wrap it around the same tree," Will says. "I can anchor it on my end to the chimney of the main lodge."

"If you could do that," I say, "at least they'd have a rope, something to hang on to in the worst-case scenario."

I picture the bare trunk of the Jeffrey pine, its first row of branches at least twenty feet above the roof level of Cabin Eleven. The trunk is so close, my mom could lean over and wrap a rope around it, just as she must have done before. Yeah, at least it would be something. . . .

Boomer executes a swift no-hover landing in the field, and Beanie directs Kevin and Thomas out of the helicopter.

"If you could drop me on the roof, the crossbow is still up there, and I have another rope in my pack," Will says.

"Will do," Boomer says.

Will puts his hand over his ear, then presses the push-to-talk switch on the radio attached to his chest harness. "Mono County Sheriff, Whiskey One, relay to the victims that we're firing over another line. Like before, fishing line first, attached to a rope. I'll pre-rig the rope with carabiners, so tell them to take the line around the tree and back-clip the carabiners to the rope, over."

"Mono County Sheriff copies. Tawny's on the far side with the bullhorn and will relay."

"Beanie, are we good?" Boomer asks.

"All set in back, sir."

Boomer lifts, flying toward the main lodge in what is now a murky twilight, which means it won't be much longer until we have to use our searchlight. And adding to our visibility woes, the rain is congealing now, a liquidy sleet that the wipers struggle to push away.

"I'm gonna do a one-skid, so you can step off, Will," Boomer says.

Two trees border the main lodge, on the highway side, but the roof is so wide that we can hover on the river side and get low enough to do this.

"Got it," Will says, retreating into the cabin.

Boomer executes his approach and hovers about one foot above the roof of the main lodge. It's a quick transition as Will hops out. Boomer then lifts, and we fly toward Jack.

The raft is long gone and Jack looks as if he's being gulped whole by a fantastic morass of twisted detritus, woven thick with branches and twigs and who knows what else. Thank god he's wearing a dry suit, as his lower half looks to be completely underwater.

Boomer pulls into a hover and turns the aircraft to put the nose to the wind. From here, I can see Will, who at this very moment sets his stance, raises his crossbow, aims, and fires. I can't see the fishing line pay out, but I do see my mom and Celia scrambling forward to retrieve it.

"Sending Hap down on the hoist," Beanie says. "Hoist is on the way down . . . halfway down . . . he's at the man . . . stand by."

And while our helicopter works to rescue Jack, I look to the other side of the river, where my mom and Celia pull and pull, drawing the fishing line across, which draws the rope across in turn.

"Steady on the hover. Hap's having trouble with his footing," Beanie says.

My mom grabs the end of the rope, moves to the corner of Cabin Eleven, and begins to tie it off to the tree. At the same time, Celia begins jumping up and down, waving her hands above her. Oh, no—

Whipping my head back to Will, I see him secure the other end of the rope to the chimney of the main lodge.

"Will, the cabin!" Tawny shouts.

Crrrrrrack! I nearly shoot out of my seat as water crashes and snarls around the front of Cabin Eleven, pulling it under, dissolving it.

No! Mom!

"They're on the rope! They're on!" Will shouts. "Kelly, Tawny, I need you on the roof of the main lodge ASAP!"

"On our way!" Kelly says.

My mom and Celia cling to the rope, not hanging quite like the cat-poster cat, but more like upside-down opossums.

The radio keys, and I look over at Will, who stands atop the roof of the main lodge, hand pressed to his chest, to his radio.

"Rescue Seven, Whiskey One. How much longer?"

"Whiskey One, stand by," I say. "Beanie, are we close?"

"Negative. Jack's tangled in the debris, and shit's movin' all over the place. His harness and backpack are wrapped in practically everything. Hap's tryin' to cut him out."

As Beanie reports, two tiny athletic forms leap from the highway to a cottonwood tree located at least six feet from the asphalt. Kelly and Tawny then use this tree as a springboard, jumping to a second tree, and finally to the window ledge on the first floor of the main lodge, the water lapping just below. They scramble up the side of the house, using moves reminiscent of Will's when he did his Spiderman thing on Mount Morrison.

"Whiskey One, Rescue Seven, negative. Jack's tangled in the debris. Hap's cutting him out, over."

I glance quickly at my mom and Celia, my heart in my throat. They hang without harnesses, beyond exposed, over water that speeds beneath them. Based on the movement of debris on the surface, I'd say the water runs at twenty-five miles per hour, easy.

Even more disconcerting, the cottonwood tree just behind the Jeffrey pine that anchors the rope they hang on has snapped in half.

I turn my head to find Will, spotting Kelly and Tawny as they join him on the roof.

"Rescue Seven, I don't know how much longer we can rely on that tree anchor," Will says.

I'm sure he sees we're down to only one tree now, too.

"We're gonna send Kelly over on the line," Will continues. "She can at least get them hooked to the rope. We might even be able to bring them back across this way."

"Rescue Seven copies. I don't think we have another choice."

"Helpless" doesn't begin to cover it—watching my mom and Celia hanging in the breeze—and we can't do a thing about it.

"Rescue Seven, Whiskey One, Kelly's on."

A tiny, rain-slicked figure in pink begins a quick shimmy across the rope—a classic Tyrolean traverse. She's attached to the rope by a carabiner connected to her harness, and she carries slings and carabiners with her that can be used to secure my mom and Celia to the rope. She moves with urgency, legs hooked around the rope, moving hand over hand, fast like a cat, getting pounded with sleet.

Tawny's voice—a memory—registers in my head. *Girl power, yeah?*

Yeah.

The family of three remains clustered on the roof of Cabin Ten, so isolated. It's the only structure that remains in the middle of the canyon. God, please let it hold.

I do a quick scan of the engine gauges. Flickering low-fuel lights.

What else?

I fast-forward, adding up the time to finish hoisting Jack, move over and hoist Celia and my mom, drop the three of them off, then return for the family of three.

We should have time. Have just enough fuel.

But then I turn away from my mom, shifting to look behind me, to the space between the highway and the main lodge. The water is now above the window that Tawny and Kelly jumped to earlier, and the middle tree is . . . gone.

Wait. What? When did that happen? They just climbed that tree! And the second tree, the one closest to the highway, is bowed, almost lying flat against the surface of the water.

The exit path for Will, Kelly, and Tawny has vanished.

Which means . . . we're going to have to pick them up, too.

Holy shit . . . We're not going to have enough fuel. . . .

"Sir, easy left three," Beanie calls. "Easy left two, left one, steady. Steady right there. Hap's still tryin' to cut Jack from the debris."

"Mono County Sheriff, Rescue Seven, over."

"Go ahead, Rescue Seven," Walt answers.

"Any word on that fuel truck?"

"Stand by."

No way we can fly to Carson City for fuel. No way we can leave our victims. The fuel's going to have to come to us or it's not coming.

"Hover's lookin' good, sir," Beanie says. "Hap's almost got him free."

"Rescue Seven, Whiskey—" *Crrrrrrack!*

Shit! The detached garage—the one that Will, Kevin, and Thomas stood atop just five minutes ago—finally loses its hold. The river picks it up and slams it into the side of the main lodge, knocking Will and Tawny flat on the roof.

The main lodge shudders.

The rope sags.

Kelly, midway on her traverse, dips, swaying perilously close to the water.

"Kelly, get back! Get back now!" Will shouts, finding his feet. "Mono County, Whiskey One, need to re-rig the anchor. This house isn't gonna hold! Rescue Seven, we need you fast!"

We can't move. Hap is untangling Jack. *Shit. Shit. Shit!*

Jack—my father—snarled in debris. My mother—dangling on a

rope. My aunt—clinging next to her. Will—standing on a roof that's going to collapse at any moment. . . .

My family. This is my *family!* And for one terrifying moment, I'm overwhelmed by the images of losing them—my entire family snatched by the river in one fell swoop.

I bring my ungloved hands over my mouth to stifle the panic . . . and that's when I feel the rapid exhalations beating against my bare palms. This physical sensation—this here-and-now feedback—snaps me back to reality. *What the hell are you doing, Ali?*

I turn to look at Boomer, a model of concentration, focusing on keeping the aircraft still. Then Beanie's voice registers. "No rise, no drift. Hover's lookin' good, sir," Beanie says.

Clark also flashes through my vision—Clark, who kept it together when all was crumbling around him, when he knew all was lost.

My family still has a chance. . . .

Okay, Ali, head in the game. Head in the game!

Embarrassed that I let my attention slip, even for a few seconds, I adjust my scan to find Will. The main lodge shakes while he frantically pulls slings and a rope from his pack, looking wildly about as he does so, searching for another way to anchor the rope should the main lodge collapse. Tawny leans over the edge of the roof, shouting and encouraging Kelly, who scrambles, hand over hand, upward toward the roof. My mom and Celia continue to hang on for dear life at the other end of the rope.

The roof quakes beneath Will as he attaches a secondary rope to the main rope.

"Kelly, when you get to the roof, stay hooked to the rope no matter what!" Will says. "Tawny, you, too!"

There is no answer from Kelly, but I'm sure Tawny heard, as she, too, clips herself to the rope using the carabiner on her harness.

Will runs to the corner of the building, paying out the new rope behind him, the one he has attached to the main rope right near the chimney. What is he—?

He steps up to the roof's ledge, and based on the direction he faces, it seems that he's looking at the giant cottonwood tree downstream of the main lodge and adjacent to Cabin One—a new anchoring point.

But the tree is at least twenty feet away, maybe twenty-five. There's no way he can—

He jumps.

With the rope lying in coils over his shoulder, he plunges into the icy river.

Will!

My heart drops to the bottom of my stomach and stays there for several excruciating seconds as the river propels him downstream . . . and straight into the trunk of the cottonwood.

The last thing I see is Will wrapping his arms around the tree—his body submerged, a body without a dry suit, only his head above the surface.

"Okay, Hap's got Jack cleared. He's hooked up . . . ," Beanie says. "We have a thumbs-up . . . hoist is on the way up . . . he's halfway up . . ."

To my right, Kelly approaches the main lodge, scuttling upward, now about twenty feet from the roof. Craning my neck around, I see the reflection of Will's white helmet through the branches of the cottonwood. In the time it took Beanie to hoist up Jack, Will scrambled up at least thirty feet above the water. His bright orange gloves visible, his arms fly, wrapping the rope around the trunk. Good god, how did he make it up there so fast?

Kelly touches down on the shaky roof, but keeps herself attached to the rope as Will instructed.

A splitting. A splintering. A thundering *crrrrrrack!*

Like an invisible hand taking a knife to the middle, the main lodge splits in half, caving toward the center. If the rope remains looped around the chimney, it will pull Kelly, Tawny, my mom, and Celia with it.

"Break the anchor! Tawny! Break it!" Will yells.

Tawny pulls the main rope out of the carabiner that holds it to the chimney, freeing it. The rope snaps taut, Will's new anchor at the cottonwood tree now holding the rope. In a blur of movement, Kelly and Tawny grab tight to the rope as the main lodge folds beneath them.

40

From cottonwood tree to Jeffrey pine, a distance spanning at least seventy yards, a rope holds four women above the raging Walker River. Actually, two ropes. The new rope Will tied to the giant cottonwood near Cabin One is tied to the original rope, and this, of course, is tied at the other end to the Jeffrey pine on the far side of the river.

"Men are inside, we're clear to go," Beanie says, indicating that Hap and Jack are now in the aircraft.

Boomer slides the bird across the river and swoops down immediately over my mom and Celia. As the helicopter twitches and yaws in the wind, I think how Will has just saved four lives. Had he not made a new anchor, when the main lodge went down it would have taken the rope with it, and everyone attached. They would have—

But they didn't, Ali. So get on with it.

"Hoist is on the way down," Beanie calls. "Steady . . . halfway down . . . steady. Hap's at the women."

I scan from side to side as Beanie hooks up either Celia or my mom, I don't know which. Two structures remain—Cabin Ten, just next to us, still with the family of three on its roof, and Cabin One, on the far side of the river. Will is in the cottonwood tree—a temporary safe haven next to Cabin One.

"Temporary" is the key word, because this "haven" resides under a set of power lines. Will knows very well that we can't lower a hoist cable through a set of power lines, so even though I can't see him now, I'm sure he's making his way to Cabin One for pickup.

That settled, I tune in to Beanie, who's calling that Hap and the first woman are at the skids. I twist in my seat to look out my window, watching as Beanie pulls Celia into the cabin.

I glance at the gauges. Good power now. *Thank you, winds.* "Boomer, I think we can get Kelly and Tawny, too, after we're finished here."

"Agreed. But the fuel," he says, referring to the low-fuel lights that glow orange—lights that flicker so fast, they're almost solid.

"I know," I say. "Let's just do what we can do."

And just a quick two minutes later, Beanie is calling Hap and my mom into the aircraft. *Thank god . . .*

Boomer rolls the aircraft to the left, flying across the river, and flares to a stop, pulling into a hover directly over Kelly and Tawny.

As Beanie and Hap go to work to get the girls, I check on Will's progress. I suspect he's pacing on the roof of Cabin One now.

But I search and squint, and the roof is empty. My eyes go back to the tree. I see his helmet. He hasn't moved.

Nor has he spoken on the radio since he directed Kelly and Tawny.

Something curls in my stomach.

"Whiskey One, Rescue Seven, over," I say.

I wait. And I wait . . .

It's then that I notice something I hadn't before. Mojo. I never knew he was here, but he runs toward the water's edge now, skidding to a halt just before the highway moves underwater. He maintains a staunch barking stance—all of his energy directed toward Will's location, about thirty yards up-canyon from him.

"Whiskey One, Rescue Seven, do you read, over?" I ask, as Beanie reports that Tawny is now in the aircraft and the hoist is on its way down again for Kelly.

"Go ahead," Will says, but something is off in his voice. Something terribly off.

"Whiskey One, Rescue Seven, you need to get to Cabin One. We can't hoist you if you're under the power lines, over."

Wait. Wait . . .

"Whiskey One, Rescue Seven, you need to get to Cabin One, over," I say, attempting to keep my voice level, but the alarm bells are ringing.

"Rescue Seven, I can't feel my hands," he says. I imagine him having to push the talk button on his radio with his wrist, just as I had to do when I couldn't work my hands on Basin Mountain.

But the resignation in his tone is so startlingly clear, my breath catches, my chest tightening. How long has he been in that tree now, soaked through, gloves probably useless, in bitterly cold rain, the wind howling? He can't feel his hands, which means he can't use them, or not effectively, anyway. Not in a way that would allow him to get to the roof of Cabin One.

He knows he's stuck. He knows we can't get him. He knows . . .

Shit! Think!

". . . I have a thumbs-up," Beanie says. "Hap and Kelly are on their way up."

Beanie is leaning over the side of the cabin, his hand loosely guiding the hoist cable, as he gives the final calls to bring Hap and Kelly into the bird.

"They're at the skids," Beanie says. "Stand by. Bringing 'em in."

"Guys, we have to figure out how to get Will out from under those power lines and over to Cabin One," I say.

"Rescue Seven, Whiskey One," Will says, an uptick in his voice. "Can you get me a rope?"

"Whiskey One, stand by."

A rope for what?

"Hap and Kelly are in the bird," Beanie says. "They're strapping in."

"Beanie, can we get Will a rope?"

"We have a rope, ma'am, but—"

"Rescue Seven, Whiskey One, I have Jumars," Will says. "If you can anchor a rope to the chimney and throw the other end to me, I think I can get over."

"I think I know what he wants to do, ma'am," Beanie says. "I can hoist Hap down to Cabin One, and he can set it up."

"Do it," I say as Boomer slides the aircraft to Cabin One.

"Whiskey One, Rescue Seven, we're lowering Hap now. He'll set up the rope. Then we'll have to leave to unload the pax and return for you, over."

"Whiskey One copies."

Boomer hovers, and Beanie lowers Hap to the roof of Cabin One. He secures one end of the rope to the chimney and throws the rest of the coil to Will—about a fifteen-foot toss.

Hap gives us a thumbs-up that Will has received the rope, we hoist Hap back into the aircraft, and Boomer noses over and accelerates to our drop-off point, the same field at the edge of the canyon.

"Beanie, what's Will's plan?"

"Ma'am, he can use the Jumars to attach himself to the rope we threw over. I don't know if you remember from rock climbing that day, but those things are like claws. Even if his hands aren't working right, if the Jumars are clamped on one end to the rope, and on the other end to his harness, he'd be hands-free. Maybe he can swing over or something. That's what I'm guessin'."

"As long as it gets him clear of the power lines, that's all we need," I say.

My breaths come easier now that I know that Will has a rope and a plan.

That is, until I look at the solid orange low-fuel lights. Boomer's looking at them, too. We lift our eyes to meet each other's, and he looks at me knowingly before shifting his attention back to the field, setting up his approach to land.

"We have fuel," I say. My voice, as steely as it's ever been, belies the unease I feel deep in my gut.

Low-fuel lights in a helicopter work as they do in your car. They flicker when you're approaching a certain level of fuel, then glow solid when you reach some predetermined, almost-empty level.

And that's all well and good, but equating it with flight time is another matter altogether. Depends on burn rate.

Solid low-fuel lights could indicate fifteen minutes of fuel remaining or five. I don't know, because I've never purposely taken off with low-fuel lights to find out. You're not allowed to. *Strictly* not allowed to.

And six months ago, if you'd asked me if I'd take off with solid low-fuel lights, I would have said not only "No" but "Hell no!"

But that was six months ago. . . .

"We have fuel," I repeat, probably trying to convince myself more than anyone else.

"I was hoping you'd say that," Boomer remarks with the hint of a grin.

Boomer lands, five people run out from under the rotor arc, and I'm witness to the moment when my mother's body stills, her face frozen in stunned recognition, as she realizes who stands next to her, who was with her in the helicopter all along—Jack.

It's loud, it's sleeting, it's cold, but Jack removes his helmet anyway, his eyes never leaving my mom's. The seconds stretch, neither moving. And then the air contracts. They reach for each other at the same time, a crushing embrace.

"Beanie, are we clear to lift?" Boomer asks.

Snap. Blink. Back to now.

"You're clear, sir."

Boomer lifts, turning our searchlight on in the process.

I shift my focus to the fuel gauge. *It's going to be okay. We have enough fuel. We can get this done.*

"Mono County Sheriff, any word on that fuel truck?" I ask, wondering why I'm even bothering. If we stopped to fuel now, it's not like Will and the family could wait around for that to happen. If we're going to get them, it has to be now.

"Rescue Seven, that's a negative," Walt answers. "But I don't think you'd have time anyway." *My thoughts exactly.* "You're gonna need to get back to Cabin One ASAP."

"Rescue Seven copies," I say, shuddering. Has Will moved over yet? And if he has, will Cabin One continue to stand until we get there?

"How's Cabin Ten holding?"

"Holding for now," Walt answers. "Not great, but holding."

"Rescue Seven copies. Inbound to Cabin One."

Boomer raises the searchlight to shine on Will's tree just as he leaps from it, Tarzan-style. The rope goes taut, the one that Hap tied off to the chimney, and Will arcs down and away from the power lines, his useless, orange-gloved hands wrapped loosely around the rope while his weight is held by the Jumars. He slams hard into the side of the building, his legs splashing in the water, and the current immediately rips him sideways, pulling, pulling . . .

"He's clear!" I shout, and Boomer is already flaring, making his approach to hover over him. Beanie is also ahead of me, calling that Hap is on the hoist and being lowered.

Will uses his wrists, his elbows, struggling, clawing his way up, using the eaves of a second-story window to move himself away from the water.

"We're losing Cabin Ten!" Walt shouts. "We're losing Cabin Ten!"

"What?" I say.

"The siding's going! We can see it from here!"

Will looks up, our eyes meet, and we know. He only has to shake his head to confirm.

In the blink of an eye, the priorities have flipped, Cabin Ten now the higher risk.

"Boomer, go!" I say, willing the words out.

Boomer grits his teeth. He knows we have to do it.

"Bringin' Hap in," Beanie says. "Sir, you're clear to go. I'll hoist him in on the fly."

Boomer starts forward, and seconds later Beanie calls that Hap is in the bird.

"Copy," I say, reeling from the shock of having to leave Will. I left him. . . .

Stay focused, Ali. Stay focused!

I look ahead, the father waving his hands wildly on the roof, the woman with a tiny bulge in her jacket. The baby . . .

Two trees remain near Cabin Ten, which is good because it protects the cabin by breaking up the flow of water, but bad because they're so close that we can't one-skid. We're going to have to hoist. But with a baby . . .

"How are we gonna bring up the baby?" Boomer says. "A harness won't work."

"Stand by," Beanie says.

I look over my shoulder, watching Beanie and Hap as they confer. Just behind them, an old equipment bag . . .

"The equipment bag!" Beanie and I say at the same time.

Hap pounces on the olive-green canvas bag, unzips it, and dumps the contents—ropes, harnesses, and slings. He and Beanie rush back to the main cabin door, the one that has remained open since we lowered the hoist the very first time at the garage.

"Easy forward ten," Beanie calls. "Easy forward five, easy forward three, two, one, steady. Steady right there. Sending Hap down . . . he's halfway down . . . he's on the roof."

It runs through my mind for about a nanosecond, the stringent engineering and testing that goes into the design and deployment of rescue harnesses, strops, ropes, and litters. All of them stress-tested, checked, and rechecked. And we're about to throw an infant into an old equipment bag. . . .

"Baby's in the bag," Beanie continues. "He's hooked on the mom, they're on the hoist, bringing 'em up."

Why it hits me now, I don't know, but it's honest-to-goodness dark. Maybe it's that I'm craning my head to look back at Cabin One—to see if it's still there—and I realize that I couldn't see it anyway.

". . . they're in the bird . . . sending the hoist back down . . ."

Please be there. Please be there. Please be there. I harbor the same thoughts I had as I sped to the airport to find Will, before he boarded a plane. *Please still be there.*

". . . dad's on, Hap's on, bringing 'em up . . . halfway up . . . they're in the bird . . . clear to go!"

Boomer wastes no time, spinning and moving back to Cabin One, which now, thanks to the searchlight, I see still stands.

We've got this. We've got this.

I pivot in my seat briefly to look back into the aircraft cabin. The mother unzips the equipment bag, and a tiny head, topped with fine blond curls, peeks out, offering a curious smile.

No way. A smile? That baby's got to be destined to join a SAR team when he grows up.

Quickly, I return to the task at hand, watching Boomer flare into position over Will. Simultaneously, Beanie is sending Hap down on the hoist, no time to lose.

The searchlight illuminates the side of Cabin One, and Will remains almost exactly where we left him.

Thank god . . .

His body still shakes, which is a good sign. After all he's been through, his body could easily have shut down by now due to hypothermia, so the shivering is good.

Hap continues his descent on the hoist cable, and he's just above roof level when Will's eyes suddenly widen. It's the only warning I have before the *crack!* and the *whump!* as the cabin disintegrates, crashing over Will, and pulling him into the river.

41

I choke on my scream, unable to breathe. *Oh, dear god. Will!*

"Mother fuck!" Boomer shouts.

He shines the searchlight on the biggest pieces of the cabin, trying to follow.

"Fuck! Fuck! Fuck!" he yells.

I look frantically downward, seeing only a jumble of wood and brick tumbling in the mud-thickened, now-black water.

This can't be happening. It can't be—*Think, Alison! Think!*

The nose of the aircraft snaps to the left as the number-one engine revs up, whining—taking the load for the number-two engine. *Shit!*

"We lost number two!" I say, watching the needle on the gauge for engine number two wind down to zero, flaming out, out of gas. Shit, shit, *shit!*

Boomer reacts, dropping collective and nosing over to gain airspeed. He turns and lines up for the square-shaped field, where we've been off-loading our pax.

It's cold and we're low, but I don't know if we're light enough to be single-engine-capable, not with the family on board. Which means Boomer will have to make a perfect no-hover landing.

Which he does.

Hap rushes the family out of the rotor arc, but it's not until Boomer rolls off the throttle for the number-one engine, and the aircraft rocks as the rotors slow, and all motorized sounds die away, that the enormity of what has happened hits me. We only have one engine. We can't take off now.

The nauseated feeling overwhelms.

No. No, no, no. Don't give in to this. Don't give up!

I key the radio before Boomer switches off the battery. "Mono County Sheriff, Rescue Seven, request status of fuel truck, over."

"Rescue Seven," Walt says. "The roads are all closed. The fuel trucks can't move. They tried to cross the pass near Topaz Lake, but couldn't get through."

Okay, so what else? What else?

A long shot.

I switch the frequency on the second radio.

"Rescue Six, Rescue Seven, over."

"Rescue Seven, Rescue Six, go ahead," Clark says.

"Clark, what's your status? We need help. We need fuel."

"We're shutting down at the hospital heliport in Carson City. The weather's crap."

"Can you fly here?" I ask, just shy of panic. "We need you!"

"Negative, the weather's—"

"We're out of fuel! We have a man in the river! We need your help!"

"Alison, I don't—"

"Please! Clark, please! It's Will. Will's in the river!"

The radio goes silent, the pause so long that I wonder if Clark has just switched off his radio.

"I, um, I'll try. But I can't promise anything," he says.

Boomer turns to me, and we share a long, torturous look.

I put my hand to my chest, something to try to fill an unfillable hole. *Holy god . . .*

My gaze drifts to Jack and my mother, standing arm in arm, and Boomer follows my line of sight.

Jack has removed his dry suit and stands in the bright green jacket I remember from Palisade Glacier an eternity ago. His chest harness with his radios and gear hangs loosely over his shoulder. Celia, Kelly, and Tawny are there. Kevin and Thomas, too.

We've touched down less than a quarter mile from the cluster of police cars and ambulances, so rescue personnel have moved to our landing spot to receive the family of three that Hap escorts now.

After handing them over, Hap turns to Jack, relaying the news.

Jack looks to me to confirm. Slowly, and while gritting my teeth to choke down the emotion, I shake my head.

Jack's body appears to buckle. My mom grabs him, and so does Celia, to hold him upright.

Boomer looks away from Jack, then slams the instrument console. "God damn son of a bitch!" he yells.

I have no words, my mind blank. All of my ideas, the planning, everything leaves me, and my body grows heavy, turning in on itself with ache.

I register movement as Jack regains himself and stumbles under the stationary rotor blades, climbing into the cabin. There is no sound save the sleet that continues its relentless pounding.

"Alison," Jack says, moving from the cabin into the little space between the cockpit seats. He puts a hand on my arm, but when I meet Jack's eyes—my father's eyes—I can't hold the tears back anymore.

"I couldn't—" I say, gagging on the words. "I tried. I tried. I did." The tears stream out the corners of my eyes.

"I know you did," Jack says. "I know—" He stops, removing his hand from my arm to wipe at his face.

I drop my head in my hands, sobbing, barely noticing when my door is opened. I hear a familiar voice, feel the comforting pull of arms around my shoulders. My mom draws me to her, squeezing and rubbing my back, just as she did when I was little. Only this time, she can't fix it.

Damn, this incessant sleet! Rain! Whatever! Will! Oh, dear god, Will . . .

My mom hugs me closer, and I shake in her arms. Visions of the rescue mission from beginning to end flicker and flash through my brain. The unchecked efforts of so many people to help save lives despite the danger. And I think of Rich, who never would have put himself in this position. Will would and did. Heroic, brave, selfless. And I lost him because of it.

No! Will!

The visions shimmer and morph. Will stands on Donner Summit. He unfolds his arms, standing taller. *"You missed something."* And I see myself running. Blinded by rain, darkness, out of breath—

A wet, golden blur streaks under the rotors, Mojo's wolfy bark rising. He leaps into the main cabin behind me, issuing a series of yelps, before bounding out once more, sprinting a complete circle around the bird, and returning to the cabin.

He leaps in again.

"Mojo!" Jack says, falling backward this time as Mojo launches straight into his chest. "Calm down, boy. Calm down."

Jack's attempts at subduing the Lab prove futile, as Mojo yips and woofs, scrabbling to keep his footing on the metal flooring of the aircraft. Then, quick as flash, he darts from the aircraft once more, turning circles, jumping, barking, in front of the cockpit window. A sprint ten yards toward the right, toward the river, a manic dash back.

But it's Mojo's sudden stillness that causes me to sit up straight. Stable on all fours, he looks up, meeting my eyes, and stares, waiting, alert.

Beep . . . beep . . . beep . . . beep . . . beep.

Like Mojo, we still. Boomer and Jack breathe in, hold it. My mom straightens. And we listen.

Beep . . . beep . . . beep . . . beep . . . beep.

Jack bolts up, and his hands fly to his chest harness, which now lies on the cabin floor. He had been carrying it on his shoulder, having removed it from over his dry suit. He picks it up, fumbling with it.

BEEP . . . BEEP . . . BEEP . . . BEEP . . . BEEP.

The beeps grow louder as he pulls the fluorescent orange avalanche transceiver from its holder.

"It's Will," Jack whispers in disbelief.

"What?" I say, not daring to hope, but damn it, the spark flares. "Wait, Jack. What are you saying?"

"I'm saying, this receiver is beeping because Will turned on his transmitter."

"He's alive, then," I say, my breaths coming fast. "Jack, where is he? How far?"

"Less than four hundred yards."

"Maybe he washed up on shore," I say, unstrapping. "Maybe—"

"Alison, don't get your—" Jack starts.

"Which way?" I say, leaping out of the aircraft. But then I realize I don't need to ask. I just need to follow Mojo.

The dog sprints away, toward the broad plain that fans out away from the canyon, and I follow. Freezing rainwater soaks my flight suit, and I labor to run as mud from the soggy field sucks and pulls on my boots.

One hundred yards? Two hundred? Up and over a bridge that's somehow still standing, the water rushing just beneath.

But the longer I run, the greater the dread. What if the avalanche transceiver was ripped from Will's vest and floats on its own. Or what if it's still attached to Will, but he's been pulled underwater or remains trapped under debris. It could be all of these things.

Another fifty yards. Mojo skitters to a stop in a marshy quagmire of a field that borders the widened river, barking nonstop.

"Where is he, Mojo? Where is he?"

I pull the flashlight from my survival vest, but it doesn't have near the intensity that I need. Then, from behind, a high-powered beam shines on the water. Kevin and Thomas run up behind me with Beanie, Boomer, and Jack on their heels. Kevin carries a portable spotlight, which he sweeps across the river.

Jack holds the avalanche transceiver in front of him. BEEP . . . BEEP . . . BEEP . . . BEEP . . . BEEP.

"He should be right there!" Jack says, pointing.

Please, please, please . . .

"I think I've got something!" Kevin says. "I have an orange glove!"

We snap our heads in the direction of the light, to the top of an unmoving mess of debris, piled high, like a beaver dam. The only thing between the glove and us . . . fifty yards of uncrossable river.

"It's gotta be . . ." But then Kevin's voice trails away.

"It's just a glove," Thomas says.

Mojo continues to bark toward the pile.

"Remember—and I've seen this several times—the gear you see on the snow could still be connected to the victim, like a hand in a glove."

"What if he's buried? He could be beneath all that!" I say.

"The transceiver's pointing right there!" Jack says. "It's gotta be him!"

"Well, let's get him! How are you guys gonna—" I stop, when I see their faces.

"I don't think there *is* a way," says Kevin. "Unless . . . Jack?" He turns to him. "Any ideas? There's nothing to anchor to here."

We're joined by Kelly, Tawny, Walt, Hap, and Celia, who begin brainstorming how to get to Will. Assuming it is Will.

It has to be Will. It *has* to be.

Mom is here, too, and I watch in awe as her search and rescue training kicks in. She jumps right in with the group, throwing in her two cents, trying to find a solution.

The conversation recedes into the din, and my mind whirs, click, click, click, as I tick through takeoff performance charts in my head. And the idea returns, the one I had dismissed originally. Not because it's strictly forbidden, but because I didn't think it would be possible.

I jerk my head up, locking eyes with Boomer, and I see it in his face when what I'm thinking registers with him, too.

"Boomer—"

"Alison," he says, raising his hands. "I already know what you're thinking. What you're gonna—"

"Number one still has fuel.

"No way. You have no idea how much time you'd have."

"It's cold enough."

"No."

"We're low enough."

"Still no."

"If it's just two people, we're light enough."

"Goddamn it," he says, walking away with his hands on his hips before turning and pacing back toward me.

"It could work," I say.

"What could work?" Jack says, the conversation around us suddenly absent.

The sometimes rain, sometimes sleet continues to fall, but oddly, no one shivers, even though, to a person, we're soaked.

"We could fly single-engine to get Will," I say. "Me and one other person."

"I'll do it," Jack says.

"You can't," I say.

"I can," Jack says.

I stare at Jack. He stares back.

"Boomer, we need to strip the bird," I say, my eyes shifting to his.

"Goddamn it," he mutters again. We stare at each other long and hard before he throws up his hands. "I think I trained you *too* well."

He turns and jogs toward the bridge, yelling over his shoulder. "Come on folks, we've got work to do! The doors! All of it! We need it gone!"

"Kevin," I say. "Stay here. Keep the light on that pile."

"Will do!"

"Jack, you can't," I say as we turn to follow the group that chases after Boomer.

We jog side by side, my mom next to him, and Mojo in front of all three of us.

"I have no idea how much fuel is left. This has crash landing written all over it."

"Do you really want to ask Beanie or Hap to go?" Jack says. "Do you want to put them at risk?"

"But I don't want to put you at risk, either."

We rush over the bridge.

"And what if we need to hoist or—"

"This is one-skid all the way and you know it," Jack says. "Someone just needs to step off the aircraft, grab him, and put him in. I can do it just as well as they can."

"But you just found—" I point to my mom.

He puts a hand on my arm, bringing me to a stop. "I just found you, too." He looks at my mom briefly before returning his gaze to me, swallowing. "I won't abandon you again, Alison."

Behind Jack, lights flicker through the sleet, rescue personnel swarming the aircraft, working to strip it.

I start to shake my head again, but he stops me with a light touch to the cheek.

"Please, let me be there for you. For once."

I blink, my eyes watering, and I find myself nodding, understanding what he's willing to sacrifice—the love he had thought lost, but now found—for Will's sake . . . for my sake.

"Please," he says.

"Okay, Alison!" Boomer yells.

I turn to my mother. "Mom?"

"Go on," she says. "Both of you."

Boomer smacks the nose of the aircraft. "She's all ready!" he bellows.

"But Mom—"

She takes my upper arms in her hands and looks at me squarely. "He's the best person to help you. Now go get it done."

I sense no reservation, no hesitation whatsoever in my mom. Same with Jack. They're not worried about the what-ifs. That there isn't a security net. That there aren't any guarantees. And in this, my mom, Jack, and Will are cut from the same cloth. They're not afraid to put it out there. To risk. To fail. Their energy directed solely—fiercely—on doing the best they can in a given situation. And then, the chips fall where they fall. But there are no regrets. Because at least they've tried and given all of themselves in the effort.

"Okay," I say. "Let's do it."

42

Jack leans into the cockpit from the main cabin. I flick on the battery switch, and we test that he can hear me.

"Radio check, over," I say.

"Loud and clear," Jack says, pressing the switch on his radio. He has it attached to his chest harness, which he has donned again, strapping it over his green jacket.

As soon as the rotors start turning, Jack pulls the avalanche transceiver from his harness, and holds it over the main console, where I can view it, the arrow pointing to the left. I pull up on the collective to lift, flicking on the searchlight.

I make a beeline for the debris pile, homing in on the searchlight that Kevin keeps trained there. We cross over junk-ridden water that roils beneath us, and all the while Jack's beacon beeps louder and faster as we close on Will's position.

Jack retreats into the cabin to look out the side door.

"He should be right below us!" Jack shouts, his voice muffled by the wind and sleet that shoot sideways through the aircraft.

My eyes are riveted on the "beaver dam" that sits in the middle of the flow. Made up of sticks, aluminum siding, trees, and other detritus, this mound of blockage sends the water swirling into a violent, crashing wave on the downward side, chewing up any object unfortunate enough to spin through there, before sucking it beneath in one satisfied gulp.

My stomach churns, much like the water that devours all in its path below. Shit. This is so unstable.

"I've got the glove!" Jack shouts.

"In sight!" I say, descending.

As we move closer, the rotor wash kicks up sticks from the surface of the debris pile . . . and there he is, bright yellow jacket, orange glove at the end of the sleeve. He lies unmoving, his lower leg bent at an odd angle.

"There he is!"

"Got him!" Jack says.

I move to hover just feet from Will. He's so clear in my vision as I look to the right, no door to block my view.

"Getting set in the back," Jack says.

I don't have to worry about working the searchlight, since Kevin keeps his spotlight on the pile. But . . . *What's this . . . ?* The cyclic presses into my left thigh, it—

"Jack! The pile's moving! Shit! It's moving!"

Because it's night, because I'm referencing only the debris pile, I didn't notice our drift. I've been moving the control stick to the left to stay with the pile, without even realizing it.

But now it's obvious, as the pile begins to break up. And it occurs to me that the rotor wash that helped uncover Will has also disrupted the delicate balance of materials holding the debris pile together.

"Shit!" Jack shouts.

"Throw him something! Anything!"

"Stand by!" Jack says.

Surely, this pile is only moments from exploding into nothingness.

The engine hiccups. Oh no.

"Jack, the engine—"

I don't even know if he heard me, because he's already flying in midair when I say it, an anchoring rope trailing behind him. He lands on top of Will, clips him to his harness, gives me a thumbs-up, and I go.

I pull collective and slide left, the mound of debris dissolving into the torrent.

"We're riding about five feet below the skids!" Jack says.

My heart stops as I watch the caution panel light up like a Christmas tree, systems going off-line, and the engine begins to whine. *Keep moving, Ali. Turn the nose forward so you can slide head-on!*

Dry ground is ten yards away, nine, eight . . . The low-rotor-rpm horn blares. Beepbeepbeepbeep! The rotors are slowing. Seven yards to dry ground, six, five . . . beepbeepbeepbeep! The beeps come faster as the rotor speed drops below eighty-eight percent, eighty-six percent . . .

"Jack, cut the rope! Cut it!"

I can't control the landing—if there's a landing at all—and if they dangle beneath us, the helicopter will crush them.

Four yards, three yards, beepbeepbeepbeepbeep!

Two yards, one yard. I drop the collective, and the bird thuds to the ground, sliding forward on the wet grass. I manipulate the cyclic as the helicopter tips and yaws, the right skid lifting precariously high before slamming down again. The rotors slow, and so does our momentum, just as the aircraft slides into a rise in the sodden earth and slams to a stop.

I yank off my helmet and pull my harness release, falling, stumbling over the side of the aircraft in my haste to get out. Twenty yards behind me, a tangled heap lies in the dark. I run to them, and from the opposite direction a rescuing army charges to meet us, Mojo leading the way. I drop to my knees, and Jack opens his arms, Will spilling out next to him.

I lay my ear to Will's chest, feeling for a rise, listening for a heartbeat. My head moves up, then down, lifted by Will's inhalation and exhalation, his slow heartbeat reverberating through every cell in my body.

"He's alive," I say.

Mojo approaches cautiously, and when I don't protest, he continues forward, smothering Will's face in warm licks. Apparently, that's all Will needed.

His head rolls to the side and he meets my eyes.

"You're okay," I say. "You're okay."

But in the back of my mind, I know it's not okay. The roads are closed. Will needs a hospital. . . .

Hap is the first to reach us, and he goes to work immediately on Will's medical assessment.

Will's lips move, but I can't hear, due to the resounding *whop* of helicopter blades. A helicopter?

A searchlight illuminates our position as Longhorn 06 makes an approach to land. Clark! He came! Despite the dangers of flying through mountainous terrain, at night, in a storm . . .

The aircraft settles quickly. Sky jumps out of the main cabin and runs toward us, followed by Clark. Tito remains in the bird on the controls.

"We need the litter!" Hap yells to Sky, who spins around and sprints back to Longhorn 06.

Clark drops to my side. "Sorry we couldn't get here sooner," he says, breathless.

"You came. . . ."

Rain and sleet rush over his helmet, splashing in the mud.

He switches his gaze to Will, then back to me.

His eyes glisten, bittersweet.

Sky arrives with the litter, and he and Hap begin the preparations to move Will.

Clark clears his throat and the compartmentalization kicks in again. "Um, so, we need to get outta here. We're running on fumes."

He motions to Will. "Don't worry. We'll get him to the hospital. He'll be fine." He gives me a squeeze on the arm before rising and jogging back to the aircraft.

I return my attention to Will, watching as Sky, Hap, and Beanie lift him onto the litter. Hap has already fashioned a quick splint, so his leg is secure, and they work now to cover him in several layers of blankets and to strap him in.

"They're gonna take you to the hospital," I say. "You'll be—"

He pulls his arm from under the blankets, and reaches up to me, his hand stiff, cold, shaking. I take it, pressing it to my cheek.

"You need to cool it on the hero antics," he says in rasp, and god knows how, but he's cracking a smile.

"You first," I say, stupid tears leaking. I hope he can't see them, mixed as they are with the rain on my face.

He wipes under my eyes—noticing them, of course, which just makes it worse.

"What am I gonna do with you?" he chuckles.

"*How* are you laughing right now? You're insane!"

"Not really. I'd say life is pretty good right now, wouldn't you?"

I squeeze Will's hand, the tears shamelessly falling now. "Yeah. Yeah, I guess it is."

"Okay, ma'am, he's all set," Hap says.

I give a quick kiss to Will's hand before lowering it and tucking it under the blankets.

"Thank you," Will says.

I smile. "Anytime."

43

We approach the front door to Jack's house under a clear night sky flush with stars. The air is scented with vanilla and shades of apple, a product of the giant wreath adorning the front door—the one made from fresh boughs of Jeffrey pine. Music slips through the walls, light and muffled, but music I've come to know well.

I crane my head around to Will, who stands behind me, leaning on his crutches. "Randy Travis? Again?"

"Sounds like it," he says. "Can never have too much of Mr. Travis."

"It's growing on me, you know," I say, setting my shopping bag on the deck. I turn to face him, sliding my arms around his neck.

"Country music?" He grins, the movement tugging at the healing scratches and rashes on his face.

"Well, yeah, that . . . and you."

Our eyes hold, his gaze shifting from warm to smoldering. The chill of the night air evaporates, our bodies inching closer, my head angles to receive him, and his mouth covers mine. His lips are warm and perfect, an invitation to come in and stay awhile. So I do. For so long, in fact, I start to remind myself we're standing on someone's front porch. But when his hands reach to my hips, drawing them flush with his, the concern dissolves, just like the space between us. It's the first time we've—

"Welcome, you two!" Jack announces. I whip around to see Jack holding the front door wide open.

"Great to see you," Will says to Jack, none to enthusiastically.

I pick up my bag, and Will and I share a to-be-continued look and a couple of deep breaths.

"Ha! Fair William! You wear your heart on your sleeve. But I would have it no other way."

Jack, awash in laughter, pulls me into an enormous hug as Will hops in on his crutches. And, oh . . . sweet heaven. I pull away from Jack and turn toward the aroma—the mouthwatering smells of a traditional Thanksgiving feast. Turkey and stuffing and . . . wait. My mom's stuffing. My *mom's* stuffing . . . in Jack's house.

I shake my head, blinking.

"What is it?" Will asks.

"I just—"

Mom emerges from the kitchen, and Jack leaps down the stairs to join her, sliding his hand into hers.

My mom and my dad. I'm looking at *my mom and dad.* Holding hands.

Will moves his hand back and forth in front of my face. "Hello in there," he says.

"That . . . ," I say, pointing. "I'm just trying to get my head around . . . that."

"Is it okay?" my mom says.

I nod. "It is. It's very okay."

"Well, come on down then," Jack says. "I'd say alcohol is probably in order."

"Fine by me, except I don't think we've been formally introduced yet," Will says, looking at my mom.

"You haven't . . . ," I start. "Oh! You haven't!"

After Will was taken to the hospital, my mom went home with Jack. And once our crew returned to Fallon, I drove back to Carson City to stay with Will, who suffered clean breaks to both the tibia and fibula.

The surgeon said he didn't anticipate any healing complications—the word "lucky" was spoken several times during his prognosis—and now Will wears a cast, while sporting some rugged-looking scratches on his face for good measure.

I start down the three long stairs that lead to the sunken living room while Will carefully negotiates the steps with his crutches.

I meet my mom for a strong embrace, then step back. "Mom, this is Will," I say, a blush rising. "Will, this is my mom, Candice."

My mom forgoes any formality, wrapping her arms around Will. "It's so wonderful to finally meet you."

"And you," Will says.

My mom steps away, looking back and forth between the two of us, which causes me to shift a bit, nervous for some reason. Will reaches his right hand to me, which I take, and he pulls me to his side, all while balancing his crutch under his arm. My insides glow, warming like a luminaria at Christmastime.

She doesn't have to say a word for me to know what she's thinking. *Right choice.*

"So, let's go get something to drink," Jack says, putting his arm around my mom and guiding her into the kitchen.

What a marked difference in my mom's demeanor. She never looked like this in Nick's arms, almost as if they held each other as brother and sister. But it looks as if she's suction-cupped to Jack, like she fits there perfectly. She leans into him, he bends over and kisses her forehead, so sweet and tender, and very, very real.

"Actually, Jack," my mom says, "I'm gonna steal Ali for a second."

Jack's gaze shifts to the tiny jewelry box on the counter, and my mom nods, smiling.

"Take your time," Jack says sweetly. "Will's gonna help me set the table."

"I am?" Will gives his best sympathy-garnering look, motioning to his crutches.

"Oh, please," Jack says, pointing to the cupboards. "Get to work, mister."

"I didn't think that would work," Will says, shrugging. "Ah, well."

He gives me a quick kiss on the cheek before moving forward for his kitchen duties, just as my mom scoops up the box.

"Oh, Will," I say, remembering. I hand him my bag and whisper in his ear. "Hide this somewhere for me, okay?"

"Will do."

My mom and I make our way downstairs, lowering ourselves to sit on the same couch where Jack and I held our heart-to-heart conversation three weeks ago. A homey fire crackles in the fireplace, as it did then, and—ah! There's Mojo!

"Come here, you," I say. My mom and I pet him well before he takes his leave, returning to his spot next to the fire.

"Here," my mom says. "This is for you."

"What's this?"

"It's something I wanted to give you at the lodge."

"But what—"

"Just open it."

I lift the lid. An antique silver locket rests in soft, white tissue.

"This is . . ." I lift the locket by its silver chain, letting it dangle in front of me. ". . . exquisite. Where did you . . . ?"

"It was your grandmother's. Jack's mother gave it to me, when we were married."

I lay the locket on my palm, smoothing my finger over its oval shape and the etched design in the center.

"Is this what I think it is?"

"A larkspur flower, yes. His mother's garden in Bielsa was filled with them."

"A larkspur . . . ," I whisper, admiring the intricate and perfectly rendered flower. "But I can't take this. It's yours."

"No, it's yours now. Look inside."

I open the locket, focus, blink, refocus. And then the image blurs as my eyes water over.

"Your dad loved to take you on walks near the river. He would perch his little Magpie on his shoulders, and off you'd go, up and down the Walker. He'd carry you for hours."

"He told me, but I just couldn't remember."

"Grandpa Alther took that photo of the three of us, before we set off on one of our hikes."

"You used to hike," I say, noting the backpack she wears in the photo. "You climbed. You served in search and rescue! Jack told me all of that. I never . . . I never knew."

"It was so hard for me to go back to the lodge," she says, her voice cracking.

I look up, and the tears are streaming freely down her cheeks.

"Every time, I had to face the biggest mistake I'd ever made in my life. But I couldn't undo it. I'd married Nick. . . ." Her breath catches. "I did it for you. I thought I was doing the right thing."

"Mom—"

"I'm so sorry. I'm so—"

"Mom, don't. Please. It's okay. I understand."

"I wanted to show you this," she says, pointing to the locket. "Tell you about our time as a family in Walker Canyon. Do all of it right there at the lodge. Tell you everything. Apologize. But now it's gone," she says, wiping her eyes. "It's gone, and now, we can't go back."

"You're right," I say. I scooch closer to her, wiping the wetness from her cheeks, tucking the loose strands of hair—the same auburn color as mine—behind her ears. "We can't go back. But we *can* go forward."

She nods, sniffing.

"And why would we look back, anyway? I mean, Mom, look where we are now."

She smiles through her tears, and our arms fly around each other.

"Are you guys finished yet?" Celia says, peeking around the corner. "I'm starving!"

"Celia!" I say, rising to give her a hug. "When did you get here?"

"Ben just picked me up at the hotel. Just got here."

"Ben? Who's—?"

"You know. Boomer."

"Oh, oh yeah. But hotel? You stayed at a *hotel*? Mom, what's up with that?"

"We begged her to stay here, but she insisted. Sort of like you insisting Jack and I not come to the hospital," my mom says, eyes narrowing. "Same reasoning."

"Ah," I say. Nice that Celia was thinking like I was on that one, allowing my mom and Jack some getting-reacquainted time.

"So are we good here?" Celia asks.

"I'd say we're pretty good." I glance at my mom. Yep, we're in the same—very good—place. "Did you see what she brought me?" I say, holding the locket out to Celia.

"I did. Here, let me help you put that on."

She takes the locket, steps behind while I pull up my hair, and places it around my neck.

"Did you know this is why your mom wanted to have Thanksgiving at the lodge?" Celia says as she secures the hasp.

"It wasn't *my* idea," my mom says. "It was Celia's. And it took a lot of convincing. I never would have gotten to the lodge—never would have gotten to that point *mentally*—without her."

"Yeah," Celia says, head dropping. "Too bad I wasn't there—"

"Stop, Cee," my mom says. "You were there for me *exactly* when I needed you."

Celia rolls her eyes, clearly unconvinced.

"So, am I gonna have to call Dr. Grant on *your* behalf or what?" my mom says. "I will, if you don't stop the moping."

"Says you," Celia answers with a playful shove on my mom's shoulder.

"Says me." My mom shoves her back.

"What is going *on* down there?" Boomer says. He tromps like a pregnant bear down the stairs. Tromp. Tromp. Tromp. "Let's *go*, ladies!" he says, stopping on the bottom step. "I need to eat, ASAP!"

I lean back, stretching my legs under the table, blissfully stuffed with stuffing. Will reaches over, laces his fingers through mine, and pulls our entwined hands to his lap. Throughout the evening, Will has laid a gentle hand here, stroked my cheek there, while Boomer has regaled the group with another retelling of "the rescue."

We finally learned why my mom and Celia were in Cabin Eleven, not in the main lodge as I thought they would be. I guess the hero business runs in the family. They sacrificed their chance to leave the main lodge safely, instead choosing to run to all of the other cabins to ensure their guests got out first. They were on their way to Cabin Ten when the river exploded around them, trapping them in Cabin Eleven.

So many close calls. So many . . .

I think that's why Will and I are so touchy tonight. Just making sure, still there, still there. The image of the cabin pulling him into the river is one that won't soon fade, I'm afraid. Embarrassingly, I woke up shouting Will's name in his hospital room after having fallen asleep there the first night. It happened the second night, too. And, yeah . . . last night, as well. I think he can even sense when I'm thinking about it, like now, as he gives me a reassuring squeeze of the hand.

It's happening across the table, too. Mom and Jack, holding hands, stealing glances, sharing smiles.

I'm looking at my mother and father. My *mother and father* . . .

They catch me staring.

"I'm sorry," I say. "This just hasn't sunk in yet. It's so beautiful, but it's hard to believe it's really happening."

"That makes three of us," Jack says with a chuckle. "But you know what? We're gonna have a long time to get used to this. Your mom and I have decided to live together again."

My mom beams. Celia does, too.

"Now that's news worth drinking to!" Boomer says, raising his glass.

"To new beginnings," Celia says.

As we bring our glasses to our lips, I think of my mom's real-estate business, flourishing, successful. She's worked so hard for all she has. . . .

"Will you be moving to Sacramento, then?" I say.

"No, Ali," my mom answers. "I'm coming here. I'm coming home to Larkspur."

"You're coming . . . here? But what about—"

"What I've built in Sacramento is nothing compared to what I have here," she says, looking up and smiling at Jack. "If I ever feel the itch to do real estate, then I'll just start over, because I know where I want to be. I know where I belong." She winks at Jack, "*And* I've got an in with a construction company that's building some beautiful new homes!"

I reach up, as I've done most of the evening, to finger the locket on my neck. *Where I belong.* That's what it feels like. The missing piece has been found. And as I squeeze Will's hand, I know that on this Thanksgiving, everything I've ever wanted to say thank you for is right here at this table. I have to blink as my eyes start watering. Again.

Yikes. What is it with the waterworks?

"Ali . . . ? Ali?" my mom says.

"What's that? Sorry?"

"I said, and as a bonus, I'll be closer to you and Will." She looks at Will. "You know, Jack's told me so much about you."

"Uh-oh," Will says.

"It was all good, I promise." She then returns her gaze to me. "Ali, honey, as happy as you are for Jack and me, we're overjoyed for you and Will. Truly."

"I'll drink to that!" Will says.

"So how about dessert?" Boomer says.

We all start to rise to help clear our plates, but Jack shushes us down. "Keep your seats, guys. We'll get this."

He and my mom go about clearing, acting as if it's the most wonderful thing they've ever done together, while Boomer goes back to storytelling mode. "Oh, and that reminds me," Boomer says, stopping midstream. "Totally different subject, but Alison, your detailer called, while you were out."

My detailer?

My detailer . . .

My detailer!

"He . . . he did?" I say, nursing the oddest sensation—a spider scurrying under the skin. "What did he say?"

"That he hasn't had any luck on your transfer request. Although, I suppose that would be good news now wouldn't it?"

I let out the breath I didn't realize I was holding.

"Your detailer?" Will asks. "Transfer?"

"That was before . . . us. Obviously, I don't want to leave anymore."

"Well, don't forget to call him when we get back to work on Monday, then," Boomer says.

"I won't. Trust me."

Whoa. Just five weeks ago, I would have leaped at orders transferring me from Fallon. And how long have I pestered the detailer? Thank god he was thwarted in his efforts.

"Alison, did you want to bring out your presents?" Will asks.

"Oh, yes!"

"Cupboard on the far left," he says.

I stand and move to where Will stashed my surprises.

"I just have a little something for our two acrobats here." I give one box to my mom and one to Celia, both stamped with the logo from the hospital gift shop.

They open their boxes, lifting out identical mugs. "Cat poster!" they say in unison.

"Can you believe they had the 'Hang in there, baby' mugs in the gift shop?" I say.

"Well, that pretty much sums it up," Celia says.

"Not something I'll soon forget," my mom adds.

"And we're definitely having cider," I say.

"Would we have anything else?" my mom says.

"I'll boil the water," Jack says.

"But what about dessert?" Boomer asks. "I mean, just bringing us back on topic."

"Would you like to do the honors?" Jack says. "I mean, since you brought it."

"Hell, yeah." Boomer rumbles over to the kitchen as I retake my seat.

He returns shortly holding a large sheet cake-size box that he places in front of Will and me.

"Go ahead. Open it," Boomer says.

Will lifts the lid, and our faces broaden into matching beaming smiles. Inside, one dozen heavenly pieces of glazed doughnut perfection.

"Grabbed 'em up fresh from Schat's this morning," Boomer says.

Will motions for me to pick first, then turns to me, his eyes sparkling the way they did the first day I met him. "How much you wanna bet that'll be the best doughnut you've ever tasted?"

"I have no doubt about that," I say, raising it to my mouth. "None whatsoever."